HOLOTRIAL
Alan M. Wishnoff

2025, TWB Press
https://www.twbpress.com

DEDICATION

For my parents, Sylvia and Fred Wishnoff

ACKNOWLEDGMENTS

Many thanks to my collaborator, motivator, torturer, and sister, Flory Wishnoff Herman. And to my fantastic initial developmental editor and co-musician, Jason Kirk, whose birthday and mine ended up being quite serendipitous.

Supreme thanks to my incredible wife, Wendy, for her support, reviews, critiques, motivation, and love.

"For every complex problem, there is an answer that is clear, simple, and wrong."

H. L. Mencken

ADMINISTRATIVE ORDER OF THE
CHIEF ADMINISTRATIVE JUDGE OF THE COURTS

Re: Holotrial Pilot Program

Commencing January 1, 2023, all civil trials in the Supreme Court, Erie County, 8th Judicial District, shall be recorded in holographic form prior to jury selection. Upon completion of the recording, all objections, rulings, inadmissible testimony, and colloquy shall be edited out, and the remaining testimony, jury instructions, and opening and closing statements of counsel shall be condensed into a single holographic video, or "Holoscript." Jury selection shall commence within one week of completion of the Holoscript, which shall be shown to the jurors immediately after the jury is picked.

Expedited pre-trial procedures: As part of the Holotrial Pilot Program, all pre-trial procedures, including discovery and motion practice, shall be concluded within two months of commencement of the action.

Following review of the efficacy of this Program, the Office of Court Administration shall consider expanding it to other parts of the New York State Unified Court System, either as a continuing Pilot Program or by adopting the "Holotrial" system for all courts in the New York State Unified Court System on a permanent basis.

Dated: August 1, 2022   Hon. Raymond Frankhauser,
                                Chief Administrative Judge of the Courts

Chapter 1

PRIME FOODS SUPERMARKET
Buffalo, New York
Friday, June 30, 2023
3:15 p.m.

T he case started in a quiet supermarket parking lot on a warm summer day. Who could have foreseen that the cold autumn evening of November 10th would bring the day of reckoning?

Jennifer Talbot, twenty-one years old, still sporting her high-school cheerleader's body, but now with purple instead of blond hair, loaded her groceries into the trunk of her shiny new yellow Hydro. It was amazingly high-tech, though majoring in art had left her technologically challenged. All she knew was, it ran on hydrogen and never needed anything but water. Or did it run on water and just make hydrogen? Either way, it was economical; she knew that much.

After she slammed down the trunk, she picked up the adorable little girl in the shopping cart and gently placed her in the baby carrier in the back seat. Allison Talbot, two months old, already sprouting a beautiful mane of golden hair, had a smile that could melt icebergs. She was the apple of everyone's eye. Everyone, that is, except Jennifer's father, Bill. Yes, *that* Bill Talbot, the U.S. Senator. No one knew what Allison's paternal grandfather thought of her, because no one knew his identity. In fact, no one, presumably other than Jennifer, seemed to know the identity of Allison's father.

After the required buckling of buckles and snapping of snaps, Jennifer satisfied herself that the baby was secure and promised she'd be right back. She locked the doors. As she was pushing the empty shopping cart to the return kiosk, a sixtyish man pushing his own loaded cart whistled a catcall, followed up with "Very sexy." Jennifer forced a half smile. This happened a lot, ever since her cheerleader days when she had started to fill out. Truth be told, she'd grown tired of it, especially when it came to old geezers like this. It *was* a little surprising that someone of his generation would appreciate her purple hair and the small titanium studs, two millimeters in diameter, one on each side of her nose. She therefore felt only mildly disappointed when he nodded toward the Hydro, clarifying it was the car's sleek lines that excited him, not hers.

"Didn't know they were out already. Like to get my hands on one of those."

"It was a present," Jennifer replied.

"Lucky guy."

"From my dad."

"Oh."

Having returned the shopping cart, Jennifer started back to the car, waving and shouting, "On my way back, Allie." She doubted the child could hear her from inside the airtight Hydro a hundred feet away. Jennifer, or "Jenny" as her friends and family called her, spoke into her key fob. "Engine on."

The shockwave knocked her down immediately. A split second later, Jennifer understood that her car had exploded into a massive inferno, scattering pieces of metal, plastic, and fabric all over the parking lot. Orange and black flames rose thirty feet in the air. Still dazed, ears ringing, Jennifer picked herself up and ran toward what little was left of the car, screaming, "Allie!" over and over. But the searing heat prevented her from getting anywhere near the vehicle.

She fell to the ground, crying in anguish.

A hand gently touched her shoulder. It was the old man who'd admired the car a few moments earlier. There was nothing he could do or say to calm her down.

She lay on the ground, crying out, "Mommy, I'm sorry, I'm so sorry."

She fainted.

Chapter 2

IN A WHITE ROOM
Monday, October 2, 2023
9:10 a.m.

E ven though Sara Mitachi had presided over hundreds of trials, she'd never felt this level of anticipation. She wondered just how different it would be with fake surroundings, simulated weather, and everything filmed in 3-D. Above all, Sara was honored that the Administrative Judge had picked her as one of the ten judges assigned to the new Holotrial Pilot Program. The courtroom was being prepared for her. She had an extra spring in her step as she walked from her office to the door that would open on her first Holotrial.

***

The room was the size of a basketball court. Only, with no basketballs. Or hoops. Or foul lines. Or *any* lines, for that matter. Nothing discernible at all. Because the entire room was white from top to bottom. Floors, walls, ceiling, all white.

However, if you craned your neck upward, it was possible to see a bank of lighting fixtures, strange-looking cameras and projectors, and other unrecognizable electronic equipment running the entire perimeter of the room, just below the thirty-five-foot ceiling.

A discerning eye, after adjusting to the alabaster glare, might eventually pick out a few additional features in what otherwise appeared to be a shapeless, formless landscape of absolute nothingness. It was like trying to solve a jigsaw puzzle with all the pieces the same color. At the front of the room sat a large desk—white, of course—and a chair with a railing around it just to the right of the desk. Two tables were positioned in front, facing the desk. On the right side of the room ran a railing with seven bulky chairs behind it. The tables, railing, and chairs were also white, blending into the white abyss.

Suddenly a crackly voice filled the room, like a pilot over a plane's intercom: "Control, HTR, initiate VRC on three, two, one." Like a movie set, which in the final analysis it was, the stage lights illuminated, and a loud solenoid *pop* filled the room, transforming it in an instant. The plain white walls and ceiling now appeared to be covered in rich oak paneling, the floor in marble tile. The large desk, now obviously a judge's bench, turned to beautiful aged mahogany, a relic of earlier days. One could imagine it reeking of ancient pipe and cigar smoke, a spittoon at its side. Framed portraits of judges long gone appeared on the side walls of what now looked like a traditional courtroom. A gorgeous floral rug ran down the center aisle, from a double door at the rear of the room all the way to the bench. Above the rear doors hung a large clock, actually, the *image* of a large clock. An inlaid black walnut door rose behind the judge's bench.

Four-foot arched windows, their paned rectangles topped by half-moon panels, appeared halfway up the side walls. Regardless of the conditions in the real world outside, it was always a sunny afternoon in the courtroom. Only the occasional simulated flock of birds or passing clouds broke the monotony of the weather visible to the trial participants.

The Holotrial courtroom was designed to mimic, indeed be indistinguishable from, a normal trial courtroom. Perhaps an unusually exquisite one, yet a courtroom just the same. Judge's bench in the middle. Counsel tables facing the bench, witness box to the right of the bench, and jury box running along the wall on the right side of the room. The chair for Juror Number One was parallel with the witness box, about ten feet away. The chairs for jurors two through seven continued along the wall toward the rear of the courtroom. Unlike the rest of the well-lit room, the jury box was in shadow.

All that was missing were people.

The door behind the judge's bench and the double doors at the opposite end of the courtroom opened simultaneously. In her long black robe, Judge Sara Mitachi of the New York Supreme Court, Erie County, swept into the virtual courtroom, her clerk in tow.

About five-foot-two, 67 years old, with brown rimmed glasses and jet black hair speckled with bits of gray, Judge Mitachi ran a tight ship. She suffered no fools.

Her parents had immigrated from Japan many years ago, for reasons she didn't fully understand. They still talked about the "homeland" in glowing terms. Sometimes. Her father always said America offered a more "forgiving" society than the rigid one they'd left behind. She suspected it also had a lot to do with "The War," as her parents were teenagers when Hiroshima and Nagasaki were demolished by the first, and so far only, atomic bombs dropped in anger. But they never spoke of it, so neither did she. She had learned discretion, which had helped her legal career and ultimately her ascension to the bench.

Judge Mitachi's courtroom was in the Holotrial Annex Building, or "HAB," a special courthouse designed for Holotrials. She marveled at the wizardry that could transform a stark white room into this magnificent courtroom, the most elaborate she'd ever presided over. It wasn't her job to understand how it was accomplished. All she knew was that LEDs, or some such things, were embedded in all of the courtroom's surfaces.

From her perch on the bench, Judge Mitachi sat stoic as she viewed the clock on the rear wall: *9:15 a.m.* A small troop of lawyers and clients entered from the back of the room, just under the clock. She valued punctuality above all. And woe betide the lawyer or witness who showed up even a minute late. Once the proceedings began, Judge Mitachi could tolerate, to a degree, spurious objections, inadmissible testimony, the odd interruptions from clerks scurrying to and fro through the courtroom. Such nonsense would be edited out of the Holoscript anyway. But tardiness was verboten.

As the lawyers took their seats at the counsel tables, Judge Mitachi frowned, her lips pinched, leaving no question who was in charge.

In addition to the sparse furnishings, ten additional chairs were brought in to form a spectator gallery, as some of the parties' relatives and the attorneys' legal assistants were expected to attend the proceedings. Court personnel didn't normally bother to set up a gallery for a Holotrial. They rarely had any spectators, though, as with any regular trial in a normal courtroom, the general public was free to observe its judicial system in action.

The two defense lawyers at the table on the left side were not readily recognizable. Not so for the dark-haired fortyish man at the plaintiffs' table on the right. Adam Simons—law professor and reasonably well known, if not outright famous, civil rights attorney—looked unsure of himself as he whispered to the attractive young, freckled woman with the shoulder length red hair in the seat next to his. He appeared nervous, out of his element, though the courtroom usually felt like a second home to him. His son, Pete, sometimes complained that it was more like Adam's first home, and the classroom his second, while the four-bedroom house where he and Pete slept each night played third fiddle. If that.

Judge Mitachi nodded to her court clerk, who bellowed, "Holotrial H23-104C, Talbot versus Vertex Corporation et al. All counsel present. Preliminary instructions complete."

At least they allow me a human clerk.

It was comforting to begin with a vestige of normal court procedure amidst the artificial environment of a Holotrial courtroom. Judge Mitachi addressed the lawyers, only one of whom was familiar to her. "Gentlemen, and lady, we are ready to proceed. Anything I need to know?"

One of the defense lawyers jumped to his feet. "Yes, Your Honor. There is. There certainly is."

***

A few minutes later, after a colloquy with the lawyers, the judge nodded to Adam. "Okay then, Mr. Simons, you may open. Bring in the jury."

The jury box, which until that moment lay in shadow, was fully illuminated in an instant, revealing seven life-like fiberglass *jurors*. They'd been sitting there all along, in the darkness, waiting for their moment to shine, and their freshly polished faces glistened in the augmented lighting.

The jurors were hauntingly real. At least their faces and upper torsos. Adam doubted they had legs, though he'd never checked. Meanwhile, special holographic cameras, high above and hidden in the walls, recorded the scene from every angle.

Adam stood to begin, as he had innumerable times before.

Strangely, he felt as nervous as a second-year law student, a *2L*, conducting a mock trial. Three things bothered him: his case, his clients, and the Holotrial procedure itself. He'd made it a rule not to represent friends or family. Yet here he was, breaking it. And he hadn't handled a personal injury case in decades. He didn't want to screw it up. Adam normally exuded supreme confidence at trial, and he hoped his inner turmoil for this trial didn't show.

Holotrials were still new to Adam, indeed, to all the lawyers in the local bar association. It was only a pilot program, but Adam feared it was catching on, at least among the administrative bureaucracy. Film the trial as a three-dimensional hologram. Then present it in crystal-clear, life-size holographic form with a nice bow on top to a live jury, who could then typically view the entire trial in a day or two at most.

The distorted symmetry of the Holotrial system seemed perverse. The *real* Adam addressed a *fake* jury. Then a week or so later, the *fake* holographic Adam would address a *real* jury. A trial pieced together like a Frankenstein monster, part dead, part living. The Office of Court Administration loved it.

Adam hated it.

What the hell do they know about conducting a trial? They haven't seen a courtroom in 20 years. If ever.

He took one last peek at the outline on his iPad before walking to the jury box. He was momentarily distracted by *Juror Number Five*, whose features resembled those of his young co-counsel. "May it please the Court," Adam began. "Ladies and gentlemen of the jury. You are about to hear a story unlike anything you've heard before. A story of greed. Of profit. Of death. Of sordid..."

Chapter 3

SUPREME COURT, ERIE COUNTY
Talbot versus Vertex Corporation et al.
Holotrial Annex Building, Part 7-HT
Main Street, Buffalo, New York
Live Jury Session
Thursday, November 9, 2023
Morning

The holographic image of Adam Simons, virtually indistinguishable from the real Adam, continued his opening statement in front of the seven real human beings now in the jury box. "...so-called businessmen who would sacrifice human life for a few extra bucks. Think it sounds like a cliché, my friends? A bad movie maybe? But it ended in the tragic, horrifying death of a..."

The Holotrial had finished filming two days ago.

The holographic cameras had done their work well. This *Adam* was just a beam of light, but to the jurors, he was a flesh-and-blood lawyer standing in front of them. The detail was so lifelike they found it hard to believe they were staring at a bunch of photons.

Six of the jurors would ultimately decide the case. The seventh was an alternate should one of the others become unavailable for deliberations, a rare event under the Holotrial system. The jury's viewing of the Holoscript would be completed in one day, during which it was unlikely that any of the first six jurors would get sick, have a dental appointment, or go into labor.

About seven minutes in, the holographic Adam picked up a jagged metal remnant and showed it to the jurors. "It was murder, plain and simple. It's sad. It's tragic. And it's why you're here."

After opening statements, Judge Mitachi wasted no time moving the proceedings along. "Thank you, Mr. Simons. You may call your first witness."

Chapter 4

FOUR MONTHS EARLIER
BUFFALO AND ERIE COUNTY NAVAL & MILITARY PARK
Friday, June 30, 2023
4:35 p.m.

C al Dryer was still in awe of the ships, though he'd walked their bows and sterns with his grandfather innumerable times as a child. Now, as a college student, he was reliving that childhood, though Grandpa Max was no longer around.

The two gray, hulking Navy ships—Fletcher-class destroyer USS *The Sullivans* and the guided missile cruiser USS *Little Rock*—floated majestically above the harbor, bristling with armament. Batteries of five-inch diameter guns protruded menacingly from their turrets, and depth charges, anti-aircraft emplacements, torpedoes, and machine guns threatened any who might dare attack the Buffalo waterfront. However, there was little chance of such an attack, as no foreign power had stormed the United States mainland since 1812, and an attack on Buffalo was unlikely, in any case, since an enemy would first have to land their navy in the middle of the Great Lakes. The only access from the ocean was to navigate the Saint Lawrence Seaway, one ship at a time through the locks, a dubious military strategy. On the other hand, plunking a naval fleet directly into Lake Erie, presumably from the air, would seem to pose even greater logistical problems.

The World War II-era ships had been mothballed long ago and brought to the Buffalo & Erie County Naval and Military Park in 1977 as floating museums. The destroyer, named after the five Sullivan brothers from Waterloo, Iowa, was the first ship in the Navy to be named after more than one person. Contrary to the Navy policy of separating siblings, the five brothers were all assigned to the light cruiser USS *Juneau*, and all five lost their lives when a Japanese submarine sunk the ship during the Battle of Guadalcanal, causing the greatest military loss by any one American family during the entire war.

The destroyer was in a sense a contradiction in terms—a gargantuan steel behemoth from the outside, but on the inside, a Lilliputian maze of narrow corridors, tiny rooms, small windows, and hammocks stacked in threes. Vignettes of life at sea were placed throughout the ship, including life-size mannequins in WWII uniforms huddled over maps plotting the ship's course, cooking the evening meal, doing the voluminous laundry generated by 300-plus sailors, and performing the numerous other tasks necessary for survival at sea.

On this sunny summer day, tourists flocked up the destroyer's gangplank and disappeared into its deep bowels and winding self-guided tour paths. In a variation of *follow the Yellow Brick Road*, visitors were supposed to follow yellow lines and arrows painted on the decks of the ship if they did not want to get hopelessly lost and become permanent residents of the boiler room.

Cal and several of his college buddies jammed into a narrow walkway on the second level below the main deck, peering into rooms *manned* by seamen, petty officers, ensigns, warrant officers, lieutenants, and an occasional admiral or captain. The college kids' jeans and T-shirts were printed with what they thought were clever sayings. Cal's read: YOU CAN MAKE ME GO TO SCHOOL, BUT YOU CAN'T MAKE ME THINK. Lisa, always the idealist, wore: POLITICIANS ARE LIKE DIAPERS. THEY SHOULD BOTH BE CHANGED OFTEN AND FOR THE SAME REASON.

They were done with finals, and Cal had suggested the trip to the Naval Museum. It brought back memories of Grandpa Max, dressed in a threadbare Navy uniform dripping with medals, proudly showing Cal around the ships, describing them with the Navy jargon Max had picked up during the war. Cal recalled how Max stood up just a bit straighter when the volunteers checking tickets at the bottom of the gangplank saluted him, always responding with his own razor-sharp salute.

Mitch, a fellow senior, asked, "Hey, Cal, like, wasn't your father in the Korean War?"

"It was my grandfather, you putz. And it was, like, World War II."

Ron chimed in. "You're the putz. You couldn't last, like, a day in the Navy."

Cal couldn't resist the challenge. "Bet you fifty bucks I can last a night."

Barry moaned. "Here we go again."

"Fifty bucks says I can stay on this big floating tin can 'til, like, tomorrow morning," Cal said. "Pick a hiding place, get some sleep, done and done. See you at morning light. Bottom of the ramp. Be there."

Lisa insisted, "No paying off security. Like last time."

"Like, totally scrotally legit. So, fifty each? Whadaya say, you all in?"

***

When Cal's friends left the ship, ninety percent of his bravado went with them. He was a bit freaked out. Alone in these empty skinny passageways, he wondered if they'd turn the lights out after visiting hours. He wouldn't have admitted it to the gang, but he hadn't outgrown his childhood fear of the dark.

Brushing aside his fears, Cal descended one level and cased out various rooms for a good hiding place. Ruling out one after another, he eventually came upon a sick bay that looked promising. A mannequin sailor in a WWII lieutenant's uniform lay on the examining table, mostly covered by a gray blanket. A second one—a white-coated doctor in outfit and stethoscope right out of the 1940s—peered over the *patient*. Cal let himself in and peeked back out the doorway, just enough to scan the corridor. The coast was clear.

After quietly removing the blanket from the *patient*, Cal changed into the lieutenant's uniform. He stowed his folded jeans and T-shirt, along with the naked seaman, in a closet. Cal climbed on to the examining table and covered his torso. The blanket didn't cover his head, so he lay face down. He could only hope that any lingering interloper wouldn't notice his too-lifelike hair and skin, though it was unlikely he'd have any guests after visiting hours.

Listening intently and hearing nothing, Cal took out his phone and pressed the contact for "Tina." After four rings, her message came on. "Yo, Tina here. Well, maybe not exactly *here*. You know the drill. Like, spill your guts at the [BEEP]."

"Hey, Tina, it's me," Cal whispered. "Gotta cancel our date night. But I'm gonna make a hundred fifty bucks. I bet the assholes—" He stopped abruptly, stiffening. A slow staccato of footsteps made its way down the corridor, approaching the sick bay. Cal briefly imagined his friends had outed him in a reverse prank. *I should have figured those fuckers might pull some shit like this.*

Cal didn't know it, but the approaching footsteps belonged to Damytro Gura, 47, ex-Ukrainian mob soldier, a veteran of the violent and unpredictable underworld of Kyiv with a proclivity for sadistic violence and general psychopathy. To Cal's dismay, the man's footsteps stopped right outside the sick bay. Cal shoved his phone into his pocket, turned his head toward the door, and held his breath. Squinting, he saw an imposing figure—probably six-foot-four, 240 pounds—enter the room, fiddling with his phone. A scar ran across the man's forehead. His gray jacket sported a VERTEX SECURITY logo. A bulge behind the logo outlined the gun in his shoulder holster, a Makarov PM liberated from a Ukrainian army barracks.

As Gura entered the room, Cal quickly turned his head face down. He slammed his eyes closed, weighing the risks of remaining still or revealing himself. He didn't want to startle his guest. If the man was not exactly friendly, there was probably no one on the ship to help him.

Gura approached the examination table and stood next to Cal's right leg. He leaned back against the table and propped himself up with one hand, his fingers just inches from Cal's calf underneath the blanket.

Cal, his heart beating like a drum roll, prayed his uninvited guest wouldn't touch his leg.

Sweat formed on Gura's forehead. His hands trembled as he placed a call. Cal barely heard four rings, then a curt voice answered. He couldn't make out the words, but he heard Gura respond. "*Pryvit shefe.* Mr. K, you not believe what—"

Chapter 5

HOME OF ALEX KURTOFF
Stonecliff Court, Clarence, New York
Friday, June 30, 2023
4:45 p.m.

Alex Kurtoff, captain of industry, sat alone in the well-appointed dining room of his three-story, 9,000 square-foot mansion. He'd initially balked at putting the Vertex plant in Buffalo. But when he had seen the tranquil suburbs like Clarence, where he now lived, he was sold. Not that Buffalo proper was so bad. It had a funky downtown with historic houses and architectural gems, a symphony orchestra, sports stadiums, art museums—all the trappings of a major American city. But after living in crowded Kyiv and New York City, the quiet burbs felt like an eternal Zen session.

Also, Western New York didn't have hurricanes, tornadoes, earthquakes, forest fires, floods, or other natural calamities that wiped out various communities elsewhere in the country from time to time. He could live with a little snow. Like that line from the cartoon all the kids watched incessantly: "The cold never bothered me anyway." His choice of Buffalo also allowed him to keep a close eye on the competition, the New Millennium factory in Niagara Falls.

Though only about five-foot-eight, Kurtoff nevertheless cut an imposing figure. The fierce deep-brown eyes and general aura of tension that he exuded gave the impression of a coiled rattlesnake ready to strike. He had a prominent nose, and his pale skin was offset by dark brown hair, a mustache, and short sideburns. Like Gura, Kurtoff had scars on his forehead, though his were hidden by thick bushy eyebrows.

Everything was just so in Kurtoff's private palace: inlaid maple dining room table, lace curtains, immaculately polished silverware, cloth napkins folded with perfect creases. He'd managed to infuse his home with a veneer of civilization that was part of the remolding and repackaging of Alex Kurtoff, respected businessman, CEO of Vertex Corporation.

Arriving in the U.S. a mere decade ago, an unpolished thug with murderous instincts and a wad of cash large enough to choke a horse, he'd since managed to refine his accent somewhat and his image a lot. That included softening his name from Alexi Kurtov to Alex Kurtoff. Slowly but surely, he climbed the social and financial ladders of the New World. He also attended night sessions of law school, thinking that he so often operated at or beyond the fringes of the law, he might as well learn about its inner workings in America.

Many of his Ukrainian mob associates had also made their way to the States, and they helped him launder and multiply his money with investments in various iniquitous undertakings. Drugs, gambling, prostitution, loan sharking. Everything he'd learned in Ukraine also applied here. America was not as lily white as it liked to portray itself.

Kurtoff had parlayed his dubiously earned fortune into part ownership of Vertex Motors, an electric car manufacturer, ultimately converting his dirty money into squeaky clean stock to become the majority shareholder and CEO. As the world continued its green march toward energy-efficient transportation, Vertex became more lucrative than Kurtoff's nefarious enterprises. He ceded his criminal operations to his second in command, retaining a 10% share of the profits. So many millions flowed in from Vertex legitimately, he had reasoned, why take the chance of a criminal conviction? He'd laundered his dirty money to buy his interest in Vertex, and Vertex, in return, had laundered his not-so-clean image, though rumors of his past still abounded.

The evening news was playing on a wall-mounted TV, the volume low enough that Kurtoff could enjoy his supper without distraction. His plump housekeeper placed a soup bowl on the table, then scurried off before she could receive a nasty reprimand for something she'd done, real or imagined. Kurtoff was taking his first sip when the news broadcast returned after a commercial. The soup was delicious. Life was good. After savoring a spoonful, he looked up at the screen to see a sea of flames engulfing what was left of a smoldering yellow vehicle.

Judy Murano, local television anchor, provided the voiceover:

"explosion of a Hydro, the brand-new hydrogen-powered car from New Millennium Motors, took the life of an infant late this afternoon at the Prime Foods Supermarket."

Kurtoff choked on his soup as he leapt to his feet. He picked up the remote and raised the volume to an almost piercing level and turned on the closed captioning to be sure he'd understand every word. "*Layno.*"

Murano and her co-anchor Don Williams now appeared on the screen. She continued, "the world's first self-sustainable hydrogen-powered vehicle. Its only fuel is water. The exact cause of the disaster is unknown. Questions *have* been raised whether New Millennium rushed this vehicle into production without adequate safety testing."

"You're right, Judy," Williams added, "didn't that consumer advocacy group call for a delay in marketing the Hydro until more testing could—"

"Sorry to interrupt, Don. We're getting word that the car belonged to Jennifer Talbot, daughter of United States Senator William Talbot of New York. The child was his two-month-old granddaughter, Allison." An image of the little girl's face appeared on the screen.

Kurtoff had seen enough. He flung the bowl at the wall, completely shattering it. "*Shit. Shit. Shit.*" His flustered housekeeper rushed in with a mop and rags, but Kurtoff screamed, "No. Not now." As she hurried away with her head down, Kurtoff's phone rang. It was Gura. Kurtoff tried to control his mounting rage before finally picking up after four rings.

"Yes? *Tak?*" After listening for a few seconds, he shouted, "*I believe you are idiot.* How could this happen? *Explosion. Kill little girl?* I do not like to be disappointed, Damytro. And I *am* disappointed, is not? *Extremely so.*"

When their conversation ended, Kurtoff returned his attention to the screen. He'd frozen the playback on a frame of the destroyed Hydro. What had happened to their plan?

Chapter 6

BUDDY'S HOBBY PALACE
Main Street, Amherst, New York
Monday, July 3, 2023
7:38 p.m.

Pete Simons, fourteen years old, Adam Simons' precocious only child, was in hi-tech teen heaven. Racetrack tables, computer games, gigantic screens, robots, drones, and other gadgets abounded. As did the youngsters. Dozens of them. This week, twenty tables were arranged in the middle of the room, each with a two-lane racetrack. The deafening din of whining electric toy car motors, mini hover vehicles, whirring robots, video game explosions, and screeching adolescents made it nearly impossible to hear yourself think.

Pete, smart beyond his years, and his friend, Aidan, were raucously engaged in a car race near the back of the room. Pete was of average height for a ninth grader but significantly overweight. Too many sugary soft drinks, cookies, candy, ice cream. Too little parental supervision. He had few boundaries, allowing him to indulge in the immediate gratification of untempered youth.

Except for his weight, Pete took after his mother, with soft brown hair, brown eyes, and prominent cheeks. His smarts he got from both parents. Yet his grades didn't match that intelligence. He preferred to goof off and play class clown, in need of constant attention. Homework was boring. He had better things to do.

With a dark glint in his eye, Pete roughly elbowed Aidan aside. Ignoring Aidan's yelp, "Dude, *no!*" Pete brought his racecar to a stop and stuffed a firecracker in its tailpipe, adhering it to the car with the wad of gum he'd been chewing. Pete ignited the fuse with a cigarette lighter, another vice he'd snuck past his father. Sparks flew from the fuse, and the car screamed down the track before finally exploding and spewing tiny pieces of metal and plastic all around.

The children at the nearby tables screamed and winced as pieces of Pete's car rained down on them. In the cacophony of sound and motion, they were unsure of the source of the mess. The bored proprietor sitting at the cash register, the late Buddy's grandson, was deeply engrossed in a comic book and the hip-hop playing in his earbuds, so he didn't notice the chaos.

Aidan stared at Pete with a combination of admiration and deep reproach. "Dude. *What* the *fuck*?"

"Bored," Pete replied. "Follow me." He carried the laptop, which he always had with him, toward a corner of the room where he took a new piece of gum from his pocket and stuffed it in his mouth.

Aidan picked up his intact car then followed along. His phone rang. It was his mother's ringtone. "Yeah, Mom. C'mon. How 'bout 11?...10:30?...C'mon, Mom, please?...Okay. 10:15. Yeah, he's here...I know...I will be..." Aidan lowered his voice to a whisper. "It wasn't his fault. The kid lost his balance. Don't worry. Pete likes me. I'll be careful. Promise... No, honestly. The kid lost his balance, that's all."

When Aidan caught up with Pete, they sat down on the floor. Pete remained nonplussed about the destruction at the racetrack table, but Aidan wasn't. "*Dude.* What's your dad going to say about the car?"

"You think he gives two shits? Forget it. Watch and learn. This will take your mind off it."

Pete opened his laptop. *CALL OF DUTY 14: ZERO GRAVITY COMBAT, THE MOON* appeared on the screen. Pete logged out of the game and deftly maneuvered his touchpad to display a naked woman with immense and undoubtedly augmented breasts lying on a heart-shaped bed draped in plush red velvet. Two snarling tigers sat on the bed, on either side of her, presumably Photoshopped in. Nevertheless, they leant a sense of danger to the lewdness of the scene.

"Like, *dude,* how do you get away with *this*?" Aidan asked

"Since my mom died...I told you. Not two shits. Not even one. Totally clueless. I could set his stupid hamster on fire, you think he'd notice?"

Pete typed feverishly, and a stylish woman replaced the

seasoned pro with the tigers. About mid-30s, silky brown hair, with a smile as wide as the ocean. When Pete hit [play], the picture remained static, but the voice of his father spoke.

"Hi, Beth. We haven't spoken in a bit. I'm sorry. It's been pretty hectic at work, and taking on a summer class hasn't helped. Let's see, um... News. We're up to our fifth Hamilton since you've been...gone. They don't live very long, do they? Not like humans. At the pet store, they said gerbils are hardier than hamsters, so maybe next time. Believe it or not, I'm actually thinking of teaching full-time and closing the office. They've got this ridiculous new system called Holotrials..."

Pete paused the playback. "Didn't make the daily report. Again."

Aidan asked what they were listening to.

"My dad's diary."

"*No way.* Isn't it password protected and encrypted and...how'd you—"

"My Uncle Mac," Pete explained. "He taught me lots of things. He was an Army ranger. And not one of the wimpy ones. Get this. Last year my dad had an affair, and when they broke up, she went to Switzerland to have a baby."

"No shit. So *dude,* you have a little brother? In Switzerland?"

"Shhh. Actually it's...doesn't matter. I had to do extra special research to figure that one out. My dad doesn't even know about the kid. More competition. All I need. The freaking hamster's enough. Maybe I *should* set it on fire."

"What kinda' research?" Aidan asked.

"Told you. My Uncle Mac. He's the coolest dude ever. Well, like, coolest over twenty. We're gonna shoot each other tomorrow."

Chapter 7

HOME OF JEROME ("MAC") MCMILLAN
Auburn Avenue, Buffalo, New York
Saturday, July 8, 2023
10:30 a.m.

Mac—a.k.a. Jerome McMillan, though no one called him that—was having the dream again. It never ended well. He stood on the sidewalk, clutching a red plush toy in his left hand. He called it *Dinobird*, or just *Dino*, because it was hard for young Mac to pronounce *pterodactyl*. His right hand grasped another, larger, hand. He couldn't see any more of the person than a vague purple dress.

Suddenly a strong wind blew Dinobird into the middle of the street, into oncoming traffic. Mac started to run after it, but then he remembered the hand and the purple dress. He wanted to save Dino, but he couldn't, wouldn't, let go of the hand. A diesel truck was fast approaching. Mac tried to reach for Dino, still holding on to the hand. His arm stretched into the street like Pinocchio's nose, but the closer his hand got to Dino, the faster the truck approached. Dino wasn't going to make it. But he couldn't let Dino die. Yet he couldn't let go of the hand. But he couldn't let—

The ding of a text message on Mac's phone woke him from the dream. It was Pete, reminding him of their outing this afternoon. Mac sluggishly rose from the bed and surveyed the room. To call it slovenly would be a compliment. Empty beer bottles lay everywhere. One even sat atop the parakeet cage. The parakeet was God knows where. The previous week's wardrobe was all over the floor.

Mac staggered through the door labeled LATRINE. Gathering his wits, he shakily picked up a razor, then paused to stare at his image in the mirror. "Not bad." Mac could always muster compliments for himself. At six-foot-two, he had a balding head laced with fringes of hair around the circumference. He'd retained much of the musculature he'd developed way back in boot camp, as well as a sprinkling of scars from hand-to-hand combat and a couple of entry and exit wounds.

Mac tried to stay in reasonable shape. Old habits, like old soldiers, never died. These days, he rarely got into physical altercations on the job, but the muscles came in handy for his weekly arm-wrestling contest with Freddie, Adam's paralegal extraordinaire. No money wagered, just for bragging rights. If asked after a match, each would say he'd won.

At 75—at least Mac believed that was his age, having lost track somewhere in the progression of foster homes—he might have lost a step or two. But his vision was still damn near perfect. He'd never needed glasses, which had served him well during his three years as an Army sniper. The glare reflecting off eyeglasses could reveal one's position and turn the shooter into the target.

Mac's Army skills would come in handy today. Once fully dressed, he opened a concealed panel in the living room wall, revealing a large safe that contained a formidable display of weaponry. He chose a dependable handgun and a somewhat exotic rifle for this afternoon's activities. He would need them to kill Pete and his comrades in arms.

Chapter 8

NIAGARA WAR GAMES
Wheatfield, New York
Saturday, July 8, 2023

Mac and Pete were suiting up in the prep room. Mac knew he was pushing the envelope by bringing him here. *Hell, what Adam doesn't know won't hurt him. Pete won't tell, that's for sure.* Intimate father-son moments were rare for Pete and Adam. Nevertheless, as far as Adam knew, they were at the zoo.

Each of them wore a tac vest with extra magazines for their rifles and handguns. Pete's vest was blue, Mac's green. Pete carefully loaded the clip for his AK-47. Mac checked out his ASG Scorpion EVO 3 A1 ATEK rifle. Each of them had an Elite Force Glock 17 Gen 5 handgun and a helmet, as well. Pete's resembled a black skull, with black impact-resistant goggles, excellent for fading into the scenery. Mac went for a more basic helmet with a tinted face shield. The vests and helmets would protect their torsos and heads, but their arms and legs were fully exposed, covered only with ordinary street clothes. Pant legs and long sleeve shirts wouldn't do much to stop a successful shot. Before they entered the arena, each checked the other's weapons and tightened the straps on their helmets. Neither wanted to chance a stray *bullet* ricocheting through a gap and taking out an eye.

Mac suggested they start with their usual target practice. Pete complained that it was too boring, they'd logged gobs of hours on the practice range already, so they agreed to skip it and go directly into battle. As they proceeded to their separate entrances for the blue and green teams, Mac yelled at Pete, "Halt, soldier. Extricate that gum from your mouth and secure it in the nearest disposal unit. *Now.* The enemy can hear *you* chewing from two clicks away. If *you* spit it out on the battlefield, you will have marked your location."

Pete did as he was told.

Mac then gave his standard advice. "Eyes behind your head. Watch the terrain. No distractions."

Pete emerged from a winding tunnel into the Blue Team's staging area, the second floor of a bombed-out brick building. He held his rifle with both hands, his Glock in its holster, just as Mac had taught him. Two Blue Team members were already there, a thirty-something on his day off from the Amherst Police, and an Air Force retiree seeking the thrill of combat that he'd never had as a mechanic working on drones at Holloman Air Force Base in New Mexico. Each carried an M4 carbine.

When he saw this teenage kid playing soldier, the Air Force weekend warrior rolled his eyes. Seeing this, the cop set him straight, telling him this *kid* had saved an entire platoon from an ambush the week before. He'd also fashioned a mortar out of scrap pieces of broken weapons. The teenager was a wizard, could build anything they needed, the cop insisted.

With Pete's bona fides established, the three formulated a plan to find and extinguish the Green Team. They gathered next to a shattered window to get a better view of the battlefield. It wasn't easy. The Niagara War Games folks had done their best to give the converted Walmart mega-store the feel of a genuine combat zone, filling it with smoke, burned out buildings, destroyed tanks and Humvees, as well as ear-splitting sounds and blinding flashes of light from simulated artillery and air strikes.

The policeman volunteered to run recon. When Pete advised him that Mac was on the Green Team today, the cop's face got a little green, but pride made him stick to the mission. They found a large black tarp on the floor, cut a hole for his head, and draped it over him like a Rambo-style poncho for camouflage. It was not quite long enough to reach the floor—the bottoms of his legs, from the calves down, were still exposed. After a round of *good lucks*, he descended the broken stairs and slithered out the battered front door, crawling on his belly until he reached a demolished Bradley Fire Support Vehicle lying on its side. He started sprinting to another burned-out vehicle about ten yards away, but the moment he left the cover of the Bradley, the distinctive crack of Mac's rifle rang out.

Sure enough, Mac had targeted his prey's left calf. Falling to the ground, the cop grabbed his leg and shrieked in pain. Those airsoft guns might not kill, but they certainly gave a good sting.

***

As they removed their gear, Mac began his usual post-combat quiz.

"Okay. Let's review your training. Then we'll grab some chow. Ready? What's the primary goal of hand-to-hand combat?"

"Kill the other asshole first. It doesn't work so well in reverse."

"Zactly. What's more accurate, a sniper rifle at 200 yards or a handgun at ten?"

"C'mon, Uncle Mac, too easy. The sniper rifle. *Duh.*"

"What's *most* accurate?"

"A knife at one yard."

Mac smiled at his protégé as he disassembled his rifle. "You see an IED on the side of the road, ten yards away. What do you do?"

"Call in an EOD unit. *Unless* one of your grunts is WIA and can't evac. Then you take it apart and defuse it yourself."

"Negative, Pokey. If you're not wounded, you run like hell and call in ordnance disposal. Let EOD handle it."

"Uncle Mac, I can take apart an IED in my sleep. Jeez, I read the manual like a year ago. No need to wait for EOD. *Never shall I fail my comrades.* The ranger creed."

"Negative, Pokey. You get the hell out. You're not leaving your buddy behind. The disposal unit's gonna take care of him. And *you're* gonna live to fight another day and help the rest of your comrades."

"Yeah, whatever."

"Soldier. Respect a superior officer. You got that?"

"I'm sorry, Uncle Mac. I mean, yes, *sir.*" Pete snapped to attention and executed the laser sharp salute Mac had taught him.

"Okay, Pokey. You're in the National Military Command Center at the Pentagon with a five-star general and the President of the United States. The general gives you an order. The President gives you a contrary order. Which do you follow?"

"The President."

"What's the matter with you, soldier? You want permanent latrine duty? You would take orders from a goddamn civilian over a five goddamn star general?"

"Yes, sir. Would, sir. The President is the Commander in

Chief, sir."

Mac smiled. "Perfect. Okay. Let's try it this way. You're in a bird, about to do a drop. I'm your commanding officer this time. The President's there. We give conflicting orders. Which do you follow?"

"The President's. But..."

Mac eyed him quizzically. "But *what*, soldier?"

"But I'd prefer to follow your orders, sir."

"Good answer. Okay, chow time."

"How about we get a couple of beers first, Uncle Mac."

"Sure thing, Pokey. I gotta finish changing. You wait for me outside...for about seven years."

"Ah, c'mon, Uncle Mac. Just one?"

"Let's stick with Mighty Taco today. Not to mention your dad. It'd be bad enough if he knew you were here."

"C'mon, Uncle Mac. The dude don't give a shit what I do."

"He's a dad, not a dude. Don't forget it."

"Yeah. He couldn't care less. Maybe if I was a hamster—"

"Pokey, you have no idea how much your dad loves you. He's just had a hard time since... You don't have a clue what a blessing it is just to know who your old man is."

"All right. But Uncle Mac, just one lousy beer?"

"No beer. Tacos. Let's go back to my place first, and we'll take the Porsche."

With the thought of riding in Mac's awesome sports car, Pete's eyes lit up. It would hardly have been his first beer, anyway.

***

As they walked to Mac's very uncool Chevy, Mac replayed the dream in his head once again, straining to resolve the woman in the purple dress. Her face. Eyes. Hair. Something. Suddenly, he didn't know how—a sixth sense maybe—he was sure she was alive, as if he'd willed her into existence. It didn't make any sense. He didn't believe in such nonsense. Yet he was sure. And he swore more forcefully than ever that he'd find her.

Chapter 9

STATE UNIVERSITY OF NEW YORK ("SUNY")
AT BUFFALO LAW SCHOOL
Room 304
Amherst, New York
Monday, July 10, 2023
10:00 a.m.

Adam Simons, now in full-on professor mode, stormed into the noisy classroom. *"Creatures."* The chattering stopped abruptly. These students were 3Ls. In summer jobs, they'd all seen some semblance of the legal world, but they were still in awe of Adam. He was that special brand of professor who had made a difference in their lives, and the students appreciated him. Most of the girls had a crush on him, and the boys wanted to be him, vice versa in some cases. Though a 45-year-old professor seemed ancient to them, he was in reasonably good shape: five-foot-ten, wavy brown hair, and a pleasant square-jawed face made for the movies. More significantly, he was a fount of legal knowledge and a brilliant trial lawyer. Brains were sexy. Adam's brain was particularly sexy.

He loved teaching summer courses. The students were in a better mood and more attentive because of their lighter class loads. The days were longer, sunnier, warmer, and the smell of freshly cut grass permeated the air on the university's sprawling North Campus in Amherst, a northern Buffalo suburb.

The classroom was laid out like a small movie theater, a slanted floor with ten rows of seats and a *stage* at the base for the professor. Adam always entered through a door built into the back wall of the stage. On the door was a large poster that had been on the refrigerator in Adam's law-school apartment, twenty-three years ago: FOR EVERY COMPLEX PROBLEM THERE IS A SIMPLE SOLUTION...AND IT IS WRONG. The message had been in front of his nose for three years, whenever he retrieved the prior night's cold chicken wings, but it didn't sink in until he started practicing law and realized just how true it was.

Adam briefly glanced at the poster before pivoting to address the class. "Okay. Everything you need to know about trial technique in a three-second mantra. There used to be this TV infomercial I got a kick out of, one of those real estate get-rich-quick schemes. The conman giving the sales pitch had a simple formula for how to get rich. *Look at what the poor people are doing...and don't do it.* So, go down to the courthouse and catch a trial or two. Watch what the bad trial lawyers are doing. And don't do it."

The class chuckled, as they always did at Adam's humor. He could mesmerize them as well as he could a jury. He didn't need silly lawyer jokes, though he had plenty if he needed them. And what he didn't have, Mac did.

"Creatures. Creatures. Simmer down. Let's address the woolly mammoth in the room. The Holotrial. What do we think of it?" Adam brought up a power point slide on the large interactive whiteboard in front of the class: HOLOTRIAL = HOLLOW TRIAL.

A nerdy student in the fourth row piped up. "Why, Professor Simons? It sounds great. For the jurors, the taxpayers, everybody."

"Anyone else? Creatures?"

Kelly Martin raised her hand from the third row. She was an excellent student, top of her class, editor-in-chief of the *Law Review*. With her eye on the professor.

"Ms. Martin?"

Kelly gave Adam a big smile. "Finally brings efficiency to the legal system after a few hundred years."

"Yes. Makes the trains run on time. You're probably too young for that one."

"C'mon, professor." Kelly scoffed. "You think we didn't study World War Two? Mussolini. The '69 Mets. Hula hoops. Give us a hard one."

Adam wondered if she'd intended a double entendre. He was used to student crushes. *As bad as patients falling in love with their psychologists. And just as unethical if acted upon.* "Okay, Ms. Martin. Let's get back to the subject at hand. Holotrials. Who can tell me the first specifically guaranteed right pertaining to trials in the New York State Constitution? Anyone?"

Adam paced back and forth, seeking a volunteer. A few

students tentatively raised their hands but soon lowered them. Adam changed the slide on the whiteboard: TRIAL BY JURY IS INVIOLATE FOREVER. "I've paraphrased slightly, but you get the gist. Inviolate *forever*, creatures. By my Apple Watch, forever includes today."

A male student in the seventh row challenged him. "We don't study state constitutions in law school, professor. Anyway, you *do* have juries in Holotrials, and you pick them just like before."

What's his name again? Oh yeah, Sammy Wong. "Mr. Wong, you most definitely *do not* pick them just like before. When the justice system was *sane*, before Holotrials, juries would be chosen prior to beginning the trial. We could observe the jurors throughout the entire proceeding, as evidence was introduced, not to mention during our opening and closing statements. Now we don't pick them until after the trial is *over*. It's like having the umpires come out on the field after the game has been played."

***

Adam had just finished a trial in Monroe County, where the Holotrial system had *not* yet been adopted, and which amply demonstrated the virtues of being able to observe real-time juror reactions. He'd defended a defamation case for a newspaper that had used a photo of a hog feeding at the trough to represent a congressman accused of mishandling public funds. Falsely accused, as it turned out. The congressman claimed the public had come to identify him with this particular hog, and it was hurting his re-election chances.

While Adam cross-examined the congressman, a sixteen-square-foot cage was wheeled into the courtroom. Adam asked the congressman to identify which of the five hogs within it was the one from the newspaper. To the congressman, and everyone else in the courtroom, they were identical. Even the congressman laughed. The widespread dissemination of this scene in the traditional media, as well as every imaginable social media platform, served to show the congressman's human side and increased his popularity. In fact, it probably got him re-elected. So losing the defamation claim didn't sting as badly. The next night, Adam was booked as a guest on *The Tonight Show* and dutifully brought the pigpen with him. The studio audience, like the congressman, had fun trying to pick out the offending animal. Though perhaps they weren't trying too hard, because the winner got to take home the hog.

***

"Listen creatures, a trial is a play, not a movie. You have to react to your audience in real time. Never forget, the jurors are the six most important people in the world. You've got to know them. Smell them. How do they react to your witnesses? The other side's witnesses. To you and your opponent? To the judge's rulings. Do they like humor? How do they feel when a lawyer challenges the judge? Do they get it when a witness is lying, or do you have to spoon-feed them? If you can't observe them during the trial, you're flying blind."

He didn't know it yet, but in about seven hours, he would be asked to fly blind. By a pretty powerful man.

Chapter 10

HOME OF ADAM SIMONS
Tudor Place, Buffalo, New York
Monday, July 10, 2023
5:40 p.m.

Adam whistled as he entered his stately Tudor-style home. It had been a long day, teaching his *creatures* at the law school and running his one-man specialized law practice. Hanging on the side wall in the front hallway were two small baskets labeled SUSTAINED and OVERRULED. He threw his keys into SUSTAINED, took a tiny candy out of OVERRULED, and went straight to the hamster cage in the living room. "Hi, Hamilton. Want a treat? Treat? How's my boy?" Hamilton gobbled up the treat and returned to his hamster wheel. Adam marveled at how the little fellow could run on the wheel with such enthusiasm for hours on end, without getting anywhere at all. The analogy to his own daily battles, at the law school and in court, did not elude him.

His house had been built in 1910. Like the other Tudor homes on the street, it had a white stucco exterior accented with dark brown timbers. The house had seen two World Wars, the Great Depression, the Roaring Twenties, the Kennedy assassination, the moon landing, the blossoming of the civil rights movement, and countless other historical milestones. In fact, the original owner of the home had been a Civil War veteran. From the winning side. Adam loved that sense of history. *If these walls could talk.*

Adam had done well for himself. Not as well as those class-action lawyers with their billion-dollar settlements, but well enough to lead a comfortable lifestyle, a universe apart from the tiny apartment in the Bronx where he'd spent his childhood.

His parents didn't have much, but what they had, they had given to Adam and his sister. The family didn't summer in Europe, or even the Hamptons, but they scraped enough together to visit the

Alan M. Wishnoff

Bronx Zoo, Coney Island, Catskill Game Farm, and other attractions within a day's drive in their second-hand car.

With the help of full scholarships, Adam excelled at Princeton, and then Yale Law School, where he fell in love with two things: Beth, and the United States Constitution. In that order. Beth was the most wonderful thing God had put on earth. The Constitution, remarkable as it was, ran a distant second. Its guarantee of individual freedoms including freedom of the press, speech, and religion, would spur him on to a career defending those rights. Those eighteenth century geniuses had composed a document embracing a brand new structure of government that was still viable more than 230 years later, in a modern computer-driven society many times the size of revolutionary America. Nevertheless, the irony didn't escape Adam that, when this utopian guarantee of freedom and equality was adopted in 1791, a large part of the American population was enslaved, with no rights of any kind, by another part of the population.

Even now, 247 years after the Declaration of Independence, the Founders' vision of equal rights for all was far from achieved. Adam knew this from his own observations and from listening to Beth's impassioned speeches on the subject, first in class, then in his dorm room, then in his bed, and ultimately in their apartment.

During the summers after their 1L and 2L years, Adam followed Beth to summer jobs at the ACLU and the NAACP Legal Defense and Educational Fund. Upon graduation, he had his choice of high-paying mega-law-firm jobs but instead went to the U.S. Justice Department Civil Rights Division in Washington D.C., where Beth had gotten a job at a non-profit. In five years he'd risen to Assistant Director, which made him realize he enjoyed the taste of battle in the courtroom infinitely more than pushing papers around a desk. They moved to Buffalo, Beth's hometown, where he opened a law firm specializing in civil rights matters. When the Dean of UB Law School came calling, Adam thought he'd give it a try, and he actually found teaching to be more enjoyable than practicing law.

Over the years, Adam's practice branched out to all sorts of constitutional issues. He became famous not only for his string of victories, but for his textbook cross-examinations, openings, and summations, his masterful and often unorthodox legal analysis, and the ease with which he could charm judges and juries and make unpopular causes and clients popular. His sense of humor helped, and he would wield it in the courtroom when appropriate. Even in the most serious cases, perhaps especially in those cases, it could be helpful, on occasion, to lighten the mood with a little levity.

***

Adam relaxed on his couch, listening to a Rachmaninoff piano concerto. The phone rang, and when he answered, he heard a voice he hadn't heard in a long time: Adam's law school roommate, Bill Talbot. *Senator* William Talbot, of the Great State of New York. Bill had a request, and when Adam heard it, he immediately knew he shouldn't do what the Senator wanted. But he probably would.

Chapter 11

LAW OFFICE OF ADAM SIMONS
Parkside Avenue, Buffalo, New York
Tuesday, July 11, 2023
7 p.m.

Adam's office was in a two-story red brick building on Parkside Avenue, a no-frills utilitarian structure circa the late 1940s. It was close enough to the downtown courts to get there fast, yet distant enough for Adam to avoid being accosted on the street by lawyers bragging about their latest war stories every time he went to lunch. He also liked being in a largely residential area with a lovely park across the street.

The name of the street alone brought back fond memories for Adam because of his soft spot for the Parkside Candies shop. Built in 1927, it was famous for its old-fashioned ice-cream parlor ambience, as well as its delicious chocolates and other confections, including chocolate-covered sponge candy, a Buffalo delicacy. Yes, Buffalo had more than chicken wings to offer the world, though most of its home-town offerings, including "beef on weck" and fried bologna and onion sandwiches, would make a dietitian wince.

The sweet shop played an immensely important role in Adam's life. It was there that he had proposed to Beth, in the romantic booth in the rear of the store. They'd been living together for over seven years and were madly in love, as far as Adam was concerned, but his proposal was met with stone cold silence. After pausing a bit to tease him, Beth happily accepted, smiling and giggling. Her mischievousness was one of her most endearing qualities, and Adam couldn't be mad at her once he was engulfed in the ecstasy that her "Yes" brought him. He couldn't imagine being mad at her under *any* circumstances. And he never was. Not that he hadn't pretended on occasion, to no avail. She could see through him like plastic wrap.

Holotrial

***

Adam sat behind his tidy, organized desk as he awaited his guests. A few framed photos graced the desktop. A beach scene, a picture of Beth from 2007, and a hamster, Hamilton III. The photo of Pete, age five, hadn't been updated since Adam had lost Beth. He gazed out the window at Delaware Park, watching the joggers, the old men playing bocce ball, the fledgling parents nervously pushing their strollers, the pickup basketball games. So carefree.

Adam had made it a rule not to represent friends or family. Yet, in marched his friends, Bill and Katherine Talbot, with their daughter, Jennifer. Katherine looked devastated. Eyes red and moist, an empty stare. Jennifer appeared detached, almost surly. *Interesting. The grandmother taking it harder than the mother.* Bill was stone-faced, typical for him when he wasn't on the campaign trail, glad-handing potential voters and kissing babies. Meticulously quaffed lest a member of the press capture him looking anything less than perfect, every strand of Bill's dark black hair was in place, his tailored suit freshly pressed.

Adam hadn't seen Jennifer in many years, long before the purple hair and nose studs. He had no doubt that Bill was less than pleased. To the Senator, she would be a detriment to his campaign, though his aides had undoubtedly told him her new image was good for capturing the youth vote. *I wonder if this is an act of rebellion, or simply a reflection of her personality. That's all I need, another rebel to deal with.*

The Talbots came to a sudden stop, trying to decide which of the three chairs in front of Adam's desk they'd each take. The Senator, exhibiting a chivalry that seemed forced, let the ladies sit first. Katherine chose the chair directly in front of Adam. She was an attractive woman, a 45-year-old version of Jennifer, except for the purple hair and nose studs. They shared the same blue eyes and athletic body, though Katherine's was more filled out, in all the right places. She'd put on a smidgen of weight since Adam had last seen her, but it didn't do her looks any harm. Her breasts were particularly prominent. *No doubt overeating to compensate for life with Bill. Some people cope that way. When I'm depressed, I stop eating. Oh well. Chacun à son goût.*

Katherine quietly sipped from a bottle of Voss Artesian Still

~33~

Water. Adam sensed from the Senator's repeated glances at his watch that he was more invested in planning his next campaign rally than the legal claim for the loss of his granddaughter.

As Adam was about to speak, Jennifer pulled an e-cigarette from her purse and started puffing a cloud of mango-flavored vapor.

"Jennifer..." Bill snapped. "I told you to leave that thing in the car."

Jennifer peered at Katherine.

Katherine frowned. "Bill, leave her alone. Adam, is it okay if she vapes?"

"Adam isn't her father," Bill insisted. "*I* am. And as long as I support, feed, and clothe her, *and* pay her rent, she'll follow my rules."

Adam was shocked by Bill's tone. *Jennifer deserves some slack after her recent tragedy.*

She put the offending e-cigarette away, though her eyes continued to shoot daggers at her father. From her purse, she took out a piece of gum and started chewing it, loudly.

Like my own rebel at home. Even the same flavor gum. He hoped to cut through the tension. "Bill, Katherine. Jennifer. I can't tell you how sorry I am. Really. There are no words. If there's anything I can do..."

Notwithstanding his apparent reticence about the meeting, the Senator adopted his usual take-charge demeanor. "That's why we're here, Adam. You're going to represent us."

"Bill, I want to help. And I will. Any way I can..."

Jennifer was surprised to hear Adam address her father as Bill. She was used to people subserviently calling him Senator, or at least Mr. Talbot.

"But honestly, you'd be far better off hiring someone with real personal-injury experience. I'm a civil rights lawyer. The last PI case I handled was mock trial in law school. Let me give you some names—"

"Come on, Adam..." Bill barked, "you can do this in your sleep."

"I wouldn't sleep too well, Bill. Frankly, with these screwy Holotrials, I've a mind to quit the trial business altogether. It's not only the lack of live jurors, but the harebrained program has an accelerated pre-trial period, just two months to prepare for trial.

They call it the *Rocket Docket*." Adam turned to Katherine, whose face was anguished. "I'm sorry, I shouldn't be whining about *my* problems. They're nothing compared to what you've been through. Losing a child like that...Jennifer, again, I'm so sorry. Listen, if I thought it made sense, I'd handle this, Holotrial be damned. But I don't do PI, and I also don't work for friends or relatives. You're not only friends. You're like family. I'm simply too close. It would be like a doctor operating on his own child."

Katherine choked on a sip of her expensive water. The Senator appeared not to notice.

"Adam, we need your transcendent trial abilities," Bill pressed. "Your sense of discretion."

That seemed like a curious thing to say, but Adam let it go, for now. *What secrets could there be? The car blew up. There was a video.* He couldn't believe Jennifer was at fault. What could need discretion?

"We go back... Adam, remember our first day of law school? I thought a tort was something you buy in a bakery. I'm not one to call in chips with friends..."

Adam barely suppressed a laugh at this bald-faced lie.

"But you *do* remember how I saved your ass in that faculty-student football game. If I hadn't blocked that obese contracts professor, you would've been dead meat."

Katherine sniffled.

Bill seemed oblivious to the crass irony of his comment.

Katherine finally spoke. "Please, Adam. Here." She slid a photo across the desk. "This is Allison. Our Allie."

Adam gazed at the photo of the tiny child's face, so full of life. "She has your smile, Katherine. You know, she looks a lot like Pete at that age."

Katherine choked up again, her eyes imploring.

Adam felt helpless. As much as he wanted to hug Katherine and tell her that things would be all right, it was Bill's place to comfort her. If Adam tried, it would just make Bill jealous, harkening back to the trio's serial dating at Yale so many years ago.

Bill chimed in again. "Adam, it's straight *Res Ipsa.*"

Jennifer gave her father a puzzled look.

"*Res Ipsa Loquitur*, Jenny. It's Latin for *The thing speaks for itself.* Cars aren't supposed to explode. If they do, the manufacturer was negligent. Case closed. You don't even need to prove specifically *what* they did wrong. The law assumes they screwed up. Adam, a 3L could handle this."

"Then maybe you should get a 3L," Adam replied. "I'm sorry, it's just—"

"Mr. Simons..." Jennifer finally spoke up.

"Please. Call me Adam."

"Um, Adam, would I have to testify?"

Adam understood her concern. What mother would want to relive such an event on the stand? Risking blame for killing her own daughter by a practiced and unscrupulous cross-examiner?

"It could come to that, Jennifer." Adam realized what a clone Jennifer was of the young, vibrant Katherine that he'd met in the Sterling Memorial Library as a 1L when Katherine was getting her masters in anthropology. Adam hadn't needed to be there. He had all the required law books in his dorm room, but he was observing the time-honored college tradition of hanging out in the school library, pretending to study while spending his time scanning for romantic liaisons. Adam had been oblivious to the fact that Katherine was pursuing the same strategy. She'd had all the anthropology books *she* needed in *her* dorm room.

Adam returned his attention to Jennifer. Something about her struck a chord. Not just her resemblance to Katherine. Was it that they'd both experienced the tragic loss of loved ones? "Jennifer, I'm sure you'd do fine. It's natural to be nervous. Every witness is. Believe me, we'd go over everything ahead of time until you were thoroughly comfortable. Anyway, I wouldn't worry about it. These things mostly settle out of court. I think your father's right, it's probably a *Res Ipsa* case, so it wouldn't make a lot of sense for them to fight too hard and get more bad headlines."

"So you're taking the case?" Katherine sighed with relief.

"Bill always *was* too persuasive for me." Adam kept his gaze on Katherine. They both knew who'd convinced him.

As the Talbots left, Adam was already replaying the meeting in his mind, as if reading a deposition transcript. Something was wrong. He'd never had such a strange feeling after a client meeting. "I'm guilty of breaking my rule about representing friends, is all," he told himself. But the strangeness of the meeting went beyond that. He just couldn't peel off enough layers to reach the center of this onion. Not yet.

The Talbots were headed for the staircase when Katherine exclaimed, "I'm sorry. Left my purse in Adam's office. Not thinking straight."

"You'll work it through," Bill replied coldly. "Meet you at the car."

As she turned back, Katherine muttered under her breath. "You work it through, you son of a bitch."

As Bill marched down the stairs, he nearly knocked over a man passing him on the way up. The man, in his early seventies but still bearing much of the muscular physique of his youth, steadied himself against the rail and offered a pleasant smile to Bill's gruff apology. Bill stared at him for a moment. "Excuse me, have we met?"

Freddie, Adam's paralegal, just smiled. He'd grown used to this. "I think I'd remember, Senator."

"You're sure?"

"I get that all the time. Must have one of those faces."

"Well, here. Take one of these." Bill withdrew a TALBOT FOR PRESIDENT button from his breast pocket and handed it to Freddie.

"Thank you, Senator." As the Senator continued down the stairs, Freddie proceeded to the second floor and, not so gently, deposited the campaign button in the nearest trash can.

***

Adam was surprised to hear a knock at the door so soon after the meeting. He had nothing else scheduled. As he opened it, Katherine glided past him, their shoulders almost touching. She stopped on a dime and spun to face him, close enough that Adam could smell her perfume, feel her warm breath. This close, he detected a tinge of alcohol.

"Please close the door, counselor." It was more of a command than a request. When he complied, Katherine spoke in a whisper, her despondency replaced by an icy calm. "Listen. As our lawyer, there's something you should know. You always say you have to dig up the dirt in your own yard first. I read it in that fluff piece the *Times* ran on you in March." She looked out the window at the park.

"Kate—"

"Shut up, counselor." Katherine turned to Adam and locked eyes with his. "*Shut up and listen* for a change. About a year ago, I had an affair. Bill knows about it. I couldn't hide it from him. But I never told him who, and he's never asked. So my paramour need not worry. There's no point quizzing Bill about it. You won't learn anything more. And that's all I will ever say on the subject."

Adam swallowed hard. "Kate—"

"I just thought you should know." She touched his arm. "As our lawyer."

***

Katherine sat in the plush leather seat of the black Lincoln Town Car limo with U.S. Senate license plates. The Senator closed the privacy window, then scrutinized Katherine, trying to read her face. "Did you tell him?"

"No. He doesn't need to know."

"Agreed."

Chapter 12

MAC'S HOME
Auburn Avenue, Buffalo, New York
Thursday, July 13, 2023
11:00 a.m.

Mac was having the dream again. The anguished choice between holding on to the hand in the purple dress or saving Dinobird from the fast-approaching truck.

His phone's Army-anthem ringtone woke him with a start. The caller ID indicated Adam Simons. Trying to break through his morning haze, Mac barked at the phone in his gravelly voice, "Jesus Christ, Chief, it's eleven hundred. Not even on my first Scotch. Not operational. What can't wait?"

His Army training had taught him to awaken and be ready for battle at a moment's notice, but that was a long time ago. He was a civ now, a noncom. He liked his sleep. In fact, he treasured it after all those years sleeping with one eye open and one ear to the ground.

"This is an all-hands, Mac."

"One sec, Chief. Had a late one. Gotta clear my head."

Mac put the phone down and walked into the latrine. He steadied himself on the sink and filled a glass with water. Which he proceeded to pour over his head. With his wits awakened, if not fully revived, he returned to the phone.

"Okay, back on duty, Chief. Wadda' we have? Some asshole invoking his constitutional right to sit naked on a school bus?"

"I'm buying. Crawdad's. Twenty minutes."

***

Adam began using Mac's services shortly after he set up his law practice in Buffalo. It didn't take long for them to admire each other's excellence in their respective jobs, and Mac became a full-

Alan M. Wishnoff

time member of Adam's staff. When Beth died, their bond became irrevocable. And Mac became a regular at the Simons' dinner table. Pete loved his new *Uncle* Mac's jokes and war stories, and Mac provided a sounding board for Adam's raging battle with the world. Meanwhile, Pete and Adam became the family Mac had never had in the various foster homes he'd passed through as a child.

***

Now in his standard private investigator attire—muted colors, conservative, nothing to see here, folks—Mac closed the front door behind him, squinting into the bright sunlight. He paused on his front stoop to pull a torn photo from his wallet. The little boy's face stared up at him, serious eyes, half smile, his left hand holding Dinobird, his right hand extended into another person's palm. The photo was torn in half near the middle, right where the woman's wrist would have been. Mac traced the jagged edge of the photo with his finger, trying to conjure up the person in the missing half, the woman with the purple dress from his dream.

***

Twenty minutes after Adam's call, they were seated at a corner table in the rear of Crawdad's Restaurant on Allen Street. An old habit, but Mac wanted to be as far as possible from the other patrons of the restaurant, in a spot where he could see anyone who entered.

A waitress came to take their order. Mac didn't need the menu. "The usual, Syl."

"Usual lunch or usual dinner, Mac? Or are you still on breakfast time?"

"Lunch, Syl..."

She took Adam's order and walked away.

"Okay, so what's the operation, Chief?"

"New Millennium Motors."

"Oh yeah. That's the, uh, they make the—"

"Hydro. The hydrogen car. The one that exploded."

"Holy shit. *That* case? It's practically 24/7 on CNN. You chasin' ambulances now?"

"Just this one. Old friend from law school. You know Senator Talbot."

~40~

"Who doesn't. Guy's a whore. He'd screw a Moroccan monkfish to be President."

"Mac. A little deference? Bill's my friend. Or he was."

Mac remembered a vague story about a shared girlfriend.

"Forget it. Mac, I need info on New Millennium. I thought there might be a quick settlement, but they've literally got billions at stake. This car *is* the company."

"Who you tryin' to impress, Chief?"

"I told you. Favor for a friend. Honestly, I can't get the dead child out of my mind. She's the spitting image of...forget it. Anyway, sounds like a simple case. I just want to dot the i's and cross the t's."

"I once knew a lawyer who said there were no simple cases, only simple lawyers. I think the same lawyer also said *never work for friends*."

"Well, only a fool never breaks a rule. By the way, Mac, how's it going with your mother?"

"*Bupkes*. But I got a new app that might be promising."

"You know, at the age she'd be now, there's a good chance she's not alive."

"True, Chief. But people do get to their nineties and beyond these days. If all I get is her name, *my* name, that'll do. Who knows, maybe I have siblings, cousins, a niece or nephew somewhere." Mac didn't mention his premonition about his mother being alive. He'd have felt foolish.

"Mac, I'm sure I don't have to tell you, if there's anything more I can do..."

"Yeah, I appreciate it."

***

Mac was almost done eating when his attention was suddenly drawn to the large television screen on the wall, displaying a picture of New York State Attorney General Susan Stevens. The news anchor provided a voiceover: "Attorney General Susan Stevens announced the indictment of two prominent Wall Street brokers for violations of the Dodd-Frank..."

"Jesus. I can't look at her." As Syl walked by, Mac half-pleaded and half-demanded she change the channel, or just turn the damn thing off. "Please, Syl. That broad gives me the creeps."

Adam was calmer. "We haven't been up against her for a while, Mac. Give it a rest."

"Chief, it's always a pissing contest with her, and you'd think that's one game the guys would win."

"She's just stubborn. Like you, Mac. You know, I think you'd make a beautiful couple."

Mac's reaction was predictable, if crude. A raised hand with a single raised finger.

"And Mac. Be careful. New Millennium's got billions on the line. You never know what people will do to protect that much cheddar."

As they rose from the table, Mac made his usual parting gesture to the waitress. "Hey, Syl. Heard about the new restaurant on the moon? Great food. No atmosphere."

Chapter 13

SUNY AT BUFFALO LAW SCHOOL
Room 304
Amherst, New York
Friday, July 14, 2023
10:00 a.m.

Adam moved behind the podium in the small mock courtroom set up at the front of the lecture hall. The mock courtroom had been a demand in his second contract. The Dean told him they couldn't afford both the courtroom and a raise, so Adam chose the courtroom. It was the single most important tool for producing competent new trial lawyers who one day might turn into *great* trial lawyers. Adam was too modest to add *like me*, even to himself. Modesty had been drummed into him by his father, and Beth made sure he never forgot it.

They'd been driving home from a bar association banquet at the Hyatt, where he'd received an award for his pro bono work. Smiling broadly, chest puffed out, he had asked Beth, "Honey, how many truly great men do you think there are in the whole world?"

Her reply had been instantaneous: "I don't know the exact number, honey, but I *do* know there's one less than you think there is."

Adam stood in front of the lecture hall's *Complex Problems* poster, surveying the class for an appropriate candidate.

"Before we start, I need a second chair on the Talbot case. Preferably someone with some science background. Unless you've been living under a rock with no cable or Wi-Fi, I assume you're familiar with the case. I'd say it's relatively straightforward, but as you know—"

"There are no simple cases, only simple lawyers." The class spoke as one, as if delivering a responsive chant in church. Excited chatter broke out, along with the numerous raised hands at the prospect of working on such a highly publicized case.

I've taught them well.

"You might want to put those hands down, because we're in the Rocket Docket, so it's a Holotrial. God help me." Much to Adam's chagrin, the possibility of litigating a Holotrial excited them more. *They know not whereof they speak. I'll try to bring them back to earth.* "Now where did we leave off? Of course. Holotrials. I'll give you an example of how important a live jury is, though it's undoubtedly an apocryphal story."

Adam brought up a cartoon on the whiteboard. A lawyer was finishing his summation. In the jury box, all of the jurors but one were extending their necks toward the door at the back of the courtroom. The lone juror was staring at the defendant, who had a big grin on his face. Adam often displayed such puzzling images, which seemed to defy explanation. No student had ever figured one out on their own.

Staring at the sea of blank faces before him, Adam explained. "A defendant was on trial for murder based on circumstantial evidence. The police never found the body. The trial was almost over when the defense attorney dramatically announced that his next witness would be Mr. Brown, the alleged murder victim. All eyes turned to the courtroom door, but no Mr. Brown. In his summation, the defense counsel explained, 'When I called Mr. Brown to the stand, you all looked at the courtroom door, which means you all have reasonable doubt as to whether he's dead, let alone murdered.'"

Paul Pankowsky, always a kiss-ass, exclaimed, "Pretty clever, professor."

"Not quite. In twenty minutes, the jury unanimously rendered a verdict of guilty, Murder One."

"But how?"

"Precisely what the defense attorney wanted to know. When he ran into the jury foreman in the hallway, the foreman told him, 'When you called Mr. Brown to the stand, everyone else watched the door, but *I* watched the defendant. *He* wasn't looking. *He* knew Brown wasn't gonna walk through that door.' Take my word for it, creatures. *Holotrials* are an elevation of practicality over principle, convenience over justice. An abomination."

Chapter 14

SUPREME COURT, ERIE COUNTY
Holotrial Annex Building, Jury Selection Room
Main Street, Buffalo, New York
Friday, July 14, 2023

The life-sized three-dimensional hologram of Dante Russell, retired NFL Hall of Fame wide receiver, expounded on the benefits of the Holotrial system to the hundred or so prospective jurors gathered in the bullpen. "It's a remarkable, time-saving, economical, and fair method for achieving justice. The Holotrial has revolutionized our judicial system."

Charles, a seventyish owner of a computer repair shop, had always wanted to serve on a jury. It looked so exciting on TV. When he'd finally received his jury summons, he was told to report to the HAB on Main Street, where they filmed Holotrials. The new Holotrial pilot program was guaranteed to pique the jurors' interest, and it had certainly piqued Charles'. *Wait 'til I tell the boys at the club. I think I'll spring it on them after the 18th hole, when we're back in the clubhouse, sipping Arnold Palmers and kvetching about the shots we should've aced.*

Charles had been exposed to technology throughout his career. Nevertheless, he was extremely impressed. Dante Russell looked as alive as the attendant who'd ushered them in. *If I didn't know better, you could tell me the attendant was the hologram and Russell was the real person.* The sole reason he knew which was real was that he'd seen the attendant walk onto the stage, whereas Mr. Russell had appeared out of thin air.

Russell had played twelve years for the Buffalo Bills. He was an idol among Bills fans, perfect for getting the potential jurors' attention. Russell's holographic image continued to dote on Holotrials. "We've made your job a lot easier by packaging trials in pre-recorded, three-dimensional holographic presentations. Much like myself here. A three or four-week trial can now be viewed as a six or seven-hour holographic video called a *Holoscript*, usually in a single day."

Russell's image dissolved in front of their eyes, replaced by a miniature version of a Holoscript, about five feet high. Two of the mini-lawyers were arguing with each other. The mini-judge banged his gavel. The detail and clarity were extraordinary. Charles *was* a little disappointed by the size. He'd hoped for something a little grander if he was going to brag about his experience.

Then, as if the Court Administration programmers had read his mind—which, essentially, they *had,* with the help of human behavioral experts—the mini-courtroom scene expanded to life size. This elicited the usual gasps from the audience.

A pest even in a courthouse, Charles turned to the fortyish woman sitting to his right. "Why are there only seven jurors? Don't they need twelve?"

The woman whispered back, "Keep your voice down. Twelve is for criminal trials. This must be a civil case, where they only need six jurors. The seventh is an alternate in case one of the others dies or something."

"Interesting. How do you know all this?"

"My brother-in-law's a lawyer. Don't ask."

While they spoke, the courtroom scene dissolved and the life-sized image of Mr. Russell reappeared.

Charles, a die-hard Bills fan who'd lived through the glory years of the "Bickering Bills," commented to the gentleman on his left. "He looks smaller than when he was playing."

"*Shhh,*" a woman sitting in front of him hissed.

Charles answered, "I don't think he cares. He's a holo-whatever."

"*Shhh.*"

The hologram of Mr. Russell continued, oblivious to the whispering jurors, indeed oblivious to everything going on in the room. "Ever watched an NFL football game? They take about three hours. How much meaningful action is there? About eleven minutes total. That's all. That's the length of the edited game films we study each week to prep for the next game."

Charles longed for the days when Russell played football instead of giving speeches to jurors. He couldn't help thinking out loud. "We could'a won those damn Super Bowls with *this* guy."

The irritated woman turned around again. "*Shhh.*"

"He can't hear me."

"Well, *I* can."

Charles turned again to the woman on his right. "Hey, if this is the Supreme Court, why do they have trials? I thought it was just for appeals."

"New York does things differently," she replied. "In most other states, the Supreme Court is the highest court. In New York it's the lowest court where the trials are conducted."

"How'd you know all *that*?"

"I told you. My brother-in-law. Don't ask."

Dante Russell's image morphed into a video excerpt from an edited football game that the Bills had been kind enough to donate for the jury presentation. Exactly as he'd told them, it showed back-to-back plays with no delays in between. It was strange to watch. A quarterback would throw a thirty-yard pass, leaving players scattered all over the field, and a second later, like magic, they were all back at the line of scrimmage to start the next play. The jurors leaned forward in their seats to get a better look. Charles, a bit OCD, as well as nudgy, tried to figure out if he'd attended this particular game.

After five rapid-fire plays, the football video disappeared, and Mr. Russell returned. "Same for jury trials. For every four hours of court time, there's roughly one and a half hours of usable testimony. On *average*. Not to mention the down days to accommodate the judge, the jurors, the lawyers' schedules, weekends, holidays, et cetera. In a pre-recorded Holotrial, jurors don't have to sit through objections, rulings, lawyers arguing with the judge and each other, and other wasted time. All objections are ruled on during the filming and edited out. Basically, anything that isn't admissible testimony, jury instructions, or statements to the jury from the judge or the lawyers is deleted. So, the Holoscript, the final product you'll be watching, is a lean, clean trial machine."

Charles started chanting under his breath, "Mean Machine, Mean Machine." He ignored the glare from the exasperated woman in front of him.

Mr. Russell, immune to the ramblings of his audience, continued. "Prior to Holotrials, if the judge were to strike improper testimony, it might be too late to cure the problem. Sure, the judge would instruct the jury not to consider such evidence, to wash it from their minds, but you can't put the ketchup back in the bottle. If the testimony is prejudicial enough, it could result in a mistrial or a reversal on appeal. Either way, you'd have to start the trial all over again. Now, with Holotrials, improper testimony is removed from the Holoscript *before* the jury ever sees it. No mistrial. No reversal.

"Oh yeah, I forgot to mention that you'll all have stand-ins while the trial is recorded. A bunch of fiberglass dummies, no offense intended, fabricated to simulate real people. Reminds the lawyers that, eventually, actual humans like you are going to be watching them.

"*So*. No inadmissible evidence. No lawyers arguing. No objections. No rulings. No delays or short trial days because the judge or a juror has a doctor's appointment. You get all the meat, none of the fat. As I said, lean and clean. By the time you enter the courtroom, the lawyers will have already given their opening statements and summations, the witnesses will have testified, the judge will have given preliminary and final jury instructions, and you're set to go. You're on a bullet train to justice. See you all in court."

And with that, the affable Dante Russell dissolved into thin air.

Chapter 15

CHILD & FAMILY SERVICES
Genesee Street, Cheektowaga, New York
Monday, July 17, 2023
9:20 a.m.

Mac shunned the elevator and bounded up the steps, two at a time. There was still some spring in the gray-haired warrior's body, at least when he was at work and not out *havin' just a few*. In this case, his task was way too important to be impeded by alcohol. When he got to the fourth floor, he scrambled down the corridor to the Records Office.

He quickly sized up the woman behind the counter. Obvious stick up her ass, but she had a nice figure for, what, mid-fifties? Name tag: SHARON. Mac was convinced there was a smile buried somewhere underneath the government-issue grimace displayed by all such clerks behind all such counters.

"Sir, may I help you?"

"You sure can, sugar."

The grimace became a scowl. "Do you have legitimate business here?"

Hmm. Need a better icebreaker. "Hey, sugar, why is there an expiration date on sour cream?" Her scornful visage didn't change a whit. Nor did she respond. *I thought for sure that would do it.* Mac switched to a business-like tone and employed that trick he'd learned from Adam, to use Sharon's favorite word. "Yes, uh, Sharon. I need the records for a foster child, to find his biological mother."

The woman's face puckered up even more. "And you are?"

"A close relation, Sharon. Call me Mac."

"Sir, I assume you have written authority to perform this search?"

"Absolutely. Grade A. No standard issue here."

"Name?"

"Jerome McMillan."

She typed it into the computer. "Did he go by a different name perhaps?"

The expression on Mac's face went from swagger to puzzlement, if not introspection. "You know...I don't... I guess that's why I'm here. McMillan's the only one I know." Mac could tell from the sudden softening of her face that she understood. She'd been won over by sympathy rather than charm. *What the hell? Any port in a storm.*

Former foster kids regularly came to the agency searching for their bio-parents. It rarely ended well. They'd find no peace, no closure, once they identified the biological parents who'd abandoned them to the foster care system, or whose drug problems meant they were dead by now. Of course, lots of parents *did* keep in touch with their children and plucked them back from foster care when they were able. But for those who didn't, the children often ended up with a sad, lonely, and ultimately unsuccessful quest.

"Just when were you in foster care, Mr. McMillan?"

"Call me Mac. Well, let me see. First foster family, about seventy years ago. First of six. Moved around a lot. Not *always* my fault."

"Mac, you don't look old enough to have been *around* seventy years ago."

Well, well, well, the Ice Queen hath melted.

Sharon typed another command into the computer, after which her newly pleasant countenance resumed its frown. "That explains it. I'm sorry, Mac. The records from that time were lost in a fire before they could be scanned. If there's anything else—"

"Well, let's give it a try. Here." Mac pulled the torn half-photograph from his wallet, offering it to his new friend Sharon. Her eyes moistened as they lingered on the photo. "I'm sorry, but there's no way I would...we don't keep photographs."

Mac chuckled. "Not the boy. The *intersection*. I wouldn't dare think you were old enough to remember this runt, Sharon. I've got twenty years on you, easy. Maybe thirty."

Sharon smiled at the obvious flattery, but she shook her head. "I've lived here forty years, but I've gotta say, this intersection isn't familiar. I'm sorry. I wish there was more I could do."

"You and me both. So, what time you get outta this place?"

***

As Mac exited the building, he was nearly run over by two investigators from the State Attorney General's office. He knew one of the bums. The other looked like a rookie.

"Jesus, you mutts tracking me?" he taunted them. "Don't ya know I'm retiring? I got nothing goin' with the AG."

Tom Jiara, the familiar one, responded, "C'mon, Mac, you think if we were on you, you'd snag us this easy?"

"I think you couldn't find an owl in a Hoot factory. I'm here on personal business."

The rookie who'd almost knocked Mac down tried to smooth things over. "Our business is kind of personal, too."

"What, you gonna adopt each other?"

"Somethin' like that. Direct orders. From the top. Can't say anything more."

"Well, talk to me again when you have a new boss." Mac sneered. "One without fangs."

As he walked to his car, Mac's premonition grew stronger. He *knew* the purple dress was still alive, waiting for him. But where?

Chapter 16

A PHONE CALL
Friday, July 21, 2023

While Mac spoke with Adam on the phone, he continued multi-tasking, thumbing through newspaper clippings that referred to Senator Talbot's presidential ambitions and his successful early career prosecuting organized crime.

"Chief, what if we're barkin' up the wrong tree? Maybe New Millennium had nothing to do with this. They've already sold five thousand of those suckers, and none of the others turned into an IED. You know, the Senator's gotta have enemies. Some bruiser he put in the can? Political opponent?"

"The car, Mac. Stick with the car."

"Why don't we check both? What is it, one out of every seven Presidents faces an assassination attempt? Or a success. Maybe they're getting an early start on him. How 'bout I run background on Talbot and his wife? Everybody's got somethin' to hide. 'Cept for me and my monkey."

"Mac. The coroner said it was an accident. The police investigated and found *nada*. They put *three detectives* on it. That's what being a Senator gets you."

"Chief, I love those assholes, but you think they have any fuckin' idea how this car works? What it would take to blow it up? I sure don't."

"No, Mac. Keep off the grass. My dime."

Before Mac could ask again, Adam abruptly hung up and put his feet on the desk. He already knew one of the bigger Talbot secrets, since he had a starring role in it. A secret even Bill Talbot didn't know, thank God. No need for Mac to dive in.

Mac's phenomenal when it comes to sniffing things out. Could he be right, a deeply buried secret come back to haunt Bill? A thug he put away in his U.S. attorney days? An enemy he made climbing the political ladder? No. It's gotta be the car. The police haven't remotely suggested foul play.

Speaking of secrets, why is Pete so secretive? What's that kid doing behind my back? No. It only looks secretive because I'm not paying enough attention. Well, I'm paying more attention than he thinks. I know about the cigarettes. And the beer. I should put a stop to it, but the boy's suffered, losing his mother before he really ever got to know her. Better save my ammunition for bigger problems.

***

Adam's thoughts meandered back to Pete's fourth grade band concert. All the students were excited about playing on the main stage of Shea's Performing Arts Center. They'd arrive by school bus, and their parents were supposed to pick them up at the baton drop. Before Pete got on the bus, he made Adam triple promise he'd watch the whole concert. "When you get to Shea's, turn off your phone, Dad. Not just the ringer. *All* the way off. Wait. Just give me the SIM card now." Adam didn't hand over the SIM card, but he did triple promise.

About an hour before showtime, though, he took a client call, and spent way longer than he intended, trying to talk her off the ledge. Every time he thought they were done, she'd start grumbling anew about the government subpoena she'd been served. Meanwhile, the clock ticked, closer and closer to 2 p.m. At 1:45, he told her he had an emergency hearing in court, but he'd call back later. He sped over to the theater, parked illegally, and rushed into the massive lobby running from Pearl to Main street.

Shea's, the crown jewel of the Buffalo Theater District, had been designated a National Historic Site. Built in 1926 with the *Mighty Wurlitzer Organ*, it had lush European baroque architecture designed by the world-renowned Louis Comfort Tiffany: domed ceilings, gold-painted plaster ornaments, lavish crystal chandeliers and wall sconces, and fantastical carved, molded, and hand-painted elements throughout the huge theater. Intended to resemble a European opera house and originally built as a grand movie palace for silent films, the theater graduated to vaudeville and, ultimately, Broadway touring shows. Every time the forty-five-foot curtain rose into the 110-foot-high ceiling, the audience was in for a treat.

Adam barely made it to a balcony seat before the concert began. He was about to turn off his phone when Katherine's ringtone started playing. His internal struggle lasted two seconds before, against his better judgment, he answered. Bill was out of town again, on a week-long fundraising *excursion*, his euphemism for simultaneously whoring and raking in donor money. "Can you come over?" Katherine asked. "It feels like we've been apart forever."

Adam knew it had actually been four days.

"Where are you anyway? It sounds so noisy."

"Just the supermarket, Kate," he lied. *There's 3000 people here, minimum*, Adam then rationalized. *No way Pete could tell if I'm here. I'll only be an hour or so. Should be back well before the concert's over. Not like the time I told him I had to be in Philadelphia for a week on business.*

Katherine pressed, laughing. "C'mon, counselor. What's it gonna be, boy? *Yes or no*?" It was one of their in-jokes, quoting from Meatloaf's iconic song.

Trying to stifle his uneasiness, Adam said he'd be right over. It was rare for Bill to be gone for so long, and they had to take advantage of it. He could stay about an hour, he told her, then he had a client meeting. *How many lies have I told to how many people today?*

Katherine pretended to pout, but they both knew she was kidding. "A quickie, huh? What, you think I'm that easy? Well, lucky for you, today I *am*. Get over here *now*, counselor."

Adam ended up staying longer than planned. He barely made it back to Shea's before the concert ended, leaving his car in a no-parking zone again. After picking out Pete from the rest of the band members—identically dressed in white shirts and black pants—they walked back to the car, where Adam was relieved not to see a ticket on the windshield. *Parking enforcement must have the day off. My luck is running good today.* As they started for home, Pete asked Adam how he liked the concert. "*Fan-tastic*," Adam sang. "When I closed my eyes, I thought it was the BPO itself."

"Wasn't my solo cool, standing up in front of the whole band? Did you notice I almost fell off the stage?"

"Like a pro. I was very proud."

Pete's face reddened, and Adam immediately realized that his son had pulled his *own* trial lawyer move on him. "Dad. There was no solo...You *triple* promised. *Triple.*"

Adam had no answer. The rest of the ride home, Pete just looked out the passenger window, his eyes moist. Neither spoke a word.

***

The phone rang again, putting an end to Adam's bad memories. It was Mac. He didn't give up easy.

"Chief, it's just, I have a sixth sense about the Senator."

"Well, I have a seventh sense about the car. Stick with that."

"Chief, how 'bout just a little second-level noodling? No one will know a thing."

"*No*, Mac. Sorry. The car. Not the Talbots. It's the car."

"You always say dig up the dirt in your own yard first. I read that in—"

"I know, Mac. Let's leave the Talbots' yard alone. For now."

"You know, their daughter's a piece of work herself. They've managed to keep it quiet, but she's been busted for shoplifting four times, possession twice. I think she's bad news from Sunday."

"Mac, just leave them alone. *Please.*"

"Okay, Chief. Hey, Chief. you heard about the pony with the sore throat? He's still a little hoarse."

Adam hung up without another word. Mac continued to stare at his phone. He still had a bad feeling about the Senator. He was sure he was on the right track. But was it the right train?

Chapter 17

ADAM'S LAW OFFICE
Parkside Avenue, Buffalo, New York
Monday, July 24, 2023

Mac practically skipped into Adam's office, a broad smile on his face.

Adam instantly perked up. "What? Tell me?"

"Simons says keep off the Talbots, I keep off the Talbots. You say look at New Millennium, I look at New Millennium. Take a look at this." Mac took a thumb drive from his jacket pocket and inserted it in Adam's desktop computer. "We're goin' to the movies, Chief."

"Tell me, Mac, is this *Chief* stuff your idea or Freddie's? At least I'll know which one of you hates me more."

"I'd probably say it was Freddie. He'd probably say it was me. One of us would be lying. Maybe both."

"Let's make it simple. Just stop calling me Chief. Okay?"

"Sure thing, Chief."

"This video. Has New Millennium produced it?"

"No, Chief. Technically it's not from their files. They outsourced it. BDT Technologies. You'll see why." Mac wheeled an office chair next to the desk and sat on it backward, his chest pressed against the chairback. He was excited, anticipating Adam's reaction. One didn't often find evidence this good.

The video started with a gray car parked on a crash-test track. Notwithstanding the numerous external monitors sticking out all over, Adam knew it was a Hydro. The car started moving down the track toward a crash wall, picking up speed, the four crash-test dummies, two adults and two children, oblivious to their fate. The car went faster and faster and then... A ball of flame, metal, and dummy parts flew everywhere.

"Holy shit, Mac, that's unbelievable. How'd you get this? Where did... No, don't tell me. I guess we should subpoena this from

BDT."

"I don't know, Chief. This goes public, it could endanger their fat contract with New Millennium. It might be in their interest to accidentally on purpose lose it in a data dump or something."

"You know, maybe we could get this in at trial if it were already in the public domain. I'm just saying. Let's get Freddie in here."

Mac smiled. "Already got that covered, Chief."

***

Freddie was on his way to Adam's office when a client in the waiting area got up from his chair and impolitely stared at him. "Excuse me, but do I know you?"

Freddie sighed. "I get that all the time. Sorry. Got one of those faces."

Looking mildly disappointed, the client sat back down and resumed watching the ballgame on the waiting room TV. Freddie thought, as he often did on such occasions, *Should I take this as a compliment or an insult? Could go either way.*

Adam didn't even give Freddie a chance to sit down before he pointed to the computer screen. "Freddie, you understand how helpful this video is. I assume you also know, from conspiring with Mac behind my back, that it might disappear from BDT's files if we subpoena them. New Millennium may have been smart enough not to retain a copy, physical or electronic. *They* haven't turned it over in discovery. That much we know."

The tone of Adam's voice made Freddie uneasy.

"We need to *find* this video independently. Maybe Instagram? YouTube?"

Freddie raised an eyebrow. "You sure about this, Chief? It's not like you to—"

"Sorry, Freddie. I know. But the picture Kate showed me of the little girl, it haunts me. I can't get her out of my head. If we run a couple stop signs, that's on me. Listen, New Millennium should've provided the video to us in the first place. We're just ensuring they don't bury it. Righting a wrong. That's what the law's all about, isn't it?"

"You're the lawyer, Chief." Freddie looked down at the floor.

"Freddie, look, it's not like we're manufacturing evidence. I'd never ask you to do that. This video is real, authentic, relevant, and *immensely* important. We're simply ensuring that the jury gets to see it. As they should."

"I...guess so. I think YouTube's the best place to find it."

Adam pushed the envelope. "I think it would have the most impact if it had been posted before the explosion of Jennifer's car. Say, four or five months before. Prior knowledge, you know. Always helpful to flesh out a negligence claim."

Freddie stared at him. *This wasn't like Adam. Why's he have such a hard-on for this case? The Senator sure doesn't seem to give a damn if they win or lose.*

"I'm sorry to have to ask, Freddie. Extreme circumstances call for extreme measures. All I can tell you is, don't ever represent friends."

"Okay. But you double damn sure, Chief? We've never done anything like—"

"I think you're confused, Freddie," Mac cut him off. "With all the crap happening in the office, the long hours you're putting in. *I* inquired about this, not the Chief. I don't think he knows anything about this, at all, unless we find it on the internet and bring it to him. Let's get out of here before he says otherwise."

Chapter 18

ADAM'S HOME
Tudor Place, Buffalo, New York
Tuesday, July 25, 2023
8:36 p.m.

When Adam answered the doorbell, there stood his old friend and classmate Bill Talbot. "Adam, thanks for seeing me. I hate to intrude on your family time. It's sacred for me, too."

Sometimes one says the opposite of what one means. This was one of those times. "Not a problem, Bill, any time at all."

"I think you ought to know...it has no direct bearing on the case, but Kate might be overly emotional, with the pressure of the trial, and all. When she gets like that, you don't know what she'll say. I should tell you, as our lawyer, that about a year ago, Kate had an affair. I was a bit harsh in my reaction. But all is forgiven now, both sides."

"Bill—"

"No telling what it would do to my chances if it came out. I took fairly extreme precautions to keep it quiet, and I know I don't need to tell you about confidentiality. Just, um...if Kate seems a bit out of sorts, she hasn't totally gotten over it. That's all."

Adam blinked. *Hasn't gotten over it? I guess she does miss me. And it looks like she was telling the truth when she said Bill didn't know about us.*

***

Their complicated relationship had begun with Adam's brief crush on Katherine during their first semester at Yale. He thought it was the real thing, until he met Beth. Not that it mattered, because Bill snagged Katherine out from under him shortly after their first date. Adam and Katherine had been munching on an *Everything* pizza, sans onions, at a favorite student haunt in downtown New Haven, when his suave roommate just happened to drop by and join them. Proving all is fair in love and roommates, Bill proceeded to schmooze Katherine for the next hour. She evidently saw greater potential in Bill, and Adam couldn't blame her. What was more attractive, a 3L who might, someday, become a successful trial lawyer? Or one with lofty political ambitions, who knows, maybe all the way to 1600 Pennsylvania Avenue.

***

Adam escorted Bill to the door, letting out a sigh of relief as it closed. Bill could be an obnoxious, lying asshole. But how could Adam really be mad? *I should be thanking Bill for diverting me from Kate and putting me on the course to Beth.* He knew he couldn't have been as happy with Katherine. Nor, ultimately, as heartbroken. *Maybe that wouldn't have been so bad, after all. You can't miss what you never had, right? No Beth, no devastating end, no... No. Never think that. Even if the despair of that final year overwhelms the joy of the first thirteen.*

Anyway, Adam and Katherine would circle back eventually. Twice.

Chapter 19

HOME OF WILLIAM AND KATHERINE TALBOT
Lincoln Parkway, Buffalo, New York
Sunday, July 30, 2023

The two Talbots sat at their dining room table, staring down at their plates, up at the walls, anywhere but at each other.

The Senator finally broke a seven-minute silence. "Please pass the ketchup."

"Please pass the ketchup, *Katherine*. You can't even say *my* name, can you?"

"You've been drinking again. Or more accurately, you haven't stopped."

Katherine picked up the ketchup bottle and threw it at the Senator, missing her intended target.

One more day she regretted the choice she'd made at Yale.

***

Adam and Katherine's full-blown affair began on New Year's Eve, 2017. Adam was surprised to get a call from her. She begged him to come over, so he made the short drive to the Talbot house. Bill, a Buffalo native, had retained his home and established his Senate office in Buffalo.

When Adam arrived, Katherine was decked out in a glamorously arousing outfit. That didn't surprise him. At first. After all, it *was* New Year's Eve. However, there was no Bill in sight. Katherine ushered Adam in and made him a drink. And then another. And another. After their third—or fourth—Grey Goose martini, he asked what had her so upset.

"Bill's on the road again. Why spend New Year's Eve with the wife when you can..." She stopped to sniffle. "I've finally determined where I stand in Bill's pecking order. Political career clearly comes first. I figure I'm somewhere between the new stick vacuum and the toaster."

The next thing Adam knew, he woke in the Talbots' comfortable king size bed—Katherine naked beside him—wondering when Bill was expected back. She hadn't told him that possibly significant tidbit of information. She slept so peacefully that he didn't want to disturb her, so rather than wait to find out how imminent Bill's return was, Adam quietly dressed and slipped out the back door. As it turned out, he needn't have worried. Bill was on a two-week political junket on the West Coast.

Adam and Katherine would have many more such nights, until Katherine abruptly broke off the affair on Christmas Eve, 2022. Another holiday during which Bill had abandoned her, for yet another political function, or so he said. When Adam arrived, he found Katherine despondent. That alone didn't raise any alarm signals as, more often than not, their evenings began with Katherine nursing a grievance about Bill's latest slight or abandonment of her in favor of either his political cronies or whatever *femme du jour* he was banging at the moment. Of course, who was Katherine to point fingers?

Adam sensed something was up when Katherine didn't start the evening with her usual complaints about Bill. In fact, she said nothing at all for a few minutes. Then she told Adam, very coldly, in an almost trance-like state, that she could no longer cheat on Bill. It wasn't fair to him or his career. At first, Adam thought she was joking, given the contempt with which she usually spoke of Bill. But it wasn't a joke. She would no longer see Adam. She was sticking with Bill. Period. End of story.

Though she tried to project an icy demeanor, the tinge of sadness in her voice, and in her eyes, told him there was much left unsaid.

She's trying, but she can't hide it. She's not happy with this supposed change of heart. Where did this come from? Everything was fine a few nights before. What isn't she telling me? Had Bill discovered the affair and threatened her, financially or otherwise? Did they have a pre-nup that allowed him to screw her if she didn't play the loyal politician's wife? Did he give her some kind of ultimatum?

Adam had actually thought that Katherine wanted to leave Bill, and he'd anticipated that being a topic of discussion that Christmas Eve. They'd been sneaking around for five years. He thought they had something special. It just didn't make any sense. Here she was, abandoned by Bill on another major holiday, pledging fealty to him. Adam tried to probe, but Katherine was resolute in her refusal to discuss it any further.

On the cold, lonely drive home, Adam could think of nothing else. *What the hell just happened? Kate's suddenly devoted to the man she hated most?* The only explanation he could come up with was that she'd changed her mind about the First Lady gig. She wouldn't be the first woman to endure a loveless marriage to attain that title. But this conclusion was shaky at best. They'd discussed the *First Lady question* a number of times, and Katherine had repeatedly insisted that having a position with no duties, no actual legal status, and no significant accomplishments wasn't worth being tethered to Bill for four—or God forbid, eight—years in the White House. Adam was left with no logical conclusion about Katherine's about-face.

***

Bill wiped a few specks of ketchup from his pants and glared at Katherine.

She sneered back. "I made a mistake, and you made me pay for it. *I* committed adultery. But *you*. You're a goddamn murderer."

"You watch yourself." Bill seethed.

"What, you gonna lock me up again? Where to this time? The gulag?"

"Just *watch* it."

"Threaten me all you want. You've already done your worst."

"*Katherine.* This lawsuit won't bring her back. I think we should drop it, put this behind us. It's best for all of us."

"You mean best for you, don't you, *Senator*? Who gave you the fucking right to nix the abortion anyway? Are you running for President or God? You think those fuckin' holy-roller voters give a shit? They already know what a hypocrite you are. They'd stick with you for one lousy abortion. Then there'd be no Allie, and no need to kill her. What *was* the plan, Senator? Was Jennifer supposed to be in the car, too? Was it just luck that saved her? Was she supposed to

~63~

go with Allie, erase the whole goddamn episode? No witnesses, no loose ends? Except for me, of course. Was I *next*? What did you have planned for your loving wife?"

Bill jumped out of his chair, staring daggers at Katherine. "*Jesus,* you're not just drunk, you're insane. You should know me better than that. At least when you're sober you do."

"Who gave her the car? Who insisted she drive that damn hydrogen-filled car?"

"It's not hydrogen-*filled*. It's...screw it. Enough bullshit from you. I mean it."

"What should I believe, William? Tell me, Senator Talbot. *President* Talbot. Rolls off the tongue, doesn't it?"

"You're out of your mind."

"Am I? You've hated her since she was born. You're a powerful man, William. Men have done things for you, things we never speak of. Is this one of them, William?"

"*Jesus Christ,* I'm telling you for the last time. One word of this idiocy and the campaign could go up in smoke. So forget it. *Now.*"

"Will I, Grandpa Bill?"

"*That's enough.* You'll keep your mouth shut if you know what's good for you."

Chapter 20

EDEN CORN FESTIVAL
Eden, New York
Tuesday, August 1, 2023

K elly and her classmate Jalissa Jones, JJ to her friends, lazily picked their way along Route 75 in Kelly's beat-up Prius. They were on the final leg of their trip, if a 25-minute drive could be considered long enough to have legs. Kelly was salivating at the thought of their destination: Eden, a quiet little town, population 8,000, sixteen miles south of Buffalo. Once every summer, though, it wasn't quiet at all. The famous Eden Corn Festival drew about 100,000 hungry visitors from miles around. Kelly thought it was great that things were relatively back to normal, with festivals like this, after that ghastly pandemic. They'd been limited for so long to online learning, no socializing, afraid to go out in public for fear of a virus that caused serious illness and death in millions. How wonderful to be able to experience ordinary pleasures again.

Kelly wondered if Eden truly had the best corn, or if it was simply that anything dipped in a vat of hot butter was bound to taste good. *Who cares? It's once a year.* She remembered that Mae West line that her grandfather had often repeated. "I never give into temptation...unless I can't resist."

***

Kelly had met JJ in a study group for their Civil Procedure class, and they were BFFs at first sight. Jalissa was from Jamaica, so Kelly offered to give her a tour of Western New York. They hit the usual suspects: art and science museums, the zoo, Frank Lloyd Wright mansion, Canalside, Shakespeare in the Park, the Anchor Bar—where chicken wings were invented—the majestic Buffalo

City Hall, the locks on the Erie Canal, and, naturally, Niagara Falls.

Kelly's tour showed JJ that Buffalo had a lot to offer, even if no one had heard of it back in Kingston. Its past was even grander. Buffalo had been a center of commerce, dating back to the late 1800s. Located on Lake Erie at the terminus of the Erie Canal, Buffalo was once the *Gateway to the West. Millionaire's Row* on Delaware Avenue had been one of the preeminent neighborhoods in America. Two of Buffalo's citizens, Millard Fillmore and Grover Cleveland, had become President, and a third President, William McKinley, had been assassinated in Buffalo. How many cities could say that?

***

Kelly and JJ sat at a splintery picnic table beneath a large tent, sinking their teeth into butter-soaked ears of corn. JJ quizzed Kelly about her relationship with Professor Simons. Kelly was ecstatic that he'd chosen her for the second chair position in the New Millennium trial, but it was all business, she insisted, though she held out hope that it might blossom into something else.

"Come on, Kell, you think it's a coincidence the great professor just happened to choose the hottest girl in the class?"

"First of all, you're the hottest, JJ. I'm number three. He went for brains. My undergrad degree in chemistry sealed the deal."

"Oh yeah, I forgot you didn't choose one of the usual bullshit pre-law majors. Like poli sci. Like I did."

They both laughed.

JJ continued her interrogation of Kelly's romantic intentions. What was it like working with the professor? Kelly tried to be nonchalant. "Nothing special, you know. Mostly boring." They both burst out laughing again, but Kelly realized that JJ was employing one of the cross-examination techniques that Professor Simons had taught them: targeted questioning buried among a seemingly innocuous line of inquiry.

"Hey, Kell, what's the story on that killer witness?"

"Adam would kill *me* if I told you anything about him."

"Is he cute?"

"*JJ.*"

"Sorry. So Kell, what does the great professor have you doing on the case?"

"You know, that's an excellent question. I can't go into detail, but it feels like all my assignments are largely duplicative of his. Like, preparing witnesses, meeting with experts, researching hydrogen vehicles. I think the one thing I'm doing that he's *not* is reviewing medical records. Sometimes I wonder why he bothered to create this second chair position."

"It couldn't just be an excuse to have a bit of alone time with his favorite 3L, could it?"

Kelly ignored JJ's comment and soldiered on. "I assume I'll be useful at trial, like, bringing up photos and videos on the courtroom monitors and shit like that. Though Freddie, he's Adam's amazing paralegal, Freddie could do that for him. Probably better than me."

"Better maybe, but not prettier."

"Oh, get stuffed."

They both laughed again.

"You had any late-night sessions, like at his house? You two doin' the old boolooloop?"

"JJ, I'm not underneath the mango tree. I've heard that song."

"Seriously, Kell. You *gotta* tell me before I die. Are you doin' it? Yes or no? Just for my ears, girlfriend."

"Look. Adam, Professor Simons, I told you, it's strictly professional." Kelly was getting misty-eyed. "You know, sometimes he seems to go out of his way to avoid me. After he picked *me* to help him on the trial. I don't get it."

"I don't care, Kell. You wanna hook up with the professor, you go for it. If people want something bad enough, they find a way."

That was the story of JJ's life. And Kelly's as well.

***

Both their lives had been heavily influenced by their fathers. In *very* different ways.

JJ had grown up in a tough neighborhood in Kingston when that city was setting new homicide records every month. Her parents had scant time for her or anyone else in their household. She was reminded on a daily basis that a woman's place was at home, and that's what she should expect: caring for parents, grandparents, siblings, nieces and nephews, all of whom lived in their tiny home.

That included helping with the chickens that they raised, and ultimately slaughtered, in the backyard.

JJ's father was usually tired and irritable after working two shifts at the bauxite plant. He was responsible for the nine or ten people who lived with them, depending on the day, and his gruff personality derived from those responsibilities. It scared the rest of the household, including JJ, though in truth, her father wasn't a mean man, just fatigued and often overwhelmed.

JJ's high school classmates saw in her an enormous potential that eluded her family. For three years they had scraped together a secret *JJ education fund*, until there was enough money for a college application and a flight from Jamaica to the U.S. To JJ's amazement and delight, she obtained a full scholarship to the University of Miami, including room and board. She had no funds for discretionary expenses, but that was okay. Perhaps she'd get a job in the school cafeteria to eke out enough for a night on the town with her classmates every now and then. All that mattered was that her dream of higher education, *in the States*, was becoming reality.

She thought about leaving Jamaica in secret, pondering how harsh her father's reaction might be, but ultimately, she couldn't leave that way. She was no coward, nor was she ungrateful. The man had given her food and shelter for seventeen years. He deserved better. She'd tell him to his face, whatever the outcome. Two days before she left, she asked to speak with him privately.

There was rarely time or space in their crowded house for private conversation, so they went to the back porch, where her father shooed away several children and chickens before sitting down on one of two rickety chairs. JJ sat, and then outlined her plans and dreams. At first she didn't think he comprehended what she was saying at all. None of them had ever taken a plane ride, let alone gone to college. It was so wildly beyond their imagination that anyone in the family could accomplish so much.

JJ's father remained calm throughout her presentation. When she finished, he stood up, towering over JJ, and said in a gentle voice, "You go with God, little girl. Go with God. You make somethin' of yourself. You make us proud. I know you will." With that, he reached into his pocket and retrieved two greasy Jamaican $500 bills, his entire discretionary budget for the month. "I'm sorry, this is all I got, little girl, but you take it. You better than this place.

You gonna be somebody, I know it. I think I know before, but I know it now for sure."

With tears in her eyes, JJ took the money. It was slimy and smelled of fish, and was worth practically nothing in the States, but they were the most beautiful bills she'd ever seen. She hugged her father tight. "Thank you, Daddy. Thank you. Thank you."

She spent the next seven years in Miami and then transferred to UB law school. And every month, like clockwork, she'd received an envelope with two crumpled Jamaican $500 bills. Once in a while, there was a poorly written note. Usually not. JJ swore to herself that when she graduated from law school, she'd repay every dollar. In shiny American greenbacks.

***

Kelly was on her third ear of corn, hoping JJ would get off the topic of Adam. Even if Kelly let something slip, she assumed JJ would adhere to the ancient and sacred BFF code of confidentiality. She had thought her crush on Adam was imperceptible to everyone, including JJ.

I guess not.

After more questioning, Kelly figured, *If I'm not fooling her, I might as well seek her advice.* "JJ...do you think it *could* work? Me and him? I mean, like, with the age difference and all. Could it? He's so brilliant. You should see how he prepares summations. Exactly like he told us. Before he knows most of the facts, he's got a whole outline. And you should see him interview a...oh, who cares? You know, what the hell? When the time is right, I'll just tell him how I feel."

JJ smiled. "You go, girl. Hey, Kell, just one more question. You said I'm the hottest in the class."

"Yeah."

"And you're number three."

"Yeah."

"So who's number two?"

Chapter 21

OFFICE OF DR. MARCEL SAPERSTON
Youngstown, New York
Wednesday, August 2, 2023
8.30 a.m.

The jokingly self-proclaimed dream team—Adam, Mac, and Kelly—made the thirty-six-minute drive to Youngstown in twenty-five minutes. Mac was at the wheel. Watching the scenery, Adam understood why Marcel Saperston had chosen to put his private office here in this quaint historic village, population about 2000, just across from Niagara-On-The-Lake, another beautiful little village, on the Canadian side of the Niagara River.

Youngstown was also the home to Old Fort Niagara, originally built by the French in 1726, and later occupied by the British, then the Americans. It had been restored and brought up to code for guided tours. Fort Niagara protected the U.S. from Fort George, its counterpart across the river on the Canadian side. The tranquil beauty of the area belied a considerably more combative past. During the War of 1812, American troops captured Fort George and burned Niagara-On-The-Lake to the ground. The British and their Indian allies later recaptured Fort Niagara and burned down part of Youngstown. Those sorts of things didn't tend to happen these days.

Dr. Saperston's office looked as timeworn as the Fort. Once inside, Adam made the introductions, and they were ushered into the professor's office. It was cluttered with papers and piles of books, basically Mac's living room with scholarly treatises instead of empty beer bottles. A card table had been set up in the middle of the room for the meeting. Saperston hastily removed a small television from the table and replaced it with his laptop.

"I hope you'll excuse me," he said. "I was up late watching the Yankees. Double header."

The folding metal bridge chairs' ripped vinyl seats didn't

surprise Mac. The rickety one under him seemed ready to collapse. Each of them had a cup of coffee, though Mac's had a funny aroma, a little extra *flavoring* from a flask he kept inside his jacket.

Adam had used Marcel Saperston's services before. The professor, with PhDs in molecular physics, chemistry, and chemical and electrical engineering, was a perfect expert witness. In private with Adam, he told it like it is, leaving no meat on the bone. On direct examination, he was masterful, the consummate college professor explaining intricate scientific principles in plain language that juries could understand. On cross-examination, he had a wonderful ability to thread the needle, never telling a falsehood while trying not to give up too much, either.

Perhaps most importantly, he had the one trait that all trial lawyers longed for in their witnesses and aimed for themselves: he was likeable.

Adam opened up the discussion. "Professor, thank you for having us. A physicist who knows his way around a hydrogen car, *this* hydrogen car...well, let's just say you're not a dime a dozen."

"Well, it may not be a dime."

"So what can you tell us?"

"I've created a few slides to help us along. They're based on the plans and schematics you obtained from New Millennium. First of all, calling this a hydrogen car is a bit of a misnomer. It's really an electric car that runs on water. Hydrogen is sort of the middleman in the process."

Saperston called up a diagram on his laptop and positioned it so his three guests could see the screen.

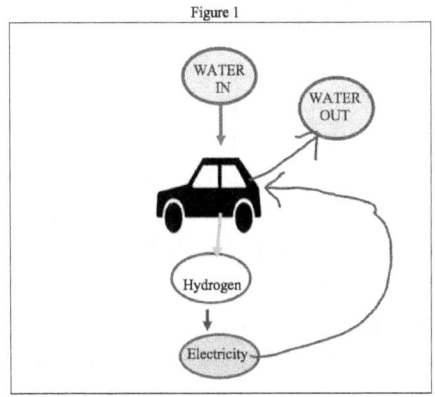

Figure 1

"As you can see on this *extremely* simplified diagram, Figure 1," Saperston explained, "you put water in the car, the water is used to create hydrogen, the hydrogen is used to create the electricity that runs the car, and the only emission is water. Water in, water out."

The next slide was more thorough.

Figure 2

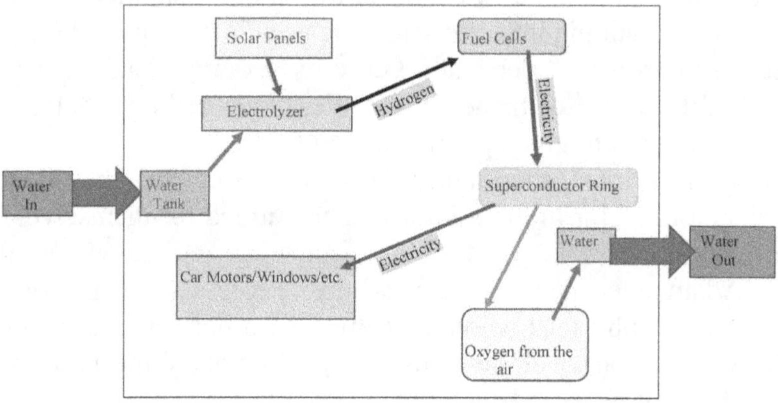

"Figure 2 here shows the process in a little more detail, including the proprietary modules created by New Millennium. This is where the true magic lies. *Really* quite exciting." The seventy-four-year-old professor sounded like a child with a new toy.

Adam and Kelly carefully scanned the diagram from left to right. Mac just stared at it, puzzled. "A *little* more detail, Doc? This looks like the plans for D-Day...on *Mars*."

"Believe me, Mr. McMillan—"

"Call me Mac, Doc."

"Yes. Well. As I was saying, this is still a very simplified version, but it gives you the highlights. The process starts with water being pumped into the car, shown on the left. The water is then fed into a component called an electrolyzer, which splits the water molecules apart to create hydrogen. Anyone remember high-school chemistry?"

"I think I missed that day, Doc."

Saperston raised an eyebrow, his only discernable reaction. "Yes. Well. Moving along. The hydrogen generated by the electrolyzer is then fed to the fuel cells, over here on the right. They employ a chemical process to convert the hydrogen to electricity, which ultimately runs the car's motors, powers up the dashboard, radio, door locks, and so on. You don't need an external hydrogen source, or a hydrogen tank, because the car makes its own hydrogen. You also don't need an external source of electricity for the electrolyzer, thanks to the unprecedentedly efficient solar panels, shown at the top."

"I don't get it," Kelly interjected. "If you have solar panels, why not just use *them* to power the car?"

"Smart girl," Saperston noted. "She's a keeper."

Kelly couldn't help but blush.

Adam remained deadpan.

"Because, my dear...can an old man say *my dear* these days?"

She frowned.

"Because it takes considerably more electricity to run the car motors than solar panels can provide, but they have plenty of juice to power the electrolyzer. New Millenium's solar panels do have an ungodly efficiency rating, but even with that, if you tried to run the car on solar panels alone, they'd weigh down the vehicle so much it couldn't move. Much more efficient to convert the hydrogen into electricity in the car's fuel cells and store it with an extraordinary bit of innovation called a *superconductor ring*, shown here. The ring stores an enormous amount of electricity, exponentially more than a standard car battery. In essence, it is a *super battery*. This is what provides enough electricity to run the car, even at night or in overcast conditions when the solar panels aren't functioning. Plus, we already have all-electric cars. That would be boring. The Hydro is thrilling. For a scientist, anyway."

Kelly continued probing. "So, essentially, with the solar panels and the superconductor ring, you're using electricity to make electricity?"

The professor gave her another look of admiration. "That's a bit of an oversimplification, but essentially, yes."

"And no emissions other than water?" Adam queried.

"Pure water. Totally nonpolluting. You can drink it if you like. The environmentalists love it because it's clean. The public loves it because water is abundant and cheap. And New Millennium loves it because it sells."

"Hydrogen cars have been around for a while," Kelly said. "But there's been no demand for them."

Adam looked at her and smiled.

Mac just sipped his coffee.

"Again, smart girl," Saperston said. "That is true. Producing electricity from hydrogen is nothing new. In fact, it goes back to 1839. What they called a *gas battery* back then, today we call it a *fuel cell*. There have been advances over the years, but the Hydro has made quantum leaps, realizing what has long been only a dream of physicists and car makers. A car that runs on water. Nothing like a little capitalism to encourage scientific curiosity. It is a virtual perpetual motion machine, as long as there is water around. And sunlight. Simply remarkable."

Adam cut to the chase. "So, what went wrong here? Why did this perpetual motion machine explode?"

Saperston walked over to the desk and pulled a much more detailed schematic of the Hydro from the top drawer. It was covered with Saperston's scribbling, and CONFIDENTIAL PROPRIETARY INFORMATION was stamped all over it. "Thanks again, Adam, for obtaining these. Frankly, based on the design, it's hard to fathom what could have caused such a cataclysmic event. Nothing pops out. But I haven't finished my investigation. Your paralegal said he's getting me those police pictures of the car remnants tomorrow. Perhaps I'll be able to tell you something then."

As the dream team exited Saperston's office, Mac couldn't resist. "Hey, Doc. Never trust an atom. They make up everything."

Chapter 22

CRIMSON COFFEE CAFÉ
Youngstown, New York
Wednesday, August 2, 2023
9:55 a.m.

T he dream team found a coffee shop about a mile from Saperston's office and plunked themselves down in a quiet corner. Kelly was still high on adrenaline from her first meeting with an expert, yet surprised that nothing had really been resolved. They'd barely sat down when she began speaking at a clipped rate. "Professor Simons, what do you think? I mean, I just wonder why, didn't you expect him to—"

"Whoa. Slow down there, Kelly," Adam said. "You know, if we're going to work together as colleagues, you should call me Adam. I'll call you Kelly. Outside of class, naturally. And we keep it strictly professional. You okay with that, Ms. Martin? I mean, Kelly?"

Kelly wasn't crazy about the *strictly professional* part, but she was excited to be on a first-name basis with her brilliant professor. She was about to respond when her attention was drawn to a yellow car passing the shop window. It looked like a Hydro. In fact, it looked identical to Jennifer Talbot's Hydro. Kelly followed it with her eyes until it crossed the next intersection...*and exploded in a fireball*, sending a charred empty baby seat flying through the air. When she blinked, the yellow car, the baby seat, and the explosion had all disappeared.

There's the proof, ladies and gentlemen. A litigator too invested in her case. Professor Simons always said not to get personally involved, or you'll act out of emotion rather than reason. Though he himself is helping friends in this case, another rule he'd taught us and has now broken. What did he say about representing friends or family, again? Oh, yeah, an elephant.

"Often the closer you get to an object, the less you can see of it," Adam had said. "Stick your nose right up against an elephant's hide and try to tell me what the tusks or the tail look like. All you can see is gray elephant skin. Friends and family do the same thing. You can be so close to them, you don't see their faults, your case's faults, you don't realize how they're affecting your judgment. They can make you act out of emotion and loyalty when you should be employing logic and law. Avoid them at all costs, creatures."

While Kelly pondered the litigation traps posed by friends and relatives, Adam was remembering the moment he first fell in love.

***

He was smitten at first sight, but true love began about a month after they started dating. At a birthday party for Beth's four-year-old niece. Somehow Beth convinced him to dress up as a clown to entertain the children, proving once again that she could get him to do pretty much anything. Adam's only relevant skill was a rudimentary ability to juggle, but they bought him an outfit, Beth made up his face and put a green wig on his head, and off they went.

While the kids were eating birthday cake, a little girl hesitantly approached Adam and Beth, who were having an animated legal debate in the corner of the room. The girl looked up at Adam, her eyes wide with wonderment and adoration at seeing an actual clown up close. "I love the clown."

Without skipping a beat, Beth knelt down to face her. "I love the clown, too." When Beth looked up at Adam, the clown's heart had melted.

That sealed the deal for him.

They would start their journey a month later, when they moved in together, but it would be derailed fourteen years later. A single child was born of their union, after years and years of trying. It was obvious something wasn't right, but it took the doctors a long time, *way too long*, to figure it out. The birth had been difficult, though Adam didn't believe it caused Beth's cancer. He didn't blame Pete, but when it was all over and perpetual darkness blanketed Adam's world, Pete became a constant reminder of Beth, their struggles, their far-flung hope against hope that *this time* the magic potion would work. And the ultimate defeat.

After Beth's death, Adam didn't consciously shun Pete, but their interactions grew less and less frequent, and less and less meaningful. Unintentionally or otherwise, Adam acted selfishly, his grief for Beth superseding his fatherly duties just when Pete needed his love most. Adam was oblivious. On the plus side, while some might have been driven to drink or chemical diversion, Adam dealt with his bitter memories by plunging headlong into his work.

***

Kelly told herself Adam *must* have feelings for her. *Why else pick me? Out of everyone in the class. And now to be on a first-name basis? Score.*

"So Adam..." She loved saying his name. "Do we have a case or not?"

"I'll let you know on Friday," he replied. "When Marcel Saperston lets *me* know."

Chapter 23

OFFICE OF DR. MARCEL SAPERSTON
Youngstown, New York
Friday, August 4, 2023
7:00 p.m.

D r. Saperston welcomed Adam, Kelly, Mac, and Freddie into his office. The desk and filing cabinets were strewn with papers. The television had been removed from the card table and placed on Saperston's desk. A baseball game was on, but it was muted. While Adam and Freddie watched a few pitches, Saperston thought about how to break the news to them.

He had counted on Mac not attending, given Mac's apparent boredom at the prior meeting. *I'm sure he's likable under the right circumstances, but those circumstances don't include a serious scientific discussion. Or perhaps any discussion in which I'm a participant.*

The young lady, on the other hand, was a pleasant surprise. *A law student capable of grasping some pretty difficult scientific concepts. Maybe there's hope for the younger generation, after all. Once they figure out what music is.*

Before he could get started, Saperston's attention was diverted by Freddie. "Have we met before?"

"Nope. Sorry, Doc. Just got one of those faces."

"Are you certain? I still have a pretty good memory."

"Sorry, Doc. I'd remember meeting *you*, for sure."

Adam opened up the discussion. "I gather you've reviewed the police photos of the vehicle remnants?"

"That, as well as the debris inventory, and the security camera's video of the accident. And the police grid, showing where the car components were found." Saperston knew they were looking for a simple answer, but there was none. *Might as well announce the verdict now, rather than build up false hopes.* "I'm sorry to be the bearer of bad news, Adam, but I have read the report from the defense expert, this Ditenzo, and I tend to agree. It turns out there *was* a defect in this particular vehicle, but the defect couldn't have resulted in the sort of catastrophic explosion we had here."

Kelly lost her cool. "But the car blew up. The little girl—"

"Marcel," Adam said, "she has a lot of youthful enthusiasm, but she also has a point. The Hydro is still just a machine, and every machine has faults. You're telling me a hydrogen powered vehicle *can't* explode that way? What about the Hindenburg?"

"Adam, you may allude to that in your jury presentation if you wish, but the Hindenburg had seven million cubic feet of hydrogen in its gas cells. Because the Hydro creates its own hydrogen, there's only a thimble-full stored at any given time, making the chance of an explosion remote, if not impossible. You might get a firecracker-sized pop, under the right conditions." Saperston held up a photo of Jennifer Talbot's car engulfed in flames. "But *this*? No."

Adam pressed him. "Didn't you say there *was* a defect?"

Saperston anticipated Adam's reaction the moment he uttered the word *defect. When a lawyer hears it, his pulse soars, he salivates, and he dreams of large checks. He'll cling to that defect like a dog with a bone.* "There was a defect. Strangely, inexplicably, they put an extra electrical cable in this car. It ran from the superconductor ring to the right rear motor." *Adam's sharp, though. Once he stops salivating, it'll make sense to him why this couldn't be the proximate cause of the explosion.*

This time Adam asked for clarification. "In English, please."

"I've made a diagram identifying the defect." Saperston opened his trusty laptop.

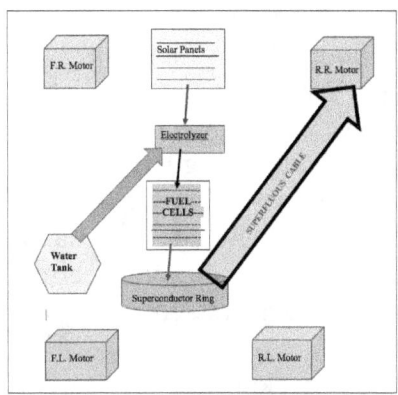

"You see this cable here? Labeled superfluous cable? That's precisely what it is, superfluous. It shouldn't have been there. It's not in New Millennium official illustrations of the Hydro, and there's no reason it would be. It serves no function. But what it *did* was continuously feed electricity to the right rear motor, even when the car wasn't in operation. This could have overheated the motor and caused a fire. But an explosion? No. And before you ask, I've identified no other flaw in the design or manufacturing of this particular vehicle."

Adam wouldn't give up. "This cable, it must do *something*?"

Saperston looked quizzical. "That's just it. As I said, there's nothing like it in the schematics. It's not supposed to do anything because it's not supposed to be there. In any event, however it got there, it couldn't have caused the explosion."

"So we have a defect, yet it's irrelevant," Kelly stated calmly.

Just a student, and she's already got defect fever. "The extra cable is no more responsible for the explosion than a defective radio."

"Freddie," Adam said, "show the professor the video. Let's see if we can move the needle for him."

Freddie opened his laptop and entered several passwords in succession. A video appeared, the crash-test video that Mac had found. The five of them watched in silence, with a communal gasp at the end when the car exploded in a ball of flame. Except Saperston.

Lay people shouldn't be allowed anywhere near science. "It's interesting, but we have no idea what prototype stage we're looking at, how similar it was to the final product that Jennifer Talbot drove. I'm sorry. My opinion is unchanged."

Kelly gasped. "Interesting? That's all?"

Adam gave her a sharp look. "Like I said, Marcel, youthful enthusiasm. Kelly, I've never known Marcel to take me down the wrong path. He's as reliable as Big Ben."

Saperston looked down at his waistline, then quickly looked back up. "There are innumerable phenomena in nature and physics that cannot be explained. Science is not a perfect...well, science."

"So this cable," Adam pressed, "it's possible it *could have* caused the explosion?"

"Based on my current knowledge of physics, no. Is it possible it *did*, in a manner that I don't currently understand? Possible. Though unlikely."

"Well, if *your* current knowledge of physics isn't good enough, no one's is. Any other ideas, Marcel? Can you reverse-engineer the explosion? There must be another angle to look at this."

"I have given it some thought."

"I knew you would."

"One possible scenario comes to mind. Fairly simple, actually. You could get a buildup of hydrogen inside the car if you ran a Y-shaped tube from the electrolyzer, diverting hydrogen to the interior of the car through one branch of the Y, while continuing to send hydrogen to the fuel cells through the other branch."

"Yeah, Doc," Mac said. "Simple."

I'd almost forgotten about that bozo. "In this scenario, a tiny spark, perhaps a buildup of static electricity, or just starting the ignition, *could* result in an explosion of this magnitude."

Adam and Kelly both started to speak. Kelly deferred, letting Adam have the floor.

"Why a Y-shaped tube? Why not a *single*, uh, tube running from the electrolyzer to the interior?"

"For technical reasons that I won't go into at present, the New Millennium electrolyzer can have only one exit tube. Thus, under this scenario, you'd need a single tube exiting the electrolyzer that would bifurcate with one branch going to the fuel cells as designed, and the other to the interior of the car. If a single tube diverted the hydrogen to the interior, no hydrogen would flow to the fuel cells and the car wouldn't run. Here, I've drawn up a diagram. Again, an exceedingly simplified version. The hypothetical Y-tube is labelled."

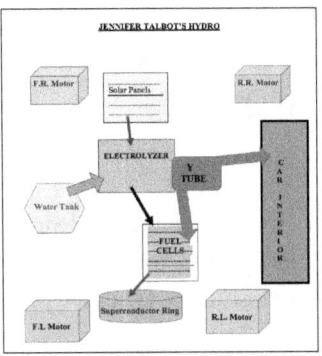

Adam pressed Marcel. "Is it possible the extra cable found in the wreckage could have done the same as this hypothetical tube?"

Saperston felt for Adam, but facts were facts. "No, Adam. They are two completely different things. The cable found in the wreckage was a solid electrical cable. The Y-tube in my hypothesis is a hollow tube that could transport hydrogen into the car interior."

Saperston, seeing the furrowed brow on Kelly's face, expected another good question, and he got one.

"Doctor Saperston, wouldn't you smell it before enough hydrogen accumulated to blow up the car?"

"Good questions, but hydrogen is a colorless, odorless gas."

Kelly persisted. "They don't use the mercaptan they add to natural gas to make it stink so people don't blow up their houses?"

Saperston's admiration moved up another notch. *Maybe I should grab her for the physics program, instead of letting her waste her time learning to argue for a living.* "They do not, young lady. Since there is a miniscule amount of hydrogen in the Hydro at any one time they don't bother to odorize it. In any event, there are, at a minimum, two significant problems with the Y-tube scenario."

The professor paused in thought for dramatic effect, as he often did at trial, so Adam made the obligatory inquiry. "And the problems...they are?"

"First, I can't imagine why anyone would do such a thing. It makes no sense. It's not in the plans and not necessary for operation of the vehicle. In fact, as I explained, it could be quite detrimental. And second, no such tubing, or anything like it, was found in the debris. So this remains a hypothesis in search of facts."

Adam sighed. "Better to find out now than at trial. Thanks for your time, Marcel. You know that we can't retain you for trial."

"As I expected. And I understand."

"Hey, Doc," Mac said. "If electricity comes from electrons, does morality come from morons?"

***

Walking back to the car, Mac had an idea. One word of Dr. Saperston's Y-tube discussion rang in his head: *branches*. Mac would forget about it for a while. But not forever.

Chapter 24

THE BUFFALO CLUB
Delaware Avenue, Buffalo, New York
Saturday, August 5. 2023
6:39 p.m.

The dark wood-paneled walls were adorned with oil paintings of past Club presidents, some of whom were also U.S. Presidents. The Buffalo Club's intricately patterned blood-red carpeting, fourteen-foot-wide staircases, and gleaming chandeliers were even more opulent than the ephemeral simulated décor of the Holotrial courtrooms.

Founded in 1867 by Millard Fillmore and a number of other exalted gentlemen of the day, The Buffalo Club reeked of old money and past grandeur. Over a century and a half after its founding, the successful and important and well-connected still gathered there for celebrations, business meetings, and casual liaisons. The building's understated red-brick facade merely hinted at the exquisite elegance inside.

Adam felt Kelly deserved a treat for her hard work. Why not something special, like introducing her to The Buffalo Club? On the one hand, he feared this might feed her crush. On the other, he hoped that, if he kept it professional in this one-on-one setting, it would crush the crush. He was wrong.

As he had feared, Kelly got the wrong message from the moment she entered the Club. Just ascending the elegant staircase to the second floor left her wide-eyed, and her broad smile and pause on each step to drink in the surroundings told Adam that such settings were not a normal part of her childhood.

"Prof... Adam, this place is magnificent," Kelly said. "I can imagine the Queen of England and her entourage descending these stairs for a lavish royal ceremony. I can't believe you brought me here. This is special. Let's make it a special evening."

***

Unlike JJ, at no time was Kelly under the illusion that she had a supportive father, or even a remotely nice one. Brad Penner was with the U.S. Border Patrol, stationed at the Canadian border crossing at Rouses Point, New York, a sleepy little village sitting right on Lake Champlain in northeastern New York. He basically did desk work. After two tours of duty in Afghanistan, he'd returned without a left arm. But he did have the right one, and it was useful for all sorts of things: shaving, eating, bowling, texting, tweeting, and beating on Kelly's mother, Erin.

It had started almost the moment he returned from his second Afghanistan tour. His first morning back, while he was getting dressed for the day, Erin began gently fastening the buttons of his shirt. It had been a morning ritual from long before he'd gone to war, long before he'd lost an arm. Brad's response was to swat her hands away and push her violently to the floor.

As Brad watched his colleagues perform various functions that a one-armed man could not, he graduated from swatting Erin to punching her. When he lost his job and upped his alcohol consumption, he began pushing her down the basement staircase.

Kelly had been two years old when Brad did his first stint in Afghanistan, and she was five when he returned the second time. Kelly often noticed the bruises on her mother's face and arms, but she didn't make anything of it. People got bruises. She got them. Her friends got them.

Once Kelly grew old enough to understand the situation, she begged her mother to leave Brad. Her mother would hear nothing of it. "I signed up *for better or for worse*. He's been through a lot, honey. It's more my fault than his. I'm probably not giving him enough support. Or care. We'll be back to *better*. We just need to give him time."

Kelly wondered, if they gave him time, how many more broken bones and drunken rages it would lead to. She did find it strange that Brad never harmed *her*, saving all his wrath for her mother. As she grew older and more perceptive, she sensed that on some level, Brad was afraid of her, that he sensed an inner strength that Kelly herself did not realize she possessed.

Kelly was fifteen when the straw broke the camel's back. It

was a sunny Friday afternoon. She was walking home from school, chatting with friends about their weekend plans. About half a block from home, she heard loud bangs like gunshots coming from her house.

Kelly ran inside to find her mother handcuffed to a kitchen chair. Brad had placed an apple on her mom's head, mumbling about William Tell and the Sheriff of Nottingham. Not surprisingly, he was mixing up his fables. When Kelly burst into the room, he was yelling at Erin not to move, that she was throwing off his aim. There were bullet holes in the wall and cabinetry. Erin screamed at Kelly to leave, but she wouldn't budge. She calmly dialed 911 while her father reloaded. Before he'd finished, she grabbed a kitchen chair and smashed it on his head, knocking both the gun and a stunned Brad to the ground.

The sheriff's deputies took Brad away that day, though Kelly knew he'd be back. Even after this dangerous and humiliating episode, Erin didn't leave him. Kelly had to take matters into her own hands. She went to the *big city* of Plattsburgh, population 19,500, the nearest thing to a metropolis, to find a lawyer. It was her introduction to the legal profession. The first four lawyers on the list that she'd Googled wouldn't give her the time of day: who wanted to deal with a fifteen-year-old with no money who wasn't old enough to sign a binding client retainer agreement? Kelly needed to head home soon. It was getting late in the afternoon, time for her father to return from his *day shift* at the bars. She thought she'd give it one final try with the next lawyer on her list, a Mr. Barber.

As she entered the front door of his office, she was nearly run over by Mr. Barber, who was calling it a day. When he saw the desperation in her eyes, he did an about face and ushered her inside. There he listened to an all too familiar story. The next day, Kelly brought Erin back with her. Erin apologized for her impetuous daughter, attempting to downplay the seriousness of the situation at home, which was belied by the bruises on her face and the long-sleeve shirt and jeans she wore on that warm spring day.

Mr. Barber gently coaxed Erin's story out of her, bit by bit. No job, little education, virtually no money, just a few hundred dollars in coins she'd hidden from Brad in the attic. Mr. Barber asked if Erin intended to get a job once she escaped her current situation. She said she would, if she could find one that suited her meager skills. The attorney beamed. She just happened to qualify for his working client payment plan. She could pay off her legal bill without any interest, once a year on December 31, shooting for $500 a year if she could afford it. If not, any shortfalls would be left for the end of the payment period.

Kelly smiled when she heard this. *Major props to me. I couldn't have picked a nicer lawyer.*

Erin asked, in a quiet shaky voice, "What is the payment period?" She'd never handled financial transactions more complex than checking for better prices on Amazon. And she'd never spoken to a lawyer before. Brad had drilled into Kelly and Erin not to trust lawyers, that they were slimy creatures who were trained to be tricky. This kind, helpful lawyer confirmed Kelly's belief that Brad's entire outlook on life was complete bullshit, the ravings of an angry, unhappy, drunken, disheveled mind.

Barber assured Erin that the length of the payment plan was adjusted based on each individual client's circumstances, with the client's best interests being the guiding factor.

Kelly, already wiser than her mother in the ways of the world, immediately understood that Mr. Barber didn't care if he ever received a nickel from Erin. That was the moment she decided to become a lawyer. She wanted to help people, too, like Mr. Barber was helping them. To *pay it forward*. She would also literally pay it backward and see that his bill was satisfied. She promised herself that this nice man would get every cent he was owed once she graduated from law school.

After convincing her mother that Mr. Barber could be trusted, Erin signed the retention papers. That afternoon, Mr. Barber got a restraining order, and the next morning, he filed a divorce action for Erin and a criminal complaint against Brad. He was as efficient as he was nice, and soon Brad was out of their lives.

With Brad gone, Kelly started going by her mother's maiden name, Martin. Mr. Barber offered to change it legally, but Kelly wanted that to be her first professional task once she got her law license. It would complete the exorcism of Brad from her life, which would be more meaningful if she did it herself.

But Kelly's troubles were far from over. The scars from dealing with Brad didn't heal overnight. She went through a period of recklessly seeking affection from every Y-chromosome within a

50-mile radius. At her high school, she gained a reputation as a major slut. Her girlfriends slowly but surely drifted away. It took months for Kelly's misbegotten foray into the world of promiscuity and self-destruction to end, but eventually she was almost back to baseline, before Brad-world had turned everything upside down and inside out. Kelly's subconscious search for a father figure would continue, but she'd no longer pursue random sexual encounters as a means to that end. Maybe just an innocent flirtation—well, mostly innocent—with, say, a law professor, would fill the bill?

***

Adam and Kelly were seated by the maître d' in a quiet corner of The Buffalo Club's largest dining room. At Kelly's shy request, Adam had ordered a bottle of wine for the table. The moment they sat down, Kelly tried to set the tone. "Adam, I love that you've brought me here. Thank you *so* much. I feel really special. I hope I am?"

To her dismay, Adam ignored the question and began discussing the case in such business-like fashion that Kelly's initial elation descended into a somber mood. *Okay, let's talk about the trial. Just for now. Maybe Adam will come around, so let's get that wine.*

"Adam, this is a great place," she said, "but what is there to celebrate? I mean other than you and I making a great team? It's so frustrating. The car blows up. The girl, she's *dead.* And New Millennium, they get to walk, no questions asked?"

"What are you talking about, Kelly?"

"It's over, isn't it? We don't have a *defect.* Isn't that the primary requirement of any product liability case?"

"It's *not* over. Far from it."

"But the case. Dr. Saperston... Are we not even paying him?"

"We *are* paying him," Adam clarified. "As a consultant. We just can't retain him as a trial expert. He understands. If we retained him for trial, we'd be obliged to disclose his opinion to New Millennium's counsel. So that we're on the same page, if anyone asks, we are getting background information from Dr. Saperston, who's acting as a general consultant, *not* as a trial witness. But I doubt anyone will ask."

Kelly frowned. She didn't want to get caught up in anything improper before she even passed the bar. And how could Adam suggest such a thing? He'd repeatedly pounded into his students that they adhere to the highest ethical standards at all times. "Purer than Caesar's wife," he'd say. She knew about Mussolini and hula hoops, but that one she hadn't heard before. *Was this another principle he was abandoning, like not representing friends?*

Lucky for Adam, Kelly didn't know how Freddie had *found* the crash-test video on YouTube. Sometimes ignorance *is* bliss. If this business with Saperston had her this much on edge, there's no telling how she would have reacted to the crash video's provenance.

"Kelly, this is perfectly kosher," Adam said. "It's done all the time. We're only required to disclose experts who are expected to testify at trial, not experts we consult for background."

"Isn't that why we met with him in the first place, hoping he'd be our expert witness?"

She truly loved working on the case, not just getting to work next to Adam. It was her first real case in her first real courtroom, not to mention that she cared about Jennifer and the loss of her child. Kelly weighed all that against starting her career with disbarment.

"Kelly, if you feel uncomfortable, you can withdraw," Adam promised. "I won't hold it against you. However, I assure you, again, this is standard practice. We went to Marcel with the dual purpose of considering him as a consultant and *possibly* as trial witness. We decided against the trial witness role. He continues as a consultant."

"No, prof...um, Adam. I'm sticking around. I can't abandon these people. Or you. And *Jennifer*. I can't imagine, like, *to lose a child that way*. But Adam, none of it matters without a theory of the case. We have no defect."

"We don't *need* a specific defect. *Res Ipsa Loquitur*. You're familiar with that from torts, I assume?"

Kelly blushed. *Idiot. And in front of Adam. What must he think of his star student now? Some editor-in-chief of the law review. Well, maybe that's my excuse. Brain overload. Between this trial, classes, choosing articles for the* Review...

She regrouped and tried to dispel the notion that she'd slept through her first year of law school. "Yes, *Res Ipsa Loquitur, the thing speaks for itself.* Cars aren't supposed to explode in huge balls of flame. If they do, the car maker had to be negligent."

"Perfectly stated."

"But is this ethical? Our own expert told us that a defect didn't cause the explosion."

"Kelly, that's *not* what he told us. You know, you asked some great questions in there. The *true* art of cross-examination lies in listening to the answers."

"I didn't know I was cross-examining him."

"We all were. You heard him. Marcel said it himself: science can't explain everything. He doesn't know how the extra cable could have caused the explosion, but that doesn't mean it didn't, and it also doesn't rule out another defect that Marcel can't identify because our current scientific knowledge doesn't recognize it. The only other theory he has is the Y-tube, which doesn't exist. Look. This Hydro is filled with new technology. Marcel understands how the car works. But neither he nor anyone else understands everything that could happen when it *doesn't* work."

Adam pointed at Kelly's empty wine glass. She nodded, and they both reached for her glass to hold it under the wine bottle. Her hand got there sooner, and instead of grasping the glass, his hand enveloped hers. She would later deny to JJ that this was anything but accidental, but was it? *Did I see his hand coming and beat him to the bottle?*

They both froze, Adam wondering how to get out of the situation, Kelly wondering how to make sure it never ended.

"Would either of you care for dessert?"

Adam and Kelly hadn't noticed the waiter. Adam swiftly pulled his hand off hers. They were hardly the restaurant's first pair of amorous customers, though their age difference did seem eye-opening. Finding no takers for dessert, the waiter proceeded to another table.

The spell broken, Kelly could think of no smooth segue, so she plunged right back into the case. "Where were we? Oh yes. *Res Ipsa Loquitur*. The doctrine was made for a case like ours. No need to prove exactly what the negligence or defect was. It's assumed."

Adam concurred. "In fact, we have a far stronger *Res Ipsa* case than usual, since we *have* in fact identified a defect. We just don't know precisely how it caused the explosion. That's where *Res Ipsa* comes in. We don't *have* to know."

Listening to Adam's reasoning, which sounded almost like a

summation for a jury, Kelly snapped out of her romantic fantasy and into its close cousins, admiration and idolatry.

Adam continued. "Do I wish we understood what the defect did? Of course I do. But that's beside the point. Listen, we may be walking a fine line here, but I don't think we're crossing it. Anyway, I'm doing it for a friend. Sometimes friendship trumps everything."

"I thought you and the Senator had drifted apart."

"It's a long story. A very...long...story."

It must involve Katherine. Their chemistry is palpable. How did that not register with me? I know he'd like me more if he didn't already have a thing going with Kate. I know he likes me. I just know it. He won't show it in front of Kate. Maybe that'll blow over. Wonder if they're doing it? Oh God, now I sound like JJ.

But Adam was all business. "I have a new assignment for you, Kelly. This could be supremely important if I'm guessing right. Find out how many Hydros have been sold to date...and how many have exploded."

Chapter 25

SUPREME COURT, ERIE COUNTY
Talbot versus New Millennium, Inc.
Holotrial Annex Building, Part 5-HT
Main Street, Buffalo, New York
Monday, August 14, 2023
9:35 a.m.

The assemblage of lawyers, clients, and Talbot family members stood as Judge Thomas Arturo shuffled into the courtroom from the door behind the judge's bench. He was twenty minutes late, a new record for him. For promptness, that is. His slow gait and wrinkled face reflected his 69 years. Some at his age remained energetic and nimble, but Judge Arturo was an old 69. Perhaps because of this, he was considerably *laissez-faire* in his courtroom. He didn't have the energy, mental or physical, to impose rigorous discipline on attorneys or engage them in complex legal discourse. It was considerably easier to defer a ruling and let his law clerk research it later. Better yet, just let the evidence in and leave the Appellate Division to deal with it. *What do I care about reversal rates? I'm retiring in three months, for God's sake.*

Adam and Kelly represented the plaintiffs, Jennifer Talbot and the estate of Allison Talbot. All three Talbots were seated next to Mac and Freddie in the peanut gallery. New Millennium was represented by Michael Chun, an up-and-coming partner at Burstein, Wang, and Torreti, as well as a male associate from the firm. Adam always chuckled at the firm's name. It sounded like the punchline to a multi-ethnic joke. But the firm was no joke. It specialized in product liability litigation. Adam wished he could say the same for himself. The corporate representatives for New Millennium, also seated in the gallery, were Dr. Joan Perry, its CEO, and the in-house General Counsel, Dan Toler. They were taking this case quite seriously.

Alan M. Wishnoff

Judge Arturo fumbled with some documents. He was never going to be comfortable with the computer age that his children and grandchildren had adapted to so well. He liked the feel of paper. The look of paper. Reading off computer screens gave him a headache. Finally, he got down to business, nodding to his court clerk to begin the proceedings.

The clerk dutifully announced, "Holotrial H23-85C, Talbot versus New Millennium, Inc. All counsel present. Preliminary instructions completed."

Judge Arturo took over. "You esquires gonna give me any headaches? This gonna be a long one?"

Michael Chun, ever quick on his feet, replied, "It should be over before you can say *directed verdict*."

"Well, I've never known Mr. Simons not to have a case," Judge Arturo retorted. "Or, to correct the record, I've never known Mr. Simons not to *think* he had a case." The judge picked up on Chun's worried face. "Don't worry, Mr. Chun. If Mr. Simons is keeping score, I'm confident I've ruled against him more often than not. And we actually crossed swords when I was a swashbuckling litigator myself. Yes, it may be hard to believe, but once upon a time, these old bones cut a rug through the trial courts. Not these Holotrials, mind you, but the real thing. Isn't that so, Mr. Simons?"

"Your Honor is being modest. I wouldn't want to tangle with those bones, then or now."

"Guess I asked for it. Flattery will get you nowhere, though I won't stop you from trying. In all seriousness, Mr. Chun, I *will* say this is an unusual case for Mr. Simons to take. But I guess even Mr. Simons has to eat."

Adam replied, "Your Honor's concern is touching."

"Okay, then. We might as well get going. Anything we need to address before we call in the jury?"

Adam and Michael Chun replied in unison. "No, Your Honor."

Good. The judge smirked. *If we can get through this one quickly, I'm gonna take a week before the next trial to do a little fishing, Rocket Docket be damned. No reason to kill myself so the widow can collect my pension. Let the Administrative Judge get off his ass and take the next trial if he doesn't like it. I'm out here on the firing line, keeping up his stats while he sits on his fat ass behind a cozy desk. Lazy bastard.*

Holotrial

***

Like all Holotrials, this one was recorded in the specially constructed annex to the Erie County Courthouse. It was two miles from the main courthouse on Delaware Avenue, but it might as well have been two lightyears. The main courthouse was an elegant gothic stone building erected in 1875. The Holotrial Annex Building, or *HAB*, was an abandoned red-brick warehouse that had been converted to its current purpose in 2022. Unlike the old granite courthouse with its 270-foot clock tower and arched entranceways, the annex was a drab, windowless cube. If not for the sign at the entrance, nothing would indicate to passersby that it was a courthouse or, for that matter, a building of any consequence whatsoever.

If the HAB was pure Rust Belt on the outside, inside it had the feel of a modern twenty-first century office building: freshly painted walls, laminate flooring that resembled top-of-the-line Brazilian Cherry, newly installed HVAC system, and a state-of-the-art glass-walled control room in the center of the building, partitioned into ten cubicles, each with a designated console assigned to one of the hi-tech courtrooms, Parts 1-HT through 10-HT. The building was, in essence, a large television studio.

Judge Arturo hoped the Holotrial experiment would catch on and go from Pilot Program to SOP. *So much easier not having to deal with pain-in-the-ass jurors. They always wanted breaks, food, having exhibits passed around. And there was always at least one sneezing juror who seemed likely to give me the flu.*

"Mr. Simons, you may now give your opening statement. Bring in the jury. So to speak."

As Adam approached the *jury box*, additional lighting turned on and made the seven shiny juror faces more vivid. Just the same, no one would confuse them with living, breathing human beings. The *jury* included four *men* and three *women*, each with a different face, age, hairdo, and clothing. Two of the men and two of the women wore suitcoats. A couple of middle-aged men sported polo shirts, and a twentyish woman wore a hoodie. Two jurors were black, two Caucasian, two Hispanic, and one Asian.

This was Adam's fourth Holotrial. The first had been a challenge, trying to emote to a bunch of lifeless dummies who never smiled, frowned, or reacted in any way to his oratory. How an actual human jury would respond was guesswork, at best, or as he told his students, flying blind. Once again, Adam prayed for a return to the traditional procedures that had served everyone just fine for hundreds of years.

At Adam's first Holotrial, the fake jurors and the holographic video replay, or *Holoscript*, were the most striking aspects of the pilot project. By his second trial, Adam had more subtle questions. For example, why bother transforming white surfaces to mimic wood, glass, carpeting, etc.? Why not just use a real mahogany bench, oak-paneled walls, and glass windows? When he had put the question to the young genius from Disney who'd developed the Holotrial system, the obvious answer made Adam feel exceptionally foolish.

"You have to understand," the savant had explained, a Holotrial courtroom serves two distinct, and essentially opposite, purposes. It's both a film studio, in which the Holotrial is recorded in front of the substitute jurors, *and* a movie theater for later projecting the finished Holoscript to the live jury. For the same reason that standard-format movies are projected on white screens, Holotrials needed to be projected on white surfaces. Using real furniture would present a hopelessly complicated viewing surface, with multiple colors and textures that would make playback unwatchable. The essence of the Holotrial concept was to make it as realistic as possible for the jurors. Presenting them with a distorted grainy image of the trial, bearing scant resemblance to real life, would defeat the whole purpose.

It made sense to Adam, but it didn't make him like Holotrials any better. He held that thought as he addressed the inanimate jurors. "May it please the court, ladies and gentlemen of the jury."

***

The lawyers having finished their opening statements, Jennifer Talbot was called to the stand. Adam would literally start off with a bang, the car's explosion, to immediately capture the jurors' attention.

They'd gone over her direct testimony five times in Adam's office. Nevertheless, Jennifer was a bundle of nerves. She was fidgety, her eyes darting all over the room, fingers tapping on the railing of the witness box. It wasn't just the subject matter of her testimony that concerned her. Like most people, she'd never been inside a courtroom, let alone been a witness at a jury trial. Not to mention that this didn't resemble any courtroom she'd ever seen or heard of. Adam was a little surprised that the toughness she'd exhibited in his office utterly disappeared in this setting. He'd seen it before, though. This bizarro simulated courtroom with the plastic jurors was enough to throw anyone off their game.

Jennifer knew that the wood paneling, the marble floor, the windows, the rug—none of it was real, though she had no idea how they did it. *Guess I understand this as well as I understood that damn car. What the hell made me accept it from him? The rotten bastard. I shouldn't have listened to Mom either.*

Jennifer was seated a few feet from Juror Number One, made up to look like a frumpy middle-aged man in a white shirt, red bow tie, and navy blazer. She pictured him as a boring insurance exec who sat behind a drab desk all day, at night strumming wildly in a *Goo-Goo Dolls* cover band. She couldn't get over how lifelike he appeared. It was like being at the Tussaud's Waxworks museum in Niagara Falls. That preppy from the library with the bad breath had taken her there for their first, and only, date. She had found the wax characters macabre, and now there were seven of them sitting in judgment of her. *I wonder if these jurors are based, like Tussaud's, on real people? Or do they have special fake-juror artists to design them? Is that a thing?*

Adam walked to the end of the jury box so that Jennifer would be facing all of the jurors as she testified. It was an old lawyer's trick, designed to make your witness more relatable to the jury. On cross-examination, you did the opposite. Stand to the left of the witness box, forcing opposing witnesses to testify with their backs to the jury.

Q: Jennifer, how old was your daughter Allison on June thirtieth of this year?

A: This year? You mean now? She'd be about four—

Q: No, Jennifer, I'm sorry. The question is how

old was your daughter on June thirtieth when
your car...when the incident with your car
occurred in the Prime Foods parking lot?

A: Oh, I'm sorry, Mr. Simons. Allie was...like, she
was two months old.

Q: And she was your only child?

A: She was very precious.

Q: You're doing fine, Jennifer, but you need to
listen closely to the question. Allison was...
You didn't have any other children?

Mr. Chun: Leading, Your Honor?

The Court: Well, kind of preliminary. We'll let it
go.

Q: Jennifer, do you remember the question?

A: No, no other children.

Q: Jennifer, who gave you the car, the Hydro?

A: That was, like, the...New Millennium company.
They make, they made—

Q: I'm sorry, Jennifer, I probably wasn't clear
enough. Who did you get the car from? Was it
a gift?

A: Oh yes. That's right. From my father.

Adam peered at her quizzically.

Jennifer stared back. *I understand your frustration. You don't understand mine. What I'm doing, what I have to do. What I've been told to do. Why the fuck did I listen to them?*

Q: Jennifer, on June 30 of this year, did you park
your car in the Prime Foods parking lot at
approximately 2:35 pm?

A: Yes. I did. Yes.

Q: Jennifer, we have some closed-circuit video
from that parking lot on June 30.

Adam gave Kelly a slight nod, and she manipulated a small control panel on their counsel table. A video of the supermarket parking lot appeared on monitors on the counsel tables, the bench, and two screens in front of the *jury*.

> Q: Jennifer, is that your car, the yellow Hydro,
> pulling into the spot there?
>
> A: Yes.
>
> Q: And I think we can all see that is you exiting
> the car, holding Allison?
>
> A: Yes, Allie. Yes.
>
> Q: Okay, we will fast forward. We see you placing
> your daughter back in the car.
>
> A: Yes. She's back in.
>
> Q: And now we see you walking to the shopping
> cart corral?
>
> Mr. Chun: Your Honor, a lot of leading.
>
> The Court: Yes, but I'll allow it. The video is
> doing the real talking. And under the
> circumstances, kind of preliminary.

While common for judges to permit a reasonable amount of leading on direct examination for so-called *preliminary* matters that are not in dispute, such as a witness's age or education, Judge Arturo had an exceedingly expansive view of what was a preliminary matter. He'd made it into an art form in his courtroom.

> Q: And now you've finished putting away the
> empty shopping cart, and you're starting to
> walk back to your vehicle?
>
> A: Yes. I mean, correct.
>
> Q: And then you took out your key fob. What did
> you do with it?
>
> A: It was a...like, a special kind of...you talk into
> it. To start the car, you say *engine on*. That's
> what I did.

Q: And is this what happened next?

The video continued, showing the Hydro explode in a tremendous ball of flame. Jennifer fell to the ground. Adam instinctively turned to see the jurors' reactions to the explosion. Of course, there were none. Just a reflection of the orange flames on their shiny plastic faces.

Q: Jennifer, I'm sorry, but for the record, is that what happened next, what we saw there?

A: Y-yes, Mr. Simons.

"Thank you, Jennifer. Nothing further. This next gentleman, Mr. Chun, is going to ask you some questions now."

The Court: Mr. Chun, cross-examination?

Mr. Chun: Yes, thank you, Your Honor.

Q: Ms. Talbot, do you find it curious the father of your child is not a party to this action?

Mr. Simons: Objection, Your Honor. Curious?

The Court: No, I'll allow it. Preliminary.

Q: Can you answer the question, Ms. Talbot?

A: I'm sorry—

Q: Ms. Talbot, you are the only plaintiff here, correct? Allison's father is not participating in this lawsuit?

A: Yes.

Q: And why is that?

A: I, I don't know. You'd have to ask him.

Q: Well, who *is* the father, Ms. Talbot?

A: I...I don't know.

Q: You don't know? Were there too many—

Mr. Simons: Your Honor.

Mr. Chun: Never mind. We'll move on.

Q: Ms. Talbot. Was the car ever in the shop prior

to the explosion?

A: I only had it for, like, a day. I don't think—

Q: Well, do you know who modified your car? Are you aware there was an extra cable in the engine compartment that wasn't put there by the factory?

Mr. Simons: Objection, Your Honor. Assumes facts not in evidence. There's been no testimony that this occurred outside the factory.

Mr. Chun: Oh, there will be.

The Court: Fine, Mr. Chun. Then let's wait for that testimony. For now, objection sustained.

Q: Okay, Ms. Talbot. Do you know of anyone who could have placed that cable in the car after it left the factory?

Jennifer scowled. *I think I know damn well who did it, the bastard, but I can't say it. They won't allow it.*

A: I think...I think...

Jennifer looked toward her parents sitting in the gallery.

A: Uh, sorry. I think I was confused. No, I don't.

Chapter 26

SUNY AT BUFFALO LAW SCHOOL
Room 304
Amherst, New York
Tuesday, August 15, 2023
10:10 a.m.

A dam smiled. *Time for a Greek history lesson.* "Alexander the Great. Battle of Gaugamela. Anyone?"

Blank stares filled the classroom.

"Alexander had about 50,000 soldiers. Estimates of Persian King Darius's army go as high as a million. What was the best strategy for Alexander? Probably run and hide. Did he do that? No, he didn't. Outnumbered maybe twenty to one, no chariots or other heavy weapons, fighting on a battlefield chosen by the Persians to their advantage...Alexander had the Persian army right where he wanted them."

The class giggled.

"Because Alexander had one huge advantage. He knew how King Darius thought, his expectations from years of commanding the Persian army in battle. So Alexander prepared some surprises. For one thing, he knew Darius assumed the Greeks would fight the way everyone had always fought. Armies of the day were typically arrayed in straight lines, facing each other, so Alexander lined up his battalions at a forty-five-degree angle. Right away, before the battle even began, the Persians were off balance, seeing this strange angled wedge coming at them, unsure of what they were facing. The Greeks ended up winning an astounding victory. What's the lesson here, creatures?"

A smiling student responded, "Think like Alexander."

Adam frowned. "No. Exactly the opposite. Think like your *opponent*. Think what *she* thinks you're going to do. Then, *don't do it*. Do the unexpected. Let's take cross-examination of expert witnesses. Kelly and I have one coming up soon in our trial against New Millennium. You all know, the Talbot case. How should I start the cross of their expert?"

A hand shot up from the fourth row. "Show that their expert went to worse schools than yours. Maybe your expert was their expert's teacher. Or he's never testified about this subject before. Or published anything on it."

"Perfect examples," Adam replied, "and perfectly wrong. That's the way most lawyers do it. Let me suggest something different. Start in *cut-to-the-chase mode*. Confront the witness straightaway with decisive questions about the ultimate issues in the case. Don't let them ease into your cross-examination with the usual banal introductory puffery about the witness's employment history, education, favorite cookie, etc., as the defense counsel has undoubtedly done in its preparation of the witness. An uncomfortable witness is likely a helpful witness. On the *other* side, that is. Anyone?"

A number of eager hands rose. Adam picked one from the back of the class, Jack Poltowski.

"How about, 'Are cars supposed to blow up?'"

"Excellent. Perfect idea. I may have to split my fee with you." Adam chuckled. "Starting off with a game-set-match question like that also demonstrates another important trial strategy. Primacy and recency. Start your trial with the most significant witness's most significant testimony. Get the jurors' attention immediately. Get them on your side. And you end your case with very compelling testimony that will be the first thing they think of when they start deliberations.

"Primacy and recency works for individual witnesses' testimony, as well. On cross as well as direct. We'll use Jack's excellent question for the New Millennium expert: should cars blow up and kill their occupants? That's an attention grabber. Ending the cross-examination is a little trickier, but if you get it right, it pays priceless dividends. Present a summary of all the helpful admissions you've eked out of the witness, and get him or her to agree, so the jury hears the best elements of your case coming from the mouth of your *opponent's* expert. Taking the example we've been working with, 'Dr. So-and-So, based on what you've testified to today, I think you can agree that cars are not supposed to blow up and kill their occupants, that it would be negligent for an auto maker to produce a car that could blow up and kill its occupants, that you know of no modification to the car by the plaintiff or anyone else after it left the factory, and that Ms. Talbot's car did in fact blow up the day after it left the New Millennium factory and kill her infant daughter.'"

A hand shot up from the fifth row. "Can that ever really work?"

"You'd be surprised. Oh, by the way, Jack, your question also demonstrates another interesting counterintuitive trial tactic. What's the golden rule of cross-examination that even school children seem to know?"

The class responded, almost as one: "Never ask a question if you don't know the answer."

"Exactly. *However*, there are what I call *no lose* questions, usually yes-or-no questions, when you don't care what the answer is. When diametrically opposite answers are equally helpful. A variation on the classic *When did you stop beating your wife?*. Jack's suggestion is a perfect example. If the witness answers 'No,' meaning that cars are not supposed to blow up, it helps to establish your case. If the witness answers 'Yes,' meaning that cars *are* supposed to blow up, he'll look like a callous fool and lose all credibility with the jury. I'll tell you Friday which path New Millennium's expert chooses. Stay tuned."

Chapter 27

SUPREME COURT, ERIE COUNTY
Talbot versus New Millennium, Inc.
Holotrial Annex Building, Part 5-HT
Main Street, Buffalo, New York
Thursday, August 17, 2023
9:45 a.m.

After two days of mundane testimony from police detectives and the National Transportation Safety Board (NTSB), and grisly testimony from the Erie County Medical Examiner, New Millennium Motors Chief Engineer Dr. Paul Ditenzo took the witness stand. Since he was called by the plaintiffs, his testimony was technically a direct examination. However, as he was obviously a hostile witness, it was essentially treated as cross-examination.

Adam slowly rose from his chair at the counsel table, scrutinizing Ditenzo for any sign of nerves, or uncertainty, any potential weakness. *It's hard to attack an expert full bore when your own expert agrees with him. I've got to earn my fee this morning.*

"Good morning," Adam began:

Q: Tell us, Doctor, should cars be designed so they don't blow up and kill their occupants?

Dr. Ditenzo stared at Adam before responding.
He's smart. He senses a trap.

A: Is that a serious question, Mr. Simons?

Q: Dead serious. Please answer the question. Should they?

A: Of course.

Q: Are well designed cars supposed to blow up and kill their occupants?

A: Mr. Simons, really, is this necessary?

Q: As a matter of fact, it is. So please tell the jury, should well designed cars blow up and kill the occupants?

A: Of course they should. I mean, that is, they *shouldn't* be designed that way, to blow up or kill occupants.

Q: Should cars be *manufactured* to ensure they don't blow up and kill their occupants?

A: I think you know the answer to that one as well, Mr. Simons.

Q: So you say. Let's make it clear to the jury. Yes or no, Doctor?

A: No, they should not kill the occupants.

Q: Would it be negligent for a car manufacturer to market a car whose design made it possible to blow up its occupants under normal driving conditions?

Mr. Chun: Objection, calls for legal conclusion.

The Court: Well, somewhat preliminary. Why don't you try to rephrase, Mr. Simons, and save us all some trouble.

Q: Dr. Ditenzo, would it meet the standard of care expected of the automobile industry to design a car that would blow up its occupants under normal driving conditions?

A: Well, put that way, of course not. But there was no such design flaw here.

Q: Yes, Doctor, so you say. Let's get some more *preliminary* matters out of the way first. Would you say that a car that does blow up and kill its occupants has some type of defect?

A: Um. Not necessarily. There could be an external stimulus.

Q: Doctor, is it fair to say that, while car accidents such as head-on collisions have external stimuli by definition, most car *explosions* involve a defect?

A: I'm sorry, Mr. Simons, I'm not up on those statistics.

Q: Let's keep it simple. Is it fair to assume that most car explosions involve some sort of defect rather than external stimuli?

Mr. Chun: Objection, Your Honor, calls for speculation.

The Court: Well, he's the top engineer over there. I would think he'd have some idea. Anyway, kind of preliminary. Go ahead.

Q: Can you answer the question, Doctor? Do you need it read back?

Before answering, Ditenzo looked at Michael Chun and then smiled very slightly.

A: I'm sorry Mr. Simons, I'd just be speculating on the percentage caused by defects versus external stimuli.

Q: Doctor, you examined the accident scene. You examined the debris from the car, the police report, the video. I assume you have done everything within your power and expertise to analyze the destruction of Ms. Talbot's car. Would you agree you left no stone unturned in trying to find the cause of this accident?

A: That was my intention.

Q: And did you identify any external stimulus that could have caused this car to explode?

A: Well, it depends how you define external. There *was* an extra electrical cable in this car's engine. It had to be placed there after the car left the factory.

Adam had been glancing down at his outline, but his head shot up when he heard Ditenzo's answer. *Now the external cable is a cause? Let's take a gander at your report, Doctor.* Adam brought up Ditenzo's expert report on his iPad. *Thought so.*

Q: Dr. Ditenzo, are you stating within a reasonable degree of scientific certainty that this cable caused the explosion?

A: Put that way, I suppose not.

Q: You suppose? Doctor, do you have any theory how this extra cable could have resulted in the destruction of Ms. Talbot's car?

A: No, I don't.

Q: And did you state in your report here that in your *expert* opinion, this cable could *not* have made the car explode? Or was that before you came up with this theory that the cable was somehow placed in Ms. Talbot's car after it left the factory?

Mr. Chun: Your Honor, really.

The Court: Yes, Mr. Simons, you know better.

Mr. Simons: I'm sorry, Your Honor, but this expert has contradicted his own report, which he submitted to counsel and to this Court.

Mr. Chun: He certainly has not.

The Court: Please, gentlemen. No more speeches. And please address the Court, not each other. Mr. Simons, you may continue your examination. But no speeches.

Mr. Simons: Yes, Your Honor.

Q: Dr. Ditenzo. Let me read from your report. Page 1, paragraph 1. "Within a reasonable degree of scientific certainty, the cable running from the superconductor ring to the right rear motor in Jennifer Talbot's car could not have caused it to explode. In particular, it could not have caused the explosion of her car on June 30, 2023." Did I read that right?

A: Yes. You know you did.

Q: And do you still stand by those words?

A: I, um...yes, I do.

Q: Every one of them?

A: Yes.

Q: So then you agree, Doctor, that there is no way this particular cable caused the destruction of Jennifer's car and the death of her little girl, no matter who put it there or where the car was when the cable was inserted?

This time Kelly's head shot up. She gave Adam a long stare.

A: Well, we don't know what we don't know. But, given that. Given that, I would have to say yes.

Q: So I will ask you again, now that we have ruled out this cable. Did you identify, *can* you identify, any external stimulus that could have caused the explosion?

A: No, sir. I have not.

Q: Are you aware of anyone who has?

A: No, sir. I am not.

Q: And you've talked to the police, NTSB, the FBI, and BDT Technologies about it?

A: Yes, I have.

Q: And not one of them identified an external cause of this tragedy, did they?

Mr. Chun: Objection, hearsay.

The Court: No, I'll allow it, part of the investigation to formulate his expert opinion.

Wow, Tom, you've expanded your repertoire.

The Court: Basically preliminary anyway.

There you go. Gave you too much credit. I should'a known better. Hey, isn't that a Beatles song? Mac would know.

Q: Do you remember the question, Doctor? Let me make it easy. Has anyone, including New Millennium, NTSB, FBI, BDT Technologies, the police, *anyone* identified an external cause of this explosion?

A: I'm, uh, not aware of such a finding.

Q: So are you able to state, within a reasonable degree of scientific certainty, that there is no known external stimulus that could have caused the explosion of Jennifer Talbot's car and the death of her young child?

A: Put that way, yes.

Adam leaned toward Kelly and whispered, "There's our *Res Ipsa* case."

Q: By the way, have you ever had your engineering license suspended or revoked?

A: I've never been disciplined. Outside of my marriage.

Everyone in the courtroom, except the *jurors*, laughed.

Q: I've been there.

The Court: Yes, we've all been there. On that note, let's take ten. No. Make it twenty.

Chapter 28

SUPREME COURT, ERIE COUNTY
Talbot versus New Millennium, Inc.
Holotrial Annex Building, Part 5-HT
Main Street, Buffalo, New York
Thursday, August 17, 2023
11:05 a.m.

K elly could barely contain herself during the short walk to the attorneys' conference room. Before Adam could sit down, she shouted, "What was *that*? I thought we were going with the cable as the defect. Everyone agrees it wasn't supposed to be there. No one has an alternative explanation. And now you do a 180, getting him to confirm it *wasn't* the cable?"

"Kelly, remember what I said about paying attention to the answers? Wasn't it obvious, from the way Ditenzo was fudging, that they think they can somehow prove the cable was inserted after the car left the factory? If the jury believes it's an *aftermarket* cable, *and* that it caused the explosion, there goes our case. I don't know what proof they have, or if it's just some kind of a bluff, but I'd rather not guess when there's no need to."

Kelly slowly eased into one of the conference table chairs. She was getting a real-time education in trial technique that was impossible to duplicate in the classroom. Why hadn't she picked up on the need for a new strategy, as Adam had done on the fly? *He's drummed into us to be ready for surprises, changes in testimony, uncooperative witnesses...and at the first sign of trouble, I panic. How does he remain so calm?*

"Better we take the cable out of the equation, Kelly. After all, no one really believes it caused the explosion anyway. Not even Marcel. Why argue against the scientists' conclusions when we don't need to? When their opinions can actually help us. If the cable didn't cause the explosion, who cares how or where it got there. It won't affect our case. Ditenzo ultimately admitted it. He can't think of any external cause, including the cable. That just leaves the car. *Res Ipsa*. Speaks for itself. The end."

"I'm sorry, Adam. I didn't mean to suggest you didn't know what you were—"

"It's fine, Kelly. Really." Adam gave her a warm smile. "I've been doing this a long time. I don't remember my first case, but I'm sure it wasn't pretty. I didn't come out of the womb a trial lawyer."

A little smile started to form on Kelly's face. "I don't know, Professor. Um, Adam. We all think you *did* pop out and head straight to court."

"I wish. Listen, you've been doing great in prep. You've been exposed to battle. Believe me, it will get easier. I get your reaction to the change in strategy. You've been trained in Torts, perhaps overtrained, to cling to the concept of *defect*, but in a *Res Ipsa* case, you don't *need* one. Sure, the case is a lot sexier if you can point to a specific defect like the cable, but it's tough to ride that pony in both directions. A wonderful theory if it was installed in the factory, but case dismissed if it happened later. I don't know exactly what New Millennium had up its sleeve, but I *do* know we've checkmated it. Let's stick with the scientists. Ruling out the cable just means no one can identify *any* cause. Which leaves only the car, and a fine *Res Ipsa* case. For every complex problem—"

"There's a simple solution. And it's wrong. Where have I heard *that* one?" Kelly teased him.

Adam smiled. "The answer to this one is both simple *and* complex. It may be true that no one knows what the defect was. But there *had* to be one."

***

The Court: Mr. Simons, any idea how long you're gonna take? Will it interfere with the lunch break?

Mr. Simons: I'm afraid it might. I'll try, but I can't guarantee.

The Court: *Ugh.* So be it. Let's get going then.

Kelly teed up the crash-test video.

Holotrial

Q: Dr. Ditenzo, you invented the Hydro?

A: It was a team effort, Mr. Simons.

Q: Don't be modest, Doctor. You were responsible for most of the important breakthroughs, weren't you?

A: I did play a role—

Q: I'll say, Doctor. New polymer electrolyte membrane, proprietary anode catalyst, super-efficient solar panel, revolutionary superconductor ring. And I gather you ran challenge/de-challenge scenarios?

A: I see you've done your homework, Mr. Simons. Yes, the engineering process requires one to rule out potential bugs.

Q: Bugs, Doctor? You were checking for catastrophic failures, weren't you?

A: That is one of a number of parameters and outcomes we test for. It's mostly done by computer these days. Don't use many crash-test dummies. Though there is an abundant supply of lawyers if we need any.

The courtroom, Adam included, again burst into laughter.

Q: I'll take that as a compliment. We're going to get to crash tests very shortly, Doctor. For now, did you find any bugs, as you call them?

A: Not in the design. Nothing significant.

Q: Significant? Would you call a bug that resulted in a fiery explosion, destroying the vehicle and killing its occupants, significant?

A: Of course we would. If we identified such a bug, it would obviously be significant. But we found none. This type of incident simply didn't occur.

Q: Didn't occur? What about this?

Adam nodded to Kelly. The video that had made such an impression on them, though not on Professor Saperston, played on the courtroom monitors. Adam watched the Hydro with the four crash-test dummies moving down the track, building up speed. It never made it to the crash wall. About 20 feet short, it exploded, burst into flames, and tossed pieces of car, sensors, and test-dummy parts in all directions.

Chun burst from his chair, his face red, shouting.

> Mr. Chun: Your Honor, please. Move to strike this exhibit. It wasn't produced in discovery. It's a blatant disclosure violation. There should be sanctions.

> Mr. Simons: Not produced in discovery? Are you *kidding*? It *should* have been produced in discovery, all right. By *you*.

> Mr. Chun: It's confidential proprietary data from BDT Technologies. New Millennium outsources crash testing to them. They're not a party here. They weren't required to turn over anything.

> Mr. Simons: And New Millennium has no copy in its files? *Come on,* Michael.

> The Court: All right, gentlemen, you both know better. Please, address your objections and comments to the Court. So what about it, Mr. Simons? Where did you obtain this video?

> Mr. Simons: My assistant found it on YouTube. Ms. Martin?

Kelly brought up a YouTube page on the courtroom monitors. It showed the opening frame of the crash sequence under the title "You Gotta Be A Dummy to Get in This Car."

> Mr. Simons: I thought the caption was somewhat insensitive for this proceeding, so we left it out. I believe it was posted in May 2022. Anyway, Mr. Chun's histrionics demonstrate that they knew about this video all along, as one would

expect for a crash test of their *own* vehicle. It's shameful that they didn't produce it.

The Court: Okay. We'll allow it for now. But we may revisit this as necessary. I may have my law clerk look into it.

Just as he was about to order a resumption of the testimony, the judge did a doubletake and addressed Freddie in the gallery. "Have you been in front of me before, sir?"

Freddie gave his usual answer. "Just got one of those faces, Your Honor."

The Court: Hmm. Well. Back to business. Dr. Ditenzo, you are still under oath, do you understand?

Dr. Ditenzo: Yes, sir. I mean, Your Honor.

The Court: Do you want it read back, Mr. Simons?

Q: I actually don't think I got a question out before Mr. Chun sprang up so valiantly. So, Doctor. The explosion in this video was similar to what happened to Ms. Talbot's car at the supermarket, wouldn't you say?

A: This was a crash test, and an early one. The Hydro design was significantly changed before we went into production. Unlike Ms. Talbot's vehicle, the prototype in the video had a large hydrogen tank, and a number of other differences. And unlike Ms. Talbot's car, the vehicle in the video was moving, accelerating. Ms. Talbot's car was stationary in that parking lot when the...totally different circumstances.

Q: Okay. That's plenty of information I didn't ask for and none of the information I did. Was that intentional on your part, Dr. Ditenzo?

Mr. Chun: Your Honor.

The Court: Yes. Move along Mr. Simons.

Q: Okay, Dr. Ditenzo, let's try it again. Would you

agree that the explosion in this crash-test video looked similar to the explosion of Ms. Talbot's car, which killed her baby?

A: I suppose all explosions look similar to some degree. But again, you can't compare the two cars.

Q: Well, let's give it a shot. First off, was the crash-test car a Hydro?

A: Yes, but—

Q: Was hydrogen the primary fuel that ran the test car's motors?

A: Yes, but the real external fuel was just water.

Q: And that was true of Ms. Talbot's car, too, wasn't it? It also had water as its external fuel?

A: Yes. Mr.—

Q: Okay, let's make it simple, Doctor. I'm going to list several components and processes and ask you at the end if they all apply to the vehicle in this crash test. So bear with me. I think we can agree, you said it yourself, the car in the video is a Hydro...a Hydro that uses water as its external fuel. You can also agree that the Hydro in the video works as follows. Water is fed into an electrolyzer that gets electricity from super-efficient solar panels. The electrolyzer splits water molecules to produce hydrogen, which is sent to the fuel cells. The fuel cells convert the hydrogen atoms to create electricity, which is initially stored in a superconductor ring, and eventually used to run the car. Now, is it fair to say that each of the processes and components I've just described applies to the crash-test Hydro in the video?

A: Yes, but there are other—

Q: Dr. Ditenzo, I'm sure Mr. Chun is capable of following up on this questioning. So please confine your answers to the questions I ask, okay? Is it also fair to say that each and every one of these processes and components I've just described for the crash-test Hydro also applied to Jennifer Talbot's Hydro?

A: As far as that goes. Yes.

Q: And is it fair to say that both the crash-test Hydro and Ms. Talbot's Hydro both exploded without striking or being struck by any object, another car, a tree, a crash-test wall, anything?

A: Yes, in that respect, the incidents were similar, but—

Q: "Incident?" You can call it an explosion, Doctor. The jury knows what this incident really was.

Mr. Chun: Move to strike. Dr. Ditenzo doesn't need any instruction in the English language from Mr. Simons. Nor does he know what the jury knows.

The Court: Well, they do look attentive.

Once more everyone in the courtroom laughed.

The Court: But, yes, Mr. Simons, you know better.

Mr. Simons: Apologies, Your Honor.

The judge's joke made Adam think, for the umpteenth time, that there had to be a better way to give attorneys the feel of a real jury. Why bother putting pretend humans in the jury box? Why not just project *them* as holograms so they could breathe and fidget around and change expressions now and then. When he had asked the Disney techno-master, he'd been told that projecting a hologram and filming it at the same time with the specialized holographic cameras would largely cancel each other out.

While Adam was pondering the oddities of the Holotrial system, New Millennium's CEO Joan Perry practically ran down the faux carpeted aisle from the back of the courtroom to where Mac was sitting in the gallery and started whispering to him. Mac listened with his mouth agape.

Adam blinked. *I've never seen anything make Mac react like that. Whatever Perry's telling him must be damned good.*

Judge Arturo banged his gavel and cast a disapproving eye, at which point Mac and Dr. Perry virtually ran in tandem up the aisle and out the back door. With that disruption over, cross-examination continued.

Q: Dr. Ditenzo, did you watch Ms. Talbot's car being made?

A: Of course not.

Q: Did you work on her car yourself?

A: Mr. Simons, I'm a Chief Engineer. I don't work on cars.

Q: Did you set your eyes on *any* part of Ms. Talbot's Hydro? Top, bottom, rear, front before it left the factory?

A: I have no way of knowing about any individual car. We make thousands. Did I...okay, unlikely.

Q: So Dr. Ditenzo, is it fair to say you don't have the slightest idea whether the factory made any mistakes in manufacturing Ms. Talbot's Hydro, which then burst into flames with her two-month-old daughter in it?

A: My job is not to work on individual cars. I've told you. That's all I can say. I designed the car. We have an excellent manufacturing team.

Q: Let's try to wrap this up. Dr. Ditenzo, as you sit here today, under oath, can you swear, based on your own observations, that the New Millennium factory followed your design to the T in manufacturing Ms. Talbot's Hydro?

A: I told you, I don't observe individual car assembly.

Q: So your answer is no, you can't swear that the design was correctly followed.

A: I assume it was, based on all the practices I have observed in the plant for years. As to this particular car, I don't have such personal knowledge.

Q: I have a few hypotheticals for you, if we can switch gears now. No pun intended. Dr. Ditenzo, if hydrogen were diverted to the interior of the car, could that result in an explosion?

A: If hydrogen were diverted to the interior instead of the fuel cells, the car wouldn't run. It would never leave the factory.

Q: Doctor. Again. I would like you to answer the question I asked you, not the one you'd like to answer.

Mr. Chun: Your Honor.

The Court: No, Mr. Chun. I think that's a fair characterization of what this witness has been doing. I gave him one bite of the apple, but he can't keep chewing. Overruled.

Wow, Arturo, you've grown a pair.

Q: Dr. Ditenzo, to be clear, my hypothetical involves hydrogen running to the fuel cells as well as to the interior of the car.

A: It can't be done. The design allows only one conduit to run out of the electrolyzer. You can either feed the fuel cells or the interior, but not both.

Q: I may have a solution for you. Maybe not very elegant, but a solution. What if one put a Y-shaped tube at the electrolyzer's output, so it could simultaneously feed hydrogen to the fuel cells *and* to the car interior?

A: That's absurd. No one would do that.

Q: Can you answer the question I asked you?

A: There's no such part anywhere in the Hydro production line. Not anywhere in the factory, for that matter. Not to mention that there was no such part among the debris from Ms. Talbot's car. All of the components were accounted for.

Q: Are you saying your floor engineers, with all their expertise and the raw materials and tools at their disposal, couldn't design such a Y-shaped tube?

A: Is it physically possible to create one? Absolutely. My high-school shop class could do it. We have the best engineers in the world at New Millennium. I handpicked most of them myself. If you can think of it, they can build it. But again, there's absolutely no reason in the world to do such a thing, unless perhaps you're trying to sabotage the car.

Adam's eyes widened. He could tell from Ditenzo's slight blush that he was embarrassed, as he'd probably been told not to volunteer unnecessary information, but now he'd given Adam an idea for a whole new line of inquiry.

Q: So it's possible a disgruntled employee...maybe didn't like his Christmas bonus, passed over for a promotion, whatever...could have sabotaged the vehicle in this manner?

A: *Sir,* the caliber of our employees is carefully evaluated during our hiring process. We take no one if there is *any* significant question about their character. I can't contemplate such behavior by any of our people. Even if one rotten egg got through, it wouldn't make a difference.

Q: And if two rotten eggs got by?

A: Mr. Simons, each car is inspected multiple times by multiple persons on the floor before it goes out the door. The type of Y-tube you are suggesting would be obvious and would raise all kinds of red flags and alarm bells. Impossible.

Q: Let's get back to the original question. If the interior of the car filled with hydrogen, could that result in an explosion?

A: Under that scenario, yes, it could.

Q: Doctor, you are familiar with the Automobile Consumers Association of America?

A: I am indeed. We try to implement their suggested standards.

Q: Then you're aware of their claim that New Millennium rushed this car into production because the company was running very low on capital?

Mr. Chun: Objection, Your Honor. I thought Mr. Simons was going to invoke an industry standard. Apparently he cannot, and chooses to rely on hearsay instead.

The Court: Well, I'm not sure what knowledge the witness has on this subject, but I'll give Mr. Simons a bit of latitude. For now, it's preliminary. Let's see where we're going.

Adam tried to control his smile. *God love him.*

Q: Let's do it this way, Dr. Ditenzo. New Millennium was incorporated barely two years ago, with an initial public stock offering that brought in about four and a half billion dollars, correct?

A: Yes.

Q: As of October, 2022, cash on hand was down to a hundred and fifty million, wasn't it?

A: I don't concern myself with financial matters, Mr. Simons. I'm a scientist, not a bean counter.

Q: The company was about to go under if they didn't rush—

Michael Chun started to rise in his chair, an objection forming on his lips.

Q: Sorry. Excuse me. The company had a significant chance of going stone-cold broke if it didn't get the Hydro off the drawing board and into the showrooms, true?

A: Again, not my department.

Q: I understand you're not in finance, Doctor, but are you telling us you heard no inkling about the company being near bankruptcy? Not around the water cooler, the locker room, anywhere?

A: Honestly, Mr. Simons, I don't think about money, and I refuse to participate in gossip. I stay focused on my drawings, component development, production statistics. Not the chattering of the idle classes.

Q: Okay, Doctor. Let's focus on science then. Isn't it an industry standard that it takes three to five years to design and manufacture a new car model?

A: I don't think industry standards apply to the Hydro. It's quite unique in many ways, it—

Q: That's precisely the point, isn't it? This car had a radical new design, including multiple components never before used in any vehicle. You don't deny any of that, do you, Doctor?

A: Yes, we had a number of breakthroughs.

Q: And you started selling this radically new car less than two years after the company was formed, didn't you?

A: Your timeline doesn't take into account that my team had been working on the design for seven years prior to the IPO. The company was able to raise the start-up capital because we had a feasible design by that time. The car was actually marketed about eight and a half years after the design work started.

Q: Suddenly you seem to know about finance, Doctor.

Mr. Chun: *Your Honor.*

The Court: Move along, Mr. Simons.

Q: Doctor, is it fair to say that rushing a car into production is likely to make it safer or less safe?

A: I can't answer a question like that. There are so many factors pertaining to safety. It's too hypothetical, too complex a question.

Q: Okay, Doctor, let's simplify it. All other things being equal, is it fair to say that rushing a car into production makes it less safe?

A: All things being equal, I would have to say it leans toward less safe. But all things are never equal.

Q: So you say. Let's take it one step further. All things being equal, is it fair to say that rushing a car with a cutting-edge design, with components never used before in any vehicle—

A: I understand. Again, though all things never are equal, those circumstances would make it less safe. Obviously.

Q: It is obvious, isn't it? One last question, Doctor. What model car did you drive prior to June 30 of this year.

A: A Hydro beta prototype.

Q: And what kind of car do you drive now?

A: That's two questions.

Q: Pardon my math. Not one of my strong points. What do you drive now?

A: An Xl54. But—

Q: Thank you, Doctor. I think we get the picture. Oh, I do apologize, just *one* more question. This time I assure you my math is correct. Dr. Ditenzo, based on your investigation of this matter...leaving no stone unturned as you said...and the testimony you've given here today, can you confirm the following? Yes or no, and please wait until I'm finished. It's a four-parter. One, New Millennium designed and manufactured Ms. Talbot's Hydro. Two, the car blew up within 24 hours of leaving the factory. Three, you have no personal knowledge about the manufacturing process for this particular car, and you therefore don't know whether the factory made any mistakes in building it. And four, no one on earth, yourself included, has identified any external stimulus that could have caused the explosion. That's all true, isn't it Doctor?

A: Limited to those parameters...I would have to say yes.

Mr. Simons: Nothing further, Your Honor.

The Court: Folks, we'll take a ten-minute break. Nature calls. Oh, look at the time. Let's make it twenty.

As the judge exited the door behind the bench, Mac hurriedly joined Adam at the counsel table. "Chief, there's somebody you gotta meet."

Chapter 29

SUPREME COURT, ERIE COUNTY
Talbot versus New Millennium, Inc.
Holotrial Annex Building, Part 5-HT
Main Street, Buffalo, New York
Thursday, August 17, 2023
12:35 p.m.

Adam, Mac, Kelly, and Freddie convened with the New Millennium group, Joan Perry, Dan Toler and Michael Chun, in the attorney conference room down the hallway from the courtroom. Already seated at the table were Larry Zack, a fellow PI long familiar to Mac, and Cal Dryer, palpably nervous and pale. The occasion marked several firsts for Cal: first time in a courthouse, first time with a bunch of lawyers, first time giving a mob boss a reason to kill him.

The two PIs gave each other a slight nod. Though they were often rivals for the same jobs, they sometimes worked together when their clients' interests meshed. Zack was an ex-cop, Tonawanda police. He'd left the force before his full pension kicked in, generating rumors that it wasn't voluntary, but whatever transgressions he might have committed were anyone's guess.

Zack had outdone himself. When New Millennium hired him to investigate the accident, no one even knew Cal existed, let alone his story about Vertex's involvement in the deadly car explosion. But like any good PI, Zack's information-seeking tendrils extended deep into the community. So, when Cal's girlfriend, Tina, made an off-hand comment to a college friend about Cal's frightening experience at the Naval Museum, and the college friend passed it along to his cousin, who mentioned it to her aunt, who happened to be dating one of Zack's former narcotics informants, Zack was at Cal's door the next morning. And now here they were at the courthouse, ready to blow this trial apart.

Joan Perry excitedly made the introductions. "Mr. Simons, meet Cal Dryer. Mr. Dryer, Mr. Simons."

"And I want to meet Mr. Dryer because..."

"Because he can tell you what really happened to Ms. Talbot's Hydro."

Adam went into witness interrogation mode. "You were there, at the explosion?"

"No," the young man replied.

"You work at New Millennium? On this car?"

"No, Mr..."

"Simons."

"No. Like, I never saw the car, Mr. Simons."

Mac intervened. "Just let him explain, Chief. I think you'll be interested."

"Okay, then...go ahead, Mr. Dryer."

Cal's eyes circled the room. *One, two, three, four...seven complete strangers. Can they be trusted? They are wearing nice suits. And Tina said it was the right thing to do. Okay.* "The day that the, uh, of the thing with, like, the car. I was hiding in one of the Navy ships. Like, on the waterfront. The big one. I was wearing a World War II uniform, um, I guess a sailor, being treated in, like, a hospital room. I know it sounds stupid. It was a bet. I was pretending to be, like, a fake sailor on an examination table when this dude walked into the room. Well, like, I guess it worked, he must have thought I was just, like, a dummy. He started talking on the phone. About the, like, the car explosion. He kept calling the other guy *boss* or *Mr. K.*"

Adam wasn't impressed. "So he knew about the explosion. It was on the news. *My hamster* knew about the explosion."

"No," Cal responded, "the explosion was... *He did it.*"

"What do you mean, he did it?"

"Like, he made it explode."

"Did you see this person?"

"I got, like, a peek at him."

"Can you describe him?"

"Tall, like over six feet. A couple hundred pounds. Um...dark hair. And he was, like, wearing a jacket with the words *Vertex Security* on it."

"Go on."

Holotrial

***

About twenty minutes later, Cal had finished his story. Adam and his team stood in complete silence, as did Michael Chun. The others, who'd already heard the story, were also silent, *still* somewhat stunned even after a second telling.

Since Cal's story had come to Adam courtesy of New Millennium and its PI, Adam treated it warily. A story was one thing, and this one was certainly out there, but proof was another. Adam addressed the New Millennium representatives. "Okay. Here's the deal. *If* Mr. Dryer passes a polygraph exam, I expect my client will discontinue this lawsuit. *If.*"

Cal's nervousness returned. Before Adam's eyes, the self-assured storyteller had regressed to the jumble of nerves he'd been when they first entered the room. Cal asked, in a trembling voice, "Mr. Simons, sir. *Mr. K*, like, that's Alex Kurtoff, isn't it? That's who he was talking to, he called him *Mr. K* and *Boss*, but that was Kurtoff, wasn't it? He, like, he runs Vertex, doesn't he?"

"Mr. Kurtoff *is* the CEO of Vertex, but we can't be certain that's who was on the phone."

"I don't, like, I don't think I wanna take that chance, Mr. Simons. I heard about this dude. Like, didn't he run with the Black Scorpions or whatever, like, in Bosnia or whatever? And now, like, if he had a two-month-old girl killed, what would he do to a witness who could get him arrested? I read, like, even the Russians wouldn't screw with him when they ran the place. Like, anyone who scares the KGB scares me."

"Mr. Dryer, I'm sure we can protect you if need be. I have just the man for the job." Adam nodded at Mac. Cal didn't appear to be comforted. Adam chuckled inwardly. He understood, at first glance, the creaky antique might not inspire confidence. Adam was sure, though, that if Cal knew what the old soldier was still capable of, he'd be less concerned.

Cal didn't express his objections, but he didn't acquiesce to testifying against Kurtoff either. "I'm sorry. Like, I'll help you figure it out, but that's all. You gotta do it in court without me."

"Let's not get ahead of ourselves, Mr. Dryer. No one has to make any final decisions this minute. Let's get the polygraph first. Then we can talk about testifying."

***

Mac took Adam aside in the hallway on their way back to the courtroom. "Chief, even if this kid checks out, you've still got a rock-solid case against New Millennium. It's easier to get a jury to buy into negligence than sabotage, isn't it?"

"I've taught you well, Mac. Yes, a *Res Ipsa* case in particular is far easier than proving an intentional tort like sabotage. But if Mr. Dryer checks out, that means it wasn't New Millennium. They're the wrong defendant."

"I know, Chief. I'm just sayin', who cares if Dryer is kosher, why not stick with New Millennium? The kid says he doesn't want to testify, he's terrified of Kurtoff. You saw his face. Why take the chance on starting a new case when your star witness might not show up. Why not just stick with the case you can prove in your sleep?"

"Because, Mac, it would be unethical to proceed against New Millennium if I know it's not supported by the facts. But you already knew that, didn't you?"

"Look, Chief, you'd never teach your students to start a case this way. How is suing Vertex without your star witness any better than staying with the case against New Millennium?"

"God, I have taught you well. Assuming this kid checks out, you know I can't keep going against New Millennium. I'm a member of the bar. I won't defraud the court system for myself or the Talbots or anyone."

"But Chief, what if the kid won't testify?"

"I don't intend to proceed against Vertex without sufficient proof, either. I just have a feeling Mr. Dryer is going to come around. If we can't convince him, it sounds like his girlfriend might."

"But, Chief—"

"Mac, I'd do the same with Vertex. I don't have a hard-on for Kurtoff. You show me someone else did this, we ditch the Vertex suit and sue that bastard. End of story."

As Mac and Adam ended their discussion, Kelly swooped in for her own tete-a-tete. "Are you seriously considering this, Adam? Just two hours ago, I thought we determined the cable did *not* cause the explosion. That no one believed it did, and we were sticking with the scientists. Are we doing another 180? Now it's the cable again?"

She had the same frown as when they talked at the Buffalo Club about Saperston's role. *I can't believe Adam would...is the whole damn system like this? I guess the old adage is right. There are two things the public should never watch being made: sausage and law. Maybe I'm not cut out for this, after all. Learning lofty principles in class is one thing. This real-world stuff, actually being in the sausage factory...I don't know.*

"Kelly, two hours ago we thought we were trying a negligence case. Two hours ago, it made sense to stick with a *Res Ipsa* theory. We didn't have to prove a specific defect. We didn't need the cable, so why put all our money on it when Marcel didn't believe it was the culprit, and, worse yet, when we saw that New Millennium might try to avoid liability by claiming it *was* the cable but that they didn't put it there? Why wade into that mess?

"Now, I don't think I have to tell you, things have changed dramatically. Negligence has turned to sabotage. Vertex was trying to destroy that car, and they used this cable to do it. Which means *they* must have figured out a way for the cable to do the job. As Marcel told us, it's possible the cable caused the explosion in some way he can't conceive of based on current scientific knowledge. I can't believe Vertex's scientists figured it out before he could, but that doesn't matter. It's still *Res Ipsa* as to the cable. When the jury hears that Vertex planted this cable to destroy the car, and the car was in fact destroyed, it's not going to question causation."

"I didn't mean to challenge you, Adam. It's just that—"

"Never stop challenging me, Kelly. Different perspectives are invaluable. When Alexander asked his old generals how to fight the Persians, they told him to fight the old-fashioned way. He needed to hear that so he'd know what not to do. It told him how conservative military thinkers like his opponent, King Darius, would fight. Okay, let's leave Alexander alone and go break the news to the Talbots."

***

Back in the courtroom, Adam and Kelly rounded up the Talbots near the jury box. Adam took a deep breath and started to explain. "We just learned something that may require a change of course. We met someone who sheds new light on what happened to your car, Jennifer. We need to check him out, but if he's the real thing, we'll have to, uh...we'll have to start a new lawsuit. Against a different party. According to this witness, it wasn't New Millennium's fault."

Katherine couldn't believe it. "What are you *talking* about?"

"It appears the explosion had nothing to do with New Millennium. The cable wasn't installed in the factory. Vertex Corporation, the electric car maker in South Buffalo, apparently, *they're* responsible. I know this sounds like a problem, but it's not. If this witness pans out, we'll have an even *stronger* case. Please don't worry. We've lost a couple of months, but we've got plenty of time to bring the new case."

Katherine wasn't satisfied. "What does *Vertex* have to do with Jenny's car?"

"It looks like this wasn't, uh, an accident. Vertex...they couldn't take the competition from the Hydro. So they tried to destroy it. In fact, it seems Alex Kurtoff himself, their CEO, ordered it."

Katherine let out a gasp. She and Jennifer stared at the Senator, sneers on their faces. Katherine turned back to Adam. "You're telling us this Vertex intentionally killed our Allie?"

"Katherine, I don't think they were after Allison. From what I've heard, the car was the target. Allison was just in the wrong place at the wrong time."

Katherine stared at Adam, then at her husband, as if weighing competing truths. "Adam, is there evidence that any third party was in on this with Vertex?"

"It's way too early. From what I've heard, though, there's no reason to suspect anyone else. Vertex had the obvious motive."

Katherine frowned. *I know someone else with an obvious motive. The bastard.*

***

Technically, Adam and Katherine's affair began back at Yale on a red-letter date—September 11, 2001. This chapter of their saga lasted a single night. Three hours, to be exact. Adam received an anguished call from Katherine that evening, which wasn't too surprising, as the whole campus was distraught. Indeed, the whole nation, the whole *world* was traumatized by the devastatingly savage attack on the World Trade Center and the Pentagon. Beth was at a candlelight vigil at the Law School, so Adam went alone. He was surprised that Bill wasn't comforting Katherine on that dismal night, until Katherine explained Bill was in Boston, attending a moot court competition with Harvard. Adam assumed that explained her distress. Not only was she all alone on this horrific day, but Bill was in the very city from which the terrorist attacks originated.

Up to that night, Katherine and Adam had been friends but nothing more. There were no hard feelings about the end of their prematurely aborted romance, because it barely got past peck-on-the-cheek stage before Bill swooped in and erased Katherine from Adam's equation. By September 2001, Adam was euphoric about Beth, and he found it hard to harbor ill will toward anyone. His world was perfect, shatterproof, or so he thought.

When he arrived at her apartment, Katherine, like most of the country, was glued to the television, toggling between CNN and the major networks' non-stop coverage of the day's calamitous events. They sat on the Naugahyde sofa she'd inherited from her grandmother, and Adam put his arm on Katherine's shoulder to comfort her. She started sobbing and leaned into him. Her lean became a hug, and suddenly she was telling him that the main source of her misery wasn't the terrorist attacks. "Oh, Adam, I think I've made a terrible mistake."

The terrible mistake was Bill. Why hadn't she given the relationship with Adam a chance? Why had she let that slick, fast-talking bastard ruin everything? She knew now that she'd have been happier with Adam. Lots happier. To Bill, she wasn't much more than a trophy girlfriend, destined to graduate to trophy wife, to be carted around to rubber chicken dinners, fundraisers, and campaign events. Just smile, look pretty, that's all they want to see, the all-American family. In this, she had been clairvoyant.

Kate's explanation made the hug incredibly uncomfortable for Adam. He tried to gently extricate himself before this mushroomed into something he'd regret. She responded by clinging tighter. As long as he lived, he'd wonder why he gave in to her that night. Perhaps the shock of the terrorist attacks left *him* not thinking straight. Perhaps, subconsciously, it was revenge for Bill stealing her from him. Whatever the reason, Adam gave Katherine the comfort she was seeking.

Afterward, ignoring her entreaties to stay, he made a quick exit from the apartment with a raging guilt, not knowing whether or how he could ever face Beth. Even if he said nothing, Beth would know instantly. He decided the only sane course of action was to come clean and pray.

Beth's reaction was no surprise. To say she was hurt was a vast understatement. Their mutual trust, the foundation of their relationship, had been shattered. Adam couldn't look her in the eye. He despised himself for the heartache he'd caused her. Without waiting for her to tell him, he packed his things and moved in with one of his friends. For weeks, Beth wouldn't so much as look at him. He wondered if she'd started up with someone else. If she did, he had no right to object. *What had he done? Given up everything for what?* He didn't love Katherine. He wasn't even attracted to her, after falling so hard for Beth. It must have been temporary insanity. But that defense, as difficult as it was to prove in court, didn't have a snowball's chance with Beth.

About three months later, for reasons known exclusively to the gods of love, Beth somehow managed to take him back. She was very intuitive and must have understood on some level that the tryst was more Katherine's doing than Adam's. Whenever the four of them had hung out, Katherine appeared jealous of Beth's relationship with Adam. It also seemed that Katherine's relationship with Bill wasn't all that solid. Not as solid as they pretended, anyway.

Adam didn't bother to promise Beth that it would never happen again. That would just have been empty words, as if his transgression could be explained or rationalized. He did swear to himself, though, that as long as he lived, he'd never let it happen again. And it didn't. Not until seventeen years later. By then, Beth was gone, so Adam felt only a little guilt. Toward Beth, that is. Cheating on Bill didn't bother him at all.

***

Katherine's reaction to the news about Vertex was puzzling to Adam. *Why would she immediately ask whether another party was involved?*

None of them noticed the judge re-entering the courtroom, so his banging of the gavel startled them. Judge Arturo may have run a lax courtroom, but it was still his fiefdom. "Gentlemen, ladies, we have a trial to finish. Please. If we can get done this afternoon, I think we can take a long weekend. We'd all like that, wouldn't we?"

Adam tried to make amends. "Your Honor, my apologies. There's been a rather significant change in circumstances. There's a good chance we'll be terminating this action, with prejudice, but we request a one-day continuance to sort out the facts."

"Mr. Simons, I know you're a critic of the Holotrial system, but if this were a regular trial, I wouldn't grant your request. Given that we have no live jury to be inconvenienced, just little old me, I'll give you the day. Tomorrow being Friday, that *does* make it a long weekend. I'm gonna get a little fishing in if you all promise not to tell the Administrative Judge. And Mr. Simons, perhaps you'll reconsider your thinking about the new technology while you're at it."

"I will indeed, Your Honor. Will indeed."

Chapter 30

MAC'S HOME
Auburn Avenue, Buffalo, New York
Friday, August 18, 2023
10:00 a.m.

The one exception to the clutter and disarray that defined Mac's home was the *office* he'd carved out of a little nook in the corner of the living room. It was meticulously ordered, clean, and appointed with state-of-the-art technology. On the sparkling white particle-board desk sat two large computer monitors and an all-in-one laser printer. A pegboard on the wall above the desk held numerous electronic surveillance devices of various sizes. Some appeared to be ordinary objects: a pencil, a pair of cufflinks, a button.

Mac had just downloaded an update for the *Geo Locator Pro* app, a sort of combination Google Earth, Historical Society archives, and geographic recognition analytics. He pulled the childhood photo out of its sacred place in his wallet, ran his finger over the boy's face, his tiny hand, and the larger mysterious hand that little Mac was holding on to. He'd searched in vain for years to find the street intersection in the photograph. After exhaustively covering Buffalo, he worked his way around the suburbs, then to Rochester and even as far as Syracuse. There simply was no such corner. Not in the twenty-first century, anyway. After all, the photograph was about seventy years old. The buildings pictured in the photo might have been razed and replaced with new structures long ago. Maybe several times. Or now it might be an empty lot strewn with refuse. There were no street signs in the photo, so that line of investigation was blocked.

The upgraded app might be just the thing to solve this mystery. It contained scanned photographs of almost every inhabited location on the globe, including historical photos, when available, dating back to the beginning of photography in the 1830s. If the manmade structures had changed over time, its algorithms could sometimes identify an area based on tiny geographic clues, often clues that were wholly opaque to the human eye and brain. The software was so precise, it could sometimes pick out a site based on a single tree or a configuration of bushes, decades after the surrounding structures had been demolished.

Mac's sacred photo had long ago been scanned into the computer. He dragged it from the Photos file into the updated locator app, which started its silent search. Thousands of photographs of intersections from the world over started streaming across the screen, a dizzying array impossible for Mac to follow. After about three minutes, the cavalcade of photos came to a grinding halt with the phrase LOCATION IDENTIFIED flashing above a photo that appeared to be the exact intersection in Mac's photo. Same buildings and all. The date on the computer photo was 1962.

Most important, it cited the address. Mac couldn't believe what he was reading. *Holy shit.* "I'll be damned." *I'm Canadian.*

Chapter 31

SILLS POLYGRAPH SERVICE, INC.
Niagara Street, Buffalo, New York
Friday, August 18, 2023
3:00 p.m.

The lawyers, along with Mac and Cal Dryer, were ushered into the examination room at Sills Polygraph Service by Bob Sills, its owner and sole operator. Bob was proud of his profession and the business he'd built. He didn't care if the ignoramus courts still refused to admit polygraph evidence. There were more than enough private companies and individuals who believed in it, notwithstanding the annoying civil rights advocates who protested some of its uses, such as screening for job applicants and employee theft.

He understood the resistance from the civil rights crybabies. There *was* something Orwellian about a machine rendering judgment on a human's truthfulness. Big Brother, not just watching, but directly hooked up to your body to unearth your inner thoughts. But even pain-in-the-ass lawyers on their high horses, like Adam Simons, sometimes recognized its usefulness.

"Thanks for taking us on such short notice, Bob."

"No problem, Adam."

Mac, never at a loss for words, asked Sills, "Hey, Doc. If one synchronized swimmer drowns, do they all drown?"

"You'll have to excuse Mac," Adam interjected. "One too many grenades bounced off the helmet."

Sills remained nonplussed. He'd seen it all. "Let's proceed."

Mac wasn't deterred, either. "While you're at it, Doc, can you find out where my second wife hid our savings account?"

"This is serious business, Mr., uh..."

"Call me Mac, Doc."

"And you may call me Mr. Sills. If Adam doesn't mind,

perhaps you'd care to participate in a little demonstration that might alter your skepticism?"

"If it's okay with the Chief, it's okay with me, Doc."

"It's Mr. Sills."

"Okay, Doc."

Adam acquiesced. "Sure, go ahead. And Mac, it was your third wife. *You* stole the savings account from your second marriage. And yes, I know. You called it a loan."

Sills hooked up Mac, who was raring to go. "Okay, Doc, let's rock n' roll."

Sills liked to get a little background information on his subjects, so he started simple. "What's your birthday?"

"September 27."

"What year, Mr. McMillan?"

"Every year, Doc."

Why did I even bother with this nut job? Sills placed three playing cards, all aces, face up on the desk in front of Mac.

"We gonna play cards now, Doc? You know you're not playin' with a full deck."

"It's Mr. Sills, Mr. McMillan."

"Call me Mac, Doc."

"It's...forget it. Mr. McMillan, you have the ace of spades, ace of hearts, and ace of diamonds in front of you. Can we agree on that? Good. I want you to pick up all three cards and hold them facing you. We will turn our backs, and you'll choose one of them to put on the table face down. Place the two remaining aces in the desk drawer. Don't let any of us see any of the cards' faces."

Mac did as he was told.

"Now I'm going to ask you whether each of the cards is the one you put on the table. You will respond yes to each question."

"Let me get it straight, Doc. You want me to say I put all three of them back on the table, when I only put one?"

"Correct. You'll understand when we're done. So, Mr. McMillan, shall we start?"

"Affirmative."

"Good. Mr. McMillan, did you put the ace of spades on the table?"

"Call me Mac, Doc."

"*Mr. McMillan*, did you put the ace of spades on the table?"

"Yes."

"Did you put the ace of hearts on the table?"

"Yes."

"Did you put the ace of diamonds on the table?"

"Yes."

"All right then. We know Mr. McMillan has just lied to us twice and told the truth once. Perhaps that reflects his normal truthfulness quotient." Sills couldn't help getting in the dig. "Give me a minute or two and we'll see." With that, he left the room.

Throughout the short questioning, little needles had dutifully recorded Mac's heart rate, blood pressure, respiration, and skin conductivity on a roll of graph paper in the next room. After analyzing the print-out, Sills returned to the examining room, a wry smile on his face.

"How'd I do, Doc? Do I win the stuffed teddy bear?"

"Mr. McMillan, I'll admit you're an unusual subject, but I had figured that when you first walked through the door."

"Call me Mac."

"Mr. McMillan's responses *all* had some level of deception. However, I was able to sort through it. Mr. McMillan's biggest lies, or should I say deceptions, pertained to the aces of spades and hearts. So, Mr. McMillan, please turn over the ace of diamonds."

With a sheepish grin on his face, Mac turned over the card on the table, which was in fact the ace of diamonds.

Sills grinned. "All right. Play time's over. Mr. Dryer..."

***

Cal sat in the hot seat, wires dangling from his chest, abdomen, and index finger, a blood pressure cuff attached to his upper arm. Sills asked Cal to turn over the ace of spades. Even though Cal had just seen it done with Mac, he raised his eyebrows, wrinkling his forehead as he did indeed turn over the ace of spades.

"Mr. Dryer, we're going to change the ground rules now. Going forward, I expect you to answer all questions truthfully. Are we in agreement?"

"Yeah. But, like, I'm kinda...a little nervous. Is that going to, like, change my results?"

"Well, what are you nervous about? Are you worried you'll

have difficulty telling the truth?"

"No. I, like, I'm worried I *will* tell the truth. Then they'll want me to testify against Mr. Kurtoff."

"Don't worry about that, Mr. Dryer. The machine takes nervousness into account. Let's proceed. Mr. Dryer, are you a student at the University of Buffalo?"

"Yes."

"Are you made of Jello?"

"No."

"Is your name Calvin Michael Dryer?"

"Yes, it is."

"Were you born in the Congo?"

"No."

"Are you over seven feet tall?"

"No."

"Are you twenty-two years old?"

"Yes."

Sills turned to the meat of the examination. Adam had already filled him in on the facts by phone, as well as the exact wording of the questions.

"Mr. Dryer, on June 30, 2023, were you on a ship called USS *The Sullivans* in the Buffalo and Erie County Naval Park?"

***

When the exam was all over, Adam had a question for the polygrapher. "Bob, what's the point of the card trick when you're going to ask validating questions on the actual exam anyway?"

"The *card trick*, as you call it, is meant to show the witness, in a memorable fashion, that we know what we're doing. That we'll catch him in a lie, so don't bother trying. It also provides an extra baseline for what his deceptive and non-deceptive responses look like on the chart, which adds an extra degree of confidence in interpreting the results. Oh yes, and it also gives *me* comfort that I know what the hell I'm doing."

Adam's impatience got the best of him. "So what do you think?"

"I think you've sued the wrong people."

Chapter 32

OH CANADA
Saturday, August 19, 2023

I t took Mac nearly three hours to reach Toronto. The Grand Island Bridge and the Rainbow Bridge at Niagara Falls had both been terribly backed up, so he'd spent over an hour just getting across the border. About fifteen minutes of that had been spent in a failed attempt to schmooze the female Canadian border patrol agent who inspected his car.

He still marveled at the two faces of Niagara Falls. The U.S. side was mostly dingy, filled with aging homes, biker bars, and a dearth of child-friendly establishments. The Ontario side was a cornucopia of schlock, but it was vibrant as hell, with tourist attractions, a towering Ferris wheel, arcades, restaurants. Also, the view of the American Falls on the U.S. side was nowhere near as good as the view of the Horseshoe Falls on the Canadian side. *Guess I should feel proud to be Canadian. Do I gotta start playing hockey, too? Or worse, curling?*

After clearing customs and giving up on the border agent, he found the QEW and proceeded to Toronto. The speed limit was 110 kilometers per hour, but Mac's old Chevy couldn't do the translation on its antiquated speedometer, so he mentally converted it to about sixty-five miles per hour. Then he drove eighty-five, and still most of the Canucks passed him easily. Canadians were supposed to be a laid-back bunch, but get them on a long stretch of pavement and watch them boogie.

As he reached the seemingly perpetual traffic bottleneck at Mississauga, Mac was engulfed in a wave of anxiety. His twenty-plus-year quest for his mother, for his identity, might actually be coming to an end. Would he feel it was worth it once he finally knew? Would he lack a sense of purpose once the search was over? Would he learn anything at all? Finding an intersection in a picture was one thing. Finding anyone alive who knew something about him and his mother, some seventy years later, was a much taller order.

Mac's heart rate went into overdrive when the tall gleaming skyscrapers of Toronto came into view, the sunlight reflecting brilliantly off their glass façades. The majestic CN Tower hovered above it all: an 1,800-foot needle, once the world's tallest structure.

Mac exited the QEW, and his GPS said he was eight minutes from the destination. Eight minutes from possibly unlocking his childhood. Mac had been to Toronto numerous times, for work and for fun. Who'd have known he'd been visiting his birthplace all along? He liked the city. It reminded him of New York, only infinitely cleaner. It had a great sprawling Chinatown, though he'd found a place in Mississauga where the dim sum was better still, and a Chinese bakery with egg tarts to die for, as Adam had said when Mac brought him there once.

He parked a block from the sought-after intersection and walked the rest of the way. When he arrived, he was amused to notice that, if the camera had been angled a couple of degrees higher, it would have caught the Royal York Hotel, now the *Fairmont Royal York*, and solved the mystery long ago.

The intersection was exactly like the photo. As if it had been taken that morning. The winds of time had bypassed this place. The two corners of the intersection visible in his old photo held old but fairly well maintained apartment buildings, perhaps condos now. Bars graced the other two corners. It was hardly the best of neighborhoods, but he'd seen worse, especially on his tours of duty in some of the godforsaken backwater places that required an elite group of Rangers to put down some insurrection or another, or start some insurrection or another.

Mac figured a bar was as good a place as any to start his research. At worst, he'd end up with a couple of beers. He chose the one on the southeast corner, called Licker Up. *Classy*. Mac sat at the bar and addressed the bartender. "Hey, buddy. What's good here?"

"Best wings in town. In fact, they were invented here, about eighty years ago. Everyone thinks it's that place in Buffalo, but my great-great grandmother came up with the idea first."

"Yeah, sure. I've been to ten different places in Buffalo that invented the chicken wing. Good luck getting a patent."

"So what can I do for you, eh?"

"Call me Mac. Give me a Molson and twenty wings, extra hot. Um, also, I'm looking for someone. Well, someone who might know someone."

"Slow down there, Mac. What are we talkin'? A girl? I can hook you up with—"

"Don't need help in that department. I have to find out about a punk who lived in the neighborhood. About seventy years ago."

"Well, I'm twenty-seven. You wanna talk to Zelda."

"Zelda?"

"Zelda Einbinder. Over there." He pointed to a little old lady with horn-rimmed glasses and a wrinkled dress, ensconced in a booth at the far end of the room. An empty shot glass sat in front of her. "Does she look familiar to you?"

"Should she?"

"Go over and see. She's a legend around here. Taught kindergarten, starting in the forties. She's about ninety-five. Might be a couple of screws rattlin' around up there, but she can still knock 'em down. She's been doing that, too, since the forties. Give it a try, eh?"

Mac had surveilled the bar when he walked in, and he'd written off the white-haired lady in the corner as nothing more than a petrified lush. Now he gave her a closer look. "*Holy shit.* You know, I might remember her."

Mac approached the old lady cautiously, as if traversing a minefield, and asked if he could join her. When he introduced himself, the name Jerome McMillan didn't seem to register at all. Why would it? Even if he *was* in her class seventy years ago, which was probably just wishful thinking, he most likely had a different name.

"Well, young man, I'm sorry, what was your name?"

"Jerome, ma'am." He had to laugh. It'd been a long time since anyone had called him a young man.

"Okay, ah...Jack, was it?"

"Jerome."

"Oh yes. Well...Jack—"

"Jerome. It's Jerome." *This is hopeless.* "I'm wondering if you remember a student from a long time ago. And his mother."

"Let's go up to my place and we'll talk. Don't worry, sonny, I don't put out on the first date."

Mac chuckled. It was also a long time since he'd been called *sonny*.

The old dame still has some juice.

They entered the building directly across the street from the bar. Zelda's apartment was exactly as Mac had predicted: musty, dusty, pre-war furniture. Pre-WWI... Maybe pre-Civil War. And yes, five cats were slinking around the apartment, jumping on the kitchen counter and dining room table, searching for scraps, he supposed. Mac had figured her for four cats.

"Believe it or not, sonny, I remember every student I ever had." She pointed a bony finger at her thin-haired head, smiling with a vividness Mac could see in her eyes. The lights were definitely back on. "Got 'em all filed right up here."

"You remember me?"

"Jerome, I remember them as they were then, not now."

At least she's stopped calling me Jack. "Yeah, I might've added a few wrinkles, a couple pounds. Lost a couple hairs, too... Here." He handed Zelda the torn photo of the boy holding the hand of an unseen woman. And a pterodactyl.

Zelda stared deeply at the photo, her eyes completely alive now. "Well, let's see what we have. Oh, let's see. Um...uh...oh yes. Yes. Um...*Jerry*. Yes, Jerry. But Jerry what? Jerry, um... Jerry...*Jerry Stevens*. Yes. That's it. Jerry Stevens."

"Are you...are you sure?"

She shrugged.

"How the hell did I end up in the States?"

"That I can't tell you. But you *are* Jerry Stevens. Or were. Come here, I can show you. I think I have the other half of your photograph."

Now Mac knew she was crazy. He'd been excited for a moment. Mac wasn't fooled easily, but even he could be duped when he was so personally invested in an outcome. *Clever con. "Jerry" from Jerome. Bet she picked "Stevens" out of a hat. How could anyone possibly remember half of a photograph from seventy years ago? Wonder what she wants.*

Oblivious to his doubts, Zelda walked him into the next room, which had multiple bulletin boards displaying hundreds of pictures of children. Maybe thousands. A plethora of smiling young faces posing at home, in the classroom, at parks, playgrounds, everywhere imaginable. It confirmed Mac's realization that this was an exercise in insanity.

Notwithstanding his skepticism, Zelda zeroed in on something in no time at all. *A torn photo.* As she took it from the bulletin board, Mac instantly sensed that its jagged edge would match his partial photo. His heart began pounding again. *Holy shit, if this is a con, it's a great one.* He'd seen stuff like this from Penn and Teller, but Zelda? With no advance knowledge or preparation? Zelda took Mac's torn photo from his hand and carefully brought the two fragments together. They merged seamlessly.

The photo faced Zelda, and it was all Mac could do not to scream at her to show him. To finally bring an end to the years of fruitless searching. But she continued to stare at the photo. Mac hoped against hope that Zelda could identify the woman in the purple dress. At last, she smiled and handed him the two halves. He held them tenderly, almost afraid to contemplate how the mystery would end...and suddenly wondering if he really wanted to know. Finally, he slowly looked.

There was little Mac, holding the pterodactyl *and* the hand of a cute, smiling young woman in a purple dress. The closer Mac looked, the younger she seemed.

"My mother?"

"Your sister."

Chapter 33

SUNY AT BUFFALO LAW SCHOOL
Room 304
Amherst, New York
Monday, August 21, 2023
10:00 a.m.

The students milled about the classroom, catching up on gossip, bemoaning their most recent assignments, planning the next off-campus party, and reminiscing about yesterday's concert at the stadium in Orchard Park.

On the whiteboard facing the class was a PowerPoint image.

THE TEN COMMANDMENTS OF TRIAL PRACTICE

1. Be prepared. More prepared than your opponent.
2. Never lie to a jury or promise more than you can deliver. Earn their trust.
3. Show the jury you believe in your case and your client. Even if you don't.
4. Expect the unexpected. There are always surprises. Deal with it.
5. Never ask a question on cross-examination without knowing the answer.
6. Violate Commandment 5 if it feels right. Sometimes, yes or no are both fine answers to the same question.
7. Don't overdo objections. You just look scared, and it annoys the judge.
8. Never let them see you sweat. Especially when the unexpected happens, per Commandment 4.
9. Get as much sleep as you can before trial starts. It may be your last until it's over.
10. Get the jury to like you. And your client. Make them root

for your case.

Adam made his usual grand entrance. "Okay, creatures. I assume each of you can turn around and recite all ten commandments from memory. Who wants to start? No one? All right. Listen. If you remember one rule, make it Rule One. Be prepared. The Boy and Girl Scout motto. If you're unprepared, the judge, your client, the witnesses, and the jury will all know it. Jascha Heifetz, probably the greatest violinist of all time, said, 'If I don't practice for one day, I know it. Two days, the critics know it. Three days, the public knows it.' The jury is your public. Don't let them know it."

The class chuckled at the analogy, but Adam pounded it in further.

"So how do you get to Carnegie Hall, to win your trial? Practice, practice, practice. But let's face it, a trial is more like a war than a violin sonata. So consider Sun Tzu, *The Art of War*. 'Every battle is won before it is fought.' Sun Tzu was right on. If you haven't got your strategy, witness outlines, evidence charts, and opening and closing statements ready ahead of time, if you're still working on the basics during the trial, you'll be hopeless when the surprises start coming. Your trial *is* already over before it's fought. If you think you've prepared enough, you haven't. If you think you've prepared too much, maybe, just maybe, you've prepared enough."

The students were mesmerized. Until they became trial lawyers themselves, trial lawyers were gods. Adam's reputation as an unerring trial advocate was well known to them, and until further notice, he was their god.

"Preparation always starts with your summation. Start working on it the day you take the case. You can't know how to get there if you don't know where you're going. Make sure it covers every element of your claim or defense, every fact you'll need to prove. Then work backward from the summation to determine what evidence to present at trial. Naturally, the summation will be modified numerous times as you gather information from discovery, interviewing witnesses, and trial testimony itself. But if you don't start prepping on day one, you'll never catch up."

The students hung on his every word.

"Opening statements are just as important. They can't just be a jumble of facts. You must put all the pieces together into a coherent story. Let's face it, the human mind is geared to like stories, ever since we sat around the cave listening to tales of the buffalo hunt. The problem is, evidence at trial is usually presented in bits and pieces, out of chronological order, and often conflicting. Our brains don't like that. It's difficult, if not impossible, for jurors to keep track of. Use your opening statement to give them a good roadmap to follow, *before* the evidence starts trickling in. It will help them make sense of the case, and they'll thank you for it.

"In the final analysis, that's all a trial is. A story. An evidence sandwich packed between your opening statement and summation. In simple terms, you tell them what you're gonna tell them, then you tell them, and then you tell them what you already told them. Any questions?"

A student in the fourth row raised his hand. "Professor Simons, you've been speaking a while. Can we have a bathroom break?"

Wise ass.

***

"Okay, creatures, let's talk about summations in a little more detail. Did you know that everyone in the world has the same favorite word? It's just four letters. Anyone want to hazard a guess?"

A lot of snickering ensued, but none of the students volunteered the four-letter words that came to mind. Then a student in the sixth row offered, "Love?"

"Nope."

"Money."

"No. *Four* letters, creatures."

"Love of money?" The class erupted in laughter.

Adam waited for them to settle down. "For each and every one of you, for everyone in the world, your favorite word is...your name. N-A-M-E. What does this have to do with trial technique? Well, in the days before Holotrials, and hopefully again after this hellish program is grounded, you knew the jurors' names before you started a trial. So, for example, you could incorporate their names in a clever way in your summation. Perhaps use them in an analogy: 'What if Mr. Orange spoke about Mr. Green in this manner? Would that be defamation?' Jurors Orange and Green will be touched that you remembered their names."

A student at the rear of the class piped up. "Does that work?"

"So far, so good. *Now* for something I forgot to mention in our last lecture. You always have to watch out for the other side's Pug Matthews."

Blank stares all around.

Adam tapped on his iPad, and the *Ten Commandments* on the whiteboard were replaced by a video of a baseball player at bat. The young black man wore the distinctive pinstriped uniform of the Yankees. He fouled off pitch after pitch after pitch. Ultimately, after what felt like an eternity of foul balls, he struck out. The video ended with a freeze frame of the batter standing there, after strike three was called, with a smile on his face.

Kelly knew nothing about baseball, yet the video struck a nerve. She just wasn't sure why.

Adam explained. "This is Pug. Pug Matthews. Say hi to Pug, creatures. Pug played for the Yankees. He couldn't field worth a damn. Wasn't fast. Abysmal batting average. But he did one thing well. He was a master at hitting foul balls. Could keep his at-bat alive sometimes for ten or twelve minutes. Most of the time he'd eventually strike out, but he'd wear down pitchers, get them to throw twenty or thirty pitches to get him out. Used up a lot of their pitch count and sent them to the dugout early."

The students were still clueless.

"So, what does this have to do with litigation? In your practices, you're going to meet lawyers who will make as many frivolous motions or objections as they can think of. Not with the hope of winning them. Just to wear you down. Divert your attention. Run out your pitch count. In pre-trial discovery, they might produce reams of irrelevant documents for you to sort through. With such distractions, you might take your eye off the ball. *Don't.*"

Adam scanned the room for any sign of comprehension.

"You want to try *your* case. Not *theirs*. So don't get Pugged. That's it for today, creatures. *Johnson versus Atlas Studios* on Wednesday. And don't forget the dissent. It's better than the majority opinion."

***

Holotrial

Adam knew Pug. Quite well. They had met in the year 2000, but that meeting was set in motion long before, back in 1983, on a family trip to Niagara Falls when Adam was five years old. One of the family's rare excursions outside the New York City area. The filming of *The Natural*, a movie about a middle-aged baseball player with a tragic past who finally made it to the big leagues, was taking place in Buffalo. At a rest stop on the Thruway, while scarfing down a hot fudge ice-cream cake, Adam's parents saw an ad in the local paper for extras. Adam's father Frank, an avid baseball fan, couldn't believe his luck. Two hours later, the family showed up at the movie location, the old War Memorial Stadium on Buffalo's East Side.

All of Buffalo was in pandemonium. Not only for the rare opportunity to have a feature film made there, but because its star, Robert Redford, and other A-listers were coming to town. Thousands of Buffalonians clamored to be a part of it. The Simons family made the cut with the assistant casting director, and they had great fun changing into their 1939 attire and sitting in the stands among hundreds of cardboard cutouts of fans sprinkled with living extras like themselves.

Adam had no memory of this event except a vague recollection of a fireworks display, which was actually the dramatic ending of the film, in which hundreds of stadium lights exploded in the outfield after Redford smashed his winning home run. Adam *did* have a photo of Redford, in his baseball uniform, patting a wide-eyed Adam on the head, and a Roy Hobbs baseball card, based on Redford's character, which he treasured along with his other favorite cards.

Fast-forward seventeen years, to 2000. It turned out to be far more than just a new millennium for Adam. He saw an article in the New Haven paper about a sequel to *The Natural*, filming again in Buffalo. And they were bringing back Robert Redford. Adam couldn't resist the thought of being an extra in both the original and the sequel. He posted an ad in the school newspaper to see if any other Yalies wanted to join him in this adventure. A bunch did, so they chipped in to rent a mini-bus and shuffled off to Buffalo during spring break. Among them was a stunning first-year student with chestnut hair, whom Adam recognized from his contracts class. He was too intimidated to strike up a conversation, but throughout the eight-hour trip, he repeatedly shot furtive glances at her when he

Alan M. Wishnoff

thought she wasn't looking.

Every so often, he tried to work up the nerve to approach her, though she'd never given him the time of day in class. *What non-banal intro can I come up with? "Your first time as an extra in a movie?" Boring. "How do you like our contracts professor?" Lame.* Adam didn't realize that the woman's primary motivation for coming on the trip was its destination, her hometown of Buffalo. He was also unaware of three other significant facts. First, the main reason she never seemed to pay attention to him in class was that she sat four rows in front of him, *not* that she wasn't interested. Second, during the trip to Buffalo, *she* snuck furtive glances at Adam almost as often as he did. And three, she *was* interested. Adam's wit, his already apparent prowess as a future litigator, and his classic good looks were a turn-on.

The War Memorial Stadium had been demolished in 1988, so the sequel was being filmed at the new downtown baseball stadium, Dunn Tire Park. Once again, Buffalo was in a frenzy over the production. It was the most excitement the city had seen since the Bills had made it to the Super Bowl—*four years in a row.*

Adam suggested that his companions stick together in a group of seats next to third base so that no one would go missing. That would also keep the young woman within striking range. His plan appeared to backfire when the now sixty-four-year-old Redford walked over to where the group was sitting, in order to watch the action from that angle. To their utter shock and delight, the larger-than-life actor engaged in brief chit-chat with them between takes. Redford seemed enchanted by the brown-haired beauty who'd been the center of Adam's attention, and Adam became feverish with jealousy. *Goddamnit, Redford just happened to mosey over to steal my girl? Jesus, Earth to Adam, as if this goddess who doesn't even know I exist is "my girl."* In spite of himself, Adam had to admit the actor still had almost unfathomable charisma and magnetism, a one-in-a-million combination of rugged masculinity coupled with that boyish smile and tousled blond mane. All of the Yalies noticed it too, including Brown Hair.

Adam snapped out of his sour mood when he saw that the producers were using retired professional baseball players to simulate the fictitious 1940 New York Knights, and one of them was his favorite New York Yankee, Pug Matthews. At the end of the day's shoot, while Adam waited his turn at an ice-cream stand set up for the extras, who showed up at the end of the line but Pug himself? Abandoning all decorum and acting as if he were still the five-year-old extra at the original film shoot, Adam rushed over to ask for an autograph, praying that Pug would also have his picture taken with him. Living up to his good-natured reputation, Pug willingly obliged.

To Adam's surprise, Brown Hair approached them. *Could this day get any better?* She asked if she too could have her picture taken with Pug. As they shook hands, Pug sensed she had no idea who he was. He figured he understood her real motive for joining their little group. She introduced herself to Pug as Beth, then turned and shyly repeated the introduction to Adam. Adam barely stammered out his own name in return.

Once the pictures were taken, Pug did the good deed for which Adam would be forever grateful. With a glint in his eye, Pug suggested that Adam and Beth could make a happy couple. "Why don't I take a picture of the two of *you*?" He then watched with amusement their awkward attempts to arrange themselves for the photo, arms hanging limply at their sides, struggling with how close to stand to each other, whether to touch, how much to glance at the other without staring. Finally, Pug took the initiative and pushed them together, shoulder to shoulder. Adam's heart started to race. Just before Pug said "cheese," Beth slinked her arm through Adam's. He shuddered at her touch. Game over.

As a parting gesture, Pug said, "If it works out, send me a copy of the picture with *your* autographs." A year later, they did.

The sequel was never released, but that didn't bother Adam. It had given him two of his most treasured relationships. That was enough. *Dayenu.*

***

Adam was back at the office for a twenty-minute pit stop between the law school and the old downtown courthouse, where he had a motion to argue. As he was running out the door, he ran into his invaluable paralegal in the hallway. "How are we coming on the Vertex discovery, Freddie? Trial starts in a month. By the way, we drew Mitachi. Could be worse."

"Caparini asked for possible witnesses. I tracked down eight hundred twelve people at the Naval Park on June thirtieth. The dossier's about two feet thick, mostly from Google, LinkedIn, Facebook, and two or three others. That should keep Caparini busy a while."

"That's great. You Pugged them."

Chapter 34

ADAM'S HOME
Tudor Place, Buffalo, New York
Wednesday, August 23, 2023
5:00 a.m.

The troops convened around Adam's kitchen table, half asleep. Mac broke the silence. "Hey Chief, is there another word for *thesaurus*?"

Adam ignored the *Mac-ism*. He was too focused on how the hell to win a case without a star witness. He wasn't crazy about cloak-and-dagger stuff, but until further notice, it seemed necessary here.

"Hey, Chief. Why can't Freddie do the babysitting?"

"I think this one requires your special expertise."

"In other words..." Mac huffed, "he's the brains, I'm the muscle."

Adam smiled. "For once I won't argue with you. We need this kid wrapped up tight. Frankly, there shouldn't be any danger. Kurtoff has no clue about Cal's identity, as far as we know. But why take chances? In the meantime, until he grows a couple of gonads, I'll try to convince him he's safer testifying than not. Which, by the way, is true."

"Don't worry, Chief. I won't let him put on his pajamas unless I've got one leg in there first."

"The kid's damn scared of Kurtoff, if you can believe it."

"I can believe it. I am too, Chief."

Adam and Kelly each raised an eyebrow.

"And Mac, based on Cal's polygraph results, we're essentially talking murder. Why don't you refer this to the Attorney General's office? If you haven't managed to piss them all off."

"No, Chief. Actually, I think I got a new contact there. Made a friend the other day."

"Good. Just avoid the Dragon Lady, and you'll be alright."

Kelly's was the only chair facing the kitchen door, which was why she alone noticed the shadow in the hallway. It seemed to be the shape of a person, with an outstretched arm holding a small object. A gun? Kelly gestured to the others to be quiet and pointed at the shadow. Mac instinctively reached inside his jacket for the shoulder holster, but Adam pressed his hand over Mac's, pinning it down before Mac could pull out his .45.

An instant later, Pete jumped into the kitchen doorway, pointing his index finger and barking, "*Blam. Die you motherfu—*"

Kelly screamed and jumped out of her chair.

Adam wasn't amused. "*Pete.* What do you think you're doing?"

Mac responded before Pete could. "Sorry, Chief. Guess I made Pete's training too real-world. We'll tone it down a notch. My fault."

Undeterred, Pete addressed his mentor. "Whada'ya think, Uncle Mac? Good ambush?"

"Check the room, Pokey. Not a Taliban in sight. You blew 'm all away. Good job."

"Just good?"

Pete and Mac recited the response together. "It ain't great if you ain't got the CMH."

"Can I come over to see yours again?" Pete asked.

Mac kept his Congressional Medal of Honor in a sock drawer. He took it out only on special occasions, such as whenever Pete visited. Which was fairly often. Only a handful of people knew about it. Fewer still had seen it.

"Sure thing, Pokey. I'm gonna' be busy with company for the next couple weeks or so. After that, come by anytime."

Pete smirked. "What's her name? Or is it, what's *their* names?"

"Not that kind of company, kid. Top secret. Level Four. Need to know. I could tell you, but I'd have to kill you."

"*C'mon,* Uncle Mac. I got Level *Five* clearance, remember?"

"Affirmative. All I can tell a Level Five is, your dad's got me operating my own Witness Protection program, the home version. Shouldn't be a problem. Just a civilian. I'll let you know if I need backup."

Adam put a stop to the banter, yelling at Pete, "Upstairs. Now."

Mac and Kelly exchanged glances, but they said nothing.

***

The doorbell rang at 6:05 a.m. Adam ushered Cal into the kitchen, where the other two dream team members, having gotten over the adrenaline rush of Pete's ambush, were once again trying to shake the sleep from their eyes.

"Cal," Adam began, "you've met Mac before. You've awakened his repressed maternal instincts, and he's going to put you up at his place. No one but the four of us here will know."

Mac barked an order worthy of a drill sergeant. "That means you stay inside, kid. No walks in the park, no midnight trips for donuts. Any provisions you need, *I* bring in. Windows closed, shades down."

Cal nodded his assent, but Mac wasn't finished.

"And you tell no one where you are. Not your mother, girlfriend, best friend from nerd school, no one. No tweets, no messages, no phone calls. Got it, kid? You behave, maybe I get you a burner phone so you can talk to the girlfriend, but that's it."

"Mr. Simons, like, are you sure, um, Mac is the right—"

"Don't worry, Cal. He may not look like much, but this Paleozoic hulk has a Congressional Medal of Honor. For what, he can't say, but I'll bet it's violent."

"It was, Chief. I was a meat eater."

"Cal, I'd trust him with my life. He's the best, really."

"I guess, like, I'll stay with him for now. But I'm not sure about testifying. Tina...that's my girlfriend, not my mom...said it's like my civic duty or whatever. She's the only reason I'm here."

Adam tried to reassure Cal. "While you're enjoying the luxurious accommodations at Mac's place, think about it this way. You're in greater danger *not* testifying. As long as you're a *potential* witness, Kurtoff has reason to stop you. Once you testify on the record, it's preserved forever. There'd be no point in harming you after that. Your testimony will live on, even if—"

"Even if *I* don't. Like, I get it."

***

Adam watched from his front door as they left, Mac already

Alan M. Wishnoff

sticking to Cal like glue. They got into Mac's car, a bright red vintage Porsche convertible, Mac's man-about-town car. Adam didn't like the idea of them driving around with only a thin tarp above their heads, but Mac's skull was pretty thick. That had been proven a number of times. Unlike the flamboyant Porsche, Mac's *work* car, a nondescript gray Chevy, was designed *not* to draw attention.

After waving goodbye, Adam turned around to go back inside and almost had a heart attack. Inches in front of him stood Pete, with a wicked grin on his face. Mac had taught him stealth all too well. "*Jesus*. You've got to stop this, Pete. It's not funny, and you could get yourself killed if Mac regains his old reflexes."

"Sorry, dude...Dad. But remember, you said if you lost a trial, we'd go on vacation. Together."

"That was three years ago. You were throwing a fit about going to school, and I was just trying to...you're not going to hold me to that, are you?"

"Well, you lost. So where are we going?"

"Actually, we bet on a *trial*. That was a *Holotrial*."

"C'mon, Dad. It's still a trial. You lost, so let's go."

Just as he would in court, Adam went to his fallback argument. "Well, the truth is, I didn't lose the case. We just discontinued it because we, uh, sued the wrong people. It's still going now, with the correct defendants."

A frown formed on Pete's face. His shoulders slumped as he turned away, mumbling, "Lost on a technicality. Again."

Adam felt sorry to disappoint Pete, but he could hardly go on vacation with the Vertex trial about to start. He couldn't do that to Katherine. Or Jennifer.

Pete turned back to Adam and said, almost in a whisper, "Dad?"

"Yes?"

"You know how Aunt Helen calls me her *number one nephew*."

"Yes. You're her *only* nephew."

"Dad, am I your...Dad, what if... No, forget it."

***

They got to Mac's place about 7 a.m.

"Yeah, I know, it's not much, kid," Mac said, "but it's home."

Cal struggled to come up with a compliment. There were clothes strewn all over the floor, beer cans on every surface, and little that bore any resemblance to actual furniture. "It's, like, it's fine. Looks just like my dorm room." He picked up a tattered middle school yearbook from the floor and found a photo of young Mac, which had a handwritten inscription: "May 27, 1961, Thanks for my first time. Love, Lisa." Cal did the math. "What's this? *First time* what? How old were you? Like, how old was she?"

"Leave it alone, kid. Here's a Kindle. Read all you want. Knock yourself out."

Mac stared intently into Cal's eyes. For a brief instant, the blazing fire in his own eyes gave Cal a glimpse of the raw power and determination that the aged warrior could still muster. *I don't want to be on the wrong side of that.* Then Cal's imagination started to run away with itself. *What if Mac's working for Kurtoff, a double agent sort of thing? After all, wasn't he a mercenary, willing to do whatever he was asked by the highest bidder? How well does Mr. Simons know Mac?*

Mac's gravelly voice interrupted Cal's lurid train of thought. "Kid, your specs are filthy. Give 'em here. I got a special cleaning solution that a pretty gal at Lens Crafters gave me. Think she was sweet on me. Not the crap they give to regular customers. This is behind-the-glass technician stuff. Top secret. Need-to-know."

They're trying to kill me, and he cares about my glasses? Cal handed the glasses over to Mac, who disappeared into his bathroom. After five minutes, during which Mac hummed the Army anthem out of tune and turned the faucet on and off several times, he emerged, glasses in hand. When Cal put them on, he had to admit they were amazingly clean. *I guess Mac has talents beyond following and killing people. What's he going to do next, cook me a quiche?*

"And remember kid, you don't answer the door, the phone, nothin'. You copy?"

"Yes...um...I copy."

As Mac was heading out, he turned back to Cal and yelled, "By the way, for breakfast I got Cheerios. Frosted or unfrosted, take your pick. Let me know if you're gonna want milk." With that, he was

Alan M. Wishnoff

gone.

Cal surveyed the room. He cast a close look at the door. It had a chain lock, like an old-fashioned hotel room. Not very reassuring. *They can't find me here, can they? Guess I shouldn't have told Tina where I was. They can't find her, can they?*

Chapter 35

SUPREME COURT, ERIE COUNTY
Talbot versus Vertex Corporation et al.
Holotrial Annex Building, Part 7-HT
Main Street, Buffalo, New York
Monday, October 2, 2023
9:15 a.m.

Judge Mitachi gazed up at the make-believe sun shining through the fake windows in her new courtroom and smiled. Her last courtroom had no windows. *I could get used to good weather all the time.* She got things going promptly, as always, nodding to her court clerk, who announced, "Holotrial H23-104C, Talbot versus Vertex Corporation et al. All counsel present. Preliminary instructions completed."

Setting the tone that said she would brook no nonsense in her courtroom, the judge sternly scrutinized the four lawyers standing before her. Equally stern looking was the middle-aged man standing next to the lawyers at the defense table with a perpetual sneer: Alex Kurtoff, Vertex CEO, wearing his trademark black suit and gold Rolex watch.

The judge began. "Gentlemen, and, uh lady, are we ready to proceed? Anything I need to know?"

Phillip Caparini, one of Vertex's two lawyers, was quick to his feet. "Yes, Your Honor, there is. *There certainly is.* The plaintiff has an undisclosed witness, whom they claim has extremely material testimony."

"What's this all about, Mr. Simons?"

"Your Honor, we *have* disclosed this witness, just not his name."

Caparini continued to protest. "No name is no disclosure, Mr. Simons. Coupled with a totally vague description of the witness's testimony."

"This witness fears for his safety, Your Honor," Adam responded. "We'd like to address this with the court in an *in camera* meeting, if the court will allow." Adam's gaze centered on Kurtoff as he made the request.

Judge Mitachi raised an eyebrow. Such a request had reversal written all over it. *Well, Simons usually knows what he's doing, so we'll see.* "Extremely unusual for a civil trial, to say the least. I guess we'll cross this bridge when we come to it."

"Thank you, Your Honor."

"Is that it?"

Adam and Caparini responded "Yes" in unison.

"Very well. Let's get going. Okay then, Mr. Simons, you may open. Bring in the jury." With that, the jury box was lit up and *came to life*.

Even with the aborted New Millennium trial under his belt, Adam still felt out of his element trying a personal injury case. That, and his feeling that something screwy was going on with the Talbots, imbued him with a nervousness that was unfamiliar to him in the courtroom. He prayed it didn't show. *Commandment Eight: Never let them see you sweat.*

Adam approached the jury box, exuding a fearlessness he didn't have. Before beginning his opening statement, he reminded himself to treat the faces in front of him as living, breathing humans. He briefly paced back and forth before settling in front of Juror Number Five, whose green eyes and red hair matched Kelly's. He turned to confirm that the real Kelly was still sitting at the counsel table and almost lost his concentration, but he quickly recovered. He'd trained himself not to react to the myriad surprises that always occurred at trial: missing witnesses, unexpected changes in testimony, vexatious objections, erroneous rulings, and even, on occasion, an attractive juror.

"May it please the Court, ladies and gentlemen of the jury..."

***

Jennifer sat in the witness box. Her direct examination had gone much like her prior testimony. The new defendants didn't change anything she knew about that woeful afternoon. Her car blew up. Allie was gone. It was that simple. But the prior trial had been a month and a half ago, and whatever confidence Jennifer may have developed from that trial was long gone. Nevertheless, they'd gotten the job done, setting the scene with the video of the car exploding.

Before the cross-examination began, Adam thought he had better raise the issue of Cal Dryer. If they couldn't somehow make Cal comfortable testifying, the rest of this was pointless. "Your Honor, is tomorrow afternoon a good time for the *in camera* meeting with the witness?"

The judge checked the calendar on her phone. "Let's do it Thursday evening, 7:30. I think we can keep this trial going until then. Okay, Mr. Caparini, you're up."

Caparini stood, a slight sneer on his face. Adam wanted to tell him not to bother trying to intimidate Jennifer. She was already maximally uncomfortable. Caparini stayed in front of the defense counsel table on the left side of the courtroom, forcing Jennifer to turn her back to the jury. She was unquestionably a sympathetic witness, having lost a child, at such a young age and in such a violent manner, so Caparini had to minimize her bonding with the jurors.

Q: Miss Talbot, you first sued New Millennium Motors for this accident, yes?

A: Yes.

Q: And you swore in a pleading submitted to this court that New Millennium Motors was at fault, yes?

A: That was because—

Q: And now you swear in a pleading in this case that Vertex and Mr. Kurtoff are responsible, yes?

A: Yes.

Q: Who will you blame tomorrow? Your hair stylist? The Pope?

Mr. Simons: Really, Your Honor, do I have to—

The Court: Mr. Caparini. I will have none of this. There's no jury here to impress anyway. Consider yourself warned. You will address

> *Ms.* Talbot with the decorum required in my
> courtroom.

Mr. Caparini: Apologies, Your Honor. When one's
clients have been so wrongly accused, one gets
emotional.

The Court: *Save it*, Mr. Caparini.

Q: So Miss, uh, *Ms.* Talbot. I understand from
reading the transcript of the New Millennium
trial that you claim you don't know who the
father of your child is?

Mr. Simons: Your Honor—

The Court: No, I'll allow it. I'm interested myself.

Adam had to admit he was interested, too. The Talbots had
staunchly maintained that none of them knew the father. Adam
found that borderline preposterous, but it didn't affect the merits of
the case, so he'd chosen to soldier on with this mystery remaining
in the background. "I trust that comment will not be in the
Holoscript."

Now the judge shot Adam a scathing glare. "Mr. Simons, you
worry about your own comments. The Court is perfectly capable of
handling itself. As you should know, all colloquy, including elegant
musings by the Court, will be deleted before presentation to the live
jury. This *is* a Holotrial. Mr. Caparini?"

Q: Ms. Talbot, uh, you remember the question?

Mr. Caparini: Your Honor, may the court
stenographer read it back?

The Court: Yes, go ahead.

Steno: "I understand from reading the transcript of
the New Millennium trial that you claim you
don't know who the father of your child is?"

A: God. I've already testified to this. And it's not a
claim. It's a fact.

Q: Yes, I know, Ms. Talbot. I read the transcript. I
don't see a direct answer there. That was a

different trial, anyway. Ms. Talbot? We need
an answer for *this* case. *This* jury needs to hear
your answer.

The fire was back in Jennifer's eyes, her face reddened, and the cords in her neck protruded as she violently swiveled her seat to face the seven inanimate *jurors*.

A: They don't need to hear anything. They're
plastic. Look at them. *Plastic*. They can't hear
me. They can't hear anything. What the hell do
you want from me?

Adam sprung to his feet to protect his frantic client. "Your Honor, a short recess? Ms. Talbot is in a very emotional state. I hope you understand. Can you—"

"Yes, absolutely," Judge Mitachi ordered. "Ms. Talbot, you may step down. We'll reconvene in ten. Or whatever you need. Take your time. We'll continue when you're ready."

***

Twenty minutes later, Jennifer walked slowly back to the witness stand, Kelly at her side with a hand on her shoulder.

The Court: Ms. Talbot, you understand you are
still under oath?

Ms. Talbot: Yes, Your Honor.

The Court: All right, Mr. Caparini. You may
proceed.

Q: Thank you. So, Ms. Talbot. Do you understand
what it means to be under oath?

A: Yes.

Q: It means you can't tell a falsehood, by
commission or omission. Can we agree on
that? Yes?

A: Yes.

Q: So do you need, one more time, to have the
question read back?

Alan M. Wishnoff

A: No... No.

Q: No what, Ms. Talbot? No, you don't need the question read back? No, you can't identify the father? No, you *won't* say?

Mr. Simons: Please, Your Honor, may we have one question at a time.

The Court: Yes, Mr. Caparini. You know better.

Q: Sorry, Your Honor. Ms. Talbot, do you know who the father of your child is? Can you answer that?

A: I *can* answer. *No.* I *don't* know who the father is. I don't. You can, like, ask me ten times if you want, Mr. Cap.

Q: It's Caparini. Perhaps you can narrow it down, to maybe two or three gentlemen? Yes? Perhaps?

A: No, Mr. Crap-*er*-ni.

Q: I just told you, it's Caparini.

A: And I just told you, I don't give a...I don't care.

Q: *Ms. Talbot,* can you narrow it down to four or five gentlemen?

Mr. Simons: Please, Your Honor, we're well past badgering now.

The Court: I have to agree. Mr. Caparini, you've made your point. Move on.

Q: Yes. Sorry, Your Honor. Miss, uh, *Ms.* Talbot. Let's pursue another possibility. Perhaps, the father, perhaps he didn't want anything to do with the child? Yes? Or worse, perhaps, did he have something to gain if the girl disappeared? No more child support, maybe? Yes?

Mr. Simons: Your Honor, really.

The Court: Is that an objection?

Mr. Simons: Yes, Your Honor.

The Court: Then please state it as such.

Mr. Simons: Objection, Your Honor. For starters, compound question...how do we know which question Ms. Talbot would be answering? Also, argumentative, harassing the witness, speculation. Calls for hearsay as well.

The Court: Sounds like you have all the bases covered, Mr. Simons. Overruled. Except as to compound. I would like to know the answers as well, but one question at a time, Mr. Caparini. And try not to flirt with unsupported inuendo. I will *not* have a young woman who's lost a child harassed in my courtroom. You're on a short leash, Mr. Caparini.

Mr. Caparini: Yes, yes, sorry, Your Honor.

Q: So, Ms. Talbot. Let us start with this. Is it possible the father wanted nothing to do with the child? Yes?

A: I've *told* you, Mr. *Crap*-ini. I don't know who the father is. I don't know what he thinks. I don't know what he wants.

Q: Perhaps there is someone else who was inconvenienced by the child's appearance on the scene? Possible? Yes?

Mr. Simons: Objection. Speculative, argumentative. Calls for mental impression of parties unknown, maybe non-existent.

The Court: Yes, Mr. Caparini, I think you've reached the end of that leash. Let's take ten.

Jennifer looked immensely relieved. Adam wondered why. She hadn't told him in their preparation that anyone was trying to harm Allison, rather than the car. Once again, he had a nagging feeling that the Talbots were somehow not forthcoming. Not by a long shot.

***

The recess was almost over, and Adam did *not* want to be late. Not in Judge Mitachi's courtroom. He was zipping up his fly when Katherine Talbot flew into the men's room and roughly grabbed him by the lapels. "Adam, *please. Don't* pursue the father question with Jenny."

"Kate, *what the hell*? You know you're in the...never mind. Why can't I... Just what are you telling me? Whatever it is, I won't suborn perjury. Listen, I love you..." his voice cracked a bit, "*all*, but I'm not going to lose my license over this. What's going on? Tell me the truth, damnit."

Katherine responded in a timid whisper. "The truth?"

"Yes, I need to hear it from you. I hope I can trust your word. Bill, well, we go back a long way, but his political instincts can cloud his judgment."

"Don't worry. Your precious reputation is safe. And so is Bill's. I swear it, Adam. Jenny doesn't know who the father is. She wouldn't lie under oath. My girl..." Katherine choked up. "My girl wouldn't... She was raised better than that, at least by me. You've got Bill pegged. He's capable of anything. *Anything.* But Jenny, she's innocent in this. There's not a speck of Bill in her. If there ever was, I beat it out of her."

Adam peered at Katherine's face. She seemed both earnest and on edge. She clearly wasn't telling him *the whole truth and nothing but the truth.* Maybe she wasn't lying, but she was leaving *something* out, presumably something important. *Somehow, somewhere, sometime, she's going to fill in the blanks for me, damnit.*

"I see you're still using that Neanderthal PI," Katherine said. "I thought they died out 40,000 years ago. Alert the Smithsonian."

Adam let her lighten the moment, as he obviously wasn't going to get anything more out of her there in the men's room. *At least she's gotten some use out of that anthropology degree.* Then his thoughts went to something that had been troubling him for the past ten months. "Kate, do you ever think about... I'm sorry, I have no right."

"You have every right, Adam. I do. Often. I didn't mean to hurt you. It got complicated."

"Complicated? To me, what we had was simple. I don't understand what changed."

"I can't explain. Not now. And Adam. One other thing."

"Yes?"

"Please don't call me to the stand. I can't testify. I *won't* testify."

"What are you telling me, Kate?"

"Please. Just. Don't."

Chapter 36

HOME OF ALEX KURTOFF
Stonecliff Court, Clarence, New York
Monday, October 2, 2023
8:15 p.m.

Alex Kurtoff couldn't believe his bad luck. It wasn't supposed to be like this. The police found nothing implicating him or Vertex. Gura had done his job there. No trail. No fingerprints, no tools left behind, no witnesses. *So how the hell did Gura fuck up? How does that fucking Adam Simons know what the police don't know? Who is this damn witness? If I find him...*

So Kurtoff did what he always did to calm down when there was no one around to shoot or torture. He went down the basement stairs, locked the soundproof door behind him, and entered *The Citadel*. There was no other room like it anywhere in the world.

It was temperature and humidity controlled to protect its prize possessions. On one side wall, various weapons hung from metal hooks, including assault rifles, knives, axes, handguns, grenades. On the opposite wall was a long row of felt-covered pegs from which hung a number of violins and violin bows. There were multiple traditional wooden violins, a pearl white electric violin, and a black carbon-fiber violin. One was a Stradivarius. Kurtoff owned another Strad, as well, which he loaned to the concertmaster of the Buffalo Philharmonic. Each was over three hundred years old. On the rear wall was a 105-inch television and a sophisticated, exquisitely expensive sound system.

Kurtoff liked to have the best of everything. The Strads met that goal and then some. He'd paid over two million dollars for the one on the wall. Electric violins were fun, but there was nothing like the genuine article. He found violins fascinating not only because of their beauty, but for their history. Even with all the technology available in 2023, no one could duplicate the quality of a Strad.

Holotrial

Violin making had reached its heights in the 1600s and 1700s, with the likes of Antonio Stradivari, Guarneri del Gesu, and Andrea Amati. And all in the same city: Cremona, Italy.

There were various theories as to why the Strads sounded so good. Some say it's the wood, that a *little ice age* was responsible for slow-growth wood around Cremona. Others believe it's the varnish. Others think it's merely the age, that sitting around for a few centuries somehow makes a violin sound better. They'd analyzed them with X-rays, CAT scans, chemical analysis, computer-acoustic tests, but no dice. Stradivari's 300-year-old secret was still safe.

Unsurprisingly, Kurtoff's involvement with violins began with violence. Specifically, the threat of violence. When he was still an up-and-coming punk taking orders, his boss Marco told him to collect a debt from the owner of a violin shop in Phillippavivska. While explaining to the owner the order in which his limbs would be broken if he didn't pay up, the young Kurtoff noticed the various stringed instruments and bows hanging on the walls throughout the store. He also realized that music was playing in the background. He didn't recognize it then, but it was the Tchaikovsky violin concerto, a piece he'd eventually learn to play pretty well.

Maybe it was the Slavic nature of the concerto, maybe the glistening polished surfaces of the violins. For whatever reason, he wished that he himself might be able to produce such glorious sounds, and he demanded that the shop owner show him the best violin in the place. The trembling proprietor pointed to a violin that looked pretty much the same as all the others. Alexi, as he was still named then, had no idea whether it was truly the best one there, whether better violins *looked* nicer or were different in some other manner than cheap ones. So, he did what came naturally. He plucked the violin from the wall, picked a luxurious violin case from the many on display, and walked out. Upon his return to Kyiv, he paid off the shop owner's debt to Marco from his own pocket. And kept the violin.

Over the years Kurtoff had become a highly proficient musician, buying better and better violins. However, it wasn't until attaining the position of Vertex CEO, where dollars fell off the trees for its executives, that he had the kind of money to get a Strad. That was the violin he chose for this evening, along with a phenomenal carbon fiber bow. Perhaps it was blasphemy to combine the two, but Mr. Stradivari was not around to object.

Before picking up the violin, Kurtoff inserted a *Symphony Soloist* Blu-ray disc in his player. Amazingly, in a digital age of streaming music and hi-res downloads, this CEO of a high-tech electric car manufacturer still used clunky old CDs and Blu-rays. Not that Kurtoff was a complete Luddite. He had a state-of-the-art sound system that was unparalleled: 34-speaker advanced Atmos array with the best amplifiers, pre-amps, DACs, and cables.

When he pressed *8K Blu-ray* on his remote, a video of a large symphony orchestra appeared on the television screen that occupied most of the back wall. At the first wave of the conductor's baton, four lone timpani strikes sounded, and the warm orchestral opening of the Beethoven violin concerto filled the room. Kurtoff had plenty of time during the long introduction to get the violin in proper position. Then he began playing, precisely on cue, and for 45 minutes, he was lost in Beethoven's world, which was far preferable to the real one. No Adam Simons. No Gura. No court. No witnesses. Only heavenly, soothing music. It was extraordinarily satisfying to have a whole symphony orchestra accompanying him. And for the mere price of a Blu-ray.

***

While Kurtoff was immersed in his music, Adam had no time for play. The cross-examination of Vertex's expert was the next step in the trial, so he called Marcel Saperston to see if the new circumstances affected his opinion. Adam didn't expect it would, and he wasn't disappointed. Saperston remained unmoved. No matter how the extra cable got there, be it Kurtoff, the stork, or the tooth fairy, it didn't change the laws of physics. The extra cable couldn't have been the cause of the explosion. The fact that sabotage was involved certainly made things more dramatic, but that's all. Of course, Saperston said, he couldn't rule out some other form of sabotage, but there was no evidence for it.

"Some other form of sabotage." The phrase kept ringing in Adam's head. *Could there be? Then why insert the electrical cable? A decoy? But why need a decoy?* Something didn't add up.

Chapter 37

ADAM'S HOME
Tudor Place, Buffalo, New York
Monday, October 2, 2023
10:15 p.m.

Squirrely was a trait Adam usually associated with his opponents' witnesses. But it defined his current clients to a T. He was positive the Talbots weren't being straight with him on a number of fronts. First and foremost, Allison's father. That seemed to be causing the most consternation, certainly in Jennifer and Katherine. Hell, not just consternation but *pure hysteria* in Jennifer.

Adam went down to the basement, to the Holoscript viewing room that he and Mac had constructed. A miniature version of a HAB courtroom, with stark white walls, floor, and ceiling, it had no furniture besides a small white chair for Adam. A holographic projector was embedded in the rear wall. All lawyers conducting trials in the Eighth Judicial District had been given one of these, and Kelly had programmed it to play relevant excerpts of Jennifer's testimony from both trials.

First up were those from the aborted New Millennium trial. Adam zoomed in to give the appearance of a life-size Jennifer sitting right in front of him, ready to strike up a conversation. Up close like this, it never ceased to amaze him. *This is unreal. Strike that. It's unbelievably real.*

He knew it was Jennifer, yet it seemed that a fresh-faced Katherine, the young anthropology major of twenty-three years ago, was sitting there. *Like she's ready for our first date. Hey, Kate, I'll meet you after my Estates and Trusts class. Four-thirty...Snap out of it, idiot. That Kate is gone. Forever. And Jennifer isn't here either. It's just a bunch of photons.*

Adam started the playback. His own disembodied voice

addressed the hologram of Jennifer. He watched as she stumbled on basic introductory questioning concerning Allison's age and the incontrovertible fact that Bill had given her the car. *What the hell was all this about?* Adam didn't recall such difficulty during their trial prep. Maybe it was such an innocuous preliminary subject that he hadn't bothered to go over it with her? Chalk it up to Jennifer's understandable nervousness about testifying in general?

Adam skipped to Jennifer's cross-examination by Michael Chun, zooming in further until the back wall of his viewing room was filled with the greater-than-life-size face of Jennifer, reminiscent of the menacing Oz Wizard's head projected on the flame-filled screen to frighten Dorothy and her three unique friends. Only this time there were no flames, and the large projected head itself seemed scared. Adam watched as Jennifer denied knowing the identity of Allison's father. He paused the playback, scrutinizing her face for a clue. Her facial muscles were rigid, eyes wide. It was hard to hone in on any conclusion about her veracity in such a state. *What was she so afraid of? Going to jail for perjury? Being embarrassed? Coming off as promiscuous?*

Adam switched to Caparini's cross-examination in the Vertex/Kurtoff trial. This time, Jennifer went berserk in response to questions about the child's father. *Why? Is she afraid of the father? Too scared to name him because...why? He's threatened her? Threatened her family?* Whatever it was, Adam was sure the jury would understand. How could anyone suffering such a loss maintain her composure?

Then it hit him. Jennifer must have been raped. *That's it, isn't it. That could explain it. She really doesn't know his name. Some stranger who attacked her in the park, or in her home? Merely talking about him causes her to relive the horrible experience?* Could a rape serve as the *unified theory of everything* in the warped Talbot universe?

Chapter 38

SUPREME COURT, ERIE COUNTY
Talbot versus Vertex Corporation et al.
Holotrial Annex Building, Part 7-HT
Main Street, Buffalo, New York
Tuesday, October 3, 2023
9:20 a.m.

Christine Morier sat in the gallery, waiting for her name to be called. She'd flown in from Pasadena the night before, to rest up. Her schedule was too busy to come to Buffalo earlier, so she and Caparini had Zoomed her preparation several times. It didn't take long, as her opinion was simple. Most of the prep focused on what this Mr. Simons might ask her on cross-examination.

Christine was a fairly striking woman, in her forties with a pleasant face. She was forceful and direct in the delivery of her opinions, with a classic Quebecois accent, courtesy of her childhood. The *true* French, especially Parisians, would look down on her accent, but then again, the French looked down on pretty much everything and everyone.

> Mr. Caparini: Your Honor, the defense calls Dr. Christine Morier.
>
> The Court: Welcome, Dr. Morier. Please make yourself comfortable.
>
> Dr. Morier: *Merci.* Um, thank you. Madame? Your Honor?
>
> The Court: Madame is fine. I've been called far worse. In fact, by some of the gentlemen in this courtroom.

Adam looked down at the counsel table, avoiding eye contact with the judge.

The Court: So, Dr. Morier, would you like to take an oath or affirmation?

Dr. Morier: I view testimony in a beautiful court such as this to be almost sacred, you know. I will take an oath, please.

The Court: May I ask, Dr. Morier, would you prefer to be sworn in on a French bible? I do keep one here.

Dr. Morier: Thank you kindly. English is fine.

Court clerk: Please put your left hand on the Bible and raise your right hand. Do you solemnly swear to tell the truth, the whole truth, and nothing but the truth, so help you God?

Dr. Morier: I do.

The Court: Thank you. You may be seated, Doctor.

As Dr. Morier was sitting down in the witness chair, Caparini walked to the end of the jury box.

Q: Dr. Morier, please tell the jury about yourself.

Though Christine had been told about this unorthodox trial system, experiencing it in person took a little getting used to. Pretend the synthetic people are human, Caparini had said, because eventually they will be. The real ones will be impressed by your credentials and enjoy your delightful accent, as well.

A: I was born and raised in a small town. Saguenay, Quebec, you know. I am a graduate of McGill University and Stanford University.

Q: McGill, that is in Montreal, yes?

A: *Oui, monsieur.* Ah, sorry. Yes sir, it is. I received a Bachelor of Science and a Doctorate in Physics from McGill, then a Doctorate from Stanford in Engineering Physics, you know. I have been at NASA's Jet Propulsion laboratory as a Senior Engineer for the past fifteen years. I am also a visiting professor at Harvard University.

Q: What is your Harvard position, Dr. Morier?

A: I teach Physical Engineering. Adjunct faculty, you know.

Q: Sounds like a big commute, yes?

A: It is. But worth it. I enjoy pursuing new frontiers in Physical Engineering at NASA. But there's nothing like *quel est le mot*...sorry, how do you say, nurturing young minds at Harvard, you know.

Q: Yes. Dr. Morier, did your education at McGill and Stanford, and your work at NASA, involve hydrogen-powered engines?

Mr. Simons: Objection, compound question.

The Court: Well, let's see where it goes.

A: Yes, all three. That was the subject of my dissertation at Stanford.

The Court: There, problem solved.

Q: Dr. Morier, did you examine the vehicle in question in this case? *Ms.* Talbot's car, yes?

A: *Oui.* I examined the pieces the police were able to recover.

Q: Yes, yes. And based on that examination, do you have an opinion as to what caused the vehicle to explode?

Because of what happened next, it would be more than an hour before Caparini's question would be answered.

Chapter 39

SUPREME COURT, ERIE COUNTY
Holotrial Annex Building, Control Room
Main Street, Buffalo, New York
Tuesday, October 3, 2023
9:45 a.m.

It was a big day in the control room. Judge Raymond Frankhauser, the Chief Administrative Judge, was visiting from Albany to see his pet project. The staff was excited to demonstrate its prowess to the big man. They didn't understand that, to him, they were nothing more than low-level functionaries, technicians. He took full credit for the entire project.

The judge had brought his grandkids, Ethan and Emma, ages seven and five, to get them out of his daughter's hair for the day. They were rambunctious, to put it mildly. He'd warned them they better behave because this was a *very* important place. If they didn't, he might have to put them in jail.

Charlie Ross, the Chief Courtroom Tech, shuddered when he saw the two urchins with large cans of Mountain Dew in their hands. However, he was not brave enough to remind the judge that neither children nor food were allowed in the control room, so he let it go and gave Judge Frankhauser's entourage the royal treatment. Their tour included the cubicle dedicated to courtroom 7-HT. At first, the children were in awe, as if they were on one of their Disney World trips with Grandpa. The control panel had what seemed to be zillions of knobs and buttons and sliders, with lights flashing all over the place. Fourteen sliders controlled the volume from various locations around the courtroom. The buttons and knobs manipulated the holographic cameras located near the ceiling and in the walls of the courtroom, ensuring that the resulting Holoscript would have pristine three-dimensional imagery.

Charlie pointed to a large green toggle switch at the center of the panel. The left side was labeled *Whitescreen*, while the right side was labeled *Courtroom*. "See this switch here, kids? It's from the ninth dimension. When you flip it, everything in the room turns from plain white to wood, glass, carpeting, all kinds of stuff. No, sorry, Ethan. We don't touch. Just for grownups."

The kids desperately wanted to play with the control panel, but Charlie's mild admonishment and a stern look from Grandpa Ray squashed those thoughts. They were also fascinated by the large television monitor on top of the console. Just like the big OLED television Grandpa had in his den back in Albany. At present, the screen was divided into five frames: a Judge, the plaintiff and defense counsel tables, the witness box, and the jury. The last was the strangest of all. It showed a row of artificial *people* seated along the wall, and a man in a dark suit, apparently human, standing next to the plastic Juror Number Seven. The woman in the witness box and the man standing near the jury appeared to be speaking to each other, though their voices weren't audible. The audio feed was confined to headphones worn by the two courtroom techs at the console.

As part of the tour, Charlie proudly gave the judge a technical dissertation on the workings of the Holotrial control room. Judge Frankhauser nodded as if he understood the process intimately, whereas, in reality, he couldn't have repeated any of it in any detail if he'd been offered the Hope Diamond to do so.

Four minutes into Charlie's oration, the children began to grow restless with their tour guide's unintelligible jargon. Their incessant need for constant entertainment was no longer being met, so they reverted to their usual course of conduct when boredom set in. Ethan started teasing Emma, alternately poking her and sticking out his tongue. With each poke, she flinched and nearly spilled her soda. The judge, immersed in Charlie's technical presentation and consumed with pride in *his* Holotrial system, failed to notice the change in the kids' demeanor.

At first Emma grew sullen, deadly quiet. That was a danger signal. Finally, after enough teasing by her brother, her mood turned on a dime to one of blistering anger. She'd show Ethan that she wasn't a baby to be picked on. With one fell swoop, she swatted the can out of Ethan's hand, sending it flying toward the console. Charlie watched in horror as his beloved control panel was drenched in Mountain Dew. Sparks flew and a loud crackling sound emanated from the control panel, followed immediately by circuit breakers tripping.

The effect was immediate. A fantastically loud electric *crack* filled the courtroom, startling everyone. All eyes instinctively looked up, and as they searched the ceiling for the source of the noise, a brilliant flash of light filled the room, and the ceiling *disappeared*. The entire courtroom essentially disappeared. With the room reverted to its original pristine white *naked* state, the glare was blinding. However, it didn't last, and a second later, after another loud *crack*, the lighting completely cut out, plunging the room into darkness, except for tiny rows of emergency lights dotting the floor and leading in two directions: toward the door behind the bench leading to the judge's chambers, and toward the double doors at the rear of the courtroom.

At first, everyone milled about in confusion, a low murmur filling the room. The rapid transformation from pure white to nearly pitch blackness was disorienting, but fortunately, the judge's court clerk had been trained for just such an emergency. He immediately led Judge Mitachi to her chambers, advising everyone else to stay put. He then returned to shepherd the remaining lawyers, witness, parties, and spectators out the rear doors and down the hallway to the attorneys' conference room.

As they crowded into the room's modest confines, still shaken, they sat down around the conference table haphazardly, intermingling. Katherine found herself directly across the table from Kurtoff. He thought he'd amuse himself by trying to intimidate her, so he amplified his usual sneer by staring directly into her eyes. She stared right back at him with a mask of hatred so deep it shook *him*, though he tried not to show it. *Alexi. A woman no less. A grandma.*

Jennifer sat across the table from her father and gave him an icy stare, chewing her gum and saying nothing.

Adam found himself next to Dr. Morier. They began a polite conversation, careful not to touch on the subject of her testimony. Adam reminisced about a long-ago visit to Montreal, how elegant he found its old-world ambiance, as if he were in the middle of a venerable European city rather than chilly North America. He didn't mention that Beth had been with him. Not that he was trying to hide anything. It simply wasn't relevant. Right? Up close, Adam couldn't help but notice how attractive the French-Canadian woman was. Soon they dropped the *Doctor* and *Mr.* labels in favor of first names. *She seems to be enjoying our conversation. I sense she likes me. On a professional level, of course. I wonder if Kate is jealous. Jesus, Adam, don't waken the noodle. Concentrate. You've got a case to try.*

Back in the control room, technicians hurriedly worked to replace the damaged parts of the control panel. It took them an hour and a half to get back on-line. Judge Frankhauser and the children were nowhere to be seen, having beat a hasty and timid retreat.

Chapter 40

SUPREME COURT, ERIE COUNTY
Talbot versus Vertex Corporation et al.
Holotrial Annex Building, Part 7-HT
Main Street, Buffalo, New York
Tuesday, October 3, 2023
11:20 a.m.

Normalcy restored, the judge, lawyers, witness, and spectators resumed their positions. Adam wondered if the courtroom meltdown had been some kind of trick by Kurtoff's people, though he couldn't figure out what it gained them, nor more generally why they might plant the electrical cable in the Hydro as a decoy for another form of sabotage. If the interruption had occurred during a particularly brilliant bit of cross-examination, that could make sense, but during a calm and seamless direct examination of their own witness?

I guess we'll have to see.

Caparini retook his position at the end of the jury box and resumed his questioning.

> Q: Dr. Morier, I believe, before the lights went out, I asked if you have an opinion of what caused the vehicle to explode?
>
> A: Yes, I do. Or perhaps, I should say, you know, I have an opinion on what did *not* cause it to explode.
>
> Q: And what *is* your opinion, Dr. Morier?
>
> A: Well, you know, I could find nothing that would explain the cause of this accident.
>
> Q: Dr. Morier, Mr. Sands from NTSB said they found some kind of extra electrical cable. What

about that?

A: *Oui*, I examined that cable. In my expert
    opinion, it might have caused the car to catch
    on fire, given enough time, but, you know, not
    to explode,

Mr. Caparini: Your witness.

Adam had the same feeling as when he'd cross-examined New
Millennium's expert, Dr. Ditenzo. He found Dr. Morier likable, and
her opinion fairly convincing, since it too coincided with Marcel
Saperston's conclusion. Her credentials were impeccable,
outstandingly so for this case. *Think I'll start off the cross on a bit
of a tangent. Perhaps better to prove what she doesn't know than
what she thinks she does know.*

Q: Dr. Morier. Who put the extra electrical cable
    in the engine of Ms. Talbot's car?

A: I have no idea how it got there, Adam. *Je
    m'excuse*...Mr. Simons.

Caparini raised an eyebrow, as did Kurtoff.

Q: So you can't rule out that it was put there by
    someone working for Vertex?

A: As I said, I have no knowledge on this subject.
    I was not retained for such opinion nor could I
    give one, you know.

Q: Thank you. Tell me, Doctor, do we know
    everything there is to know about physics?

A: Mr. Simons, there is *no* area of science in
    which we know everything. And there
    probably never will be, you know?

Q: Is it possible then, Dr. Morier, that the extra
    electrical cable did in fact cause the explosion,
    and science simply hasn't yet caught up to the
    explanation?

A: *Je suppose*...I suppose anything is possible, Mr.
    Simons. Within the rules and boundaries of the

physical universe. But, you know, there is currently no scientific basis for concluding that this cable caused the car to explode. That's the best I can tell you, *n'est-ce pas*?

Q: Scientists make hypotheses, correct?

A: That is correct.

Q: And then they try to prove or disprove those hypotheses, correct?

A: Testing hypotheses is the essence of science, Mr. Simons. The eternal quest for knowledge. I think it is fair to say, you know, once a scientist comes up with a hypothesis, more effort is put into disproving it than proving it.

Q: Is it fair to say that your opinion, that the extraneous cable couldn't have caused the explosion, is a hypothesis?

A: One could call it that. However, you know, I would have to say it is stronger than a mere hypothesis. It is based on objective, empirical evidence. We did a test at Harvard, recreated the exact scenario of a Hydro with a matching extraneous cable running from the superconductor ring to the right rear motor. We ran the test car a hundred more miles than the Talbot car had on it, you know. The right rear motor *did* overheat enough that a small fire developed in the rear of the car. That was it, you know. There was no explosion.

Adam was aware of the test from pre-trial discovery produced by Vertex. He tried to shave off a layer or two of confidence in her opinion, distinguishing the test conditions at Harvard from the real-world circumstances involving Jennifer Talbot's car. However, he couldn't really fault Dr. Morier for reaching the same conclusion as his own expert. *No one* seemed to believe that this strange extra cable had caused the explosion. Now here was someone who'd actually tested it to *prove* the negative. And she did.

Adam had one last play.

> Q: Dr. Morier, I have a hypothetical, if you don't mind following along with me. What if the same person who put the extraneous cable in the Hydro *also* placed an extraneous piece of tubing in the car. Let's assume this person inserted a Y-shaped tube running from the electrolyzer, one branch going to the fuel cells, the other to the interior of the car. Are you still with me, Dr. Morier?

> A: *Oui.* Sorry, yes. Mr. Simons. A strange but intriguing scenario, you know.

In the gallery, Adam's question had triggered in Mac's brain the same thought he'd had in Saperston's office: *branches.*

> Q: Could this Y-tube cause a buildup of hydrogen gas in the interior of the car?

> A: Under that scenario? I suppose it could happen. But, you know—

> Q: Just bear with me another second, Doctor. So, we have this Y-shaped tubing running from the electrolyzer to the fuel cells *and* to the car interior, causing a buildup of hydrogen gas inside the car. Is it fair to say that a tiny spark, perhaps a buildup of static electricity or just starting the ignition could result in a powerful explosion?

Kurtoff gave Caparini a wincing jab in the ribs and whispered, "Why you not cut this off? They not *find* Y-tube."

Caparini sprang to his feet. "Objection, Your Honor. We keep hearing about a Y-shaped tube from Mr. Simons. Y-shaped tube, Y-shaped tube. There *is no* Y-shaped tube. It exists only in Mr. Simons' imagination. Improper foundation, Your Honor."

> The Court: Well, what about it, Mr. Simons. Is there a Y-shaped tube?

> Mr. Simons: I can't say one has been found, Your

Honor. But the car was so mangled, anything might be in there.

Mr. Caparini: Mr. Simons knows that all parts of the car were accounted for by the police and by New Millennium, the car's *manufacturer*. They found no Y-tube. They don't even make such a tube.

Mr. Simons: So they say. Your Honor, a reasonable hypothesis may be propounded to an expert on cross exam—

The Court: Enough, Mr. Simons. Objection sustained. Lack of foundation. A reasonable hypothesis, Mr. Simons, must have a reasonable basis in fact. Yours doesn't. Any questioning or testimony concerning this non-existent Y-tube is stricken.

Q: Just one last question, Dr. Morier. It's a bit long. If I may summarize your testimony, you weren't asked to consider, and therefore do not know, how the extraneous cable got into the engine of Jennifer Talbot's car. You can't rule out that someone from Vertex put it there or that someone acting on Mr. Kurtoff's orders put it there. The conditions under which you tested a Hydro at Harvard are not identical to the conditions facing Ms. Talbot's Hydro on June 30, 2023. And, finally, it is *possible* that the extraneous cable caused her car to explode. Is that a fair summary, Dr. Morier?

A: As I said, there is no current scientific basis for believing that the cable was responsible for the destruction of the car.

Q: Other than that, a fair summary?

A: I suppose. Yes, I suppose, you know?

Caparini leapt from his chair. "Objection. Supposition is the same as speculation. It should be stricken."

The Court: You're objecting to your own witness's answer? I guess that's allowed. But no, I think the answer is within the bounds of expert testimony. The jury can determine what weight to give it.

Mr. Simons: Thank you, Your Honor. One last follow-up.

Q: Dr. Morier, you said you believe there is not a *current* scientific basis to implicate the cable in the explosion of Ms. Talbot's car, and the death of her two-month-old child. Is it possible, in the future, scientists may determine there *can* be such a causal connection? I believe you did testify that it's possible.

A: Possible? I suppose.

***

During the morning recess, Adam pulled Mac into the vacant Jury Deliberation Room. "Mac, do me a favor."

"You smell something, Chief?"

"Just want to tie up a loose end. I have a hunch."

"I'd go broke bettin' against your hunches."

"Mac, the cops who processed the scene, do you trust them?"

"You mean would they bury somethin' for a little extra Christmas scratch? Nah. Not that bunch, Chief."

"How about professionally. Could they miss something?"

"Possible. Nobody's perfect. 'Cept you and me, Chief."

"Do me a favor, Mac, make a second sweep. Maybe something got stuck in the fence around the parking lot. Or jammed into the fender of another car? Can you run all the plates?"

"Sure thing, Chief. Actually, I might have an idea where to expand the search. I know a place the badges might have missed."

"Good. And Mac?"

"Yeah, Chief?"

"Stop calling me Chief."

"Sure thing, Chief."

Chapter 41

SUPREME COURT, ERIE COUNTY
Holotrial Annex Building
Main Street, Buffalo, New York
Wednesday, October 4, 2023
10:35 p.m.

T he man with the big fluffy mustache entered the courthouse wearing the standard outfit of the Court's custodial department: green coveralls, rubber boots, tool belt. The badge hanging from his shirt pocket identified him as Bob Lorenzo. Damytro Gura figured the disguise wouldn't fool anyone who knew him well. He doubted that would include the yawning guard at the courthouse entrance—a college kid working the night shift who probably wouldn't find it unusual for Custodial Services to be working this late, as they were always looking for overtime.

This was one of the strangest assignments Gura had ever had, but he was not about to question Kurtoff's orders. That was never a good idea. He flashed his badge as he pushed a dolly, on which sat a large box marked *Property of New York State Supreme Court*, around the metal detector. The kid gave it a cursory glance and waved him in. Gura's guess was correct. The kid didn't know *any* of the day shift, so he probably could've picked any name he wanted.

As he'd been instructed, Gura, or *Bob*, proceeded to courtroom Part 7-HT on the second floor, where the Vertex trial was taking place. He'd never been in one of these fancy courtrooms. It was pitch black. He fumbled around in the dark for the light switch, which he'd been told was just to the left of the courtroom door. When he flipped it on, he almost fell backward from the glare of the all-white room. He picked his way to the jury box and, selecting a special screwdriver from his tool belt, detached the head of a female juror he'd chosen at random. Juror Number Five, a redhead. He then pulled a substitute juror head from the box he'd been pushing and attached it to the torso. He had to laugh, as the replacement Juror Number Five kind of matched his current disguise, a fiftyish male with a prominent black mustache.

Gura marveled once more at the boss's resourcefulness. Obtaining a maintenance outfit and toolkit was one thing, but a juror head that fit perfectly on the ones in this strange courtroom? He had to give it to Kurtoff.

After placing the redhead in the box, Gura exited the building, past the snoring guard, and returned the box to the rear of his van. Once in the driver's seat, he took off the tool belt and contorted to remove the green coveralls, revealing a crisp Vertex Security shirt. He peeled off the fluffy mustache and threw it out the window. Driving off with a smile, he reflected on a job well done. *Bob Lorenzo* was no more.

Chapter 42

SUPREME COURT, ERIE COUNTY
Talbot versus Vertex Corporation et al.
Holotrial Annex Building, Part 7-HT
Main Street, Buffalo, New York
Thursday, October 5, 2023
7:28 p.m.

Judge Mitachi, Adam, and Cal Dryer were sitting around the plaintiffs' counsel table. The judge was in a pantsuit, presumably what she normally wore under her robes. Cal was in his Sunday best, for a college student: a button-down shirt and knit slacks.

Adam knew he had a hard sell. "Thank you, Your Honor, for hearing us *in camera*. May I introduce Calvin Dryer. Mr. Dryer is in a position to provide the most direct, first-hand evidence of the defendants' conduct."

"Hello. Uh, Your Honor. Is this, like, being recorded?"

"Good evening, Mr. Dryer. No. No recording. So, tell me, Mr. Dryer, what can I do for you?"

Adam figured he'd better do as much of the talking as possible, given Cal's perpetually nervous state. "Your Honor, Mr. Dryer is reluctant to testify out of fear for his personal safety. He asks that the Court allow him to testify anonymously, with the image of his face blurred in the Holoscript."

"Come now, do you really think this is...I won't tolerate any threats in my courtroom. Has Mr. Dryer been threatened?"

"No. not yet. The defendants don't know Mr. Dryer's identity. If they did, we'd be very concerned."

"Your Honor, um, Judge Mitachi," Cal said. "Like, I've read about Mr. Kurtoff, like his connections to the Ukrainian mob or whatever. And his wife, dying in their bathtub? I know some people think it's only gossip. But, like, lots of people say it's true. I believe lots of people. Could you, like, keep him out of the courtroom if I testified, or something?"

The judge turned to Adam. "Mr. Simons, do you really expect me to invoke such a procedure?"

"Your Honor, I think Mr. Dryer has the request a little mixed up. We're not asking to exclude Mr. Kurtoff from the courtroom."

"I should hope not."

"What we *are* requesting is simply that Mr. Dryer's name not be used during his testimony, and that the image of his face be blurred in the Holoscript."

"Simply? You know how drastic that would be, Mr. Simons? The defendants would scream to the bloody rafters about their right to meaningfully confront their accuser, how it would hamstring a proper cross-examination. The constitutional implications alone would almost certainly get any plaintiff's verdict thrown out."

Adam sighed. "That's a chance I may have to take if I can't convince Mr. Dryer to testify under normal conditions."

"You know, Mr. Dryer, Alex Kurtoff is the CEO of a Fortune 100 company, a distinguished businessman. Yes, with a somewhat murky past, but it's a little far-fetched to think that he would resort to violence...not against a litigant in *my* courtroom."

"But Judge, um, Your Honor," Cal responded, "like, how can you control Mr. Kurtoff *outside* of here?"

"He's still subject to my jurisdiction and discipline when he steps foot in this courtroom. If he were to interfere with a witness, whether in or outside the courthouse, he'd be in very hot water, I assure you. Is this really a problem though, Mr. Dryer? Once you testify and your testimony is recorded on our equipment here, it's not going anywhere. There'd be no point in threatening or, God forbid, harming you. Your testimony will be preserved on the record forever. It can't be erased by Mr. Kurtoff or anyone else."

"I've told him," Adam chimed in, "but he wouldn't listen to me. Maybe hearing it from you will change his mind, Your Honor."

"You're sure I'm not, like, being recorded now? Your Honor?"

"Absolutely not, Mr. Dryer. The control room staff left an hour ago, and Charlie locks it up tight. The equipment is all turned off."

Adam nodded in agreement. He assumed the judge knew her courtroom. As it turned out, she did. And she didn't.

Chapter 43

THE VERTEX BUILDING
Boardroom
Ensign Street, South Buffalo, New York
Thursday, October 5, 2023
7:28 p.m.

T he thirty-foot table had seating for twenty-five Vertex board members, though on the rare occasions when all attended, it was a tight fit. This evening there was only one occupant, sitting at the head of the table in the plush leather chair with the brass *CEO* nameplate.

Projected on the tabletop in front of him was a holographic image of a miniature Adam Simons, about a foot tall, speaking to a miniature Judge Mitachi. "Thank you, Your Honor, for hearing us *in camera*. May I introduce Calvin Dryer." Kurtoff let out a combination sneer and chuckle. *I have him.* He picked up his phone, now with a name for his prey.

***

Even in miniature on the boardroom table, the images of the *in camera* session were stunning. The realism of the Holotrials' 3-D video was a technical marvel, eons ahead of any prior methods of three-dimensional video recording. The program had actually come about by happenstance. Judge Frankhauser had taken his grandchildren to Disney World for spring vacation. On the second morning of their visit, or *Disnit* as they were calling it, after finishing their Mickey Mouse pancakes and Goofy home fries, they caught a live show in which a cast member, dressed as a character from the most recent Pixar movie, told jokes and performed amazing acrobatics. The judge marveled at his ability to accomplish fantastic jumps and flips in what appeared to be a very clunky costume. Just as the character finished his last backward flip, *he vanished.* Into thin air. It hadn't been a cast member. It hadn't been a costume. The incredibly lifelike creature had been a hologram.

Suddenly, the judge was more excited than the grandkids. They were having a ball, but he had a Eureka moment. *This could work in court. It could. Record the trial ahead of time so the jury doesn't have to sit around twiddling their thumbs during all the wasted time that plagues every trial. We can eliminate inadmissible evidence and all the other unnecessary junk, so the jury never sees it.* Then doubts started to creep in. Projecting a hologram of a single creature on this stage was one thing, but could this be done for an entire courtroom, with multiple people, furniture, the whole enchilada? *I've gotta meet whoever came up with this.*

The next day, after pulling a few strings, the judge met with the bright young computer engineer who'd created the show, a twenty-eight-year-old named Amal, a graduate of the Rochester Institute of Technology, who'd begun his career four years earlier at Pixar. Amal had combined the 3-D wizardry he'd learned at Pixar with standard holographic techniques and a few amazing innovations he developed himself to create a mind-blowing effect. In a bit of serendipity, Amal loved lawyer movies, particularly those involving trials. *To Kill a Mockingbird* and many others graced his personal collection. He also had fond memories, from his RIT days, of trips to Buffalo for Bills games and the bars that stayed open until 4 a.m., so he was as excited about the project as the judge. Disney agreed to loan him to the New York State court system for six months. It only took him five.

***

Kurtoff was still alone in the boardroom when his assistant's voice came over the intercom. "Alexi...*Sorry, sorry.* Mr. K. That gentleman you asked for is here."

"Send him in. *Now.*"

As Larry Zack entered the boardroom, he found the situation pleasantly ironic. He'd been paid by New Millennium when he found Cal, and now he was earning more money from Vertex for disposing of Cal. *Only in America.*

Before Zack could sit down, Kurtoff barked at him, "You got

him? Where is he? Where you find him?"

Zack smiled. *Easiest money I've ever earned. Can't remember when I wrapped up a case so fast, and with so little effort.* "Right here."

"Here?" Kurtoff was befuddled.

"Before running all over town, I checked the Vertex office phone-mail. Your switchboard was off for the night, so they didn't get this message. Though, frankly, I doubt they would've recognized its significance anyway. Probably would have dismissed it as a crank call. Better I found it."

"So I pay you ten grand to check our own phone messages?"

"That's right. I think you'll find it worth it." Zack put his laptop on the boardroom table and started playing the recorded message. The voice was distorted, but the message was clear: "Cal Dryer is at 702 Auburn Avenue."

Kurtoff was both elated and suspicious. "*What*? Who that? Why they call?"

"Apparently to tip us off."

"Why?"

"Your guess as good as mine."

"Well, who then?"

"Can't tell. They're good, whoever they are. Man, woman, boy, girl? Computer-generated? Sounds like a voice distorter. Any private dick would know how to use one."

Kurtoff looked up from the laptop, "Hm...Mr. McMillan? No. He more loyal to Simons than a dog, is not?"

"You're right. I don't think it's Mac. That's Mac's *address*. Of course, it could be a trap."

Kurtoff agreed. "Yes, that occur to me immediate I hear message. Just sort of thing that slimy bastard Simons come up with, is not? I think this call for the police."

Zack looked at him quizzically.

Kurtoff motioned for him to leave the room and grabbed his phone. As he was leaving, Zack heard Kurtoff utter one word.

"*Quill.*"

Chapter 44

SUPREME COURT, ERIE COUNTY
Talbot versus Vertex Corporation et al.
Holotrial Annex Building, Part 7-HT
Main Street, Buffalo, New York
Friday, October 6, 2023
9:15 a.m.

The great showdown was about to commence. *Simons vs. Kurtoff,* the cross-examination that could make or break the case. *Or so Kurtoff believes. It would make sense to the bastard that our case lives and dies with his testimony. That if he lies and denies, we're left with a weak, circumstantial case at best. Well, Mr. Kurtoff, we have a witness coming in who'll blow the lid off the defense. You don't get it. We almost want you to lie, so Cal can show you for what you are.* Had Adam been in the Vertex boardroom the night before, he might have been more reticent.

Adam stood up from the counsel table, cross-examination outline in hand. He took a quick look at the ersatz jurors, waving and smiling at them to send Kurtoff the message that he wasn't worried, this was going to be fun. Adam was about to start the questioning when he noticed something about Juror Number Five. He came to a full stop, transfixed by the juror's face. *Something was wrong.* It didn't have Kelly's green eyes and red hair anymore. In fact, it was a *man,* with a thick black mustache. *Perhaps I'm wrong. Maybe it wasn't Number Five?* Adam scanned the rest of the jurors, but no *Kelly-eyes.* He felt certain the other faces hadn't changed.

Number Five was the outlier. As he studied it closer, it seemed to be wearing the same dark blazer worn by the *Kelly* juror. *Something's definitely wrong. Why would they replace only this juror? And only its head? Maintenance? What kind of maintenance? The jurors just sit there.*

Judge Mitachi urged Adam in a moderately harsh tone. "Mr.

Simons? Sometime today?" Adam was violating her most sacrosanct rule, dawdling about as if he were at the Erie County Fair trying to choose between the stuffed sausage on a stick and a deep fried twinkie.

Adam motioned Mac over from the gallery. They stood in front of Juror Number Five as Adam whispered into Mac's ear, after which Mac walked behind the juror and started examining its head.

The judge raised her voice. *"Mr. McMillan.* Just what in the hell do you think you're doing?"

Adam tried to run interference. "Your Honor, I know this is highly unusual, but I think we have a significant problem here. If you'll bear with us just one more minute."

The judge wasn't happy, but she held her tongue.

As everyone in the courtroom watched in varying degrees of surprise and concern, Mac found a barely noticeable compartment on the back of the juror head. He took a tool from his coat pocket, essentially a Swiss Army knife modified for U.S. Army rangers, and opened the juror's head.

Judge Mitachi reacted even more harshly. *"Mr.* McMillan. *What are you doing to my juror?* You *do* know the holding center is just around the corner. I can hold you *both* in contempt and have Mr. Wallace take you into custody right this minute."

Adam responded, "Please, Your Honor, just a bit more." After a little more fiddling, Mac gave Adam a knowing nod. "Your Honor, before we continue with testimony, may we approach the bench?"

"This better be good, Mr. Simons. And get with the program. This is a *Holotrial.* No need to approach. You may speak from the counsel table." She pointed at the jury box. "They won't hear anything."

"On the contrary, Your Honor, therein lies the problem. Unfortunately, they *will.* At least *one* of them will. May we go on the record, Your Honor? Thanks."

> Mr. Simons: Your Honor, I don't know how to say
> this any other way...the courtroom has been
> tampered with. Juror Number Five's head has
> been changed. Until this morning, it was a
> redheaded female with green eyes.
>
> The Court: So, you're partial to redheads with

green eyes. Okay. Do we need to get that head back to make you comfortable? I'm sure it's just routine maintenance, Mr. Simons.

Mr. Simons: I'm afraid something far more sinister is afoot. Mac, show Her Honor.

Mac manipulated the electronics inside the compartment he'd found in the juror's head, and it started playing a hologram right on top of the judge's bench. There, a foot in front of her, were miniature versions of Adam, Cal Dryer, and herself conducting the *in camera* conference from the evening before. The mini-Adam Simons addressed the mini-judge: "Thank you, Your Honor for hearing us *in camera*." Mac played another few seconds of the video before the judge popped up from her chair and raised an imperious hand.

The Court: *Maji. This is outrageous.* Mr. Caparini, your license is hanging by a thread. Not to mention contempt. And worse.

Mr. Caparini: Your Honor, please, I swear, I have no knowledge of any of this.

The Court: *Mr.* Caparini. If you've helped your client commit a crime, in my courtroom, no less, I don't have to tell you where that will lead. With the bar and with me. Not to mention the criminal authorities. And Mr. Kurtoff, you will face similar consequences.

Mr. Kurtoff: Your Honor, I waive attorney-client privilege for this purpose. You ask Mr. Caparini if he ever discuss such thing with me. Or with anyone else, is not?

Mr. Caparini: As I said, Your Honor, I know nothing of this. I have spoken to no one of such a thing. Not Mr. Kurtoff. No one. I've never seen this recording before.

The Court: Mr. Caparini, I may have been born on a Tuesday, but it wasn't last Tuesday. Your *offer of proof*, if that's what it is, leaves a lot to be desired. *Cui Bono*...who benefits, other than your client? For now, I'll take your word as an officer of the court that you weren't personally involved. That leaves your client, Mr. Kurtoff.

Judge Mitachi turned to Kurtoff. "*Stand up,* Mr. Kurtoff. I mean *now*."

Kurtoff wasn't used to being ordered around, *and by a woman no less.* Nevertheless, he quickly complied.

The judge pointed to the witness box. "*Over there.*"

Again, he complied.

The Court: I will advise you of your Fifth Amendment rights, after which, if you are willing to take the stand, we shall proceed with this inquiry. Your choice, Mr. Kurtoff. You have the right to remain silent. Anything you say can and will be used against you in a court of law. This court, in fact. You have the right to speak to an attorney, and to have an attorney present during any questioning. Which you already have, unless you want a different lawyer, perhaps one specializing in criminal law. If you cannot afford an attorney...

She almost choked while looking at the diamond-encrusted gold Rolex on Kurtoff's wrist.

The Court: One will be provided for you. Now, do you understand these rights?

Mr. Kurtoff: Yes, I do. Your Honor.

The Court: After considering these rights, are you willing to waive them to the extent of testifying about the tampering with this juror?

Mr. Kurtoff: Yes. Am. Is not?

The Court: Since *I* am the most aggrieved party here, I think I'll begin the questioning. Mr. Kurtoff, do you know who tampered with this juror?

Mr. Kurtoff: No. Not.

Though Adam couldn't prove it, he had no doubt that Kurtoff was lying. There were no Pollyannas on the mean streets of Kyiv or on the boards of corporate America.

The Court: *Mr.* Kurtoff, have you ever spoken to anyone about tampering with this juror?

Mr. Kurtoff: No, have not, Your Honor. Would never do such thing, is not?

The Court: Do you understand the seriousness of this matter, and the consequences if it is determined you've perjured yourself here?

Mr. Kurtoff: I do. I am member of bar, as well, Your Honor.

The Court: Yes, I know. And perjury may be the least of your problems if it turns out you were involved in this. Mr. Kurtoff, were you aware that Mr. Simons and his witness were going to have an *in camera* meeting with me last night, here in this courtroom? In sight and hearing of this juror?

Mr. Kurtoff: No. Not remember. Don't think. No. Not.

The Court: You didn't hear that? Sitting right there at the defense table?

Mr. Kurtoff: No, sorry. Not hear. Lots going on.

The Court: Mr. Simons, follow up?

Mr. Simons: Yes, there certainly is. Mr. Kurtoff, as a member of the bar, do you understand what an *in camera* conference is?

Mr. Kurtoff: I went to law school as did you, Mr. Simons. Maybe not as good law school, but I learn same law, is not? So yes, I understand *in camera*. Private meeting with judge. You go on. I not afraid.

Mr. Simons: And you say you were unaware we'd

be requesting such a conference with the court?

Mr. Kurtoff: I have already say that, Mr. Simons.

Kelly tapped Adam on the shoulder and handed him a note. Without having to be asked, she'd already located on her tablet the relevant parts of the October 2 transcript where Adam requested, and the court scheduled, the *in camera* meeting. Adam nodded to her, and she hooked up her tablet to the control panel on the counsel desk, playing the October 2 excerpts on the courtroom monitors.

Mr. Simons: Did you see yourself there in the videos, Mr. Kurtoff? Sitting at the counsel table right over there when I stated we'd be seeking an *in camera* conference?

Mr. Kurtoff: I see now there was mention, but was brief, and uncertain, is not? I apparent not believe significant and did not retain in memory, is not?

Mr. Simons: That was just four days ago. *Is not?*

Mr. Kurtoff: Yes, Monday, four days ago. Minor part. Lot going on, is not? Opening statements, Miss Talbot testify, she get upset. Minor part.

Mr. Simons: Did you also see Judge Mitachi scheduling the *in camera* conference for Thursday, that's yesterday?

Mr. Kurtoff: My answer same, is not?

Mr. Simons: Your Honor. I submit that Mr. Kurtoff's amnesia is simply not to be believed.

The Court: We're going to find out soon, Mr. Simons. I will refer this matter to the Attorney General's forensic division. Let's see what they can tell us about this juror head. If forensics doesn't find anything meaningful, I'll consider proceeding with the trial. But if we do, a cloud will still hang over it. A serious cloud. We are adjourned until further notice.

Holotrial

***

Judge Mitachi pondered whether to declare a mistrial no matter what forensics found. *Is there any doubt this was Kurtoff, and possibly his lawyers, as well?* Though she harbored this strong suspicion, as a guardian of the law, she wouldn't convict until all the evidence was in. That's what she always told her juries, and she'd abide by that principle here. For now.

***

Kurtoff still couldn't believe that Gura had been so stupid, substituting a male juror head for a female one. *The bastard better not left fingerprints, or he dead man.* They'd fucked up the first part of the plan, but it did get them Cal's identity. It was essential they act on that immediately, before Simons found out that they also knew Cal's location. He scrolled through the Q's in the contact list on his phone, stopping at Quill. It was time the sergeant earned his pay. *Cal Dryer must never see inside of courtroom.*

Chapter 45

GENOMIC FORENSIC SERVICES
Undisclosed Location
Cheektowaga, New York
Friday, October 6, 2023
10:08 p.m.

T he unremarkable house on an ordinary street in the northern suburb of Cheektowaga had no signage indicating that it was anything other than a private home. Just another two-story dwelling built in the 1950s. Dr. Prisha Singh, the sole proprietor of Genomic Forensic Services, liked it that way. Her business was solely word-of-mouth among a select clientele, and only a select subset of them had ever been to her lab. Mac was included in that subset.

Prisha was unlocking the door to the lab as Mac arrived. "You know, I wouldn't work this late for just anyone."

"That's why I love you, Sugar. When are we gonna do something about it?"

"After my next divorce." Prisha, known as *Dr. Singh* rather than *Sugar* to most of her clients, was half interested. But back to business. "So, what do you have for me?"

Mac put on a pair of latex gloves and carefully opened a large nylon bag, then removed a dirty, soot-covered piece of tubing in the shape of a Y. It was about three feet long.

Prisha enjoyed guessing the purpose of the oddball objects her clients brought her to analyze, though she'd never ask them. It wasn't hard to guess that this strange tubing had something to do with the Talbot case. She couldn't turn on her television or radio without hearing about it. *Though it doesn't look like any auto part I've ever seen. Fancy exhaust system? Heating? AC?*

She winced when Mac told her its recent history. "It's been outside, stuck in a tree, for three months now. Think you can squeeze anything out of this, Prish?"

"We'll see. I've gotta tell you, Mac, it's a long shot."

"I figure, if there's anyone could do it—"

"Okay, don't butter me up. Just pay me. Any specific databases?"

"All of 'em. State, Federal. Army, Navy, Air Force, Marines. The works. FBI, CIA, the stupid *Genes-R-Us* websites. I need a miracle."

Prisha was ex-NSA. She'd managed to retain access to the agency's DNA database, which basically incorporated all the others, governmental and commercial.

"Mac, for the record, I can't access armed forces, FBI, CIA, NSA."

"Understood." He knew what *for the record* meant from Prisha.

***

An hour and a half later, Prisha beckoned Mac over to the computer on her desk. "You're in luck. I can't identify the subject who left his DNA on this thing. I say *his* because it's got XY chromosomes. *He's* not in any database. But I did find a partial match. Fifty percent, presumably a first-degree relative."

Mac's eyes lit up. The information would hopefully allow them to work backward from the relative and identify the perpetrator. "*So?* Who is it? What scumbag's related to *our* scumbag?"

"Take a look."

Mac glanced at the screen, then re-focused his startled eyes to be sure he hadn't misread it. "*Holy shit*. No. *No fucking way. This can't—*"

Suddenly, Mac's phone alarm blared, alerting him that Cal was on the move. Mac grabbed the Y-tube and ran out the door without so much as a goodbye or thank you.

Chapter 46

MAC's HOME
Auburn Avenue, Buffalo, New York
Friday, October 6, 2023
11:30 p.m.

The ancient rotary telephone was ringing for the fourth time. Cal had been sleeping. *What time is it anyway?* He figured it had to be important. *Gotta be Mac.* But he'd been told not to answer the phone. Ever. After debating it in his still hazy mind, nagging doubts pointing him in both directions, he decided to violate Mac's order just this once, so he picked up the receiver. "Uh, hello?"

An officious voice responded, "Mr. Dryer, this is Sergeant Quill of the New York State Police. I'm coming to pick you up in four and a half minutes. Please be waiting outside the front door until I get there."

"But how? Like, how did you know—"

"Sir, my orders are to take you into protective custody and maintain strict confidentiality. That's all I know."

"But, Mr.—"

"Quill. It's *Sergeant* Quill."

"Uh, Sergeant Quill. I was told, like, never to leave the—"

"Don't worry. Mac contacted us. It's at *his* request. I can't tell you more."

The mention of Mac's name gave Cal some comfort. "Okay, I, uh, I'll be there."

Cal dressed hurriedly. He was halfway out the door when he realized how blurry the world looked. He went back to retrieve his glasses from the Amazon Prime box that passed for his night table. Even in his drowsy state he couldn't help but admire the cleaning job Mac had done on them.

***

Four and a half minutes later, a blue state police car with its yellow stripe pulled up to the curb. *Jeez, these cops are efficient.* The state trooper got out of the car, put on his felt Stetson hat and ushered Cal into the back seat. As the trooper closed the door, Cal heard the locks click. There were no door handles in the back seat, anyway. *Shit. Glad I'm not a suspect.*

Cal shook the cobwebs from his head and started worrying again. "Has anything, like, happened to Mac?"

"Mac is fine, sir. That's all I can tell you. When we get to the station, we'll see if the Captain can give you more details. Our primary concern right now is keeping you alive."

***

Cal had dozed off, until the loud ringtone on the trooper's phone shattered the silence. "Yessir, Captain...No, no problems. Turned out it wasn't stolen, just borrowed by a cousin for a joy ride... Downtown. I'm on Elmwood, passing Tupper. Yeah. Gotta check a couple things. Should be back in Clarence in about an hour and a half, maybe two. Ten-four, Captain."

Cal glanced out the window and realized that they were on the I-190 heading toward Niagara Falls. Not remotely near downtown Buffalo, as Quill had just asserted. Cal still wasn't fully awake, so to confirm that he'd heard what he thought he heard, he asked Quill, "Didn't you just say we were, like, in Buffalo?"

"Don't worry, Mr. Dryer. We're trying to keep you safe. Our pre-arranged code. Me and the Captain. Was actually Mac's idea. We didn't want to give your true location in case any of those bastards working for Kurtoff were listening."

"But, like, I thought I heard you say you're heading to Clarence?"

"Mr. Dryer, how 'bout you let me do the driving. Didn't want to take an obvious route to Clarence Station. Need to know if we're being followed."

Cal accepted the explanation for the moment. It sounded like Mac, with his covert background. Yet something didn't smell right. The road signs told him they'd just passed Niagara Falls and were heading toward the Canadian border.

***

Quill pulled off the highway in Lewiston, a few miles before the border. Minutes later, the car came to a sudden stop on the service road running along the top of the Robert Moses Niagara Power Plant, a concrete colossus looming hundreds of feet above the Niagara River. Completed in 1961, it had thirteen turbines and a capacity of 2.4 million kilowatts. When it opened, it was the Western world's largest hydropower facility.

The Robert Moses was one of a succession of power stations built to harness the nascent power of the Niagara River. The Niagara Falls Power Company built its first large hydroelectric powerhouse in 1894, backed by wealthy investors including John Jacob Astor, J.P. Morgan, and William Vanderbilt. The plant utilized the alternating current (AC) system developed by Nikola Tesla, which allowed electricity to be distributed over considerably greater distances than direct current (DC), which had been championed by Thomas Edison. In fact, Tesla served as a consultant on the construction of the original plant.

In the so-called *Battle of the Currents*, Edison went so far as to electrocute animals with AC to convince the public how dangerous it was. Some say he even electrocuted a circus elephant, though others say Edison wasn't personally involved in the pachyderm's demise. Still others claim the animal was already sentenced to death for having killed three men, and that electrocution was a more humane method of execution than the alternatives. The one agreed-upon fact is that the elephant was named Topsy. Tesla's AC current eventually won out.

Contrary to popular belief, electricity isn't made from the water flowing over Niagara Falls. In actuality, water several miles upstream from the Falls is diverted through giant underground conduits running under the City of Niagara Falls to a 1,900-acre, twenty-two-billion-gallon reservoir across the street and up the hill from the Robert Moses power station. Water from the reservoir flows down into the plant and spins turbines that power the generators, converting mechanical energy into electrical energy. Essentially a modern take on the water wheel invented by the ancient Greeks between the third and first century BC.

Cal peered out the backseat window to get a bearing on his

surroundings. The area was deserted this time of night. Now the hairs on the back of his neck were standing up. Something was *definitely* wrong. *Jesus Christ, I should have listened to Mac. Like, what the fuck have I gotten into?*

"Mr. Quill, like, why are we here? Mr. Quill? *Sergeant Quill,* I'm speaking to you. Like, what's going on?"

Quill exited the car, opened Cal's door, and barked, "*Out.*"

Cal was shocked to see Quill's service revolver pointed directly at him. The persona of helpful cop had completely evaporated. As Cal exited the patrol car, he was nauseous with fear. Quill shoved him from behind with the gun, almost knocking him down with each push, until Cal was standing inches from the edge of the precipice at the top of the power plant, looking down at the Niagara River 390 feet below. There could be no doubt as to how a fall from this height would end. *No witnesses. If a Cal falls in the forest and no one sees it...* It was pointless to start screaming.

"Sergeant Quill, I have your name and your badge number. Whatever you're doing, you're, like, going to be in big trouble."

"Yeah, whatever."

With his last molecule of fortitude, Cal made a Herculean effort to keep his shaky voice calm and stern. "You know, Sergeant Quill, Mac has, like, closed-circuit cameras in front of his house. You do anything to me and, like, they'll catch you for sure." For all he knew, maybe it was true.

Quill didn't look impressed. "Nice try, punk. You know, I *do* know Mac. And Mac *does* have a camera in front of the house." Cal's hopes rose. "I've been to Mac's home, and I *also* know Mac only uses the camera for real-time viewing, to see who's ringing his doorbell. It's not hooked up to any recording device."

Cal's hopes went from elation to deflation in a nanosecond. He was far too frightened to come up with another bluff. His panic level reached new heights as Quill described his options with dark sarcasm.

"Don't worry, punk. You get to decide how it goes. Here's your choice. I can shove you over the edge right here. Or you can go swimming in the reservoir over there." Quill pointed to the hill across the road from the plant.

Unable to stop his trembling, Cal shakily nodded toward the road. He understood that his fate wouldn't change either way, but at least he'd get a few more moments.

"Excellent choice," Quill said. "If I push you off the edge here, they'd find the body. Just a bunch of unidentifiable mush, but they might find a couple of your teeth. Somewhere. Lot cleaner to go with the reservoir. Tomorrow morning when the gates open, the water empties into the plant turbines. Two hundred thousand horsepower each. That should be enough to chop you into fish food. That's the great thing about hydroelectric power. Great for the environment. *Water in, water out*. It's a popular saying these days."

***

Quill shoved Cal forward, across the deserted road and up the hill to the edge of the reservoir. The plunge to the water here was small compared to the height at the plant, more like jumping into a swimming pool, but Cal remained terror-stricken. Quill undoubtedly had more in mind than an evening swim. Cal turned around to see Quill putting on a pair of latex gloves. Then he bent down, pulled up the cuff on his left pant leg, and retrieved a handgun from an ankle holster. He pointed it directly at Cal's chest.

"Aw, c'mon, you didn't think I was just gonna' let you take a few laps, did you? They call this a *throwaway gun*. From a dusty old evidence locker for a cold case file. No one'll miss it. No serial number. Untraceable. Comes in handy. Plant it on a dead suspect to justify a shooting. Create probable cause for a drug bust. Or get rid of pains in the ass like you."

Cal thought about jumping in before Quill could execute him, but he figured Quill would just shoot him while he tried to swim away. Better to be shot here than to be shot *and* drowned as a bonus. He closed his eyes and waited for the blast.

Bam!

He heard the report echo through the still night. Yet he didn't feel anything. *Was he already dead?* He started to move his hands over his body, searching for a wound. Then he opened his eyes to see Quill lying face down on the ground, blood and brain matter pouring from his head. A dot of white light danced on his back. About thirty feet behind Quill, someone was approaching fast, a gun with a laser sight in his gloved hands. As the gunman ran up to Quill's body, Cal realized it was *Mac*. Before he said a word, Mac put an ungloved finger on Quill's neck. Having satisfied himself of his kill shot, he threw his handgun into the reservoir and turned to Cal. "Throwaway gun."

Mac had been waiting in a clump of bushes next to the reservoir. He hadn't bothered to cover them down by the plant, because rumor had it that Kurtoff buried all his bodies in the reservoir.

"But, but how, like, how did—"

Mac plucked the eyeglasses from Cal's face then pulled apart one of the stems to reveal a tiny transmitter. "You move, it moves, I move. But what the fuck were you thinking? Was I not speaking English? Did you understand the—"

"I'm sorry. I swear, I..." Cal was so shaken he couldn't finish.

"You're an idiot, kid. Let's get the hell out of here." Mac dragged Quill's lifeless body to the edge of the reservoir and threw it in. "Fish food."

Cal took a last glance at the remnants of Quill's brain on the grass, where birds would pick at it in the morning.

Then he threw up.

Then he fainted.

Chapter 47

THE MUSIC BOX
Normal Avenue, Buffalo, New York
Saturday, October 7, 2023
4:00 a.m.

Mac brought Cal to his one remaining safe house. He'd sold the one in Lackawanna, since he'd hoped to retire soon. This one would do fine. Nondescript, multiple exit routes. And right across the street from Kleinhans Music Hall, where the Buffalo Philharmonic Orchestra played. Mac called it *The Music Box*.

Kleinhans was a majestic building, inside and out. It had a breathtakingly grand concert hall, reputed to be among the most acoustically perfect anywhere. Since its opening in 1940, all the greats had played there: Serge Koussevitzsky, Jessye Norman, Artur Rubenstein, Itzhak Perlman, Midori, Horowitz, the list went on and on. Mac thought the quality of the orchestra, particularly the brass, had gone up a notch or two when the current conductor had arrived on the scene. She was the orchestra's first female conductor, the first female conductor of any major American music ensemble. But she was no token. She was a phenomenal Music Director. And a heck of a guitar player, too.

Most of his acquaintances would be amazed that Mac could discern the quality of a symphony orchestra or its conductor. From what they knew, he was partial only to country music and rock. Which was true, initially. His love of rock and roll was firmly planted in the '60s and '70s, particularly the *big three* as he'd called them: the Beatles, The Stones, and The Who. And one obscure progressive psychedelic band called Hawkwind, which he agreed to listen to so he could get in that freshman college girl's pants, finding that he actually liked them. He still listened to Hawkwind to this day, though he'd forgotten the girl long ago.

Growing up, Mac hadn't been one for classical music. None of his foster homes played any, and he was barely aware of it before he got this safe house. But after all the years across the street from Kleinhans, he could identify and enjoy plenty of classical pieces, thanks to the ticket booth operators he'd endeared himself to, who always managed to find empty seats for him, gratis.

***

Mac had practically carried a completely exhausted and still traumatized Cal into the house. Cal collapsed on the couch the moment they got inside, and then fell into a deep sleep. Watching Cal lying there, eyes shut tight, snoring heavily, Mac thought, *the kid is kinda' growing on me. I oughta beat the shit out of him for violating protocol, but hell, he's been through a lot tonight.*

At about 4:00 a.m., Mac called Adam. He tried to discourage him from coming over, insisted that everything was under control, though he knew before he placed the call that it would be a lost cause trying to keep Adam away.

When Adam arrived, they sat at the Music Box's *dining room table,* two snack trays pushed together. "Okay, Mac. Let's think about this logically. Kurtoff had Cal's name, but not his location. Who knew where Cal was staying? You, me, Kelly. Right?"

"Don't forget Cal himself, Chief. That makes four of us. Course I checked him out first. No calls in or out of my place, except the one from Quill. Nothing on his phone, never turned it on. *Your* house is clean, too. Not even a mosquito."

"When did you sweep it? I've been there all night."

"Yeah, I can be a creepy crawler when I want to. Thought I'd check it out before I called you."

"Mac, why weren't you in your house with Cal when Quill called? What were you doing?"

Mac shuddered. "Nothin', Chief. Just personal." He didn't want to throw a monkey wrench into Adam's case, not when it seemed airtight. He still hadn't figured out how he was going to break the news to Adam about the Y-tube and its DNA results, so he returned to the main subject at hand. "Assuming Cal didn't want to kill himself, that leaves me, you...and Kelly."

"For every complex problem—"

"Yeah, I know. But what's the wrong solution here, Chief? We know it's not you or me. And I've ruled out Cal. That leaves Kelly. Four minus three is one."

"Come on, you can't think—"

"Is that your brain talkin', or another part of your anatomy?"

"C'mon, Mac, I can't—"

"If there's one thing I know, it's that I don't know nothin'. I'll check her out, Chief. Until then, I wouldn't share any intel about Cal with her."

Adam sighed. "Whoever it was, when Mitachi hears about this, she'll declare a mistrial whether we want it or not."

"Yeah...about that, Chief." Mac was almost as hesitant to raise the next issue as he was to disclose the Y-tube. First, he handed Adam a dollar bill.

"What's this for?" Adam asked.

"I'm hiring you to represent me. In the Quill matter. So everything I tell you is attorney-client confidential, right?"

"Okay. What *are* you telling me? Did it go down differently?"

"No, Chief. I mean, counselor. You can ask Cal when he wakes up. 'Zactly what I told you. Justifiable homicide, no question. I just don't feel like spending my retirement testifying at inquests and wasting time in interrogations. Or fucking up your case and making you start over again after a mistrial. Quill was a scumbag. Nobody'll miss him. One less dirty cop. So can we leave this one under the rug? I'm sure Mitachi already has Kurtoff made for the juror head switch. I don't think she can get any *more* pissed at him."

"Well, Mac, I don't think you've committed a crime. Maybe the unauthorized weapon, but otherwise, you're okay. I don't hear you telling me you're contemplating a future crime, so I'm not ethically required to report anything. Against my better judgment, I'll let it go for now. But one more attempt on Cal, and I'm reporting it to Mitachi regardless of the circumstances. You got it?"

"Affirmative Chief. I mean, counselor. Oh, by the way, Chief, it's Saturday morning now. Time and a half."

Adam handed the dollar back to Mac.

Chapter 48

THE VERTEX BUILDING
Alex Kurtoff's Office
Ensign Street, South Buffalo, New York
Monday, October 9, 2023
8:00 a.m.

Alex Kurtoff peered across his desk at Damytro Gura and Dr. Thomas Kramer, Vertex's Director of Engineering. He'd called them in on Columbus Day, when there'd be no one else around. Almost no one.

"About time I get around to you *mudaks*, is not? I thought this meeting no be needed. Until become clear you fucked up somehow. *A Senator's granddaughter.* This is like killing a fucking cop, is not? Worse. Car supposed to have fire. *Not blow up.* Supposed to scare people from buying car, *not kill them.* Where are your fucking brains? Which of you I thank for this?"

Gura's response was barely audible. "Boss, I thought you said killing Senator granddaughter make it more better, more publicity, make people super afraid of Hydro."

"*Idiot.* You try to tell me what I think? That was before they figure out explosion caused by you. By us. Is not?"

"I'm sorry, Boss."

"You *sorry*? Damytro, did I tell you to follow Senator's car?"

"Yes, Boss."

"Did I tell you to rig car so it start on fire?"

"Yes, Boss."

"Did I tell you to make car blow up and kill little girl?"

"No, Boss."

"Then why you fucking do that?"

"Boss, I do exact what Thomas say. Swear. I add cable just like he show me, like on diagram, perfect. *His* diagram. *His* plan. *His* fault."

"Mr. K," Kramer responded instantly, "I wasn't there to see Damytro's work on the Talbot car, so who knows if he followed proper procedure. I very much doubt it. The procedure *was* proper, I assure you. If he'd inserted the cable the way he was told, it couldn't have caused the car to explode like that."

The blame game continued. "I swear it, Boss," Gura insisted. "I do only what he show me. I am not engineer." He pointed at Kramer. "Was *your* plan. *You* design."

"Mr. K, the design was perfect." Turning to Gura, Kramer spouted, "What do you know of engineering, physics, that you question me? You're a *peasant*."

"That my point, Boss. I *not* engineer. I only—"

"*Enough.* I take it from fact you two idiots are alive, was no explosion when you test this in lab, is not? Though now I wish maybe there *was*."

Kramer jumped on Kurtoff's point. "That's exactly it, Mr. K. There was no explosion in the lab when the cable was inserted just as I designed it. I did some calculations. Even if this fool mixed up his connections, I don't see how the cable could have possibly caused that explosion. It had to be something else. *Had* to be."

Gura chimed in. "You hear him, Boss. He engineer. He know. Like he said. *Had to be* something else, not cable. Even if I screw up, *and I not*, explosion not possible, you hear him. Listen to Thomas. And Boss, little girl not there when I fixed it. If little girl there, I call you first."

"Damytro. This very important. Could say your future depend on it. So pay attention, is not? When you call me after explosion, where are you?"

"Ship at Navy Museum at waterfront. No one else there. Closing time. Was empty, I check."

"You sure? You bet life on it?"

Gura replayed the phone call in his mind before he answered. "No one there, Boss. No one."

"Then why plaintiff claim this Dryer overhear our conversation?"

"Don't know, Boss. But was no one there. I swear. I use standard scrambling for phone call." Gura hesitated to think, then: "Could be at your end, Boss? Someone in your house?"

"Don't you think that was first thought, you idiot? Only one person at home, housekeeper Nadia, is not? I talk to her, she know nothing. I ask three times. Fourth time, no more Nadia. But, you know, I think maybe she telling the truth. So back to you, Damytro." Kurtoff clicked a mouse and turned his laptop around to show Gura a picture of Cal Dryer. "You ever see this guy? *Ever*?"

"No. Never see him."

"You look close, Damytro. I want you be absolutely sure. No mistake. I not tolerate mistakes, is not?"

"No, boss. Never see him."

"When you call from ship, he not there?"

"No, boss, I swear it. Was alone. Never see him in my life."

"Well, you going to, is not? New number one assignment. Find him before he testify. You not, I put Petro on him. And on you."

Then a strange calm came over Kurtoff. His facial features softened. His instant mood swings were legend among the Ukrainian mob, and now among his Vertex employees. He took a silver dollar from his pocket and started flipping it in his hand. Gura and Kramer's heads nodded up and down as they followed the arc of the coin—up, down, up, down, up, down—and then exchanged worried looks. The boss's calmness was scarier than his anger, because it rarely lasted for long.

"Listen. I not such a bad guy, is not? You tell me. Go ahead. What you think? You be honest with me. Is okay. Thomas? Damytro? Maybe I too hard on you, you know?"

Neither took the bait. It could be dangerous being too honest with Kurtoff.

"They say win more friends with wine than vinegar. I give you, they call it *positive reinforcement*, is not? Damytro. Thomas. Smile. I give you present. See. I flip coin in air and one of you call it. You correct, I give you brand new Hydro. Silver. Beautiful. You call flip wrong...you get the coin. By the way, is rare coin from 1794, early America, worth about million dollars. Maybe George Washington, Bob Franklin, Tim Jefferson also hold in their hand. So you win either way. Maybe better to lose coin flip, is not? Go ahead Damytro. *You* call it."

Gura and Kramer eyed each other warily. Kurtoff had many attributes, but generosity wasn't one of them. Oh, he had his local charity work to keep up the image of a respected businessman and upstanding citizen, all of which was paid with company funds. For his employees, no image was necessary. Behind closed doors at Vertex, his bare-knuckled personality was on full display. No façade, no pretense.

Gura called heads. Kurtoff flipped the coin and it fell on the floor, tails up. "See, you both winners like I say. Damytro, you get coin. Thomas get car. Follow me for Thomas prize."

***

Kurtoff walked the two nervous employees through the executive suites and down to the factory floor. After taking a freight elevator to the sub-basement, Kurtoff ushered them into the STF, the *Special Testing Facility*, a 5,000 square-foot room with concrete walls three feet thick and blast-proof doors. Four grim-faced men wearing Vertex Security jackets awaited them. The *palace guard*. Each had a shoulder-holstered weapon.

A brand-new silver Hydro sat on a lift in the middle of the room, about two feet above a *rolling road* treadmill. A security man walked over to Gura and handed him a large toolbox and relieved Gura of the gun in *his* shoulder holster. Pointing to the car, Kurtoff exclaimed, "There, Thomas. Your new car. You like? See, I keep my word. Is silver, like I say." Then, just like that, Kurtoff's demeanor did another 180. "Okay, idiot, fucking moron." He pointed at Gura. "You do here same what you do to Talbot car. Thomas, you watch. Any mistake, you tell me."

Gura paused, trying to remember every little detail of the job he'd performed over three months ago. He knew he needed to replicate his actions perfectly. Otherwise, Kurtoff would be *disappointed*. Gura's memory was not great under normal conditions, and with the added pressure of Kurtoff's demanding eyes, his hands started to tremble.

With Kurtoff and Kramer watching his every move, Gura gingerly placed the toolbox on the floor next to the driver's door, just as he'd done in Jennifer Talbot's garage. He opened it to find the exact type of cable he'd used on her car, along with the tools needed for the job. Before touching anything else, he put on two pairs of surgical gloves, thick enough to avoid fingerprints, thin enough to do fine work.

Fortunately for Gura, the toolbox also contained the same

small diagram of the car's underbelly that had guided him on the actual job. Lying on his back, he slid under the driver's side to access the engine. At least, it was called an engine, though it wasn't like any engine he'd ever seen.

The flooring posed its own problem. Jennifer Talbot's garage had a concrete floor, whereas this Hydro hovered above a steel-belt treadmill. Its relative slipperiness might impede his ability to do the fine work necessary for this job. But he didn't complain. The Boss didn't like excuses. Even good ones.

Once under the car, Gura used the diagram to find the superconductor ring. Whatever the hell that was. He didn't care. It was on the diagram, and that's all that mattered. Carefully, slowly, he removed its cover plate using a reversible ratchet wrench with a proprietary New Millennium socket that fit the proprietary bolts. Then he quietly set the cover plate about three feet away so he wouldn't create any clatter by bumping into it during the rest of the job.

Gura performed a similar procedure on the right rear motor.

Kurtoff hollered, "*Damytro!* You going too slow. Thomas, is not?"

Kramer nodded.

Kurtoff continued yelling. "You go equal speed you did on Talbot car. Want same conditions, is not? You hear?"

Gura nodded. Kurtoff and Kramer were correct. He picked up the pace, sweat starting to pour down his brow. With the cover plates gone, Gura removed the special cable from the toolbox.

Kramer had been watching Gura intensely, changing positions several times to ensure he didn't miss a thing. Gura was sure Kramer wanted him to screw up so Kurtoff would blame the explosion on him. He wasn't sure what Kurtoff was hoping for. A proper re-creation that didn't blow up the car, to give Kurtoff plausible deniability at trial? Or a screwup to hang on Gura's neck if necessary? Gura didn't spend much time pondering this, though. He had to concentrate.

The nervous saboteur took a small cordless soldering pen from the toolbox and proceeded to solder one end of the cable to the superconductor ring, the other to the right rear motor. Then he replaced the covers for the ring and the motor, slowly turning the bolts with the ratchet wrench, careful not to drop a bolt or washer on the floor. If he did, the sound on the metal treadmill would have made a much louder clang than the concrete floor of Jennifer's garage, but Gura didn't want to have to explain that to Kurtoff. Finally, he scoured the floor with a mini flashlight for any evidence of his work. It was clean. No crumbs.

The job had taken thirty-five minutes. For the Talbot car, he had done it in fifteen. He'd also had a nip of *horilka* from his glove compartment before following Jennifer's Hydro to her house. No need to recreate that.

Kurtoff turned to Kramer. "Well?"

"You saw him, he was slow at the beginning. Otherwise, I'd have to say he followed the procedure. But how do we know this is exactly what he did on June 30?"

"I guess we just have to trust, is not? Okay. Now we see if design was problem."

Kurtoff signaled to one of his guards, who lowered the lift until the car's wheels touched the treadmill. "Now you go for spin in Thomas new car."

Gura and Kramer were escorted to the car at gunpoint. Kramer in the driver's seat, as befitted its new owner, and Gura in the front passenger seat. The guards pulled zip ties from their pockets and simultaneously secured Kramer's left hand to the steering wheel and his right hand to Gura's left. Kramer's eyes darted around the car interior. Gura's bulged in their sockets.

That was when Kramer realized that the car had no brake pedal or accelerator. The START/STOP ENGINE button on the dashboard was also missing. Kramer tried to open the window. It didn't move.

As if reading Kramer's mind, Kurtoff said, "Don't worry. We operate by remote control, is not?" He was holding what looked like a fancy TV remote. "Have a nice drive. I be back in three hours, see if you still here. Thomas, enjoy your new car." With that, he turned on the engine, and the wheels started spinning.

Chapter 49

NEW YORK STATE ATTORNEY GENERAL'S OFFICE
The Capitol
Albany, New York
Wednesday, October 11, 2023

Mac ambled up to the counter, wondering if he could break through the ice-cold visage of the clerk standing guard there, the AG's first line of defense against annoying visitors. *Like me.*

"Hey, pal, if forks were made of gold, would they still be silverware?"

The clerk's sour expression made it clear he was having none of it.

Even more severe than the gal from Child and Family. Better play it straight. I'll try the name on his shirt. "Hey, Phillip, or is it Phil? I need to see the Attorney General. It's urgent."

"You and everyone else. I'll see if any of the assistant AGs are available. May I have your name and the nature of your visit?"

"Call me Mac. And I need to see the boss lady. Can't deal with any second lieutenants."

"Sir, the Attorney General is a busy woman. If you want to see *her*, you'll need to make an appointment. We're running about three weeks out now. Here's a form. I suggest you take it home and pester someone there."

Only Mac could have sensed an opening in that response. He had the guy's attention, even as a nuisance, distinct from the nameless horde that passed through the office day after day. Mac pulled an envelope from a jacket pocket and offered it to the clerk, making those pleading-doe eyes that only an old knuckle dragger like himself could muster. "Please, Phil, just give her this. I think she'll see me. If she doesn't, you can kick my ancient ass outta here, stat."

Alan M. Wishnoff

Slowly, hesitantly, Phil reached for the envelope.

It was to Mac's credit that he could maintain a pleasant demeanor under any circumstances. A lot of ugly memories rattled around in his old skull. He'd seen every type of death and destruction imaginable, first in the regular Army, and later in Special Forces. Images of severed limbs, headless bodies, and blood-drenched uniforms littered his mind. He'd gone through fifty uniforms himself, many with his own blood, most with his buddies' or the enemy's, whoever that happened to be at the moment. The worst were the civilians. Helpless, innocent, caught up in a world of fire and iron they neither wanted nor understood. The soldiers knew what they'd signed up for. The civvies didn't ask for any of this, especially the women and the kids. Mac had killed just about everything that moved, but a two-month-old? Why the hell would someone do that? What threat could an infant possibly present? Mac had no mercy for any soldier he found to have harmed a child, no matter whose army the soldier was in.

Such memories left countless veterans bitter and hurting. And tuned out. For Mac it had the opposite effect, enhancing his appreciation of life once his Army days were in the rearview mirror. That and, if he were honest with himself, his coping mechanisms had helped, too. Drinking, constant joking, and flirting.

While Mac had slightly softened up the clerk, not so the state trooper who'd been following their interaction. His job was to protect the AG, and this big oaf, old as he was, looked like trouble. The trooper got up from his desk and approached Mac, eyeing him warily. "Is there a problem here?"

"No, everything's copacetic, Pat," the clerk said. "This charmer here thinks he can get in to see Her Majesty without an appointment. I'll humor him."

The trooper shook his head and nodded to the clerk. "Better you than me."

The clerk slow-marched to the back of the office, envelope in hand and, after a timid knock, entered a door labeled *AG*. About twenty seconds later, he exited, no longer holding the envelope, a bewildered look on his face. He walked back to Mac with new admiration, almost whispering. "The, uh, the Attorney General will see you now."

The clerk ushered Mac across the room and into the AG's

office, lingering a bit outside the door. The rest of the office strained to hear what transpired in the inner sanctum, as well.

The trooper nodded to the clerk when he returned to his station. "Whatever he has on her, I wish he'd share it with me. I could use a raise."

Chapter 50

ADAM'S LAW OFFICE
Parkside Avenue, Buffalo, New York
Wednesday, October 11, 2023

Adam sat at his desk, rubbing his eyes, trying to sort out the various conundrums confronting him. He'd never had this many in one case. The identity of Allison's father, the cause of the explosion, his relationship with Katherine, the murder attempt on Cal, Mac's killing of the state trooper, the altered *Kelly* head. He needed to clear his own head, because he'd just gotten a call from Mitachi's clerk advising that the trial would resume on Friday. AG forensics had come up empty on the switched juror head.

Adam's reverie was interrupted by a knock on the door. Assuming it was Mac or Freddie, he said, "Come in," without getting up from the desk. Instead, Jennifer Talbot strode into the room, chewing her gum furiously. *She looks like a woman on a mission.* Once again Adam longed for his civil rights cases. They never had so many loose ends or such emotional drama.

He stood and ushered his client to a chair. As she sat down, her short skirt revealed enough of her thigh to see a tattoo he hadn't noticed before. A miniature White House, about two inches wide, on top of which was a baby pissing down on the roof. *I guess that says it all.* He returned to his desk, trying not to show any reaction to the tattoo. "Jennifer, I didn't know you were coming in."

"There's something I want to tell you. But, like, can we keep this just between me and you?"

"Absolutely. Anything you say to me is subject to attorney-client privilege."

"But. But does that mean you, like, won't share it with my family? My father?"

"Technically, *you're* my only client here. Well, not just technically. *Actually.* It's your daughter who was...you're the plaintiff, not your parents. Our conversations won't be shared with them or anyone else. Not unless you authorize it. So, tell me, Jennifer, *are* you able to name Allie's father? Is that what's troubling you?"

"No, Mr. Simons. I told the truth. I don't know the father. But I..."

"Yes?"

"I-I think I *do* know who killed Allie."

That got Adam's attention. He wondered what she meant. *Don't we all know that already? She's met with Cal. She knows what he told us. Kurtoff. Vertex. We've nailed them. Haven't we?*

"Jennifer, I'm not clear why—"

"Someone who hated her."

Adam tried to make sense of this. "Who could hate a two-month-old child? Jennifer, are you saying someone at Vertex knew of Allison and wanted to harm her?"

"Not Vertex."

"Don't you think Vertex did this? The evidence is incredibly strong. From what Mr. Dryer tells us, we basically have the perpetrator admitting the crime. And we have the cable that they used. We don't often get evidence that good. I know how all this must be affecting—"

"I didn't know whether to tell you or not. I know I'm, like, the girl who cried wolf. First New Millennium, then Vertex, now...*him*. I can't prove it. Not with the kind of evidence you'd want. But I think... No, I *know*—"

"Who is he, Jennifer?" Adam asked softly.

"Mr. Simons. It's, like...even if you won't believe me, and I know you won't, but it's the truth. Like, fuck... Sorry. I hate seeing that smug face every day and I just want to...*I hate* him."

Adam tried, and failed, to come up with something comforting to say.

"It's...it's your friend."

"What's my friend?

"Your friend. My *father*."

"Bill? Your father Bill? Are you saying *he* killed your baby? His own granddaughter?" It took a lot to shock Adam, but he was stunned by Jennifer's accusation. "But why—"

"You don't know him, Mr. Simons. Not really. Not anymore.

He's not the same. All he cares about is his stupid Senate seat and winning the stupid Oval Office. He'd, like, destroy anything or *anyone* that got in his way. Allie was in his way. He hated her since the day she was born. No, I take that back, since before she was born. And he's, like, mean to my mom, too. You have no idea how mean."

Adam could easily believe Bill was abusive to Katherine, based on the interactions he'd observed recently. But *Allison*? That seemed a mighty stretch. And why? For what purpose? How could a two-month-old get in Bill's way? *Perhaps Jennifer has an emotional disorder? Off her meds*? Maybe he *would* have to talk to Katherine or Bill, not to disclose Jennifer's accusation—he'd live up to his oath—but to inquire whether they were aware of a mental disorder or drug problem. He also wondered about his rape theory, but he couldn't bring himself to broach that subject with Jennifer. For now, he'd try to piece together whatever conspiracy theory she'd come up with.

"Jennifer, why would Bill hate his granddaughter? How could he *murder* her? I can't make sense of this, given everything else we know."

"If too many questions were asked, Mr. Simons, it might ruin his precious career. He'd do anything to get in the White House. Like, *anything*."

This close, Jennifer's resemblance to her mother was even more striking. Once again, Adam could swear he was comforting young Katherine back in her apartment at Yale. In fact, Jennifer seemed to be all Katherine. Not a speck of Bill in her. Just as Katherine had said.

"Jennifer, do you think it's possible your judgment is a little cloudy, after what you've been through? That would be totally understandable. You've experienced a major trauma. I just don't see Allison being that great an impediment to Bill's career. The situation's a step removed from him, and it's not like out-of-wedlock children carry that much stigma these days."

"It's not a *situation*, Mr. Simons. It's a *murder*...I'm sorry. You've been nice to me. I didn't mean to, like—"

"Don't worry, Jennifer. They say the only thing thicker than alligator skin is litigator skin. Just... I'm not saying this because he's my friend. You're my client, and my primary...no, my *only* allegiance is to you. But Jennifer, I'll be honest, it's hard to fathom, with the evidence we have against Vertex. They put that cable in the car. Are you saying Bill was working with Mr. Kurtoff? I'm trying to understand."

"I don't know how it worked. Anything's possible with him. Maybe one of his political stooges did it and he, like, paid Cal to tell us the story about Vertex. My father could arrange something like that. Maybe he paid Kurtoff to do it. I don't know."

"That's an awful lot of speculation."

"Mr. Simons. *He's* the one who gave me the car. The car that blew up. *He* gave it to me. Said I deserved it."

Adam knew that if he accepted this story just one percent, he'd have to withdraw from the case. "Jennifer. I'm taking your claim seriously, believe me. But until we have evidence of what you're telling me, I think your case is best pursued against Vertex. And Kurtoff. All the evidence points in that direction. That's the best legal advice I can give you. I'm not trying to protect Bill. I'm trying to protect *you*. You understand, I'd need to see *some* hard evidence before I could pursue your theory."

"The evidence is he's a rotten *bastard*. Who'd do anything to be President."

"Jennifer...is there anything else you'd like to tell me? Anything important you haven't told me already?"

"I *don't* know who the father is. Period. Sorry, Mr. Simons. But I *don't*."

***

The moment she closed Adam's office door behind her, Jennifer spit her gum under a chair in the hallway and started vaping. *Who cares what the office rules are? They ought to be feeding me heroin or something, with all the shit they've piled on me.* Her thoughts meandered, as they often did, to the explosion of the car, and then back one more day to the fanfare that accompanied her receipt of it.

June 29 had been a wonderfully sunny day, not a cloud in the sky. What better way to publicize the rollout of the Hydro than give the first one to a United States Senator? New Millennium chose Senator William Talbot, who'd been instrumental in getting the company government grants for the environmentally conscious project. Jennifer had reluctantly accompanied her father to the ceremony. Her mother had volunteered to stay home with Allie, as she often did. Jennifer didn't think that Allie, only two months old, would have made it through the pomp and circumstance without a major cry. Or poop. Or both.

Her father was ecstatic. Why wouldn't he be? An adoring crowd, an opportunity to give a self-congratulatory stump speech. *It doesn't get any better than that. For him. He's living big. Meanwhile, I'm saddled with a two-month-old. Social life, dead. Grad school, dead. Career, dead. Why did I listen to my parents? I needed this kid like a case of leprosy. No, worse. Leprosy can be cured. There must be some way out of this. Has to be.*

The press conference went off without a hitch. The reporters were fascinated by the description, given by Dr. Ditenzo, of the Hydro's technological advances. Then came the pageantry. The CEO, Dr. Joan Perry, handed Jennifer's father a symbolic two-foot-long key with HYDRO NUMBER ONE printed on it. He then gave his prepared speech, congratulating the company on its formidable achievement and touting that the Hydro was designed and built by American workers in an American factory. He managed to squeeze in that, if elected President, he'd follow an *America First* agenda to encourage more such success stories. *You'd think he invented the damn car himself. He's never too shy to take credit for other people's accomplishments.*

Bill concluded with another pitch for his candidacy, mentioning that since he assumed he'd be getting government transportation in Washington D.C. for the next eight years, for now the car would go to his lovely daughter. Dr. Perry then gave Jennifer the remote, and off she drove, as planned, with a hundred cameras recording the Hydro's inaugural drive. *Off to the two-month-old anvil around my neck. Great. Why don't one of you assholes come home with me to take the next diaper change?*

***

Across town, Alex Kurtoff smiled as he watched the press conference on the television. New Millennium had made it so easy for him, identifying a target like that. *A United States Senator.*

Kurtoff couldn't pay for publicity like this. He called Gura to set the plan in motion.

Three hundred feet above Niagara Square, someone else was watching the press conference on a laptop and planning an attack on Jennifer's car. He loved it here on Buffalo City Hall's observation deck. It was no problem picking the lock after tourist hours were over, so he could ruminate in peace. The observation deck was his go-to place whenever he was sad, mad, or just needed a quiet location without prying eyes.

City Hall was a titanic thirty-two-story art deco building finished in 1931 for the then-princely sum of six and a half million dollars. It remained, to this day, one of the largest city halls in the country. Its observation deck provided a magnificent 360-degree view of the city. On a clear day, one could see the mist from Niagara Falls, sixteen miles away.

The stars aligned for him several weeks ago when the company had announced the Hydro rollout, and the Senator announced he'd be giving Hydro Number One to his daughter. That gave him more than enough time to prepare. He'd been searching for a way to destroy his prey. New Millennium and the Senator had made it easy. Fish in a barrel. He'd have to write them thank-you notes. Tomorrow his troubles would be over. One of them anyway.

***

Jennifer had left Adam's office, but her bizarre accusation lingered in the air. Try as he might, Adam couldn't give it any credence. *Bill can be an asshole, no question, but how could he—*

It seemed ludicrous on its face. The case against Vertex was solid. Hell, they had the goon on the ship confessing to the damn crime. A foot away from Cal. It was almost certain he was talking to Kurtoff. Nothing was said about Bill in that conversation. They even had the *weapon*, the extraneous electrical cable placed there on Kurtoff's orders. Saperston had no alternative theory other than the non-existent Y-tube. Nor did Mac, or the police, or New Millennium, or Vertex. Or anyone else. No one so much as mentioned Bill as a suspect or even a person of interest.

But Jennifer believes it. Underneath that mollusk shell, there's an innocence, a softness. The hatred of her father seems real. But murder? I guess anyone losing a child that way, or any way, could suffer PTSD. Jump on a wild conspiracy theory to find some meaning, an explanation. And if my theory is correct, that she'd been raped, that's just piling trauma upon trauma.

Adam knew, just from watching CNN, how much Bill had changed. Nineteen years in politics would do that to anyone. It had toughened him up, made him exceedingly cynical, and given him lofty ambitions. The loftiest. *But this? Even to gain the most powerful position in the world?*

Bill was a master at cold political calculation. It had taken him just steps from the Oval Office. What could possibly have called for the murder of his granddaughter? Taking a risk like that, because his daughter had a child out of wedlock? Is that how a savvy operator like Bill would handle this situation? If such a thing got out, and most everything in Washington leaks eventually, that's the end of his career. And the beginning of a jail sentence.

Regardless, Adam was still convinced that he didn't know the whole story of the explosion and Allison's death. This was a first for him, feeling shut out from his own case. He couldn't put his finger on it, but the pieces didn't fit together. Not just the identity of the child's father. He sensed it went beyond that. Maybe way beyond. One or more of the Talbots was holding out on him.

For every complex problem... All right, enough. The Talbots are going to have a come-to-Jesus meeting, and I'll be playing Jesus.

Chapter 51

SUNY AT BUFFALO LAW SCHOOL
ROOM 304
Amherst, New York
Thursday, October 12, 2023
3:34 p.m.

A s the last student left the classroom, Bill Talbot strode in. Adam thought, *What now?* Bill had remained fairly emotionless thus far, but today there was a look of concern on his face. "Adam. You have a minute?"

It was more an order than a request. *As if I'd refuse after Bill made the trek over to the law school to speak with me.* Bill was used to commanding office staff and jittery interns who thought they were going to learn something about politics and government, though they mostly ended up going for donuts and coffee. And to pick up Bill's laundry.

"What's on your mind, Bill?"

"Adam, this is hard to say. Jenny…well, you can imagine what she's been going through. A loss like this. She told me what she said to you. She knows it was wrong. She's apologized. I understand. I told her that."

"Why isn't Jenny here telling me herself?"

"She's embarrassed."

Adam searched Bill's face for a clue. *Is this the face of a murderer? Is he being straight with me? Not much of a test for a politician like Bill. I doubt he's totally honest with anyone about anything these days.*

"Bill, all the evidence points to Vertex. Why would she claim—"

"People say crazy things when they're upset. That's all it is. She's been off balance for a while now, even before the explosion. You know, Jenny was an aspiring artist. She was really starting to attract attention."

Adam wondered whether this was legit.

"Anyway, when the little one was born, I guess her maternal instinct kicked in. She put the art aside and devoted herself to being a full-time mother. She hasn't been able to pick up the brushes since the...she's just a lost soul."

This explanation sounded more than a little too cute. Adam probed a bit. "Bill, can I get a straight answer from you?"

"You don't honestly think I...that I'd do anything to harm my own granddaughter, do you?"

"No. Not really. It's not that. *Does* Jenny know the identity of the father?"

"No, Adam. She doesn't. And before you ask, neither do I."

"What's going on?"

"What do you mean?"

"Come on, Bill. What aren't you telling me? Listen. I want to speak with the whole family. Together. In one room. Tomorrow, 7:00 p.m., my office. There'll be coffee. Have one of your interns bring the donuts."

***

Watching Bill saunter out of the classroom, Adam came upon an idea so disgusting, so vile, he struggled to wipe it from his mind immediately. The inevitable effect of such a mental exercise was to think of nothing else. It was like telling someone, for the next fifteen seconds, don't think of a purple giraffe. Adam wished his new thought was as benign as a purple giraffe.

What if Jennifer was raped, but not by a stranger? What if it was a close relative, one with the loftiest of political ambitions? Who'd grown tired of his difficult trophy wife? And had a tremendous thirst for power over others?

Adam tried to assure himself that it wasn't remotely possible. That as much of an asshole as his friend could be, he wasn't capable of such an obscenity. But he had to admit that his idea presented something of a unified theory. Katherine and Jennifer's seething anger toward Bill. Their refusal to identify the child's father. Jennifer's inability to talk about the father without descending into hysteria. Her accusation against Bill. Maybe even Katherine's

~226~

bafflingly abrupt termination of her affair with Adam—perhaps it was all too much for her to handle, too many emotions swirling around from dealing with a deranged abusive husband and a distraught daughter dealing with the unthinkable? *Did Bill get Kurtoff to do the deed for him? For a political payoff? Maybe a huge grant like the one he'd secured for New Millennium? Politics and greed make strange bedfellows.*

Adam hadn't believed that Bill's political calculus would call for murdering his granddaughter *just* because she was born out of wedlock. However, if Bill had raped Jennifer, if he needed to suppress such a nightmare story from getting out, would that make a difference? Why not just let Jennifer get an abortion? Wouldn't that make a lot more sense than allowing the child to be born and then killing her? On the other hand, Bill does have a strong pro-life platform. Abortion *or* murder could destroy his political career. Still, if those were the only two options, why choose the one that could send him to jail for life? And if Jennifer refused an abortion, and if in Bill's mind that left no other option than murder, could that explain it.

No. I just can't believe it.

There was one major flaw in the theory. Hell, there were probably 1,000 flaws, if he wanted to find them. Assuming Bill fathered the child, which Jennifer and Katherine would have to know, why would they bother bringing a lawsuit, in fact two lawsuits, when it would only bring added attention to the matter and expose Jennifer to arduous questioning on the stand?

What am I missing?

Chapter 52

SUPREME COURT, ERIE COUNTY
Talbot versus Vertex Corporation et al.
Holotrial Annex Building, Part 7-HT
Main Street, Buffalo, New York
Friday, October 13, 2023
9:25 a.m.

Alex Kurtoff's cross-examination was about to begin, this time addressing the merits of the case, rather than switching of juror heads.

Q: Mr. Kurtoff, you are the CEO of Vertex, Inc.?

A: Yes. You know that, Mr. Simons, is not?

Q: Is it your job to see that the company is profitable?

A: Among others.

Q: You are a for-profit corporation, are you not?

A: Is correct, is not?

Q: I'm sorry. Your answer is a bit confusing.
Please tell us, yes or no, is Vertex a for-profit corporation?

A: Yes. Is. Is not?

Q: That's a yes? Correct?

A: Is not? Yes. Is correct.

Q: I'm sorry. Just so it's clear, please answer, *yes or no,* is Vertex a for-profit corporation?

A: Yes. Of course. I tell you four times now.

Q: You're not a charitable institution, an NGO, or

anything of that sort?

Mr. Caparini: Objection, Your Honor, vague.

The Court: No, I'll allow it. It's background.

Q: Do you need it read back?

A: No. We are not charitable institution, not NGO.

Q: By the way, what do your employees call you around the plant?

A: Most say "Mr. Kurtoff." A few on first-name basis.

Q: Do any of them call you "Mr. K?"

A: Sometimes.

Q: Or "Boss?"

A: Sometimes. I been called many things.

Q: I'll bet.

Mr. Caparini: Your Honor.

The Court: Mr. Simons, you know better. Don't waste valuable time here.

Mr. Simons: My apologies, Your Honor.

Q: Mr. Kurtoff, your company makes fully electric cars, the Sparx, the Charge, the Faraday, and so on?

A: Yes, we do.

Q: Last year you had a nine percent market share, correct?

A: Is roughly correct, Mr. Simons.

Q: Now, when did your company learn that New Millennium was coming out with the Hydro?

A: Was when everyone else. Last spring. They are very secretive company. Not to be trusted. No. Not trusted.

Q: Did your marketing division perform an

analysis of how the introduction of the Hydro would affect your market share?

A: Is not exact science. Largely guesswork.

Q: Well, tell the jury, what did the guesswork show?

Mr. Caparini: Your Honor. Guesswork is not admissible. Move to strike.

The Court: No. In this context, data created by the corporation in the regular course of business, I'll allow it.

Mr. Simons: It's also relevant to the defendants' state of mind, what profits they *thought* they stood to lose because of the Hydro.

The Court: Yes, thank you, Mr. Simons. That is also incorporated in my ruling.

Q: Do you want me to repeat the question, Mr. Kurtoff? Did your marketing division perform an analysis of how New Millennium's introduction of the Hydro would affect your market share?

A: I believe after one year, would be about five percent.

Q: Down from nine percent to five percent. So your market share would be cut almost in half?

A: Almost? Yes, seem to be the math, is not?

Q: And after three years, what would the Hydro's effect be on your market share?

A: Even more speculation. Yes, I know, you gonna... Speculation was, range of one to two percent.

Q: You didn't want to see that happen, did you?

A: Is serious question, Mr. Simons? No one wants to lose market share, is not?

Q: Market share means money, doesn't it?

A: Is crude way of putting it, but yes. Ultimate translation is money.

Q: And for Vertex, each percent of market share translates to about four hundred million dollars in profit, does it not?

A: Roughly. Give or take. Depend on the year.

Q: So the Hydro was going to cost your company one point six billion dollars...that's billion with a capital B, in profits, just in the first year, correct?

A: Many assumptions built into your analysis, is not?

Mr. Caparini: Yes, speculative, Your Honor.

The Court: No, he's the CEO, the buck stops there. He ought to know if anyone does. Overruled.

Q: Is one point six billion dollars about right?

A: About.

Q: Mr. Kurtoff, is your compensation based on the company's profits?

Mr. Caparini: Your Honor, what does Mr. Kurtoff's salary have to do with an exploding car?

The Court: No need, Mr. Simons, I'll save you the trouble. Mr. Caparini, I've already told you, I wasn't born yesterday, or last week. Given what Mr. Kurtoff is being accused of, his compensation obviously speaks to motive. You may continue, Mr. Simons.

Q: Do you remember the question, Mr. Kurtoff? Is your compensation based on company profits?

A: In part.

Q: What part?

A: I have base salary, plus two percent of gross profits.

Q: Help me out here, Mr. Kurtoff, two percent of one point six billion dollars?

A: Is thirty-two million dollars.

Q: You seemed to have that number at your fingertips. Sounds like you've given it some thought. Sorry, Your Honor. Strike that. So, you stood to lose thirty-two million dollars in bonuses in a single year if the Hydro was successful. Correct?

A: Is not so simple.

Q: Oh, it's simple, all right.

Mr. Caparini: Your Honor.

The Court: Mr. Simons. You know better.

Q: Mr. Kurtoff. Is it correct, yes or no, you stood—

A: The math is correct, is not? But as I say, is complicated.

Q: Mr. Kurtoff, were you thinking of that thirty-two million dollars when you orchestrated the destruction of Ms. Talbot's Hydro?

A: I do no such thing. Never heard of Miss Talbot or her car. Or little girl. Cute girl.

Q: It wasn't about one car, was it? Wasn't the plan to wipe out demand for the Hydro before it got a foothold? You didn't care what, or who, you destroyed in the process to keep your thirty-two million dollars, did you?

Mr. Caparini: Your Honor, do we still ask questions here? Is Mr. Simons giving his summation?

The Court: Mr. Simons, there's no jury here, so

there's no need for such antics. You must know that will be stricken from the record before the live jurors hear this case. Unless you've forgotten, this is a Holotrial. You can park your litigation tricks at the door. One question at a time, and no speeches. You're just wasting time.

Q: Apologies, Your Honor. A question. Here's a question. On the afternoon of Friday, June 30, 2023, at approximately 4:45 p.m., did you have a phone conversation with a man who stated he'd sabotaged Ms. Talbot's car at your request?

A: I deny that. *Nii.*

Adam noticed a bead of sweat on Kurtoff's forehead. Not such a cool customer, after all, are you? The justice system is truly a wonderful thing. Doesn't matter how rich or powerful you are. When you're on the stand, you're treated the same as any schmuck off the street.

Q: Didn't this man tell you he was surprised at the outcome of the sabotage?

A: I tell you, no conversation.

Q: Didn't this man call you "Boss" and "Mr. K"?

A: Again, no such conversation.

Q: Is that answer as truthful as the rest of the testimony you've given in this courtroom?

A: Yes, is not?

Q: Mr. Kurtoff?

A: Is. As truthful. *Tak.*

Q: And the jury can find all of your testimony, every word of it, as truthful as you are being about this conversation?

A: Yes. They can. How many times I tell you? No such conversation.

Q: Mr. Kurtoff, didn't you plan the destruction of Ms. Talbot's car?

A: I deny it. *Vicious lies.*

Q: Didn't you tell someone who calls you "Boss" and "Mr. K" to sabotage the car?

A: *Vicious* lies. *Vicious*, is not?

Q: If a witness comes walking through that door and says he heard everything I just asked you about, what would you have to say?

A: My word against his, is not? He be lying. No question.

Q: Mr. Kurtoff, why would anyone make up such a lie?

A: People try pin things on me my whole life. Frame with false, unjust accusations. I am successful businessman, is all. People, they jealous. Maybe New Millennium do this to blame me, what you call it, false flag operation. Maybe it was New Millennium engineer unhappy he cut from Hydro design team. Maybe person who not like Miss Talbot, or not like child. Maybe not like the Senator. Maybe child's father not want pay child support, is not?

Mr. Simons: Your honor, move to strike, speculative.

The Court: Well, your question asked him to speculate. You made your bed and now you sleep in it. Overruled.

A: I tell you what, Mr. Simons. I take polygraph, did I plot to blow up car? You ask me, I tell you.

The Court: Okay, hold on there Mr. Kurtoff. As a member of the bar, you know your job as a witness is to answer questions, not make

speeches. You also know, I'm sure, that
polygraph evidence is inadmissible in court.
You want to work out a private agreement, you
do it on your own time.

Q: Perhaps we'll take you up on that. For now, tell
me, was Allison Talbot the target of this
sabotage?

A: Was no target. No sabotage. I tell you again. I
not blow up car. Not kill little girl.

Q: Mr. Kurtoff, did Vertex Corporation have any
dealings with Jennifer Talbot's father, the
Senator?

A: No, sir, did not.

Q: Did you personally have any dealings with
Senator William Talbot?

Mr. Caparini: Objection, Your Honor. This is just
a fishing expedition.

*He's right. I am fishing. And without bait. I should know better
than to pursue a client's conspiracy theory without evidence. Repeat
after me: Don't work for friends.*

The Court: I agree. Unless you want to make an
offer of proof, Mr. Simons. Do you?

Mr. Simons: No, Your Honor. Nothing further. For
now. I reserve the right to recall Mr. Kurtoff. I
expect he won't be whistling Mayberry when
he hears about a conversation that has
somehow slipped his mind.

Adam didn't like the confident look on Kurtoff, his lack of
concern that Cal might show up to bring down the curtain on him.
What did Kurtoff have up his sleeve? Mac swore that no one could
find Cal at the safe house. What did Kurtoff know? Or was he just
waiting for the next tip-off? From whom? Where is the leak?

Chapter 53

ADAM'S LAW OFFICE
Parkside Avenue, Buffalo, New York
Friday, October 13, 2023
7:15 p.m.

Adam welcomed the three Talbots into his office. They lined up in a semicircle facing Adam's desk, just like they had on the day they asked him to take the case. So much had been learned since that day, yet Adam was convinced there was a lot more, if only he could somehow pry it out of the Talbots.

He addressed them as he would a student who'd been caught cheating. "Listen. There's lots of things I'll put up with, but my clients lying to me is not one of them. I've let it go too long. Probably because, as I told you at the beginning, you're like family to me. One of you isn't telling me something, maybe all of you. I want to know what it is. *Now.* Or I make my motion to withdraw from the case. Anyone?"

All three Talbots averted Adam's gaze and remained silent. Finally, Bill and Katherine both started to speak simultaneously. Katherine let her husband have the floor.

"Adam, I'm afraid we do owe you a bit of an apology. All of us."

"You *all* know the father's identity?"

"No...well, not exactly. I'll let... It's best if Jenny explains."

Jennifer looked down at the floor as she began, slowly and hesitantly. "Mr. Simons. I've been telling you the truth...I don't know his name. I mean, like, I met him, for sure, but...last year I was in a twelve-step program for cocaine abuse. You understand, with Daddy's public stand on drugs, he...*we* didn't want this to get out. That's all it is."

Adam queried, "The Brothers of Salvation clinic on Bedford? I think it's the only one for fifty miles. I hear they're pretty good."

Bill gave Adam a curious look.

"Um, yes, Mr. Simons. They were...wonderful."

"And?"

Jennifer continued, head still down, her voice shaky. "In the program, we only used first names. Jim is all I know. It's so hard to stop using, you don't know. We used sex to blot out the cravings, the shakes, the headaches. It wasn't, like, personal, at all. I guess we were just patients with benefits. I thought we were careful. But I'm not sure I always knew *what* I was doing. Anyway, nine months later, I'm done with the program, Jim's gone, and Allie's here."

Adam had spent his whole professional life ferreting out lies, and he knew he was hearing one now. Clearly, Jennifer was speaking from a script. She was obviously uncomfortable telling this yarn. It went against her nature. *How could she lie to my face like this? This must be Bill's doing. Or Kate's?* "Is this what happened? Bill?"

Bill's response was instant and forceful. "Yes, Adam. You have my word." *Bill's a politician, all right. By definition, a professional liar.*

"Katherine?"

She spoke more quietly than Bill. "Yes, Adam. What she... Yes, you have my word, too. What she said."

Adam knew Katherine better than the rest of them. Which meant he knew all her tells. Like when she blinked her eyes rapidly, as she was doing now. *Or am I just imagining this? Do I want Kate to be lying? To get back at her? To prove I'm more worthy, more pure of heart? This is exactly why I don't work for friends. Especially when I've had an affair with the friend, and her husband is sitting right next to her in front of me.*

He wondered whether Bill knew *his own* tells. It was hard enough to be in the middle of a trial, but then to have to stick with this charade he and Katherine were playing...friendly but not too friendly...caring but not too caring...looking but not staring. Every time his eyes met Katherine's, he was afraid he'd give it away. *Constantly walking this tightrope while conducting a trial on the side. Madness.*

Adam shook off his concerns, for the moment. "Jennifer, this Jim. Do you think he'd have any reason to harm your baby?"

The question seemed to make Jennifer very uneasy. "Mr.

Simons, I doubt he knew there *was* a baby. We completely lost touch after the program."

"Do any of you know of *anyone* who'd want to harm Allison?"

The three Talbots said, "No," together, though Jennifer and Katherine both glanced at Bill with a combination of anger and sorrow on their faces. *I think Jennifer wants to set the record straight, but Bill and Kate are holding her back. So, what is the truth?*

Adam still couldn't believe Bill would kill his granddaughter. Not just to hide his daughter's cocaine addiction. Assuming there was an addiction, there had to be easier ways to deal with it. Bill and his staff were seasoned professionals. Surely they could come up with a solution that wouldn't place Bill in such incredible political and legal jeopardy. So why did Jennifer seem so convinced? *Or was I right about an incestual... no, it can't be.* Adam normally would have interviewed each of the Talbots separately, but they weren't just clients, so...one more reason. "Jennifer?"

"Yes, Mr. Simons."

"About how tall was Jim?"

After a few seconds of shocked hesitation, her eyes pointed toward the ceiling. "Um, about average height. I guess."

"I see. Well, do you recall his eye color?"

"No. I'm sorry. I told you, I wasn't all there. It's been a difficult year."

Finally, a true statement. *Difficult* was putting it mildly. Losing her child, having to testify in court about it not once, but twice. Watching the video of the explosion, the obliteration of her child, twice. *I'm not a shrink, but I've got to believe such an experience could cause dissociation, maybe even psychotic episodes.*

Yet if she was making up this story, why did Kate and Bill go along? No. They weren't going along. They were clearly the inventors of this fiction. Jennifer was the one going along. But to what end? Why would Kate participate in this farce? And Bill? There had to be something in it for him.

Adam turned to Bill and Katherine. "Did either of *you* ever see him?"

"No," they said in unison.

"When did Jennifer first tell you about him?"

Katherine deferred to Bill, who answered, "We learned after

the, uh, the first sonogram."

"Jennifer, I'm sorry I have to ask, but did you have sex with anyone else in rehab?"

"No, only—"

"Adam," Bill interrupted. "Do you think I don't see what you're doing? I thought you were a friend. You *could* be more subtle."

"I don't want to be subtle." After a deep breath, Adam decided to bring matters to a conclusion. For now. There'd be no point in continuing the questioning, not while they were all in the same room.

"Bill, if you were anyone else, I'd be out of here. *Right now*. Here's what we're going to do. I'll continue with this case on one condition. No more lies. No more omissions. No half-truths. No more holding back anything you remotely *think* might be significant. I can keep confidences. For all of you. But I won't fly blind. I won't tolerate it. Do I have your word?"

A collective: "Yes."

The meeting hadn't worked out as Adam had hoped. All it did was confirm his worst suspicions. He was left with a shaky story, if not an entirely fictional one, but try as he might, he couldn't treat them as regular clients and resign from the case as he should. *Never again*. No more friends and family plan. Some rules were meant to be broken, and some rules were meant to be rules.

Adam had a sense that whatever they were hiding would answer a lot more questions. Probably questions he didn't yet know to ask. The one thing he *was* sure of was that he hadn't heard the truth. He knew that for two simple reasons. There was no rehab clinic on Bedford Avenue. And there were no Brothers of Salvation.

Chapter 54

ADAM'S LAW OFFICE
Parkside Avenue, Buffalo, New York
Wednesday, October 18, 2023
10:10 a.m.

Mac started off with a one-liner. "Hey, Chief, how come no one in Latin America speaks Latin?"

Adam could only sigh. "We'll look into it after the trial." He was more interested in Mac's research on Kelly. "Give it to me, Mac. Anything?"

"She checks out, just like you thought she would, Chief. Clean as a whorehouse display virgin."

"No links to Kurtoff?"

"None. Kurtoff, Vertex, Caparini, Ukraine. No red flags. Checked her phone, credit cards, everything. That leaves me, you, and Cal."

"It doesn't make sense, Mac. Why would *any* of us want to tip off Kurtoff? If it's not Kelly, and it's not me or you, so...Cal? Does he have some sort of death wish?"

"From what I've seen, Chief, Cal's obsessed with living, not dying. That's why he wasn't excited about testifying in the first place. So that rules out all three of us. And we're back to Kelly. I dunno. Maybe I missed something."

Adam smiled at Mac reassuringly. "I doubt it, Mac. Who knows? Maybe we're both not thinking straight about Kelly. I guess, from now on, we don't share any Cal information with her. Just to be safe."

"Jesus, Chief, what made you come around?"

"Honestly, I'm not sure." *Does anything make sense in this case? If none of us is the snitch, who is?*

***

Holotrial

At the new safe house, Cal was having his own internal dispute. When he was at Mac's place, he'd played by the rules. He hadn't called or texted anyone. He'd remained inside, window shades down. He followed Mac's orders completely. With one exception. He should have told Mac that Tina knew where he'd been staying. He'd wanted to, but the longer he put it off, the more embarrassed he felt. *How could it be Tina, anyway? She'd be the last person on Earth to give me up. Maybe one of the others let it slip? It just can't be Tina.*

Chapter 55

SILLS POLYGRAPH SERVICE, INC.
Niagara Street, Buffalo, New York
Wednesday, October 18, 2023
6:05 p.m.

Bob Sills ushered Kurtoff, Caparini, Adam, and Mac into his examination room.

Sills had handled thousands of cases, but this one was proving particularly entertaining. First, the practice exam on the big wise-cracking pain in the ass, then the terrified college boy who didn't want to testify, and now this combination CEO and mobster who was willing to be tested even though he was guilty as sin. According to Adam.

Sills could think of only two scenarios that made sense. Either Kurtoff intended to fail the exam and shove it up Adam's ass, knowing the results couldn't be used in court, a risky strategy at best. Or he knew how to defeat the process. Sills prided himself on spotting characters who thought they could fool his precious equipment.

Adam reviewed the bidding. "As we agreed, Mr. Kurtoff, the best I can do is recommend to my client that she drop the case, depending on the results here. You acknowledge this agreement before we start, correct?"

"Is deal, Mr. Simons. And you ask questions we agree to. That also deal, is not?"

"That's the deal, Mr. Kurtoff. Maybe a reasonable follow-up."

"We not agree to that."

"Let's just see where we end up. Oh Bob, excuse me, this is Phillip Caparini, counsel for Vertex. He's here to keep us honest. And I think you know—"

"Yes. Hello again, Mr. McMillan," Sills said, in a less than cordial tone.

"Call me Mac, Doc."

Kurtoff addressed Adam. "Mr. Simons, you not bring pretty young lady with red hair? I think her name Kelly, is not? She is nice girl." Adam and Mac said nothing, but each took a long hard look at Kurtoff.

Sills took over from there. "Mr. Kurtoff, please sit here."

Kurtoff, smiling and relaxed, sat and got wired up. Three aces were placed in front of him.

Too calm for one in his position. Sills went over the ground rules. Kurtoff did his part, stating that each of the three aces was on top of the desk, whereupon Sills shepherded Adam and Caparini into the next room to review the readouts. After studying them, Sills sighed. "All three responses are NDI. No deception indicated. So, he lied twice with impunity."

Adam asked, "He knows how to beat it?"

"If so, it's not any technique I've seen before."

"He did know all the questions ahead of time. Could that be it?"

"Shouldn't make any difference."

Adam turned to Caparini. "I guess that's it then. You've wasted my time. Pugged me."

Caparini's brow furrowed at *Pugged*, though whatever it meant, it wasn't good. He protested, "I assure you, Mr. Kurtoff intends to be truthful here. Ask yourself, if he could beat the polygraph, why waste that skill on this silly card test? Why not wait for the actual exam?"

There was some logic to that, Sills had to admit.

Adam was not assuaged. Back in the examination room, he glared at Kurtoff. Caparini gave him an imploring look, tinged with fright.

"As a matter of curiosity, Mr. Kurtoff," Sills said, "which ace *did* you put on the table?"

Kurtoff picked up the card on the table and fanned it out into three separate cards. He'd put all three aces on the table, stacked tightly on top of each other to give the appearance of a single card. He hadn't followed Sills' instructions, but he hadn't lied either. Nevertheless, Kurtoff's sleight of hand itself showed a degree of deception. Sills left it to Adam whether to proceed.

After a small interval of silence, Adam said, "We'll continue, though as the judge would say, there's a cloud over this exam now."

Sills gave instructions. "Mr. Kurtoff, for the rest of the examination, I want you to be completely truthful in your responses. Try to keep them simple. Yes or no, if possible. Do you understand these instructions, and are you going to follow them?"

"Yes, and yes. How that was?"

"Perfect. Okay, let's start. Mr. Kurtoff, is today Wednesday?"

"Yes."

"Is this the month of November? "

"No."

"Mr. Kurtoff, are you the CEO of Vertex Motors, Inc.?"

"Yes. Is not?"

"Is that a yes, Mr. Kurtoff?"

"Yes. Is yes."

"Is this building made of green cheese?"

"No. No cheese."

Sills then turned to the questions the parties had agreed upon. He'd been told he had to read them precisely. "Mr. Kurtoff, did you in any way cause the car owned by Jennifer Talbot to explode on June thirtieth of this year?"

"No, Mr. Sills. I not."

"Thank you. Please remember, simple, short responses. Just yes or no if you can. Next question, Mr. Kurtoff, did you in any way communicate with any person who caused the car owned by Jennifer Talbot to explode on June thirtieth of this year?"

"No, sir. Is...no."

"Mr. Kurtoff, do you know what caused the car owned by Jennifer Talbot to explode on June thirtieth of this year?"

"No. Not."

"Mr. Kurtoff, do you know *who* caused the car owned by Jennifer Talbot to explode on June thirtieth of this year?"

"I not."

Sills retreated to the next room, this time by himself, to review the graphs. Once again, all the results were NDI, no deception indicated. It was puzzling, based on the evidence Adam said they had against Kurtoff. *I guess I'll leave it to Adam to sort it out. I've done my part.*

When Sills advised the small assemblage of the results, Adam asked to speak privately with him in the adjacent room. "Don't know what to tell you, Adam, other than I don't think he beat the box. I think I'm up to date. Of course, they're always trying. Like the testers and dopers trying to stay ahead of each other in the Tour de France."

"I agree. Mac's quite familiar, too, and he didn't see anything."

"Well, what do you want to do?"

"Kurtoff was so insistent on the questions. Maybe we ask different questions."

Adam and Sills returned to the examination room to find Kurtoff and Caparini smiling.

"Mr. Kurtoff," Sills said, "a couple follow-up questions, if I may."

Kurtoff exploded. *"No. May not.* We not agree on such, Mr. Simons. I was told you are man of your word."

"And I told you my recommendation would depend on the examination results. I'm not satisfied. Mr. Kurtoff, just answer this one question and that may do it. On June thirtieth of this year, did you have a telephone conversation about the explosion of Jennifer Talbot's car with one of your employees at about 5:00 p.m.?"

"Mr. Simons, I protest. This not our agreement. Every day, I talk, maybe a hundred people, is not? I am sure explosion come up in conversation that day at every car manufacturer in country. But I tell you this, I not then, or ever, talk with anyone who cause car to explode."

"Mr. Kurtoff, can you answer my question yes or no?"

"I give you my best answer. If you not satisfied, I see you back in court. You think you scare me? Maybe I scare you."

"Are you threatening an officer of the court?"

"You take any way you want. You not know me, not absolute. Do you, Simons? *Goodbye.*" With that, Kurtoff abruptly yanked the sensors from his body, threw them on the floor, and exited. Caparini trailed behind like an obedient lap dog.

"Can this case get any stranger?" Adam exclaimed, perhaps mostly to himself.

Though Adam didn't know it, the solution to this problem *was* simple. Kurtoff's answers were truthful because he believed them to be true. In essence, they *were* true. He'd been told by his chief engineer that their sabotage of the Talbot car didn't, and couldn't, cause the explosion. It had to be something else. This was confirmed by Vertex's excellently credentialed expert Dr. Morier, as well as by New Millennium and their expert. Not to mention the test-drive that Kurtoff had given Gura and Kramer. Based on all of those sources, Kurtoff was convinced that his *special* cable wasn't responsible for the car's destruction. Hence his demand that each of the questions revolve around what caused the explosion, rather than about sabotaging the car in general.

Mac knew the answer, too. More so than Kurtoff. More than Drs. Ditenzo, Morier, and Saperston. He understood *exactly* what caused the explosion. And exactly *who*. But he couldn't bring himself to tell Adam it wasn't Kurtoff or Vertex. Nor could he tell Adam who it was...*especially not that*. At least not until the trial was over.

Chapter 56

SUPREME COURT, ERIE COUNTY
Talbot versus Vertex Corporation et al.
Holotrial Annex Building, Part 7-HT
Main Street, Buffalo, New York
Thursday, October 19, 2023
10:45 a.m.

Adam was already at the counsel table as the others returned from morning recess. He noticed Kelly having a friendly conversation with Caparini's second-seater, near the rear of the courtroom. *This character hasn't said a single word during the whole damn trial, and there he is chatting up a storm with Kelly. What's this? Hiding in plain sight? Mac just said she was clean.* Kelly and the man with no name ended their conversation and sat at their respective counsel tables.

"I didn't know you knew anyone on the other team," Adam said to Kelly.

"Oh. You mean Mr. Lukich."

"The whole trial, I didn't think he could speak. You could have introduced us."

"Oh, I've seen him at the gym on Transit doing the elliptical. I never knew his name. One time, this is funny, we use identical gym bags, and we switched them by mistake. Just as I was about to drive off, he ran over and we switched back."

"Yes. Funny." *A coincidence? Opposing counsel had access to her gym bag? Please tell me she didn't keep any trial docs in there.*

"By the way, Adam, if you're still worried about Cal, my friend JJ is moving in with her boyfriend so her apartment is available until the lease runs out in a couple months. She said I could use it. It would be a perfect place to hide Cal. There's no possible connection between him and JJ."

Adam tried to respond calmly without revealing the chill that went up his spine. "Thanks, Kelly, we'll keep it in mind. I think Cal's safe where he is for the time being."

"Oh, where did we put him now?"

"I'd rather not discuss it here. Microphones, you know."

Chapter 57

A ZOOM CALL
Thursday, October 19, 2023
11:27 p.m.

K elly addressed JJ's happy visage in the Zoom window on
the left side of her laptop screen. "Okay, lady creatures, start
your engines. The special Zoom edition of *The Price Might
Be Right* will begin in T minus five seconds." The right side was
open to the Lamborghini website. Each Thursday night, if their class
assignments didn't interfere, the two best friends held a virtual
shopping session, fantasizing about the exotic purchases they'd
make once the fees started rolling in from their lucrative future law
practices. That is, after JJ paid back her father and Kelly reimbursed
that nice lawyer in Plattsburgh who'd freed her from her abusive
father. It was fun to dream, and cheaper than buying a lottery ticket.

Zooming had gotten a boost during the coronavirus pandemic.
Kelly still appreciated the ability to have a discussion without the
other person being inside her messy apartment, particularly this
evening. The chair she sat in occupied the only free spot in her tiny
living room, as the rest of the floor was buried under materials from
the Talbot trial.

Last week they'd started with Kelly's choice, a chateau in St.
Moritz. This week was JJ's turn, and she'd chosen a Lamborghini.

"Kell, if you're gonna hobnob with the rich and tanned, why
not do it in style?"

Kelly was reticent, as some of the Lamborghini models cost
more than their future chateau.

"No worries, sister," JJ reassured her. "I'll handle it when we
get to the dealership. I bought a few cars for the family back in
Kingston. Mostly second and third-handers and a little beat up, but
a car's a car, right?"

"Sure, JJ, sure. Car's a car. Hundred-dollar car, million-dollar car, what's the difference? Okay. You picked the topic, so I go first. Check out the Huracan Evo RWD. Pretty nice for a couple hundred grand, huh?"

JJ laughed. "That entry-level, pissant Lambo. You gotta be kidding me. No gravy in that. Think big, sister. Your Huracan's just two-wheel drive. *Rear* two-wheel drive at that. Only six hundred horsepower. Might as well buy an oxcart."

"Sounds like a lot of horses to me. My Prius only has a hundred thirty-four."

"We're goin' for the moon, Kelly. Only way to fly. Scope out the Sian Roadster. *Now* we're talking. Hybrid, over eight hundred horsepower. Naturally aspirated V12 engine, not the puny ten cylinders on the Huracan. Over two hundred seventeen miles per hour for those mornings you're running a little late for class. A steal at three point six million dollars."

"Yeah. A real steal."

"Hey, Kell. It's not as if we're gonna pay full price. And don't forget the sweet trade-in we're getting on your Prius."

"JJ, I don't think they'd trade us a Lamborghini *hubcap* for my Prius."

"You're underestimating my skills. *You* try living in a house with nine people and five beds. Believe me, those Lamborghini salesmen talk a good game, but they're gonna crumble when they see two UB Law grads on the lot."

"JJ, I don't know—"

"And make sure they throw in floor mats. Always save that for the last negotiating point. Let's pick out some colors..."

***

Their shopping spree over, JJ turned to her favorite topic with Kelly. "Hey, Kell, talking about fantasies, what's up with you and Mr. Simons?"

"I don't know, JJ. I can't believe...you know, he's so...no. You're right. It *is* a fantasy. What have I been thinking? He's forty-five. I'm twenty-five. And that's the least of it. How thick can I be? It's just a one-way street."

"You're not dumb, Kell. Just a romantic fool. Big difference. So, you took an L. Now you move on. You're gonna find somebody twice as dope, for sure. And twice as young."

Both of them laughed.

Then Kelly's momentary lightheartedness turned morose again. "I guess that's that, huh, JJ?"

"I'm sorry, Kell. But you're gonna come out the other side riding them golden arches. You'll forget all about Professor what's-his-name by next week. No, strike that...by Monday, after the weekend I have planned for you."

"You're right, JJ. But is there a chance, just a chance—"

"Kell, he'd be lucky to have you. You're so smart. And hot." JJ was already contemplating weekend activities to lift her BFF's mood. "And when you find that twice as young and twice as smart boyfriend, make sure you don't go bare-back for a while," she reminded Kelly. "You don't need a bunch of cute mini-Kellys to take care of when you're getting your law practice off the ground. So put a sock on it."

"*What* did you just say?"

"I said you're gonna put Professor Big Shot in the rear-view mirror, where he belongs."

"No. After that, JJ."

"You mean about using protection?"

"Wait a minute." Kelly flew out of her chair, and JJ's Zoom window. She started rifling through papers on the floor, finally coming across the one that JJ's comment had triggered in her mind. *I was right. There it is. But how is this possible?* As her brain started to absorb the ramifications, Kelly returned to her laptop. "I'm sorry, JJ, I gotta go," she said breathlessly. "Have to check something out. We'll talk later, okay? And thanks."

"For what?"

"Just thank you."

As their Zoom windows closed, Kelly stared at a single word on the document in her hand. "Nexplanon."

Chapter 58

SUNY AT BUFFALO LAW SCHOOL
Room 304
Amherst, New York
Friday, October 20, 2023
3:32 p.m.

As most of the students were filing out, Kelly made her way to the front of the classroom. She couldn't wait to tell Adam about her discovery.

When she stopped in front of him, he cut her off before she could speak. "Kelly, I apologize, this is awkward, but I have to ask you..."

Ask me out? On a date? Finally? No, it can't be.

"Is it possible, not intentionally, but might you have told someone, maybe just let it slip out by accident, about Cal staying at Mac's place?"

Kelly tried not to show her disappointment.

"This *is* an exciting case for a law student. For me too. Perhaps you were recounting your experiences to a classmate? Your mother? A boyfriend?"

"No, Professor...can I use Adam now, since we're having a professional conversation? I guess I have my second chair hat on."

"Certainly."

"No, Adam. I understand you have to ask, but no, I'd never do that. In fact, I've barely talked with anyone about the case at all. And if I did, I'd make sure not to let any confidential information slip. You've drilled that into us pretty well." Notwithstanding her outward certainty, Kelly replayed in her mind the conversations she'd had with JJ. She'd kept it pretty generic and didn't believe she'd offered any important info. "There's something I wanted to mention, Adam."

"Yes?"

"I'm kinda stumped. I was wading through the file, and I found something that doesn't make any sense."

"And..."

"You always say to leave no stone unturned. A year before Allison was born, Nexplanon was inserted in Jennifer's left arm by her OB-GYN."

Adam just stared blankly.

Well, the great man doesn't know absolutely everything, after all. "It's a contraceptive implanted under the skin. It's effective for about three years."

"Do the defendants know about this?"

"They never asked for Jennifer's medical records. Must have assumed they weren't relevant. I would have, too. Until I found this."

"Then how did she...is it possible to have a baby with this, this what is it?"

"Nexplanon. It's ninety-nine percent effective. But I suppose it's possible."

"Can this case get any more bizarre? Well, maybe she beat the odds."

"Yes, that would be the simple solution. Ninety-nine percent chance it's wrong."

"I've taught you too well. Go forth, creature, and find me the correct, complex solution."

As she was climbing the stairs to leave the classroom, Kelly did a 180 and walked back down. She had to get this off her chest, come what may. Holding back a cry, she began, "Adam... No, for this, it's Professor Simons. I know it's only a silly schoolgirl crush. A crush on the professor. How's *that* for originality—"

"Kelly—"

"But sometimes it seems so real to me. It doesn't matter." Kelly understood from the look on Adam's face that it was not to be. Funny, though, he didn't seem surprised. Just stoic. Adam let her say her piece. "Prof...oh hell. *Adam,* even if it were real for me, I'd never be able to compete with your wife...with Beth. Or with Katherine, either. Kate as you call her when you think no one's around. So, it's a moot question when all is said and done."

"Kelly, Katherine and I are just—"

"Please, don't worry. Your secret's safe with me. Anyway,

there's no love left between Kate and the Senator. If there ever was any. And it's obvious you and Kate had something going, at least at one time. When this case is over, you should go for it, rekindle it."

"Kelly—"

"Don't worry about me, Adam. I'll be fine. Someday I'll find another dazzling trial lawyer who calls me *creature* and makes me tingle all over. One more my age. You'll be on the Supreme Court, and we'll wink at each other when I come to argue. You and Kate can have lunch with me and Superstar Lawyer-To-Be-Named-Later. Oh, was it okay I addressed you as Adam? I guess, if I'm still on the case?"

"*Of course* you're still on the case. That is, if you want to be. It's up to you. I'd understand either way."

"I do want to continue. Absolutely. I had a complex problem. I came up with a simple solution. And it's *right*."

They both chuckled, which broke the tension. They were co-chairs for the trial, good friends, nothing more. Kelly would focus on her studies, the trial, and her future nameless boyfriend.

***

Adam turned off the whiteboard and started gathering his things to go home. He was content that, at least, the *Kelly thing* was resolved. One distraction down, about twenty to go.

He replayed in his mind Kelly's cozying up to Lukich. *My imagination's gone bonkers. But it's hard to keep track of reality in this psycho case. Is there any way Bill could have been involved? Killing his own granddaughter? And how the hell did Cal and Kurtoff both pass polygraph exams with completely irreconcilable stories. What about this mysterious father no one seems to know? And Jennifer gets pregnant with this Nexplanon, a ninety-nine to one shot? Well, none of it matters a damn if we can't keep Cal alive. And get him to testify. Just how the hell did they find him? No matter. Mac assures me Cal's safe now. It would be nice, though, if we could identify the snitch.*

Chapter 59

THE VERTEX BUILDING
Alex Kurtoff's Office
Ensign Street, South Buffalo, New York
Thursday, October 26, 2023
3:12 p.m.

A s it turned out, Kurtoff didn't have to find Cal. He just had to find Mac.

Kurtoff was about to leave for a tennis match at the club when his administrative assistant popped into his office. "Mr. K, I forgot to tell you, I got this kinda strange call before lunch. He wouldn't say who he was...I think it's a he...but he, um, he did say it was urgent. So I recorded it. That's good, right? Should I play it back for you?"

"*Francesca*, someone say urgent, you get me *immediate*. Is not? Maybe this not job for you. Maybe we try welding department, is not?"

"Alexi, no. I love it here, don't—"

"I tell you before. Mr. K here. Always. No Alexi. Mr. K. You get that?"

"I'm sorry. I promise...Mr. K. Please. I'll make it up to you tonight. Anything you want."

"You play damn recording for me. *Now*. That what I want."

It was the same electronically distorted voice used on the message that Zack had found three weeks earlier. "Follow the Mac. Broadband Bar and Grill. Chippewa. 5:30. Don't be late."

Kurtoff shooed away his assistant, speaking in a harsh tone, "Francesca, you disappoint me again, that be last time. Is not?"

Privacy restored, he replayed the message in his mind.

Hmm. Broadband Bar? Never heard of it. Better get the boys over there.

Chapter 60

BROADBAND BAR AND GRILL
Chippewa Street, Buffalo, New York
Thursday, October 26, 2023
5:15 p.m.

Mac and Adam were at the newest popular hang-out on Chippewa Street. It reminded Mac of the bar in Toronto where he'd found his sister. And his name. He felt bad that he hadn't got around to telling Adam, especially since Adam had been so supportive of Mac's search. But Mac's personal news could wait. As could his news about the Y-tube. Mac didn't want to distract Adam's focus from the case with either of those revelations.

Mac felt most guilty about not disclosing the DNA result from the Y-tube. *Let's be real, I can't pretend I'm protecting him from losing focus on the case. This* is *the case. It* solves *the case. There's no question Adam should be told. I just can't bring myself to do it. No telling how he'd react. Other than not well. Very not well. Let's wait until the trial is over. Maybe then it won't matter. Maybe he'll understand.*

Mac wasn't distracted by guilt for long. "Hey, Chief, you know how many months have twenty-eight days? All of 'em."

"Good to know. What exactly *does* rattle around in that brain cage of yours?"

"You know what they say, a mind is a terrible thing to taste."

As a waitress approached the table, Mac muttered, "The usual."

"The usual lunch or the usual dinner?" the waitress asked, half-friendly, half-snarky.

"Dinner, Olive."

Ten minutes later she returned with a steak and sweet potato and three beers.

"Isn't that your usual lunch?" Adam asked. "And breakfast.

What's the difference?"

"Lunch is two beers, dinner is three."

"And breakfast?"

"Only one beer. You think I'm a lush?"

"Mac, why do I feel like I'm being played?"

"No, really, Chief. That's the menu."

"Not that, Mac. The case."

"Whada' ya' talkin about, Chief? You're gonna nail that sonofabitch. Wait till Cal gets on the stand."

"I don't mean Kurtoff. I mean the Talbots." Mac stared at him blankly. "They're being deceitful, to put it mildly. They've already admitted to withholding information from me. Then they made up a phony story about Allison's father. I still don't know what they're covering up or why, but I have a hunch it's important."

"Why would they lie to you?"

"That's just it. I don't know. Our case is as close to a sure winner as you can get, and you know how I hate to say that. We have the defendant confessing to the sabotage, a video of the explosion, recovery of the cable they put there to destroy the car. What the hell do the Talbots need to hide?"

"This ain't like you, Chief. You should take my advice."

"And that is..."

"My advice is, follow *your* advice. Don't represent friends. Anyway, I have great news. Cal's come around."

"How'd you accomplish that?"

"I'd like to take credit, but it was the girlfriend. The broad told him the obvious. Kurtoff already tried to kill him *without* him agreeing to testify. Since that plan wasn't working, his best chance for survival is to testify on the record, so that harming him won't accomplish anything. It was just like your advice, but with boobs. Makes all the difference."

"Thank God. There's no way the case could stay afloat without his testimony. Hey Mac, I thought Cal wasn't supposed to be communicating with anyone?"

"Yeah, Chief, felt sorry for the kid, let him use my cell phone to call her."

"But wouldn't that allow her to locate...oh, never mind. I'm sure you're on top of it."

***

Damytro Gura lurked in a black BMW sedan, watching Adam and Mac leave the restaurant across the street. *Good. They go in opposite directions. Mac alone now.* Gura whispered into his phone, "Heading west on Chippewa. That's for you, Santa and Rudolph. You let me know when he change direction, I pick him up. Blitzen, you stay mobile and wait for instruction. Gets you in Christmas spirit, no?"

Blitzen, loaned to him like the others from Kurtoff's *palace guard*, replied, "You bet. We nail Mac *and* witness, that's double present to hang in stockings." Blitzen was driving a taxicab, two blocks west of the Broadband Bar, ready to pick up Mac should he want a taxi or follow him should he hail a different cab.

Mac sensed he had company the minute he left the restaurant. He reflexively kneeled down to re-tie his shoelace, making it appear as casual as he could. In a fraction of a second he spotted the man in the black hoodie and jeans about a block behind him. The sonofabitch had an earpiece in his right ear, and even at that distance Mac could see him whispering into it.

If there's one, there's two. Mac stood up and resumed his walk, scanning the street in front of him this time. Not surprisingly, there was a second character in a dark hoodie and jeans about a block ahead of him, also with an earpiece. Also whispering. Both of them were pretty big. And amateurish. The tips of their guns protruded from the bottoms of their hoodies. Mac had to chuckle. *Jeez, this is the Keystone Cops. If they're gonna do sidewalk surveillance, the least they could do is dress differently.* The stooge in front of him looked back every few seconds to confirm that Mac was still there. He tried to act casual, but to Mac's trained senses it was laughable. *Or was he too obvious? Same with the asshole behind me. Were they intended to distract me from another, less obvious tail? That's what I'd do.*

Mac concluded from their distance and the manner of the surveillance that this wasn't a hot encounter. Strictly a follow-and-report job. For now. Once they tracked him to his final destination, where Cal was waiting, it was likely to get unpleasant. He didn't bother to scrutinize the street for the vehicle or two that he was sure were out there. Though he couldn't help notice a cab lingering a couple blocks ahead of him. It maintained its position as Mac continued toward it. Mac was glad he'd left Cal at the safe house. Now he needed to lose these dickheads.

Before he reached the suspect cab, Mac abruptly turned south on Elmwood Avenue. He continued down the street, seemingly without a care in the world, stopping once in a while to window shop. He didn't believe they'd made him making them. He was better at this than they were. Assuredly better than the flustered moron assigned to front him on Chippewa, who couldn't backtrack to follow Mac on Elmwood without appearing ridiculously obvious. No matter, Mac was sure someone else would pick up where that idiot left off.

He figured he could probably lose them by himself, but why not get a little help to be sure? He pulled out his phone, making no effort to conceal his actions. As far as the tails were concerned, Mac didn't realize he was being followed. How could he, after consuming all those beers they'd watched him drink?

He found Larry Zack in his contacts list. They'd helped each other out in the past. And they were already sort of working together on the Talbot case. After all, Zack found Cal in the first place.

Zack answered on the first ring. He was in a cheerful mood, and immediately offered assistance. "I'll make *sure* you get to your destination, Mac, wherever it is. I owe you one for that escort service case."

"My pleasure. But stop spreading rumors that I partook of the goods. You damn well know it was strictly professional."

"No problem, Mac. You can't blame a guy for enhancing your myth. Anyway, I have a couple blocker cars, Hummers, on standby. We'll route you by taxi to the South Grand Island Bridge with the blockers right behind you and a plain-Jane Ford Bronco in front of you. When you get on the bridge, the Hummers will have a fender bender, blocking both lanes and completely tying up traffic to keep any pain-in-the-ass tails off you."

"This sounds like the stunt we pulled in that Lockport dentist case," Mac noted.

"Roger that. On the bridge you'll switch to the Ford, which will slow down to let your cab get ahead so any forward tails will follow it to the Outlet Mall while we divert you to wherever you're going. Don't tell me over the phone. Wherever it is, I'll get you there.

Personally. You'll be gone before they can whistle *November Rain*. The poor bastards. Oh yeah, almost forgot, a pick-up location. What's good for you, Mac?"

Mac found it curious that Zack warned him not to give Cal's location over the phone. How could he even *think* Mac wouldn't know that? *Maybe he figures I'm flustered being the rabbit instead of the hound.*

Mac chose a pick-up spot that was good for a quick exit if necessary. "How 'bout southeast corner of Elmwood and West Huron?"

"Ten-four, buddy. When can you be there?"

"Make it 1900 hours even. It's about one click from here."

"Okay, see you soon. Oh yeah. Your taxi will have a Bills sticker on the front passenger door. I'll be driving."

"Thanks, Zack. I owe you one. Maybe two."

Mac was honored that Zack would go out of his way for him like this. Providing a four-fleet was over and above the call of duty. Then an odd thing happened. About thirty seconds after he got off the phone with Zack, the tails disappeared. Even the cab in front of him took off. Maybe it was legit after all. Or maybe they were better than he thought, and they'd been replaced by fresh backups, better ones. No. His experience with hundreds of prior surveillance jobs told him this one was really over. *So why did the tails drop off? Something doesn't compute.* He needed to put this picture together. Fast.

***

Mac reached the designated corner in thirteen minutes. Shortly after he got there, a cab with a big blue Buffalo Bills sticker approached, fast, as promised. When it was about 30 feet away, a shiver went down Mac's spine.

The license plate number was the same as the cab that had been surveilling him on Chippewa. He'd trained himself to be cognizant of such details, and that training had kept him alive more than once. Inside the cab were *five* occupants. That was all Mac needed to see. He wasn't going to wait around for an explanation. Things had obviously gone south.

Zack is getting sloppy. The license-plate screwup wasn't like him. Perhaps he'd been in a hurry. He hadn't anticipated Mac's call, after all. *What in the hell could have made Zack turn on me like this? Screw it. Better move now, think later.*

If Zack had been alone, or with a single other goon, Mac might have stayed to face them down. But five-to-one odds—*no*. He turned and bolted, running northeast, diagonally across the blocks, avoiding sidewalks and streets while maintaining some degree of cover by clinging to the buildings and their shadows. At Delaware he proceeded north past Chippewa, not far from where the evening had started with Adam. It seemed like he'd lost them, but Zack was good, even if he screwed up on the license plate, and Mac couldn't let up. Cutting across parking lots and alleyways, he made it to Pearl Street, where he had no choice but to use a short stretch of sidewalk to get to the Tralf Music Hall's parking lot. He went in the backstage entrance and proceeded to the lobby. When he caught his breath, he removed his reversible overcoat and turned it inside out. The bright orange coat was now black. Mac had decisions to make.

Chapter 61

Tralf Music Hall
Thursday, October 26, 2023
7:15 p.m.

The Tralf Music Hall was the successor, in name anyway, to the Tralfalmadore Café, which was universally acclaimed as one of the great jazz clubs in Buffalo history. The dank, smoky basement of the original location was perfect for ending a late night with some intimate smokin' jazz. The new Tralf Music Hall, on the second floor of a modern building in Buffalo's Theater District, was considerably more upscale than its namesake. A full-fledged night club, multiple times larger than the original.

Mac debated whether to go upstairs to the club and get lost in the crowd or cut through the lobby toward the exit on Main Street. Zack had to know about the lobby pass-through and would likely assume that Mac had chosen that route. Not to mention, Mac would be naked out there if the Main Street sidewalk wasn't busy. He didn't think his *new* black overcoat would fool them for long. If he went upstairs, though, he'd only have two exits—the nightclub entrance itself, or down the stairs to the backstage door where he'd entered.

Quick decisions under pressure were never optimal, but Mac was used to them. He bet on the club and loped up the stairs to the box office. The show had already started, so he hadn't counted on a line. To his dismay, a number of stragglers waited around the box office. *Just what I needed.* He could've tried entering without a ticket, making up some pretense or other, but he didn't want to risk drawing attention. So he waited in line, keeping one eye on the staircase landing behind him. He tried silently urging the ticket buyers in front of him to get on with their purchases or get the hell out of the line. That worked about as well as he thought it would.

An older couple approached the ticket window. The elderly

husband was a dawdler, fumbling around for his glasses and wallet, listlessly preparing the necessary cash. He got his tickets but then lingered. Mac's sigh of relief turned to frustration as his new nemesis paused again to ask the ticket seller where the seats were. It was a general admission show, no assigned seating. Mac wanted to scream.

Mac's attention was drawn back to the staircase by two burly Slavic-looking men in sunglasses trudging upward to the second-floor landing. *Shit.* Mac reached inside his coat for his .45. Then he noticed the matching blue and gold jackets. *False alarm.* Just two Buffalo Sabres defensemen, recent acquisitions from a Russian hockey team in the Kontinental League.

Finally, after ten long minutes, Mac bought his ticket and made it inside to mingle among the raucous crowd. The show featured a Beatles tribute band called the *Sgt. Pepper Pots.* An enthusiastic throng filled the dance floor in front of the stage as the band belted out *She Loves You.* As a tremendous Beatles aficionado, Mac recalled the mini-riot of teeny boppers that had broken out at Abbey Road Studios while the Beatles were laying down the song. A handful of London bobbies had tried, unsuccessfully, to control hundreds of excited teenage girls running amok through Abbey Road's corridors, the Beatles now and then poking their heads out the Studio Two door to observe the melee and break into their own hysterics. That was 1963.

This was 2023, and Mac had to make some choices, fast.

He walked around the dance floor to the opposite side of the room, where he propped his back to the wall with a direct view of the entranceway. The dancers provided reasonably good cover, though their unpredictable movements made it difficult to maintain a constant line of sight. But Mac was focused, and any bozos entering the club would have virtually no chance of immediately identifying him among the hundreds of partiers. That is, until they started to spread out and sweep for him.

Mac figured that if no one showed up in about five more minutes, he'd be safe. Maybe. Once they realized they'd lost him, they might backtrack. *Stay or go? Stay or go?* His internal debate was cut short when a young woman, probably late teens or early twenties, attracted his attention. Jet black shoulder-length hair, Mediterranean face, skin-tight jeans, deep brown eyes, and a slim

Alan M. Wishnoff

body. Except on top, where she looked to be bra-less, based on the twin points protruding from her clinging metallic halter top. A small crystal nose stud intermittently reflected the glare of the ceiling lights as she swayed to the music. *Willpower, Mac, willpower. Put it back in your pants and stay alive tonight. Eyes on the door, shithead. But damn, she's hotter than a chicken wing.*

Mac assumed she was going to hook up with the 20-something stoner standing next to him. Instead, she came to a halt in front of Mac, grabbed his hands, and yanked him onto the dance floor. He didn't know why he let her do this, except that he was immersed in two of his favorite things: Beatles music and the attention of a flaming hot gal. *She* was immersed in alcohol with a side of ecstasy. Before he knew it, they were in the middle of the wild crowd.

Mac knew he had to get back to his perch by the wall. He started to back away from the girl, hoping she'd lose track of him during a twirl and glom on to a new partner. All the while he desperately tried to keep the club entrance in sight through the tangled jumble of bodies doing the Twist, the Swim, and other '60s favs. Just when he thought he'd extricated himself, she came out of a spin and lurched forward, draping herself on him for a slow dance to the strains of *This Boy*. Or was it *That Boy*? He always got that mixed up, as had John Lennon during the Fab Four's recording of the song.

The adrenaline rush from being chased by people who might want to kill him had juiced Mac, as if ten venti caramel macchiatos with extra espresso had been pumped directly into his veins. Now it seemed to heighten his senses, to drink in every inch of the slinky body pressed against his, oscillating with the music. It created an almost hypnotic calm that momentarily erased Mac's urgent thoughts about his pursuers. He closed his eyes, gyrating erotically in sync with his partner.

John Lennon's strident, beautiful bridge snapped Mac out of his temporary euphoria. He checked the room again. All clear. *But how the hell would I know? Anyone could have slipped in while I was polishing my knob. Shit. Well, it's been about ten minutes, so maybe I'm okay.* That comforting thought was instantly obliterated by the sight of two large men in gray jackets entering the club. *Not Buffalo Sabres this time.* Clearly not there for a good time, they discarded their tickets on the floor, eschewing the free drinks included in the price of admission. They were pros. Thug number one stayed by the entranceway while Thug number two started to wander the club.

Shit, so much for this plan. Maybe they don't have the balls or the skill to subdue me among all these people. Better not wait around to find out. This was no longer a follow-and-report job. Since they knew he was onto them, they could no longer just observe. They would need to extract Cal's location from Mac by other means. With that in mind, Mac forcefully pushed away his partner, hard enough to give her the clear message he was no longer interested in their *pas de deux*, but not so hard that he'd knock her down and create a scene.

The *Sgt. Pepper Pots* were dressed in the plain black suits and ties of the early Beatles. Mac figured they must have costume changes in the back. Using the dancers as cover, he casually walked behind the stage to the dressing rooms. As expected, he found multiple outfits reflecting various stages of the Beatles' career. Including fake facial hair and wigs also reflecting the individual band members' evolution. Mac tried on a gaudy Sgt. Pepper outfit: a light blue jacket with large horizontal white stripes, along with a bright red three-cornered hat. One peek in the mirror confirmed how nonsensical that idea was. He practically split the jacket's seams, and his arms extended four inches beyond the cuffs. He looked about as much like a Beatle as a pumpkin in an onion field. *Okay. Dress-up time is over.* Mac refocused his attention on the wigs and facial hair.

Two minutes later, a tall George Harrison with hippie-phase mustache, long beard, and shoulder-length hair walked down the back staircase. Coupled with his new black jacket and guitar case, the disguise would hopefully give Mac just enough time to take out anyone waiting for him before they realized who he was. They wouldn't expect him to carry disguises with him, not for an evening that started out as a casual dinner with Adam. Sure enough, as Mac exited the stage door at the bottom of the stairs, he ran into one of Zack's troops. He didn't recognize Mac at first glance, and he didn't get a second after Mac swung the guitar case at his head, knocking him unconscious.

After removing and discarding the facial hair, wig, and guitar case, Mac hightailed it back to Chippewa Street. He knew the hippie stuff would attract unnecessary attention in a well-lit room, and he had to appear normal very shortly.

***

After getting a quick glimpse of Mac entering the lobby of the Holiday Inn Express, Zack bolted down Main Street. *That son-of-a-bitch is slippery as a greased rat. Your luck is about to run out, buddy. Sorry, but Kurtoff pays better than New Millennium.* Zack told his four associates with their Christmassy code-names to stay outside while he went in to get some info.

Zack approached the smiling woman at the front desk for assistance.

"How can I help you?"

"My friend just checked in, and he left his keys in my car. Big gentleman, about six two, mostly bald."

"Do you mean Mr. Starr?"

"Exactly," Zack responded as he handed her a set of keys. "Can you get these to him?"

"Certainly."

Zack turned to leave but walked slow enough to hear her tell the bellman to take the keys to room 634. A minute later, he and his crew entered the rear door of the hotel and hoofed it up the back staircase to the sixth floor. Gura remained in front of the hotel in his BMW, just in case Mac somehow made it past Zack's group.

Zack wondered what to make of this. *It isn't like Mac to trap himself. Unless he has recently attained cat burglar skills, his only exit from the room is the door to the hallway.* Santa used a universal key card to unlock the door to room 634. The slight whirring of the locking mechanism troubled Zack. It might be loud enough to alert Mac if he was in there waiting for them. They'd find out soon enough.

Gun drawn, Zack gently pushed open the door, inch by inch, peering into the room and seeing no one. No Mac. No Cal. As the five of them quietly entered the room, Zack saw Mac's reversible overcoat strewn across the bed, orange side up. *We have the old fool.* Zack had one of the guys check under the bed, though none of them believed Mac was *that* stupid. *On the other hand, hiding in this hotel room isn't much smarter. Poor bastard, I think he's lost a step since we worked together. I just need you to have a few left, enough to tell us where that college kid is. That's all. Then you can...go.*

Zack scoped out the room, eyeing a large closet near the front door that they'd passed when they entered. *Is Mac waiting inside, gun in hand?* Zack pointed *Blitzen* to the closet door and motioned him to open it. Blitzen approached the closet, one quiet step at a time. He was about to yank open the door when they heard the toilet flush. *Mac really has lost a step.*

The men smiled at each other, turning their attention, and their guns, to the bathroom door. One in particular was excited to get revenge for the guitar case-shaped dent on his forehead. As they waited for Mac to come out, the bathroom door slowly opened—to reveal a startled hotel employee holding a toolbox. The poor soul was frightened out of his wits, seeing the five guns pointed at his head.

"Who the hell are you?" Zack shouted.

Rudolph hurled the unfortunate man onto the bed and frisked him. "He's clean."

Prancer rushed into the bathroom, then exited a few seconds later, indicating no Mac.

The captive stuttered, "I'm, I'm...please don't hurt me. I, I work maintenance. Nights. *Please.* Mr. Starr asked me to fix his toilet, said it was an emergency, but I couldn't find nothin' wrong. That's all. Please don't hurt me. Please, I have kids."

While Zack unsuccessfully interrogated the maintenance man about the whereabouts of *Mr. Starr*, Mac was scurrying through the underground tunnel between the hotel and the parking lot across Washington Street. The tunnel was exclusively for hotel employees, and he thought perhaps Zack wasn't familiar with it. In any event, he made it to the parking lot unnoticed, hot-wired a car, and was off.

***

Fifteen minutes after *borrowing* the car, Mac was at the Music Box. He used the pre-arranged signal—three knocks, then one, then three again. When Cal opened the door, he immediately knew something had gone very wrong. It wasn't just the deep frown on Mac's face. Mac was out of breath, sweaty, and disheveled. And he wasn't wearing an overcoat on this cold autumn night. Mac wasted no time on chit chat. "Cal, we're leaving. *Now.*"

"Can I get my—"

"*Now*. I don't know how long we have, but it's not a lot."

I'm not gonna ignore Mac's instructions again. Fuck, my Oculus Quest is in the basement. No, not even gonna ask. Cal threw on his coat, and Mac guided him to the back door.

As they traversed the yard, Mac took out his phone. Cal thought he heard the word "Sis" before he moved out of earshot. He was done eavesdropping on phone conversations.

Chapter 62

BUFFALO CITY HALL OBSERVATION DECK
Buffalo, New York
Thursday, October 26, 2023
8:15 p.m.

H e took the elevator to the twenty-fifth floor, then climbed the three flights of stairs to his favorite sanctuary. Solitude. Privacy. He opened his laptop to watch Kurtoff's testimony from October 13 again. *Explosive,* he thought. *Pun intended. I'm the best there is with puns. But nobody cares.*

So far, so good. *Look over there, folks. It's Vertex. Pay no attention to the guy with the Y-tube.* His thoughts meandered back to June 30, when he'd set all this in motion. *All this commotion, thanks to little old me. Now tell me I lack motivation.*

***

Finding Jennifer Talbot's address had been no problem at all. He had everything he needed in his knapsack. The *device,* a socket wrench, soldering pen, electrical tape, and knife. He hadn't counted on anyone else being on the street at 4 a.m., let alone sneaking into the same garage he was targeting. But there he was, a burly character pulling a piece of luggage behind him. What was this all about?

The stealthy manner in which the other dude snuck into the garage told him he wasn't the only one with malicious intent this morning. He had no idea what the guy's beef was. It couldn't be the same as his. *Whatever. This could be a silver lining.* If this big man was rigging up the car, it might obviate *his* need to do it. At the very least, it could divert attention if the explosion could be pinned on whatever the other sneaky bastard was doing.

The other man vacated the garage twenty minutes later. Now certain that the street was completely empty, he quietly entered the garage, put down the knapsack, and slithered under the car. The additional cable, put there by the other saboteur and running from the superconductor ring to the rear motor, was obvious. After a minute of intense analysis, he realized it wouldn't do the job he wanted: total destruction. So he opened his knapsack and attached the Y-tube to the electrolyzer, precisely as planned. One branch to the fuel cells. One branch to the cabin. A job well done. *Now let's hope the bitch takes her little brat everywhere she goes.*

***

When he finished watching Kurtoff's testimony, he turned on the news to find he'd hit the daily double. Another explosion. *Cal Dryer was dead.* It doesn't get any better than this.

Chapter 63

SUPREME COURT, ERIE COUNTY
Holotrial Annex Building, Part 7-HT, Judge Mitachi's Chambers
Main Street, Buffalo, New York
Thursday, October 26, 2023
8:50 p.m.

Judge Mitachi was taking her evening nap on the soft leather couch in her office. Judgeship had its perks, including no one looking over your shoulder. Not that napping was a crime. There was nothing wrong with catching a few Zs in the office. After all, she was busy not only in the courtroom, presiding over trials and hearing motions, but behind the scenes in her chambers, reading briefs, doing legal research, writing opinions, preparing jury instructions. It was not uncommon to work well past midnight.

Judge Mitachi's law clerk knew better than to disturb her during the napping hour, 8:00 to 9:00 p.m. Yet at 8:50, there was an excited staccato rap on her office door. Awakened from her nap, still blurry-eyed, the judge told her clerk to come in. The young woman rushed into the room, breathless. "Sorry, Judge, you have to turn on Channel seven."

After fumbling a bit with the remote, she turned on the television. One of the nightly anchors was sitting behind the newsroom desk, his face stern. "The taxi was driving east on Delaware Avenue when it burst into flame. Attorney General Susan Stevens issued a statement that the two victims, Mr. Calvin Dryer and Mr. Jerome McMillan, both of Buffalo, had to be identified through dental records. In what seems like an incredible coincidence, Mr. Dryer was set to testify in the Talbot case about the explosion that killed Senator Bill Talbot's granddaughter. The Attorney General's office has opened an investigation. Now to the weather. Marcia?"

"Thanks, Sam. We're in for severe thunderstorms tomorrow..."

***

Out in the pristine suburb of Clarence, Alex Kurtoff watched the same broadcast, grinning from ear to ear. *Didn't think Zack could take Mac with his military, big muscles. That Zack worth every penny after all. Now I can enjoy rest of the trial. If is any more trial.*

Chapter 64

SUPREME COURT, ERIE COUNTY
Talbot versus Vertex Corporation et al.
Holotrial Annex Building, Part 7-HT
Main Street, Buffalo, New York
Friday, October 27, 2023
9:15 a.m.

Adam didn't know how he'd found his way to the courthouse. The despair was overwhelming. *I thought the bastard was immortal after all the shit he survived in the Army.* Adam had to keep it professional somehow, control his emotions, though he desperately wanted to jump over the defense table and strangle Kurtoff. *I'd lose my license, but it would be worth it.* Though the details of the *accident* were still sketchy, Adam had no doubt who was behind it.

Katherine Talbot was particularly distraught, on her second box of tissues. The defense team tried to look solemn, but Alex Kurtoff could barely conceal his glee.

How did Kurtoff find them? Only Mac and I knew where we were having dinner. Wait. I invited Kelly, too...said she couldn't make it. She was going to watch the Sabres play the Bruins. She hadn't indicated that she liked hockey before. But what the hell do I really know about her? I should have figured that revealing Mac's location was just as bad as revealing Cal's. Mac would have seen that coming. But I still can't believe she'd turn on us. The snitch must *be someone else. Yet if it wasn't me or Mac, that leaves Kelly. Three minus two is one.*

Adam scanned Kelly's face for a clue. She did seem shaken, though not as shaken as himself, or the Talbots. Then again, she didn't know Mac as well or as long as he had, and she hardly knew Cal. Nor had she lost a daughter, or a granddaughter. Was this her poker face?

The Judge was also having a difficult time holding it together. She and Mac had dated a decade earlier. Mac had always been a perfect gentleman. Their parting was amicable, and they remained close acquaintances, if not friends. She broke the deathly silence. "Mr. Simons, I...I don't know what to say. I just can't believe... Obviously, we will adjourn. I'm in no mood for business, nor do I assume you would be. I think...I think you know how this leaves your case. But that's a triviality right now."

"Thank you, Your Honor. We may need to—"

A buzzing interrupted his thought. He'd left his phone in silent mode on the counsel table, and it buzzed with a text alert. He tried to ignore it, but he got a glimpse of the message when he picked up the phone to stop the buzzing. The glimpse shook his world for the second time in twelve hours. He slowly re-read the entire message twice. *Could this be true?*

The judge was frowning. She was eager to declare an adjournment and get out of the building. Before she could speak, Adam cleared his throat and, still not sure what to believe, addressed her. "My apologies, Your Honor. Apparently, we...we would like to proceed. We have a witness to present."

"Mr. Simons, I'm really not in the mood to hear testimony this morning."

"Neither was I, Your Honor. But I think you will be. Circumstances have changed. Dramatically." Adam looked down at his phone one more time to confirm that he wasn't hallucinating. "We...we would like to call to the stand Mr. Calvin Dryer."

All eyes turned to the double doors at the back of the courtroom. And nothing happened. Silence. Now Adam really wondered what was going on. Then, to their astonishment, the doors flew open, and *in marched* Mac. Followed shortly by Cal Dryer, also alive. A woman followed them into the courtroom, but Adam remained fixated on Mac.

The courtroom erupted in a burst of emotion. All proper legal decorum was out the window. Judge Mitachi smiled broadly, then started laughing, oblivious to the disorder in the court.

Adam screamed, "Mac! You rotten bastard."

The judge didn't seem to care about his language. She had the same sentiment herself. Katherine shrieked with joy and relief. Jennifer hugged her. Kelly grinned and took in a slow panoramic view around the courtroom. At the defense table, Kurtoff cursed loudly in Ukrainian at Mr. Lukich, whose eyes bulged, his face white as a cue ball. Lukich appeared to begin making excuses, also in Ukrainian.

Amid all the commotion, Cal was a forgotten man. He marched through the mayhem as if in the eye of a hurricane, heading toward the witness box, until he stopped in his tracks, spellbound at the sight of the *jurors*. He'd been told about them during trial prep, yet seeing them *in the flesh* was still quite the experience.

Only one person showed no emotion. Senator Talbot, as usual, was stone-faced, keeping his cards close to the vest, whatever those cards were.

With a shit-eating grin on his face, Mac walked over to Adam and whispered. "Long story, Chief."

Adam grinned back broadly. *I should have known. If Mac's diet couldn't kill him, nothing could.* He grabbed Mac in a bear hug to assure himself this wasn't another hologram. He felt like a mother whose runaway child had returned home, not knowing whether to spank him or kiss him. "Mac, *what the hell?* I thought you were *gone*, you dumb bastard. Don't *ever* scare me like that again. How'd you pull this off?"

"The AG issued the phony statement about the explosion and put us in protective custody for the night. I figured Kurtoff wouldn't go after Cal if he thought he was already dead."

"But how'd you get the AG to—"

"Chief, there's somebody you gotta meet."

Mac extricated himself from Adam's grasp, then escorted him by the arm toward the gallery seats. The Attorney General herself sat there, holding a small, plush pterodactyl that Adam immediately recognized from Mac's torn photo. "Mr. Simons, meet my sister, Susan Stevens. You may also know her as the Attorney General of the great State of New York."

"A pleasure to see you again, Mr. Simons," the AG said. "This little fellow is Dinobird. I've been keeping him safe for Mac for about sixty years. Dino was beginning to wonder if he'd ever see Mac again."

***

Adam had never gotten such pleasure from watching a witness being sworn in.

The Court: Mr. Dryer, it's so good to see you.

Mr. Caparini: Your Honor?

The Court: Yes, Mr. Caparini, don't worry. That will be stricken from the Holoscript. But I must also say, off the record, it *is* good to see you alive and well, Mr. Dryer. I guess the rumors of your death have indeed been greatly exaggerated, in the words of our famous American scribe. Oh, and you too, Mr. McMillan. Welcome back to the living.

Cal's nervousness was palpable. Adam couldn't tell if it was from having to testify, or whatever Cal and Mac had been through the night before. Possibly both. Adam thought he'd start with a puffball question, using Cal's favorite word to ease him into his testimony.

Q: Cal, tell us, where do you go to school?

A: I'm, like, I'm at UB.

Q: And Cal, can you tell us where you were on June 30 of this year, at approximately 4:40 p.m.?

A: I was at the, uh, the ships.

Q: Cal, do you mean the Buffalo and Erie County Naval & Military Park?

A: Yeah, that's it.

Q: Cal, specifically where were you in the Naval Park?

A: On that ship, the big one, like, in a medical clinic room.

Q: Would that be the USS *The Sullivans*? The destroyer?

A: Yes, that one.

Mr. Caparini: Your Honor, a lot of leading going on.

The Court: Yes, but it's preliminary. I'll allow it.

For now.

Q: Thank you, Your Honor. So Cal, you said you were in a medical clinic room. Was that called a *sick bay* on the ship?

A: Oh, yeah. That's right.

Q: And Cal, what were you doing there? In the sick bay.

A: I know it sounds strange, but I was, like, pretending to be a sick sailor. On the examination table. A fake sailor, like they have all over the ships. It was a prank to show my friends I could, like, stay on the ship all night and not get caught.

The irony hit Adam. *This whole thing started with Cal being a mannequin, and now it ends with seven mannequins watching him from the jury box.*

Q: And what happened while you were lying on the examination table?

A: Well, I started to call my girlfriend Tina when somebody, like, walked into the room. So I shut up.

Q: What happened next?

A: The guy leaned against the table I was on, like real close, and he made a phone call to someone he called "Mr. K" and "Boss."

Q: Could you hear him clearly?

A: Yes. He was leaning against the table, like an inch or two away from me. I was scared shi...sorry. It was scary.

Q: And what did he say?

Mr. Caparini: Objection, Your Honor, hearsay.

The Court: I assume Mr. Simons is going to tell me it falls under the "admission against interest" exception to the hearsay rule. Is that right, Mr. Simons?

Mr. Simons: Absolutely, Your Honor.

The Court: Well, then, I'll allow the testimony conditionally, and we'll see where it goes.

Q: So, you said the man referred to whoever was on the other end of the call as "Boss" and "Mr. K?" And did they have a discussion?

Mr. Caparini: Objection, Your Honor. There's no testimony that Mr. Dryer heard the person on the other end of the line.

The Court: Let's find out. Mr. Dryer, did you hear the other party to the conversation?

Mr. Dryer: Not well...it was, like, very faint. I couldn't make out any words.

The Court: Yes, well, sustained to the extent that you will confine your questions, Mr. Simons, and your answers, Mr. Dryer, to what the man with you in the sick bay was saying.

Mr. Simons: Thank you, Your Honor.

The Court: Mr. Simons, do I really have to tell you, you needn't thank me for sustaining an objection *against* you? You can put away that litigation trick for Holotrials. You're not impressing those bubble heads over there.

Mr. Simons: Apologies, Your Honor.

The old gal hasn't lost a step. I can't forget that. Gotta stay on my toes.

Q: Mr. Dryer, let's continue. What did they talk about?

Mr. Caparini: *He* talk about, Your Honor.

The Court: Yes, Mr. Dryer, just the person in the room with you.

Mr. Dryer: Okay, should I—

Q: Yes, Cal, you can answer. The man standing next to you in sick bay. What did he say?

A: He, like he started talking about a car that had, like, exploded that day.

Q: Was he speaking English?

A: Yes, but with a heavy accent.

Q: What kind of accent?

Mr. Caparini: Your Honor, Mr. Dryer is a language expert now?

The Court: No, I'll allow it. Let's see what he can tell us.

Q: Go ahead.

A: I think, like, Eastern Europe. We have lots of students from there on campus so, like, I'm kinda able to recognize them. Like what exact country, I don't know.

Q: By the way, Cal, did you ever get a look at this Eastern European person?

A: Yes. I took a peek.

Q: Can you describe him for the jury?

A: He was big. Huge. I think over six feet tall.

Q: Did you see what he was wearing?

A: He had on a gray jacket. With, like, a logo that said Vertex Security.

Q: You're certain of that, Cal? Vertex Security? Did you get a good look at the jacket?

A: For sure. Like I said, he was real close to me. I could have stuck out my hand and touched the logo.

Q: All right, Cal, tell us, what did the large Eastern European man in the sick bay wearing the

Alan M. Wishnoff

Vertex Security jacket say about the explosion?

A: He started off saying something in his
  language, and then "Mr. K"...

***

Cal's direct testimony was over in time for lunch. It had been as powerful as they expected. Kurtoff's face had grown redder with each word. Every question or two, he'd elbow Caparini in the ribs and whisper something to him. While Cal's testimony was limited to Gura's side of the conversation, there was little question who *Mr. K* or *Boss* was. Adam asked Mac to take Cal out for lunch during the break, before Cal's cross-examination in the afternoon. Adam was going to stick around to confer with the Talbots, who were still frazzled after the death and resurrection of their star witness. They huddled around Adam in the gallery, too excited by the morning's events to sit down. Kurtoff and his lawyers remained at the defense counsel table.

While Adam explained to the Talbots that the trial would likely be over once Cal's cross-examination was complete, a text alert sounded on Kurtoff's phone. Seconds later, he jumped from his seat and smashed the phone on the table, screaming, *"Layno,"* at the top of his lungs. It startled his own lawyers as well as the plaintiffs' team. A nanosecond later, Kurtoff's scowling face transformed into a broad smile.

Adam clenched his jaw. *Very strange.*

***

Mac and Cal exited the courthouse into a heavy downpour. Fortunately, Mac had closed the top on the Porsche when he parked it that morning. As they walked to the car, Mac, struggling to hold his umbrella in the wind, congratulated Cal on his testimony. "You name the place. Lunch is on me. Well, it's on Adam, once I submit my expense report. Anyway, you've earned it."

"Wherever I can get, like, beef on weck and a flight."

"Sure thing on the sandwich. The beer will have to wait. You gotta keep your wits about you. Caparini can be crafty. Who knows what tricks he's planning for cross-examination. Hey, I bet you feel pretty relieved now you got this behind you."

"Absolutely. I'm calm for the first time in, like, months. Sort of like the buzz I get from...you know. Anyway, I'm calm."

While Mac assumed that Kurtoff would see no point in harming Cal now that he'd testified, he still took no chances, sweeping the street and the sidewalks with his trained eyes. It was difficult to see more than 10 or 15 feet through the windswept rain, but Mac figured the rain would pose an equal problem for any opposition. Even the best of marksmen would find it nearly impossible to hit a target under these conditions. Mac himself would *never* try such a shot. He could barely make out the outlines of the parked cars and a large industrial crane in the parking lot across the street, where a new office building was going up. Nevertheless, Mac looked in every direction. Every direction but up.

***

When Cal had started his testimony, Kurtoff made the same calculation that Adam had reached. There was no longer any benefit to be gained from eliminating Cal. His testimony was going into the record. So Kurtoff texted Petro, his new point man for the Cal problem, to call off the hit. Petro, foggy after a long night at the bars, was awakened by Kurtoff's text, which read, "Cal Dryer testifying. Terminate project. Repeat. Terminate immediately." Still blurry-eyed, all Petro gleaned from the message was "Cal Dryer testifying" and "Terminate immediately." The text was an unnecessary reminder of Kurtoff's obsession with this college kid, and Petro didn't want to disappoint Kurtoff. He knew what that disappointment would mean. With this impetus, Petro quickly dressed and raced downtown to the courthouse.

He knew he'd never get past the metal detectors at the courthouse entrance, not that shooting someone in the middle of a trial, with lots of witnesses including armed courtroom deputies, would make any sense. Getting off an accurate shot in this rain wasn't a viable option, either. Then, miracle of miracles, Petro saw the solution to his problem. He couldn't have conjured up a better one if he'd been given a week to plan it. The construction project across the street from the courthouse had a down day, due to the weather, which meant that the unmanned industrial crane was freely available.

While Cal was still delivering his devastating testimony inside, Petro maneuvered the crane to place the five-ton girder it was carrying directly above Mac's car, forty feet in the air. It was doubtful that Mac would see it in the rainstorm, assuming he even thought to scan the sky. And if he did see it, he was unlikely to realize what a potent weapon it had become.

***

Petro's target exited the courthouse and entered the car. With Cal in the passenger seat, and Mac walking around the rear to get to the driver's side, Petro released the girder. Mac's car, with its canvas roof, had no chance. Nor did Cal.

The deafening sound and shock wave from five tons of steel I-beam crashing onto Mac's car knocked him to the ground. His head hit the pavement, and his first thought was of some type of ordinance, maybe a car bomb? RPG? Finally realizing what had happened, Mac turned his attention, and his .45, toward the crane. No one there. He streaked back to the passenger door, hoping against hope that Cal had survived this cataclysm. No such luck. Cal's crushed and lifeless body was still in his seat. The girder had obliterated most of the car, as well as Cal. Blood was everywhere. Mac had seen enough dead bodies to recognize one here.

He brushed off the fact that he himself had almost been killed. Near-death experiences were nothing new for Mac. But Cal? *Jesus.* He was starting to like the kid.

Mac called 911, knowing it was pointless. *Jesus mother-fucking H. Christ. I went through all that shit to protect him. Took care of that asshole Quill. Nailed that double-dealing shithead Zack. The AG's office does the phony death story, puts us in Wit Pro for the night. And now this?*

After the firemen had removed the girder and the paramedics had bagged Cal's body, Mac trudged back to the courthouse, trying to think of how to break the news. The pernicious rain pelted his head, though he didn't notice it, nor the fact that he no longer had his umbrella. A paramedic, seeing Mac unsteady on his feet, stopped to check him out, but Mac waved him off. The paramedic didn't argue.

Holotrial

***

It was *déjà vu* all over again for the Talbots, mourning the death of their principal witness for the second time. Only this time it was for real. They convened in the lawyers' conference room with Mac, Adam, and Kelly. The scene of jubilation that had greeted Cal's rise from the dead, just a few hours before, had turned on its head. They hoped against hope this might be another trick, but Mac's eyewitness account, the large bruise on his head, and his rain-drenched, blood-spattered clothes squashed those hopes. Moist red eyes were everywhere. Except for the Senator who remained stoic, as usual.

At least Mac's alive. Adam felt guilty for thinking it, but it was a natural reaction. He was shocked by Cal's death, but he had barely known him. Not like Mac, whom he'd worked with for so many years. Then the real guilt hit Adam. *I shouldn't have pushed Cal to testify. He was scared from the get-go. I suppose at some point I'm going to meet the parents. At the funeral, if not sooner. And his girlfriend, too, what's her name? What the hell do I tell them?*

No one, least of all Adam, was in a mood to discuss the effect of Cal's death on the Talbots' legal options. Not that Adam needed to work it out. The case was basically over without Cal. Nevertheless, he called Mitachi's chambers to ask if they could adjourn in view of the circumstances. The judge herself took the call.

"Take as much time as you need," she said, "I'm not ready for a legal discussion right now, either. A witness in my courtroom has been *killed*. In all my years, this has never...I can't discuss with you who must be responsible without defense counsel present, but I doubt you have to guess. Whatever you need Adam, you have it."

Chapter 65

ADAM'S LAW OFFICE
Parkside Avenue, Buffalo, New York
Thursday, November 2, 2023
1:00 p.m.

Adam, Kelly, and the Talbots were assembled at the table in his conference room. Six days after Cal's death, it still felt disrespectful to discuss trial strategy, particularly when the main subject was the effect of his death on their case. But they were due back in court the next day, and Adam felt that he needed to explain the legal ramifications before they heard it from the judge or, worse, Caparini.

Adam sat at the head of the table, with Katherine to his left, Jennifer next to her, and Bill on his right. Adam abhorred having to explain the death of the lawsuit. Though the general mood was dark, there was also a sense of relief at being able to relax in a private setting without being besieged by the public and the press, who'd turned Cal's funeral into a circus.

Jennifer, perennially chewing her gum, started the conversation. "Mr. Simons. Cal's testimony was recorded, right? You said, like, he'd be safe and we'd be okay if his testimony was recorded? So we don't have to do this again?"

"Yes, Jennifer, I thought... *Goddamnit,* I hadn't counted on a lunch break before his cross-examination. Kurtoff's more of an evil genius than I thought. I'm sorry, it didn't occur—"

Katherine intervened. "Adam, forget the Jewish guilt. No one could have anticipated this."

"Thanks for trying, Kate." Adam shrugged. "But if I hadn't talked him into testifying, Cal wouldn't have been in Mac's car. He'd be alive today, hanging out with his friends, drinking beer or smoking pot or doing whatever the hell college kids do these days. Why didn't I at least tell them to eat in the goddamn courthouse cafeteria?"

Suddenly, like a dormant volcano exploding without notice, Jennifer screamed at the top of her lungs, "None of this should have happened." She glared at her parents. "No one would be dead if you didn't make me keep the damn baby."

Bill's jaw clenched, his face reddened, eyes smoldering. "Stop it, Jenny. *Now.*"

Jennie wasn't deterred. "I wouldn't need any of your crappy support, the nice little house far away from yours so no one sees the baby at your place, protect your fucking image, but no, you had to make me—"

"Enough!" Bill's shout echoed through the conference room. "I don't ever want to hear you say that again. Ever."

This wasn't the first time Adam had seen clients respond with anger to a tragedy they could neither control nor reverse. It also provided a possible solution to the Talbot enigma.

Jennifer turned to Adam. "Mr. Simons. I think you said, like, Cal was our last witness, right? So can't we finish up now? You give your ending statement and we, like, we don't ever have to do this again, right? I don't know if I could...a third time."

Katherine nodded. Bill was silent, though Adam could see the rusty legal wheels spinning inside his head. He'd save Bill the time and effort.

"I'm afraid it's not quite that simple, Jennifer. When Cal was killed, we'd only gotten through his direct testimony. The defendants were entitled to cross-examine him. That's a basic tenet of jurispru...a basic requirement for trials. It's guaranteed by the Constitution. It would be unfair to let a witness testify without letting the other party cross-examine, to see if they can poke holes in the witness's story."

Katherine scowled. "They destroyed the car. They killed Allie. What else do you need?"

"I can't argue with you, Kate. However, every litigator, Caparini included, thinks he has a good case, that he can make a silk purse out of a sow's ear, no matter the facts. Regardless of what *we* think, they had the right to cross-examine Cal. Now they can't."

"So, what does all this mean for us?"

Bill jumped in. "It means, dear, that the judge is going to strike Cal's direct testimony. And without Cal's testimony, there goes the case."

Katherine looked to Adam. "But *we* didn't cause Cal's death. The court can't blame us for Cal not being here. You know damn well Kurtoff did this."

"No question, Kate." Adam wished he had a better answer. "Of course he did it. But we can't *prove* it. That rainstorm was a godsend for those bastards. It prevented anyone from witnessing the crime, and then it washed away any evidence."

Adam had let down his guard, repeatedly addressing Katherine as Kate. Bill might not have noticed it once, but Adam's lapse continued. "Bill is right, Kate. If the defendants can't cross-examine the witness, it's almost certain Cal's direct examination will be stricken. The judge won't let the jury hear just one side's story. And without Cal's testimony, we have an extremely weak case. Almost certainly not enough to go to a real jury."

"But they talked about the explosion on the phone." Katherine's tone was frantic. "They *admitted* it. Kurtoff, that pig, he ordered it." Tears welled.

Adam slid a tissue box to her.

She blew her nose. "Adam, they killed Allie, and we all know it." She sniffled.

"Everything you said is true, Kate. *We* know it. But unless we get around the cross-examination problem, the *jury* will never know it. We have to find a way to make Cal's testimony admissible without a cross, and I'm not sure there is one."

Bill interjected. "I'm afraid Adam's right. Without Cal's testimony, the case is toast."

"*Afraid?*" Katherine shouted. "You're ecstatic, aren't you? You were against this case from the start. Worried about your damn PR, *President* Talbot."

"Now, Kate. We're all emotional. You forget, *I'm* the one who got Adam to take this case in the first place."

"Yeah, sure. You were just too persuasive."

"I did it for you, and of course for Jenny. And the child."

Jennifer snorted.

"You can't even say her name, can you?" Katherine didn't let up. "It's *Allie*. Say it. *Allie*."

"I won't listen to your nonsense anymore."

Adam had tried, uncomfortably, to play peacemaker between

his old friend and his wife, who also happened to be Adam's former lover. *Never again.* He stood up and walked behind Katherine's chair, gently putting his hands on her shoulders, hoping both to comfort her and to restrain her from physically attacking Bill. "Kate. Bill. Please, we're all upset. But anger isn't going to solve anything. I won't lie to you. Our situation is tenuous. We need calm heads. Who knows, maybe I'll try Kate's argument that we didn't cause Cal's death, so don't blame us if you can't cross-examine him." He playfully tapped her shoulders.

She gazed at him through clouded eyes, and a tiny smile started to form. "I won't even take credit, Adam. You can tell all the papers it was your idea."

***

Bill had the limo to himself. Katherine and Jennifer had taken a cab rather than ride with him. Once the limo rounded the corner from Adam's office, Bill broke out into raucous laughter, startling his driver. The dynamic between his wife and his friend, Adam, had opened Bill's eyes. They oozed intimacy. Adam had calmed her histrionics in a matter of seconds. And it wasn't just their words. Their body language, tone of voice... How had he missed it all this time?

Bill had solved a huge puzzle. *Poor Adam. He doesn't know what he's stepped in. You couldn't make this up in a million years. What a shock he's in for. If Kate doesn't tell him, I will. With relish. Let the trial finish. First things first. But there's no question those two have been at it. And I know when. Almost to the day.*

Chapter 66

SUPREME COURT, ERIE COUNTY
Talbot versus Vertex Corporation et al.
Holotrial Annex Building, Part 7-HT
Main Street, Buffalo, New York
Friday, November 3, 2023
9:15 a.m.

Back in the courtroom, a week after Cal's demise, Kurtoff barely concealed a massive grin. Strangely, Senator Talbot too seemed to be suppressing a smile. *What that all about?* Kurtoff wondered. *Who cares? The little bastard dead. No one get me now, not even great Simons.*

The court having been called to order, Caparini was quick to jump to his feet. "Your Honor. We have a motion. We are on the record, yes?"

The Court: All right, Mr. Caparini. Go ahead.

Mr. Caparini: Your Honor, the defendants move to exclude the direct testimony of Mr. Dryer. It would violate their right to Due Process under the New York and Federal Constitutions, since we have no way to cross-examine Mr. Dryer. I am sure Mr. Dryer's questionable assertions wouldn't have held up on cross. Now, there can be no cross. The jury will never know.

The Court: Mr. Simons?

Adam slowly stood up from his chair.

Mr. Simons: Your Honor, a trial is a search for the truth. Mr. Dryer's testimony exposed the most basic truth in this case. That Vertex, and Mr. Kurtoff in particular, intentionally plotted to sabotage Jennifer Talbot's car, resulting in the death of her two-month-old infant. This terrible crime cannot and must not be swept under the rug because of an unforeseeable event that was not in any way caused by the plaintiffs.

Mr. Caparini: Your Honor, we certainly don't accept Mr. Simons' characterization of the testimony, but it makes no difference. Defendants have a constitutionally guaranteed right to confront witnesses against them with cross-examination.

Adam thought he'd go for a long shot. He couldn't prove that Kurtoff had Cal killed, though everyone damn well knew it, so why not propose an alternative that might save the case?

Mr. Simons: Your Honor, the plaintiffs obviously had nothing to do with Mr. Dryer's death. The terrible rainstorm may well have caused the girder to slip off the crane, and the law recognizes that such extraordinary circumstances call for extraordinary remedies. The thunderstorm was, in essence, a *force majeure,* an act of God or Nature, which should excuse us from strict compliance with the norms.

The Court: Mr. Simons, under the circumstances, I understand why you may be grasping at straws. But of all people, I think you'd be the last to refer to Constitutional rights merely as *the norms.* You've made a career of defending those rights, virtually to the death, and it's surprising, to say the least, to hear you refer to them in so casual, if not cavalier, a manner.

Mr. Simons: I certainly didn't intend to give that impression, Your Honor. I apologize if I wasn't clear, but I suppose I was trying to state, however unartfully, that under the extraordinary circumstances we have here, one must weigh *my* client's Due Process right to a fair trial against the defendants' right of cross-examination. I *am* arguing for Constitutional rights to prevail...*the plaintiffs'*. When we have evidence of the defendants' wrongdoing, evidence of *this* magnitude, the court should err on the side of allowing the evidence and upholding the plaintiffs' right to trial.

The Court: Are you really telling us that the rain caused that girder to fall on Mac's, um, Mr. McMillan's car? That there was no human involvement?

Adam could only look down at his feet.

Mr. Caparini: Your Honor, Mr. Simons' shameless accusations aside, as you can see, he blames the rain for Mr. Dryer's death, not the defendants.

Mr. Simons: Not yet, Phil. Not yet. When we do get the evidence—

Mr. Caparini: Simons, you're just blowing smoke in the wind.

The Court: *Gentlemen.* You will address the court. This is not the Debate Society.

Mr. Simons: Sorry, Your Honor. Your Honor, the CPLR provides that pre-trial deposition testimony of a deceased witness may be used at trial provided that both parties were represented at the deposition. If a *pre-trial deposition* can be used at trial, surely testimony taken *during the trial itself* should be allowed as well.

The Court: Mr. Simons. I think you are grasping at another straw. The representation by counsel that is called for by the statute must be *meaningful* if the deceased's testimony is to be used against the defendants. At a minimum, they should have had the opportunity to cross-examine the deceased. Mr. Caparini's presence for the direct examination alone is not meaningful since a cross of Mr. Dryer is now impossible.

Mr. Simons: But, Your Honor—

The Court: No, Mr. Simons, *no*. I do give you extra credit for originality on the *force majeure* argument. But this is not a contract. It is a trial with live parties whose interests must be protected in accordance with the established procedures for jury trials, including Constitutional *norms*, as you call them. I agree with you, Mr. Simons, that it would be a crime to let these defendants walk away from responsibility for their actions.

Mr. Caparini: Your Honor—

Mitachi waived Caparini off.

The Court: But even in this civil case, I'm afraid the Constitution reigns supreme. The right to confront witnesses through cross-examination is ingrained in our legal traditions going back centuries. I'm sorry, Ms. Talbot. I'm afraid I have no choice but to grant the motion to exclude Mr. Dryer's direct testimony. It will be stricken from the record.

Kelly and Katherine gasped. Jennifer stared blankly. Adam looked like he'd been struck by lightning. Losing a motion here or there was to be expected for any litigator, Adam included, though he'd always been able to overcome such rulings in the past. That success record was in severe jeopardy now. Cal had been the only solid evidence tying Vertex, and Kurtoff, to the destruction of Jennifer's car. Cal's story had been the sole reason they'd commenced this lawsuit, and now that reason was gone.

Kurtoff turned to Caparini to whisper, "So is over? We have big celebration at my house, is not? We drink *Horilka* all night."

Caparini smiled. "We just need to get through a few formalities, and then Mr. Simons' case is gone. This shouldn't take long." With that, Caparini stood up and addressed the Court.

> Mr. Caparini: Thank you, Your Honor. We have a follow up motion, if I may.

> The Court: I assumed you would.

> Mr. Caparini: We move to dismiss plaintiffs' case in its entirety for lack of evidence. And for a directed verdict in favor of the defendants.

> Mr. Simons: *Your Honor*. How—

> The Court: Sit, Mr. Simons. Sit. There's no need. Mr. Caparini, your motion is premature. The plaintiffs have not yet rested their case. Or have you, Mr. Simons?

> Mr. Simons: Um...I don't think... If I may have a little time to confer with my client, Your Honor?

The judge looked at the clock above the rear doors, then back at Adam.

> The Court: It's 10:30. Mr. Simons, I'll give you until Monday to determine whether and how you intend to proceed. I'm not giving up any state secrets by advising you that you have your work cut out for you. Without Mr. Dryer's testimony, you haven't really tied the defendants to the cable *or* the explosion.

> Mr. Simons: Thank you, Your Honor.

> The Court: And I would note, Mr. Simons, I'm only adjourning us now because this *is* a Holotrial, so no jury is being inconvenienced. Perhaps this will change your views.

> Mr. Simons: Your Honor makes a point. Duly noted.

Chapter 67

HOME OF ALEX KURTOFF
Stonecliff Court, Clarence, New York
Saturday, November 4, 2023
11:00 p.m.

Gura arrived at Kurtoff's house, unsurprised to be summoned at this late hour. Many of their *special jobs* were performed at night.

Clarence provided a striking contrast to Gura's neighborhood in South Buffalo. Not all that long ago, the northern suburb had been mostly farmland and woods. Its quiet rural beauty presented an interesting mixture of older, more traditional houses and sparkling new homes with ultra-modern architecture set amid the green landscape that paid homage to its agrarian past.

Kurtoff himself answered the door, as his new housekeeper had gone home. The two of them were alone in the house. "I have assignment for you, Damytro, very important. Need to tie up a loose end, is not? But first, you ever see my house?" Gura shook his head no. Everyone knew Kurtoff was over-the-top proud of his home. He told anyone who'd listen that it was mostly his design, which his architect let him think. "I show you around, is not?"

There ensued an exhausting tour throughout Kurtoff's mansion. Gura lost track of the number of bedrooms and bathrooms in its three above-ground floors.

"I save best for last. I show you now The Citadel."

They walked down to the basement. Kurtoff locked the soundproof door behind them. Gura uttered a simple, "Wow," when he saw the weaponry and musical instruments.

"Damytro, we play fun game. One of these violins worth over two million dollars. See if you can pick out, is not? Take your time."

Gura surveyed the instruments with the same ignorance that Kurtoff had when he entered that violin shop in Phillippavivska so many years ago. He wanted to protest this silly game and get to the real assignment, *but if Alexi wants to play game, I play game. Never good to refuse Mr. K.* After staring at the violins for a couple minutes, Gura pointed to the one with the shiniest varnish.

"Good choice. No. Excellent choice." Kurtoff took the instrument off the wall.

Gura leaned in to scrutinize the violin up close when, without warning, Kurtoff raised it in the air and smashed it down on Gura's head. Gura stood there, stunned. Kurtoff plunged the jagged edge of the broken violin into Gura's neck, over and over, slicing through the carotid artery and eventually almost severing his head. Gura's lifeless body fell to the hardwood floor with a loud *crack.*

Kurtoff had installed the hardwood because it was great for acoustics, and also for cleaning up blood. With Gura in a bloody mess on the floor, Kurtoff called the Vertex security detail. "Anton, I need clean and erase in the Citadel... No. Just one body. Is not?"

Kurtoff hung up and sighed. Gura had been a loyal soldier, but he'd become too great a risk, a loose end to be tied off. Even though that cockroach Dryer was dead, the bastards knew about his conversation with Gura, and Kurtoff thought it best that Gura not be available to testify, cutting off Simons' only option for getting the June 30 conversation into the trial record. There had been three witnesses to that phone call. Two were now dead. That left only Kurtoff, and *he* wasn't talking.

As he climbed the stairs of The Citadel, Kurtoff took one last look at Gura lying motionless on the floor in a pool of his own blood. "At least he not pick the Strad."

Chapter 68

ADAM'S HOME
Tudor Place, Buffalo, New York
Sunday, November 5, 2023
2:34 p.m.

There are some situations that even the best of lawyers cannot overcome, and Adam was faced with one now. He was due in court in the morning, and on this rarest of occasions, he had no idea what to argue.

He had never been this discouraged. Everyone knew the truth, yet the jury wouldn't hear it. How could that be justice? He'd been wracking his brain down to the individual synapses, running again and again into the same roadblock: the sacred right of cross-examination.

What made it all the more irritating was that Adam knew Mitachi was sympathetic to Jennifer, and certainly outraged at Kurtoff. As if the sabotaged juror head were not enough, Cal's testimony erased any doubt that Kurtoff was behind the destruction of Jennifer's car and the death of her child. Nor was there any doubt that Kurtoff was behind Cal's death, but the judge couldn't act on that because any proof had been swept away in the storm.

Adam knew Mitachi would play it by the book, regardless of her personal feelings, as she'd already done by knocking out Cal's direct testimony. He couldn't blame her. He wished there were more judges who adhered so tightly to the rules. *If I could give her a reason to keep the case alive, I know she'd do it in a heartbeat. Twice now she's given us extra time to try to save the case. Very unlike her. I just wish I knew what the hell to tell her.*

In the week since Cal's demise, Adam and Kelly had reached nothing but dead ends. Kelly thought of subpoenaing the closed-circuit footage from the entrance to the Naval Park. Maybe someone else on the ship overheard Gura speaking to Kurtoff. Turned out they

Alan M. Wishnoff

still used videotape, which was recycled every two months. There was nothing left from back in June.

Adam had also asked Mac to contact as many of Cal's friends as he could find, to see if Cal might have told any of them about the conversation he'd overheard. So far, there were no takers. Not surprising. Adam thought it unlikely they'd be excited to help the people they probably blamed for Cal's death. It would be double hearsay anyway, an extreme long shot to get into evidence, but Adam was at his wits' end. Long shots were all he had left.

Kelly called to say she still had nothing. "How 'bout you, Adam? Anything?"

"Batting zero. Less than Pug. Maybe we just ask Mitachi to let the plastic jurors decide the case. They've already heard Cal's testimony, and they can't wipe it from their minds." Even in the most dire of circumstances, a little dark humor could help him get through a tight spot.

Kelly laughed at his suggestion, "Is that a simple or complex solution?"

"It's neither a... Excuse me Kelly, someone's at the door. I'll call you back."

When he opened the front door, there stood Mac, obviously happy with himself. His body filled the doorway, barely letting in any sunlight. "Chief, there's somebody you gotta meet."

Adam could only manage a slight smile through his weariness. What could Mac possibly have found? A twenty-something woman stood behind Mac, clutching something in her left hand.

"Chief, meet Tina Long."

The name sounded familiar, but Adam couldn't place it right away. Mac and the young woman walked past him into the foyer. She paused briefly to ponder the two baskets on the wall: SUSTAINED and OVERRULED.

Adam ushered them into his home office, where he addressed Mac. "And I want to meet Tina because?"

"Just listen to her, Chief."

"Okay," Adam said. "So what can I do for you?"

Mac answered. "It's what *she* can do for *us*, Chief. This is Cal Dryer's girlfriend. You remember. He called her from the ship."

"Oh, my God. Yes. Tina. I'm sorry. We met at the, uh, the wake. We're all still in shock. I'm *so* sorry for what...well, I'm

~296~

sorry."

Tina's presence revived Adam's guilt, which made it difficult for him to talk about the case, but he assumed he knew what she was going to tell him anyway. "Mac, whatever Cal told her, it's double hearsay. Tina's testifying about what Cal told her that the thug on the ship told Kurtoff. It won't get by—"

"Just listen to her, Chief."

"Mr. Simons," Tina began tentatively, "when Cal called me from the ship, like, he never hung up the phone. I guess 'cause he was interrupted by that, you know, the person he ran into there."

She had Adam's attention. Before she could continue, though, they were interrupted by Pete, who walked into the room, fiddling with his phone. No doubt, Adam thought, Pete was killing some five-legged aliens, or fighting World War V or whatever war they were up to on *Call of Duty. The kid's never around, and he picks this moment to barge in.* He wanted to shoo Pete out of the office and get back to Tina's story, but his manners got the better of him.

"Tina, this is my son Pete. Pete, say hello to Ms. Long." Pete shyly mumbled a hello, though he continued to look down at his phone. Adam considered addressing Pete's rudeness, but he had bigger fish to fry just then. "Pete, we've got business here. We need some privacy." Pete left the room, though he lingered outside, curious about the young woman Uncle Mac had brought.

"Mr. Simons," Tina continued, "the message Cal left on my phone that night was the last time I ever heard his voice, so I saved it on a flash drive. I've listened to it, like, a hundred times. I know you don't care about that. Anyway, when Cal didn't hang up, voicemail continued to record. You can kinda' hear the other man in the room talking."

Tina opened her left hand to reveal the flash drive, which she handed to Adam. He couldn't get to his computer fast enough. Could this be salvation? A simple solution to this most complex of problems? He was almost hyperventilating as he plugged in the flash drive and, with great anticipation, pressed the play icon on the screen.

Cal's message to Tina was loud and clear, followed by the faint voice of Gura and an even more indistinct voice, presumably Kurtoff. It was basically impossible to make out the words or identify either speaker.

Adam let out a deep sigh. "Mac, this is an impressive find, but what does it get us? I barely hear the shithead...sorry, Tina...the guy on the ship with Cal, and the voice on the phone is unintelligible. Might be Kurtoff. Might be my Aunt Rebecca. And how do we tie this to the Naval Museum on June thirtieth?"

"Date and time are embedded in the recording, Chief, and we have time and GPS on Cal's phone." The sound of the front door opening could be heard from Adam's office. "Oh, yeah, Chief. I asked Freddie to come over. Thought he could help with this."

A moment later, Freddie entered the room. Like Mac, he had a key to Adam's house, and had let himself in.

"Freddie, I assume you're already aware of this recording. "Why am *I* always the last to know? So, you think you can do anything with it?"

"It's worth a shot, Chief. I know a guy with some fancy equipment who can probably enhance it. Depends on the quality of the recording."

"By tomorrow morning?"

"I'll give it a try, Chief."

"Thanks. Oh, Tina, I'm sorry. This is my assistant, Freddie Matthews."

Tina stared at Freddie. "You know, you look familiar. Have you been on TV or something?"

"Well, I used to play some ball, ma'am. For the Yankees. Did some commercials too. You can call me Pug. Pug Matthews. Pleased to meet you."

***

As the front door closed behind Tina, Mac turned to Adam. "Does this do it, Chief?"

"We'll know in the morning. This is the whole case now. If Freddie's guy can enhance it so we understand what the hell they're saying, it's spectacular. If not, we've got bupkes... I'd just like to see the look on Kurtoff's face. Assuming it's not inadmissible hearsay. I've got to think about that one. Whatever happens, great job, Mac. I mean it."

Chapter 69

SUPREME COURT, ERIE COUNTY
Talbot versus Vertex Corporation et al.
Holotrial Annex Building, Part 7-HT
Main Street, Buffalo, New York
Monday, November 6, 2023
9:15 a.m.

Kurtoff was all smiles—until Adam marched into the courtroom, appearing far more confident than Kurtoff expected. *Goddamn Simons, he up to what now?*

Judge Mitachi also noticed Adam's surprising enthusiasm. "Good morning, Mr. Simons. Any more rabbits in your hat?"

"Just one, Your Honor." Adam picked up a silver flash drive and waved it in the air for dramatic effect. Kurtoff didn't know what it was, but he sensed it was trouble. "We have an enhanced audio recording of the June thirtieth conversation between defendant Alex Kurtoff and a Vertex employee, Damytro Gura, the man Mr. Dryer testified was in the sick bay with him."

Kurtoff wanted to scream. His face turned into a seething scowl as he whispered into Caparini's ear. "Jesus Christ. Now they have *recording*. Gura really fuck this one up. Not matter. *You stop this.*"

"Alexi, I—"

"Shut up, Cap. No excuse. You stop it. I do not tolerate mistake, is not?"

"Alexi, we have good arguments, you'll see." Caparini's face suggested otherwise.

"For thousand dollars an hour, I expect *win*, not *good*."

Caparini, more rattled by his own client than the plaintiff's new evidence, stood up. "Your Honor..." he said in a shaky voice, "Can we go on the record? Yes? Thank you."

Mr. Caparini: Your Honor, we move to exclude

this recording. Improper, lack of foundation.

The Court: Mr. Simons, I assume you are able to authenticate it?

Mr. Simons: Yes, Your Honor. We have a demonstrable chain of custody, starting with my investigator, Mr. McMillan, over there.

The Court: Yes, I'm quite familiar with Mr. McMillan.

Mr. Simons: So am I, Your Honor. So am I. I'd like to mark this flash drive for identification as Plaintiffs' Exhibit seventy-two. With your permission, Your Honor.

The Court: So ordered.

Judge Mitachi's business-like demeanor had not wavered, but Kurtoff sensed she was pleased with this new circumstance. *Bitch. She want to let this in. Not worry. If recording bad, no one understand. If recording good, we still keep it out.*

Mr. Simons: We were able to identify Mr. Gura by matching his voiceprint with a recorded statement taken in connection with a prior arrest. And I think everyone in this courtroom will be able to identify Mr. Kurtoff's voice.

The Court: Take your seat, Mr. Caparini. I'm going to listen to this in chambers so I know what we're talking about before I make any rulings. Mr. Simons, how long is this recording?

Mr. Simons: Approximately two and a half minutes, Your Honor.

Mitachi grabbed the flash drive, now adorned with a tag identifying it as *PX 72*, and proceeded to her chambers. She listened to it twice, each time with amazement. To call this a smoking gun was a vast understatement. More like a roaring cannon.

***

Judge Mitachi glared at Kurtoff as she re-entered the courtroom. That told him all he needed to know. Yet Kurtoff seemed less angry than before. Now that he understood what he was facing, he was fairly certain the jury would never hear it. *Smug Simons, you in for surprise.*

Back on the bench, the judge got things going again. A hint of acid laced her tone as she addressed Kurtoff's lawyer.

> The Court: *Mr.* Caparini. In the event you and your client are not familiar with the contents of this recording, we will play it for you. Or do I need to?

Caparini glanced back at Kurtoff, who remained far calmer than his lawyer. Kurtoff nodded. He hoped the recording was clear enough to hear him reprimanding Gura for blowing up the car and killing the girl. He was counting on it. *Let them hear me blame it on the dead man.*

> Mr. Caparini: Yes. Please play it, Your Honor.

> The Court: Okay. Off the record for now. Mr. Wallace, go ahead.

As the recording started, the clarity was stunning. When the playback was finished, Caparini's face was white. Yet Kurtoff wasn't all that disturbed. In fact, he almost appeared confident. *What is that crap Simon says about problems? I find simple solution here, shithead. I know something you don't know, for a change, you and your gorilla investigator both.*

Caparini stood up and cleared his throat before launching into his next objection.

> Mr. Caparini: Your Honor, you have already excluded Mr. Dryer's testimony. This recording is the fruit of that excluded testimony, so it should be excluded, too.

> The Court: Mr. Caparini, you know better than that. Mr. Simons has indicated that he can lay a foundation for the recording through other witnesses, starting with Mr. McMillan. It will not require Mr. Dryer's testimony, which

remains stricken. You have anything else for us?

Mr. Caparini: Yes, yes, Your Honor. It's prejudicial. Extremely prejudicial to my client.

The Court: *Please,* Mr. Caparini. You must have learned that prejudice alone doesn't make evidence inadmissible. *All* evidence is prejudicial to one party or another. No one brings evidence to court unless it *is* prejudicial. The question is whether it is *unduly* prejudicial. Having heard this tape, I assure you it is very much prejudicial to your client. But not unduly. Far from it.

Mr. Caparini: Your Honor, we have had no advance notice of this exhibit. It was not on the plaintiffs' exhibit list. This is an unfair surprise tactic.

The Court: Mr. Caparini, I understand that the plaintiffs themselves just came upon this recording yesterday. Is that right, Mr. Simons?

Adam nodded.

The Court: If the recording is admitted into evidence, I will give you reasonable time, perhaps a few days, for your own experts to analyze it. If you wish. After all, this is a Holotrial. No jury would be inconvenienced by such a delay. Right, Mr. Simons?

Mr. Simons: Thank you once again, Your Honor, for reminding me.

The Court: Anything more, Mr. Caparini?

Mr. Caparini: Oh yes, Your Honor. This recording is hearsay. An out-of-court statement, not sworn under oath.

Kurtoff smiled, looking more confident than ever. *I hope you like legal knots, Simons. You try untie this one.* He beckoned

Caparini over and whispered in his ear. Then he had to push Caparini away from the defense table to deliver the news.

> Mr. Caparini: Your Honor, I am led to...to
> understand that Mr. Gura, he is deceased. So
> not only are his statements hearsay, but there is
> no way we can cross-examine him now.

The judge's eyes widened. She stared first at Caparini, and then at Kurtoff. Another cross-examination dilemma, no doubt once again orchestrated by this murderous man.

> The Court: I want video on this as well as audio.
> Mr. Kurtoff, is this true? This Mr. Gura is
> *dead*?

> Mr. Caparini: Objection, Your Honor. Mr. Kurtoff
> is not on the witness stand.

> The Court: This is *my* courtroom, Mr. Caparini. I
> can and will ask questions of witnesses or
> parties whenever I damn well please. However,
> if you wish to advise your client that he needs
> to take the Fifth, that will be honored.

Kurtoff jumped in before Caparini could respond.

> Mr. Kurtoff: No, Your Honor. I not take Fifth. No
> need.

> The Court: Then what do you know of Mr. Gura's
> death, Mr. Kurtoff?

> Mr. Kurtoff: My understanding, was fishing in
> reservoir. In Lewiston. Fell in, drowned. This,
> uh, last Saturday. Big tragedy. Is not? All of
> Vertex in mourning.

> The Court: This past Saturday? Three days ago?

> Mr. Kurtoff: That my understanding.

Judge Mitachi clenched her teeth and almost imperceptibly shook her head.

> The Court: The day after I gave Mr. Simons the
> weekend to see if he could come up with other

evidence to replace Mr. Dryer's stricken testimony?

Mr. Kurtoff: Is correct, Your Honor. I know what you try to say, but just coincidence. You heard Mr. Simons. Mr. Dryer killed by act of nature, *force majeure*, rain make girder fall on him. Mr. Gura, he drown. Totally separate, not connected. You understand, Your Honor.

The Court: I think I do understand, Mr. Kurtoff. And God help you if I do so correctly. I should call a mistrial right now. The only thing stopping me is the thought of putting Ms. Talbot through all of this again. It is for that reason only, Mr. Caparini, that you may continue with your motion.

Mr. Caparini: Your Honor, perhaps, based on your comments, it may make sense for you to recuse yourself. You seem to have formed a personal opinion of my client that, well, could affect your rulings.

The Court: Mr. Caparini. If I only presided over trials involving people I like, I'd be sitting at home watching Netflix all day. I assure you that whatever I think of your client, I will give you a fair shake on your motion and any other proceedings in this case. Your motion to recuse is denied. You may continue.

Mr. Caparini: Your Honor. As I was saying, the recording is out-of-court, unsworn hearsay and, as such, inadmissible testimony. If it were allowed in evidence, defendants would be deprived of their Constitutional right to cross-examine Mr. Gura. You can't cross-examine a dead person.

Mr. Simons: Your Honor, the recording is not testimony at all. This doesn't involve a third

party like Mr. Dryer testifying about a
conversation he overheard. The recording *is* the
actual conversation of the participants
themselves, unfiltered by any witness. It is
direct evidence, not hearsay. The jury gets to
hear it straight from Mr. Kurtoff's and Mr.
Gura's own mouths. To keep evidence of this
magnitude from the jury by calling it hearsay
would be absurd.

The Court: It may be a closer question than you
think, Mr. Simons. It *is* two people talking, and
if their conversation is admitted into evidence
and played for the jury, that is *something* akin
to testimony. And Mr. Gura can no longer be
cross-examined about it.

Mr. Caparini: Exactly, Your Honor.

The Court: Mr. Caparini, I don't need any
cheerleading from you.

Mr. Caparini: Sorry, Your Honor. But that's what
I've been saying. This is unsworn testimony
and shouldn't be heard by the jury.

Mr. Simons: Your Honor, if the recording *is*
testimony, it would qualify under the hearsay
exception that allows admissions against
interest into evidence. It is assumed that people
wouldn't admit to a crime if it wasn't true. So
if a witness overhears someone admitting to
criminal activity, the witness can testify about
what they heard. I submit there can be no
clearer criminal admissions than the ones made
by Kurtoff and Gura on this recording about
their role in killing Ms. Talbot's child.

Mr. Caparini: Your Honor, even if *Mr. Kurtoff's*
recorded statements are admissions that would
qualify under the hearsay exception, the
recording would have to be excluded from

evidence because of *Mr. Gura's* part of the conversation.

The Court: You'll have to explain that one, Mr. Caparini. Doesn't Mr. Gura admit involvement in the same criminal conduct as Mr. Kurtoff on this recording? Don't Gura's statements qualify as admissions against interest just like Mr. Kurtoff's statements about the same crime?

Mr. Caparini: Mr. Gura's statements *are* admissions as to *his* conduct. But *not* as to Mr. *Kurtoff's* conduct. By definition, Gura can only make admissions on behalf of himself. He can't admit anything on behalf of Mr. Kurtoff. So, to the extent Gura's statements implicate Mr. Kurtoff, they are accusations, not admissions, and therefore are pure inadmissible hearsay that is not subject to the hearsay exception for admissions.

Kurtoff was impressed. *How come I not think of this distinction? Maybe Cap not so bad.*

The Court: If I understand what you're saying, the part of Mr. Gura's statements about what *he* did *is* admissible under the hearsay exception, but the part about what Mr. *Kurtoff* did is *not*?

Mr. Caparini: Yes, yes. Correct. The problem is, it's virtually impossible to separate the two. Nearly every statement by Gura admitting what *he* did also incriminates *Kurtoff.* There's no way to remove the accusatory part and keep the admission. The jury would be left with complete gibberish.

The Court: I agree, Mr. Caparini. That *would* be an impossible task. But your entire hearsay argument assumes the recording is testimony. As I said before, it's a close call. The inability to cross-examine Mr. Gura does trouble me,

but I am ruling conditionally, subject to further
argument, that the recording is not hearsay. It's
not testimony about an overheard conversation.
It *is* the conversation, which makes it direct
evidence, and therefore not subject to the
hearsay rule.

The entire plaintiffs' team, except the Senator, breathed a sigh of relief.

Kurtoff was less than pleased, but not distraught. *The knot still not untied, Simons.*

The Court: Anything else, Mr. Caparini?

Mr. Caparini: I'm not, uh...

Kurtoff gestured wildly to Caparini, whispering sotto voce, "*Cap, Cap.*"

Mr. Caparini: Your Honor, excuse me. May I have
a moment with my client?

Caparini and Kurtoff hunched across the counsel table, their heads almost meeting in the middle. Kurtoff rapidly chattered into the lawyer's ear, practically shoving his iPad in Caparini's face. Caparini took it and addressed the court with an objection so rarely invoked that most lawyers had never heard of it.

Mr. Caparini: Your Honor, we object to the
recording under the Dead Man's Statute, CPLR
section 4519. The statute is intended to protect
dead people from being accused of wrongdoing
when they obviously can't come to court to
defend themselves. Dead men can't talk.

Kurtoff nodded approvingly. He'd benefitted from *that* truism many times.

Mr. Caparini: The statute precludes a party like
Mr. Kurtoff from coming to court to testify
about a conversation that implicates Mr. Gura
in a crime when Mr. Gura can't be here to
respond.

The Court: Mr. Caparini. A minute ago you were

protecting Mr. Kurtoff from Mr. Gura's statements. Now you want to protect Mr. Gura from *Mr. Kurtoff's* statements?

Mr. Caparini: Your Honor, what you say is technically true, but the end result helps my client, as well. We have the same problem we had with Gura's part of the recording. Virtually all of Mr. Kurtoff's statements implicating himself also implicate Mr. Gura and, as such, they are precluded by the Dead Man's Statute. Since there's no way to separate Mr. Kurtoff's admissions from his accusations against Gura, all of Mr. Kurtoff's testimony must be excluded from evidence under Dead Man's.

Kurtoff beamed. *Gura, you finally helping me without any fuck-up.*

The Court: So let me get this straight. You are using a statute intended to protect the dead Mr. Gura from Mr. Kurtoff, to protect Mr. Kurtoff from Ms. Talbot. Do I have that right?

Mr. Caparini: Yes, Your Honor. That is what the Dead Man's Statute intends under these...somewhat unique circumstances.

Mr. Simons: How convenient.

The Court: Mr. Simons, nice to hear from you. I gather you disagree with Mr. Caparini's interpretation of the Dead Man's Statute?

Mr. Simons: I do, Your Honor. First, I question whether Mr. Caparini has standing to invoke the statute when he is, in essence, objecting to his own client's testimony. Second, the statute only prohibits testimony *against* the dead man's estate, and Mr. Gura's estate is not a party to this action. All that aside, the Dead Man's Statute has an important exception that applies here. It *does* allow a party like Mr.

Kurtoff to testify about a conversation with a dead person if the testimony of the dead person concerning the same conversation is given in evidence. That is exactly the case here. This recording has both Kurtoff's *and* Gura's parts of the conversation, so the exception applies. Mr. Gura *has*, in effect, defended himself by participating in the same testimony being played for the jury.

The Court: So now *you* are calling the recording testimony?

Mr. Simons: Only to respond to Mr. Caparini's too-clever-by-half argument. Our principal position remains that the recording is not testimony, but direct evidence of the conversation.

Mr. Caparini: Your Honor, I think an out-of-court recording of Mr. Gura's unsworn statements would not qualify as the type of formal testimony referred to in the statute's exception cited by Mr. Simons. As Mr. Simons just said, the exception would apply only if Gura's *testimony* about the conversation was in evidence. You've already ruled that the recording is *not* testimony.

The Court: So now *you're* saying it's *not* testimony? Gentlemen, did you switch clients when I wasn't looking? Mr. Caparini, if I follow the thread of your argument to its logical conclusion, it seems you are arguing that Mr. Kurtoff's statements on the recording *are* testimony implicating a dead person, but the dead person's statements on the same recording are *not* testimony? You two have created quite a bar exam question here. If the recording *is* admissible as testimony under the Dead Man's Statute exception, it is still hearsay

Alan M. Wishnoff

as to Gura's statements against Kurtoff's interests, and the defendants cannot cross-examine Mr. Gura. Which, again, raises significant Constitutional issues.

Mr. Simons: Your Honor, hearsay by definition *assumes* that the person who actually made the statement may not be testifying in court, and therefore may not be available for cross-examination. That's why it's called hearsay, because someone who heard the statement is testifying rather than the person who actually made the statement. That's not a deprivation of Constitutional rights. That's just the nature of hearsay.

The Court: Mr. Simons, it may be the nature of hearsay, but I cannot simply ignore the defendants' right of cross-examination. And we're right back to the problem of whether Mr. *Gura's* hearsay can be used against Mr. *Kurtoff*, since Gura's statements do not constitute admissions by Kurtoff. I think what we have here is what the British call a sticky wicket. There are just too many questions swirling around this recording. As the Emperor said to Mozart, too many notes in this opera.

Mr. Simons: Your Honor, I—

The Court: Is the recorded conversation direct evidence or hearsay testimony? If hearsay, does the exception for admissions allow it to be parsed out so that only admissions are introduced in evidence? Does the Dead Man's Statute trump all of that anyway? Or does the Dead Man's exception apply? If it does, does that cure the problem of Gura's words being used against Kurtoff? Does Due Process and the right to cross-examination trump all of that?

Mr. Simons: Your Honor—

The Court: I'm not blind, Mr. Simons. I'm well
            aware of the significance of this evidence and
            how it bears on the truthfulness of Mr.
            Kurtoff's testimony in this case...among other
            things. But if we allow this recording into
            evidence, the chances of a reversal on appeal
            are multiplied by all of these questions, and
            you don't want to have to try this case all over
            again, do you? As much as I hate to say it, in
            the final analysis, defendants' constitutional
            rights trump the rest. I intend to preclude the
            recording and not play it for the jury.

Katherine shouted, "No."

The judge raised her gavel to demand order, but then gently put
it back down on the bench. Kurtoff was ecstatic. He'd been
following the argument like a ping-pong match. It was hard to keep
score, even with his legal degree.

Mr. Simons: *Your Honor.* My clients' rights are
            not to be taken lightly.

Judge Mitachi gave Adam a look that had put the fear of God
into many a litigator. Adam had gone too far.

The Court: *Mr.* Simons. I don't need your
            instruction on how to do my job. You want to
            put on a robe and make the ruling, you run for
            election. In the meantime, I will let you know I
            take *no* party's rights lightly in my courtroom.

Mr. Simons: My apologies, Your Honor. I was out
            of line. I've been before you numerous times,
            and I've never seen you take *anything* lightly.

The Court: I've got a thick skin, Mr. Simons, but it
            still deserves respect. Apology accepted. In any
            event, I said I *intend* to preclude. I haven't
            made a final ruling. Here's what we're going to
            do. It's past lunchtime anyway, so we'll
            adjourn until tomorrow at 9:15. Mr. Simons,

you have until then to provide me with any
additional legal authority supporting admission
of the recording into evidence. Oh, and Mr.
Simons. Once again, if this were not a
Holotrial, our jurors would be very unhappy
staring at the walls of the jury room for the past
few hours only to find they'd be sent home
without hearing any testimony. I think you'd
agree this system has its benefits.

Adam gave the judge a half smile but said nothing. *She's right,
damnit.*

Chapter 70

ADAM'S LAW OFFICE
Parkside Avenue, Buffalo, New York
Monday, November 6, 2023
7:00 p.m.

Kelly and Adam had been at it for hours. They sat at opposite ends of his conference room table, engrossed in their laptops, searching in vain for legal authority to support admission of the recording into evidence, but all they had to show for their efforts was a half-eaten container of chicken wings.

Kelly thought back to the day that everything went off the rails, when Cal was mangled by that girder. *There was something else. Something got my attention that afternoon. What was it? Holy shit.*

"Adam. I think I have something. Judge Mitachi has had the courtroom cameras running continuously, even during down time, ever since the juror head was switched. Right?"

"Okay. What does that get us?"

"Remember when Kurtoff went nuts about some text he received? During the lunch break just before we learned about Cal's death? Don't you think the text probably had something to do with Cal?"

"And?"

"And why don't we read that text?"

"If you remember, Kurtoff smashed his phone on the desk. Not that he'd give it to us, anyway."

"Adam. This is a *Holotrial*."

"God, don't remind me. So, Kelly?"

"So, there are cameras all over the place. To produce the 3-D image for the Holoscript, there *must* be cameras in the ceiling. Pointed down *at Kurtoff's phone*."

Adam jumped out of his chair and hugged her, carefully, not too hard or for too long. "Kelly, you're worth every penny."

She loved the praise. "No charge. I volunteered, remember?"

"I do. But we still have a problem. We don't have individual camera angles. We just get the final 3-D image."

"That's why we need to get into the control room."

"At seven p.m. on a Monday? I hope Charlie Ross is in a good mood."

***

Charlie was not in a good mood. He'd worked overtime to fix a glitch in Courtroom Six and had just sat down to dinner. But he was still grateful to Adam for getting his nephew out of that shoplifting charge, and even more so for the lecture Adam gave the nephew afterward. He agreed to meet them at the courthouse in half an hour.

Charlie ushered them into his control room and fired up the Holoscript. Sure enough, within minutes he had isolated a bird's-eye view of Kurtoff holding his phone during the lunch break on October 27. Before Charlie zoomed in on the text, Adam asked him to read it to himself, to make sure it didn't contain a privileged communication with Kurtoff's counsel. Adam and Kelly turned their backs while Charlie adjusted the image.

"*Holy shit*," he exclaimed. "Take a look at this."

Chapter 71

SUPREME COURT, ERIE COUNTY
Talbot versus Vertex Corporation et al.
Holotrial Annex Building, Part 7-HT
Main Street, Buffalo, New York
Tuesday, November 7, 2023
9:15 a.m.

The holovision recorders were quietly warming up. In her excitement, Kelly had even beaten Judge Mitachi to the courtroom. They'd let her in immediately after it had transformed from stark white to an elegant courtroom. *I can't believe Adam agreed to this.* Kelly had to grab the edge of the counsel table with both hands to keep them from shaking.

The judge walked in, precisely on time as usual, though her pace was slower. She sighed as she sat down in the soft leather chair behind the bench. The case had worn her down. There had never been this much drama in her prior cases. She took a deep breath.

The Court: Back on the record. Mr. Simons. Do you have anything for us?

Mr. Simons: With the court's permission, we would like Ms. Martin to present our argument. It's really *her* argument. She is, of course, under my supervision.

The Court: Permission granted. You're up, Ms. Martin.

Adam sat. As his prodigy stood, she was almost light-headed. *My first argument before a real court. And in front of Adam. The creatures back at school are going to be super jealous. Okay. Let's make it count.*

Ms. Martin: May it please the Court. Your Honor,

I believe it is black letter law that a party
waives its Constitutional right to cross-examine
a witness if that party caused the witness's
absence. I think Mr. Caparini would agree with
that, wouldn't he?

Mr. Caparini: Yes, yes. I agree. That's the law. But
there's no evidence here that the defendants
caused Mr. Gura's absence.

Adam stage whispered to Kelly, "That's the best ten seconds
of lawyering in the whole trial."

Ms. Martin: Well, let's hold Mr. Caparini to his
word about the law. However, he's mistaken
about the facts. This argument pertains to Mr.
Dryer, not Mr. Gura. Your Honor, this is a
photo of a text Mr. Kurtoff received while he
was sitting right there at the defense table on
October twenty-seventh at 12:15 p.m. Just
before we all found out that Mr. Dryer was
dead. The text was sent to Mr. Kurtoff by a Mr.
Petro Andrich, a Vertex employee, a member
of the company's security force.

The picture of the text filled the screens of the courtroom
monitors.

> **Mission accomplished
> Mr. K.   Dryer won't be
> giving no more testimony.
> Almost got McMillan too!**

Judge Mitachi's face turned red, her teeth clenched.

The Court: *My God.* I had my suspicions, but
now...Mr. Kurtoff, you, sir, are going to jail.
Straight to jail. I will see to that. I am reporting
this to the New York Attorney General's office

immediately.

> Ms. Martin: Actually, Your Honor, we've already
> taken care of that.

Before she could respond, Judge Mitachi's phone started flashing and buzzing. She read the urgent message.

> The Court: Well, well. Looks like we're about to
> have some company.

**

Moments later, the courtroom's rear doors opened, and two state troopers marched down the faux-carpeted center aisle. As they reached the counsel tables, they executed a sharp left turn and went directly to the defense table. A brief heated conversation with Kurtoff ensued. The troopers read him his rights and cuffed him. Then they marched him up the center aisle and out the double doors.

The judge strained to hold back a smile. Adam and Kelly didn't bother to hide their jubilance. Nor did Katherine in the gallery. Jennifer just stared at her father. The Senator, in turn, focused on Adam. He hadn't even watched Kurtoff as he was escorted out. Caparini looked somber but otherwise had barely reacted.

Then the chatter started to build. The drama of the arrest behind them, everyone wondered what charges Kurtoff would face. Felony murder for Allison Talbot's death? Murder for Cal Dryer's? Illegal wiretap of a State official with the switched juror head? Destruction of state property? Attempted murder of Mac? Gura's murder, if they ever find the body? All of the above?

> The Court: Let's stand in recess. Twenty minutes.
> I don't know about you, but I need to catch my
> breath.

**

Judge Mitachi addressed the dramatic new circumstances in this rollercoaster of a trial.

> The Court: Mr. Caparini, don't bother. If you're
> going to move for a mistrial, *motion denied.*
> That would only let Mr. Kurtoff profit from all

the mayhem and murder he's responsible for.
And you may stay seated, too, Mr. Simons.
Needless to say, upon reconsideration, the
motion to exclude Mr. Dryer's direct testimony
is denied. It will be played for the jury. The
defendant's murder...I still can't, I never...the
defendant's murder of Mr. Dryer extinguishes
their right to cross-examine him. It also calls
for admission into evidence of the recording of
the June thirtieth conversation between Mr.
Kurtoff and the late Mr. Gura. That too will be
played for the jury. Mr. Wallace. Bring the jury
in.

The jury box was suddenly bathed in light. The jurors' expressions remained unchanged, impervious to surprise, stress, shock, or new circumstances, no matter how dramatic.

The judge then uttered the words that Adam had long been waiting to hear.

The Court: Plaintiffs' exhibit seventy-two marked
for identification is now admitted into
evidence. So ordered. The clerk will now play
the recording into the record for the jury.

(Kurtoff) Yes? *Tak?*

(Gura) *Pryvit shefe.* Mr. K, you not believe what—

(Kurtoff) *I believe you are idiot.* How could this happen? Explosion? Kill little girl? I do not like to be disappointed, Damytro. And I am disappointed, is not? *Extremely so.*

(Gura) Boss, I swear, I follow instructions exactly, put cable complete like he tell me. What Thomas say, perfect. I swear. From super ring thing to rear motor. Just like he say.

(Kurtoff) Did engine blow up in Thomas lab?

(Gura) No, Boss, but—

(Kurtoff) Did engine blow up after you put cable there?

(Gura) Yes, Boss, but not, I not cause that.

(Kurtoff) You must make mistake, is not? You supposed to make Senator car start on fire. Was to *scare* people, not *kill* them, is not?

(Gura) I do absolute what Thomas tell me, I swear boss. I take picture to show was correct. You see where I put cable. Like diagram he give me, you see.

(Kurtoff) You idiot. You took picture that preserve evidence against us. How big fool are you? Not enough to screw up job, now you document the crime?

(Gura) No worry, boss, they never find us. I do perfect. Make like New Millennium factory is problem, cause explosion. I did job inside lady's garage. No witnesses. Early, everyone asleep. But I not make it explode, I swear.

(Kurtoff) Damytro, you listen carefully and do exactly as I say now. As if you life depend, is not? When we done talking, erase photo, turn cell phone off. Take out SIM card, put phone and card in microwave two minutes, then throw everything in Lake Erie. You understand?

(Gura) But the microwave, boss. Nina not be happy.

(Kurtoff) *Damytro. Focus.* You get Nina new microwave. Number one job now is getting rid of evidence we kill little girl. United States Senator granddaughter. *Jesus Christ.* You screw up again, forget about microwave, I get Nina new husband. *Is not?*

(Gura) I do exactly, boss. I just, just *not* understand how this happen.

(Kurtoff) Does not matter what you understand. You do as told, no problem. You screw up, is problem. But, hmm... Maybe this better than we hope for. Blow up Senator granddaughter give more publicity. *Now* who wants to buy Hydro for sure. Is not? So maybe you mistake turn from shit to gold. *But no more mistakes,* Damytro. I bury my mistakes. Alive. *Rozumijete?*

(Gura) Okay Boss. But Boss, it wasn't—

(sound of Kurtoff's phone hanging up)

***

Adam was nearing the end of his summation. The *Kelly head*, he'd noticed, had not returned as Juror Number Five. Probably in an evidence locker somewhere, awaiting Kurtoff's criminal trial.

"You don't need an expert to tell you what happened here. Why? Because we heard it from the mouth of the defendant himself. Alex Kurtoff. In the recorded conversation with Dmytro Gura, the

Vertex employee who sabotaged Jennifer Talbot's car on Kurtoff's orders. They not only acknowledge the crime, but also the means. The extra cable they put in her car's engine.

"What did we learn from that recording? Alex Kurtoff ordered a hit on Jennifer Talbot's car. Indeed, Kurtoff ran Vertex like a crime syndicate, with a so-called palace guard of felons to do his dirty work. There's no question he intended to destroy Jennifer's car. The primary objective may have been the car, but as you heard Kurtoff say on that recording, they killed a Senator's granddaughter. I have his exact words here. 'Maybe this better than we hope for. Blow up Senator granddaughter give more publicity. *Now* who wants to buy Hydro for sure.' *That's* how Alex Kurtoff described the murder of an innocent baby, a two-month-old girl. '*Better. Than. We. Hope. For.*' To Alex Kurtoff, killing Allison Talbot was a nice bit of PR. Just another day at the office for this nightmare of a man."

Adam thought that description of Kurtoff might provoke an exception, but Caparini stayed mum.

"As the judge will instruct you," he continued, "we don't need to show motive. But you tell me, have you ever heard of a crime with a clearer motive? Vertex feared New Millennium's Hydro would make its own fleet of electric cars obsolete. Vertex was about to start losing market share, and Mr. Kurtoff was about to lose a thirty-two-million-dollar bonus, this year alone. Did he respond as a legitimate businessman would? Build a better mousetrap? Design a better car? No. He tried to kill the Hydro, literally, and in the process, he killed a little girl." Adam swallowed hard, then continued, ever so gently, "This little girl."

He nodded at Kelly, and a photo of Allison Talbot filled the courtroom monitors.

"Remember, *this* is what Alex Kurtoff did to this child."

Adam nodded to Kelly again. Jennifer and Katherine turned their heads away. Bill Talbot just stared at Adam with a mixture of venom and amusement. The video started playing: Jennifer placed Allison in the car, returned the empty shopping cart, and then—the explosion. It still shocked Adam. The car engulfed in flames, Allison inside it, Jennifer's futile attempt to get to her. He had no doubt about how it would affect the human jurors who'd soon see it.

"There's a concept in the law called *Res Ipsa Loquitur*," he continued. "You may recall that I mentioned this in my opening statement. I told you it would become relevant later, and now it is. You'll have to forgive lawyers for throwing around fancy Latin phrases, but this is actually a pretty simple concept. *Res Ipsa Loquitur* means *The thing speaks for itself.* In this case, the explosion speaks for itself. They sabotaged the car. It blew up. And no one has come up with an alternative explanation. Not Vertex, not their expert, not the police, or the FBI, or the NTSB. *No one.*"

Adam paused to scan the fake jurors, trying to extrapolate from their immutable blank stares what a human jury—with eyes, ears, and most importantly hearts—would think of all this.

"As the judge will tell you, because this case is based on *Res Ipsa Loquitur,* we don't need to prove the cause of the explosion. This isn't a physics exam. It's a trial, about a dead little girl. But there's no mystery here. We *know* it was the cable that Kurtoff's henchman placed in the car's engine. How do we know that? Because, of the *thousands* of other Hydros that have been sold, *not one* has exploded. *Not one.* Why didn't any of the other Hydros explode? Because none of *them* was sabotaged. Only *this* Hydro, the Hydro sabotaged on Kurtoff's order, ended in a burnt, twisted tangle of shattered metal and melted flesh.

"The defendants can cry all they want that something else caused this. But there *is* no *something else.* The experts can't even *hypothesize* an alternate cause. All of the parts found in the scorched wreckage that used to be Jennifer Talbot's car were accounted for in the Hydro's design, except one, the cable inserted by the defendants. That's the *only* difference between Jennifer Talbot's car, which blew up, and the thousands of other Hydros that didn't. These facts are incontrovertible and uncontested. They speak for themselves. Vertex sabotaged the car. It exploded the next morning. Allison Talbot is dead. Case closed."

Adam nodded at Kelly again, and Allison's photo reappeared on the monitors. He stared at it before continuing.

"Let's not forget, at the center of all this is a beautiful, innocent little girl who just wanted to go home and watch her mommy unpack the groceries. She didn't know from cars. From market shares. From bonuses. She had no idea there were such vile people in this world. People like Alex Kurtoff, willing to commit abominable crimes just to fatten their wallets. Allie can't be here, but Jennifer is here for her, asking you to hold Alex Kurtoff and Vertex accountable for their repulsive actions. For the murder of her child."

Adam paused. His eyes grew wet as he looked at the baby's face, her innocent smile. He wished he'd known her while she was alive, even for a day. *Okay, enough of this.*

"Allie will never have a birthday party. Not even her *first*. She'll never have her first day of kindergarten, or high school, or college. She won't run on the track team or play oboe in the orchestra. She'll never take karate lessons, or gossip with her friends. She'll never dance or fall in love. Allie will never again experience Jennifer's unconditional love or give that love back to Jennifer. There will be no wedding for Allie, no children of her own, no grandchildren for Jennifer.

"It's a terrible thing to lose one's child. At any age. It is *unspeakable* for a baby to be taken from her mother, and for no reason other than the greed of monsters."

Adam looked over at Alex Kurtoff's empty chair at the defense table. There had indeed been a monster there.

"For an intentional criminal act like this, the law allows not only what we call compensatory damages for Allison's death and her mother's pain and suffering, but also punitive damages. Punitives are designed both to punish the wrongdoers and to deter others from committing such crimes. No amount of money can bring Allie back. But money is all we have to work with here. To prevent future Allies. To that end, I submit that you should render an award of fifty million dollars in compensatory damages, and one hundred million dollars in punitive damages, so this will never, *ever* happen again."

He paused a final time, to stress that he was coming to an end.

"Allison Talbot lived in a world of warmth, of love, of soft blankets and fluffy teddy bears. Until suddenly she didn't. Allie didn't know it, but she'd run into Alex Kurtoff. She'd run into evil."

Adam took a last glance at the dead girl's picture on the monitors. Then he slowly turned his back to the jury box and returned to his seat, unable to hide his tears.

Chapter 72

SUPREME COURT, ERIE COUNTY
Talbot versus Vertex Corporation et al.
Holotrial Annex Building, Part 7-HT
Main Street, Buffalo, New York
Live Jury Session
Thursday, November 9, 2023
Morning

It had been two days since Adam gave his summation to the artificial jurors. The Holoscript had been completed in record time, thanks in large part to the nearly week-long delay after Cal's death.

In the jury room, Liz Pratt was growing impatient. The jury materials had boasted about what a whirlwind process this was. Liz had been picked for the jury yesterday, and the trial—well, technically speaking, the playback of the already completed trial—was supposed to run from beginning to end in one day, starting this morning. Yet here they were, sitting around the table in the jury deliberation room, twiddling their thumbs, drinking coffee, and scarfing down doughnuts. Like all the jurors, she'd had a brief preview of Holotrials during jury selection, and she could hardly wait to see the real thing. She taught physics at the high school, and this would certainly get the kids' attention.

Liz figured a one-day trial would hardly make a dent in her daily routine. She dropped the kids off at eight at the middle school like she did every morning, her husband would be home to greet them when the bus dropped them off at four, and she'd be home in time for dinner. The only disruption was that she'd miss running home on her lunch break to play with Pondo, the family's Italian Greyhound.

A court attendant poked his head into the jury room. "Five minutes, ladies and gentlemen."

"*Finally*," Liz complained. "I wish they'd let us keep our phones."

Juror Number Six, a professional woman in a pantsuit, responded, "I think they said it could interfere with projecting the trial. Or something like that."

Five minutes later, the attendant returned and led them down a hallway to a set of double doors. Liz hadn't known what to expect, but it wasn't *this*. At first glance, it felt like an ordinary courtroom. But on closer inspection, it was utterly freakish. There was sumptuous polished-wood paneling everywhere, ancient portraits on the walls, the complete package—but *nothing was moving*. A female judge sat on the bench. Two sets of lawyers sat at the counsel tables. Yet none of them moved an inch. Some had their mouths open, as if frozen in mid-sentence. The lawyer closest to her was halfway out of his chair.

It looked kind of like a natural history museum exhibit of early humans huddled together in a cave. The jurors were herded down the center aisle to a jury box with seven comfortably padded seats. Before sitting, Liz reached down to touch her chair, to make sure *it* wasn't a hologram.

Once assembled in the jury box, they sat in silence, soaking in their strange new surroundings. The attendant said, "If any of you needs me for anything, press the button on the railing in front of your chair." With that, he left. Liz and her six fellow jurors were alone in the large, lifeless room.

***

The realism of the holographic scene reminded Liz of a game called *Jump the Cliff* that her son played on his VR headset. The objective was to jump off a cliff that loomed above a 1,000-foot drop with large craggy rocks at the bottom. Once you made the leap, you could sprout wings and fly safely above the precipice. Liz kept telling herself she was standing with her own two feet on her basement floor, and there was *nowhere to fall*, but there was no way she could bring herself to jump off the virtual cliff. It just seemed *too real*.

The holographic courtroom looked just as real. The jurors had been told about their fabricated juror stand-ins, and Liz wondered whether the frozen judge and lawyers in front of her were also mannequins. Then, like an animatronic Disney exhibit, the room suddenly came to life. The lawyer closest to them sat in his chair. The judge started speaking. They *were* real people.

"Ladies and gentlemen of the jury, welcome to Holotrial H 23-104C, Talbot versus Vertex Corporation et al. I am Judge Sara Mitachi of the New York State Supreme Court, Erie County. I am going to start by giving you preliminary instructions about what to expect and how to perform your functions as jurors. The recording of this trial, called a Holoscript, lasts six hours and twenty-seven minutes. You will have an hour for lunch, which must be eaten in the courthouse cafeteria. I believe you've already been told, but if you need a break or have any questions, please press the button on the railing in front of your chair. Though I am currently appearing before you as a hologram, I am at this moment in my chambers and ready to respond to any questions you may have for me."

What incredible power I have, Liz thought, *to stop a trial with the push of a button. The closest I've ever come to this was the emergency strap on the subway.*

The judge began reading from the version of the New York Pattern Jury Instructions, known to lawyers simply as *PJI*, that had been modified for the Holotrial system. She reminded them this was a civil case, not a criminal proceeding. They wouldn't have to consider sending the defendants to jail, only whether they were liable to pay monetary damages for the death of Allison Talbot. She skipped the part of the PJI where the jury would normally be told not to base its verdict on motions or objections or rulings. This was unnecessary, since all such events had already been edited out of the Holoscript. Just as the holographic Mr. Russell had told them, "You get all the meat, none of the fat."

***

Five minutes later, the judge finished the preliminary instructions. Adam stood and walked to the jury bench. Liz marveled at how perfectly real he looked, standing just a couple of feet from her. Every pore on his skin, every hair on his head, the shimmering texture of his silk tie, the slight stubble on his face, all were distinctly visible. Liz was tempted to try to touch him, but they'd been told that was a no-no.

"May it please the court. Ladies and gentlemen of the jury. You are about to hear..."

***

A minute into Adam's opening statement, the gravity of Liz's responsibility hit her when a picture of Allison appeared on the courtroom monitors. *She's adorable. Imagine if I had lost my—*

Adam pointed at the photo. "Her name was Allison. Allison Talbot. Her family called her Allie. She could be your baby. She could be my baby. In fact, she looks a lot like my son at that age. He's fourteen years old now. Allie will never be fourteen. She's gone. Two months old. She had her whole life ahead of her. She never got to live that life. Thanks to the defendants."

The video from the supermarket parking lot started playing.

"On June thirtieth of this year, Allie's mother Jennifer, the young lady sitting over there, took her baby daughter grocery shopping. When they were done, Jennifer strapped Allie into the infant seat in her car and went to put away the shopping cart. That's the last time she saw Allie. The last time anyone saw Allie."

Liz watched the security camera footage: Jennifer putting Allison in the car, walking back toward the supermarket kiosk, returning the shopping cart.

"After Jennifer put the cart back, she used her remote to start the car. This is what happened."

In the video the car exploded, spewing flames, smoke, and debris. Liz and her fellow human jurors gasped, exactly the reaction Adam had anticipated and hoped for.

My God, Liz thought. *If this Vertex Company...I don't even like the sound of their name...if they did this, I know one juror who won't stand for it.*

After pausing to let the impact of the video imprint in the jurors' minds, Adam continued. "How did this happen? Because the defendants here, as repulsive as this sounds, intentionally sabotaged Jennifer's car. They made it explode in this fiery hell, taking Allie along with it. And why? Because they thought the Hydro would hurt their business, their profits, and their bonuses. It didn't matter Allison was in it. Let me explain."

Holotrial

***

The holographic Adam was nearing the end of his opening statement. Liz had listened, spellbound. She'd completely forgotten she was watching a hologram. Adam held up a jagged yellow remnant from the destroyed Hydro and walked across the jury box, showing it to each juror, one at a time, up close and personal. When he got to Liz, she again wanted to reach out and touch him. *He has to be real.*

"Please remember," Adam said. "This was not just some accident. It was not mere negligence, some engineer making a miscalculation or transposing a few numbers. It was murder, plain and simple. It's sad. It's tragic. And it's why you're here."

Chapter 73

ADAM'S HOME
Tudor Place, Buffalo, New York
Friday, November 10, 2023
9:30 a.m.

It was a splendid autumn day in Buffalo. The air was brisk. The skies were clear. Only the white contrails of the planes traversing the large piece of modern art known as the Buffalo Niagara International Airport interrupted the blue above. Families carved leftover pumpkins. Others visited the shining marble art gallery or one of Frank Lloyd Wright's well-preserved architectural gems. The *Bills Mafia*, the best football fans in the world, headed to the stadium to start tailgating a day before a rare Saturday afternoon game between the Bills and the Dolphins. "Squish the Fish" signs were everywhere. Other families completed their Christmas shopping at the funky stores on Elmwood Avenue or the suburban malls.

Not Adam. He sat ruminating in his living room, staring blankly at a one-hundred-and-fifty-million-dollar check, payable to Adam Simons as attorney for Jennifer Talbot and the Estate of Allison Talbot. He should have been ecstatic. The press coverage had been great. Not to mention bringing justice and perhaps some closure to the Talbots. And, of course, the money.

But Adam had no taste for celebrating. The case was over, and he'd won, yet he still wasn't sure what the hell had happened. It didn't add up. *Did the Vertex cable really cause the explosion of Jennifer's car? No one had an alternative explanation, but no one with any scientific background believed it, either. For every complex problem... Did this one have* any *solution, simple or otherwise? Simple solution: Gura's superfluous cable caused the explosion, though we have no clue why or how. Maybe the simple solution is correct this time.* But Adam had a nagging feeling. *What is the complex solution?* There had to be one.

He thought back to the meeting with Marcel Saperston. That was the first time, but certainly not the last, he heard that Gura's extra cable couldn't have caused the explosion. What they had thought at that time was a negligent *defect* turned out to be an intentional act of sabotage. All the same, as Saperston had reminded Adam, that didn't change the laws of physics. However it got there, the cable couldn't have blown up the car. So said Saperston. And Ditenzo. And Morier.

Adam retreated to his Holoscript viewing room, hoping he might find a clue in the expert testimony. A clue that the experts themselves had missed. Kelly had identified where anyone mentioned the cause of the explosion in the Holoscripts from the two trials. Pursuant to the Holotrial procedures—which, it still seemed to Adam, they were making up as they went along—attorneys were given the raw Holoscripts, including objections, colloquy, stricken testimony, etc., in case they needed them for an appeal.

First up was Dr. Ditenzo, New Millennium's expert from the first trial. Adam fiddled with the controls until the doctor appeared, virtually life-sized. Ditenzo echoed Saperston's opinion: it couldn't have been the cable. The virtual Adam then asked, following up on Saperston's hypothesis, about the possibility of additional sabotage with a Y-shaped tube. Ditenzo swore there was no such part in the entire factory, and that no car could have left the building without such a modification being detected.

That still left the possibility of some defect or chicanery they'd all overlooked. Saperston said he couldn't rule out the possibility of "some other form of sabotage." If Gura's cable could be inserted after the car left the factory, why not a Y-tube? *Because, moron, there is no Y-tube. Saperston may have had a good theory, but there were no facts to support it. Saperston acknowledged that himself. So, what the hell's the answer?*

Adam switched to the Vertex trial and brought up Dr. Morier's testimony. Same opinion as Saperston and Ditenzo—it wasn't the cable. Adam didn't get to try Saperston's *Y-tube theory* on Morier because Judge Mitachi sustained an objection to any such questioning, based on lack of foundation.

Adam rubbed his eyes. He was getting tired of this. *Hell, I've been frustrated the whole trial. The cause of the explosion, Allison's father, Kurtoff's polygraph test, Cal's murder, Gura's murder, just to name a few. And whatever else the Talbots were withholding from me. Repeat after me, Adam. No more personal injury cases. No more work for friends. Or former lovers and their husbands.*

He stopped the playback, and suddenly he thought he heard someone quietly breathing behind him. He sensed furtive movements. When he turned around, he almost jumped out of his skin. Pete was in the doorway, about a foot away, silently watching him.

"*Pete.* How many times have I told you not to startle me like that? You practice your stealth nonsense with Mac."

"Sorry, Dad. I just wanted to...I never saw one of these Holo things before."

"You were never interested. In much of anything. You're too...no point. I'm busy. Please."

"What're you doing, anyway?"

"Trying to solve a puzzle. Okay?"

"How's it going?"

"Not well. A complex problem without *any* solution."

Pete smiled at his father's oft-used phrase.

"And why aren't you in school?"

"Teacher administrative day."

Adam didn't know if that was true, but he'd investigate later. If he remembered. For now the enigma of the trial occupied all the attention he had.

"Can't I just stay and watch? It looks wicked. You won't even know I'm here. Promise."

"All right. But one sound, and you're out of here. And next time, you make a little noise when you approach me. Wear a cow bell or something."

Quiet established, Adam resumed his search for an answer that nobody seemed to have. Was it *possible* there was "some other form of sabotage"? Adam shook his head, puzzled. Three different experts, great credentials all, each reaching an identical conclusion. *No conclusion.* No identifiable cause of the explosion. Specifically *not* the electrical cable Gura attached to the car's engine. *How could all three experts be wrong?* Adam's gut told him to respect their wisdom. Marcel in particular had never steered him wrong before.

But if the late Gura's cable wasn't responsible, what was? Did all three experts miss something? What other form of sabotage could there be?

Adam turned around to find that Pete was gone. *Goddamnit, Mac, can't you teach him something useful for once?* Adam went upstairs and paced around the house. Eventually he found himself next to the hamster cage. Hamilton spun his treadmill, the rotating wheel to nowhere.

"You and me both, Hammy." Adam sighed.

The rodent didn't reply. But he did mosey over to the edge of the cage, hoping for a treat.

Chapter 74

ADAM'S LAW OFFICE
Parkside Avenue, Buffalo, New York
Friday, November 10, 2023
8:00 p.m.

After immersing himself in Holoscripts at home all day, and getting nowhere, Adam had gone to the office to busy himself with other work. Finalizing a brief. Outlining the next lecture for his *creatures*. Reviewing an order to show cause. Day became night, and still he sat at his desk. None of the distractions had worked. He couldn't stop thinking of the Talbot case, so he circled back to the center of the puzzle, the closed-circuit video of the explosion itself. Since the security video was in 2-D, he attached a standard video projector to his computer and placed a screen on the opposite side of his office.

Each time the footage played, Adam willed the explosion not to happen. He imagined Jennifer's Hydro starting without incident, she and Allie casually driving home, intact. He watched the explosion again and again and again, stopping at different points to hunt for clues. He'd had several glasses of wine, maybe more than several, but he did notice the door to his office slowly opening. Katherine Talbot staggered into the room, looking like she'd imbibed a lot more than Adam had. Her gait was unsteady, she struggled to maintain her balance, and she spoke to Adam in the tone of a former lover, an intimate friend, not a client.

"Proud of yourself, counselor? Hell of a trial. A truly hollow trial. You don't know how hollow." Katherine's voice was slurred, but biting.

Adam's flash of initial excitement at seeing her quickly turned to pity. "Kate. I know it's been... Please. Sit down. I'm sorry, Kate. I did all I... Let me get you something." He rose from his chair, but Katherine's next statement knocked him right back into it.

"I killed her, you know."

"What?" Had he heard her right?

"I killed her. Allie. Remember her?"

Adam was stunned. *"What are you—"*

"Shut up and listen. Let me tell you a little story, *counselor.* Think I mentioned, about a year ago I had an affair. Good-lookin' guy. Lawyer, forties, you know the type, real hot shot. Even taught at the law school, all those pretty 3Ls making goo-goo eyes at him. Anyway, Bill found out. I couldn't hide it from him. More on that in a minute. But I never said who. Never told him it was his old law-school buddy. What did he expect? All those lonely evenings, him on the campaign trail, whoring it up, me in the empty house. Christmas, New Year's, you name it. Well, *I* needed a warm body for the cold nights, too. Oh, c'mon, counselor, don't take it too hard. It was just as empty for you. Let's face it, you were with Beth the whole time. Anyhoo, let's not blame the Senator. Not for that. He has much worse to answer for."

Katherine stumbled over to Adam's desk, picked up the wine bottle in front of him, and took several swigs until it was empty. She slammed it back on the desk with a loud *crack.*

Adam's eyes remained locked on her.

"Senator Bill, maybe *President* Bill...I became an embarrassment, some nice oppo research. Not the kind you can hide for nine months. Not when your belly swells like a... Like I said, I couldn't hide it from him. So he packs me off to Switzerland, private hospital, sworn to secrecy. Registered as Mrs. Swanson or some bullshit. Even had a cover story. Nursing my sick mother back to health. If anyone cared. No one did."

"But—"

"I told you to shut up, counselor. You'll spoil the ending. Where was I? Oh yeah. We can't have candidate Bill's wife bearing a bastard child."

"Bastard? Are you saying—"

"And we can't terminate it, given his stance on abortion. So, what to do with the baby? What...to...do? *My* great idea. We pawn it off as Jennifer's. No one'll bat an eye. The younger generation, you know."

Adam burst out of his chair, eyes wide, jaw gaping. "Allie was...she was my—"

"I thought you were a quicker study, counselor, but you're catchin' on. *Your* little baby girl. Well, *ours*. I guess I killed her. If I'd stood up to Bill and kept her, she wouldn't have been in Jenny's car, and she wouldn't...you know the rest. Oh well. Spilt milk. Right, counselor? Don't beat yourself up. I wasn't gonna tell you. You barely notice Pete, so how much—"

"Of course I notice. But—"

"No, it's okay. You didn't need another kid to ignore, another reminder of our fucked-up relationship. But I knew you were driving yourself crazy over the loose ends, so I thought I'd put your mind to rest. Finally solve the riddle of the lying Talbots. You tried so hard to find the father. All you had to do was look in the mirror. There you have it. Case solved. Would you call that a simple solution or a complex one, counselor?"

Katherine wobbled over to the projector and fumbled with it, zooming in on a close-up of the car's rear window, filling the screen with Allison, *their child*, strapped into her infant seat. "Shame, isn't it?" Katherine slurred out. All the sarcasm, all the liquid confidence, was gone. She stumbled to the door, giving Adam one last lingering look. Her face was a mask of pain.

Adam stood in stunned silence as the door slammed behind her. Then he slipped back into his chair. *What just happened?*

Moments later, the door opened again. Adam thought— hoped—that it was Katherine. They had so much more to say to each other...

But it was Mac, holding a black nylon bag. He took one look at Adam's sheet-white face. "You look like you seen a ghost, Chief. You all there? We need to call in a bird for a medevac?"

"I just got some stunning news," Adam stammered weakly.

"You mean about your kid? How'd you—"

Another shock. Adam stood abruptly and grabbed Mac by the shoulders. "You *knew*? And you didn't *tell* me?"

"I couldn't. It was too dangerous, Chief. I thought it was best you didn't find out during the trial, so you wouldn't let up on Kurtoff."

Mac's not making any sense. "What are you *talking* about? Why would I let up? I'd have wanted to kill that bastard even more."

Now Mac was puzzled. "Sorry, Chief. I don't think we're talkin' about the same thing. Here. Take a look." He unzipped his bag and took out the Y-shaped tube and placed it gently on Adam's desk.

Adam couldn't believe his eyes. *"Oh my God.* You mean there actually was—"

"I took your advice, Chief. Re-canvassed the accident scene with a larger perimeter. Something Saperston said. 'Branches.' It got me thinking. So that's where I went. This was stuck way up in a tree, like ten feet outside the cops' search perimeter. Thrown there by the blast."

"So they were right all along. Saperston, Ditenzo, Morier. Even Kurtoff. It wasn't Gura's cable. This thing. *Jesus.* It's almost exactly what Marcel designed in his office. Mac, when did you find this?"

"About a month ago."

"And you didn't *tell* me? Mac. What the *fuck?*" This wasn't like Mac at all. Not at all.

"Well, there's more, Chief. Uh, we got a...a partial...a partial DNA match. For the guy who rigged the car with this tube."

"Jesus, Mac, what the fuck is going on here? Have you lost your goddamn mind?" Adam took a deep breath. And another. "All right. Who's the match?"

"It was in a government data base. Feds."

"So *who's the match*? Who's the goddamn match, Mac?"

"You are."

"What?"

"*You* are, Chief."

"Goddamnit, Mac." Adam could barely contain his anger. "I'm in no mood for jokes."

"I said *partial* match, Chief. Fifty percent. A first degree relative. You're a first degree relative of the...well, the *boy* whose DNA is on the tube."

As the word *tube* left Mac's mouth, Pete slinked past the doorway on his way to the snack room, plainly in a state of terror. Adam fell back into his chair, his legs no longer able to sustain him. He felt faint. *Pete? My fucking God. Pete? But why? Why would he kill his own—*

Then, Adam suddenly understood. And with that understanding came a wave of self-condemnation and loathing.

I did this. I killed her. My own daughter. Not Kurtoff. Not Kate.

Not even Pete. It was Pete's hand, but I pushed it. The sins of the father. If I'd only stopped wallowing in self-pity and been a goddamn father. I can only imagine his jealousy, his rage, when he learned he had a sister. But how the hell did he find out when even I didn't—

"I brought the kid." Mac interrupted Adam's train of thought. "Figured you might want him here, talk to him. Like I said, first-degree relative. Pete rigged it good, Chief. I had helped him breach New Millennium's firewall. Was supposed to be a computer training exercise. He said he'd picked New Millennium at random, sounded like a cool hi-tech company to hack."

Adam's hand started to shake uncontrollably. He gazed at the picture of Allie still on the screen, and then back at Mac. "How? Why?"

"Listen, don't worry, Chief. No one can put all this together, 'cept you and me. I know you wouldn't have turned Pete in, you'd deal with it some other way, but I didn't want you letting up on Kurtoff. The rat bastard *did* fuck up the car, after all, even if he didn't make it explode. I just can't figure out why in the hell Pete would...what *possible* connection could he have to the car? Or the Talbots?"

"He didn't like the competition."

"Competition? With the Talbots?"

"It's my fault, Mac."

"Don't beat yourself up, Chief. Pete's a good kid. I know he made a bad, okay, a terrible choice."

"A *bad choice*? Murdering a *child*? *My* child? His *sister*? A bad choice, Mac?"

"Chief? What the fuck are you talkin' about?"

"It's a long story, Mac. Kate and I—"

"Jesus, Adam. You sayin' Allison was yours?"

"Yes, she was. I'm sorry, Mac, I-I have to find—"

"Um, one more thing, Chief. Pete. Uh. He's the one who tipped off Kurtoff about Cal's location. And mine. Used a fancy voice-changing app I showed him. Jesus, I'm sorry, Chief. I've been in the middle of this thing the whole fucking time, and I didn't have a clue. I should never have taken Pete under my wing like that. I just thought he needed a..."

"A father." Adam sighed deeply. "It's okay, Mac, you can say it."

"I was gonna say crazy uncle, Chief. Really I was."

"But, Mac, why the hell would Pete want to rat out Cal? Cal provided the perfect cover story for Pete's sabotage."

"Apparently he wanted you to lose the trial. Something about taking him on vacation. I just don't—"

"Sorry, Mac." With tears welling in his eyes, Adam looked at Mac. "I have to find Pete." He stood up, walked around the desk, and left the room muttering, "Every complex problem..."

When Adam found Pete in the snack room, the boy looked like he expected Armageddon. This transgression was way beyond cigarettes and beer. He trembled as Adam knelt in front of him and gave him a hug. A tight hug. A long hug. Pete tentatively hugged his father in return, then began to squeeze harder, then as hard as he could.

Then Adam peered into Pete's eyes. Tears streamed down both of their faces. "Pete. Let's take that vacation."

"Really? Where to, Dad?"

"It doesn't matter. We both need to get away."

Alan M. Wishnoff

EPILOGUE

ANOTHER PHONE CALL
Saturday, November 11, 2023
10:45 a.m.

Mac was in a good mood. He was generally in a good mood these days. He'd even cut down on his drinking. But not on his flirting. He couldn't go cold turkey on everything.

He was having lunch with his sister in an hour. She was meeting him at his house, so he'd taken the Congressional Medal of Honor out of its usual hiding place and polished it up real nice. Hey. If your sister is the Attorney General of the great State of New York, you're entitled to brag about yourself a *little*.

After all these years, Mac's Army dress uniform still fit him fairly well. He had a little trouble buttoning up the pants, but the medals were in just the right places on the jacket. Shirt freshly starched. Pant creases perfect. He was ready for battle. The plan was to have lunch at a place she liked on Hertel Avenue, and then to catch the Veterans Day Parade. After the parade they were going to visit several of his old war buddies at the Field of Valor Annex in Forest Lawn Cemetery.

Mac's phone rang. He assumed that his sister was calling to say she was running late, but it was Prisha Singh. *Dr.* Prisha Singh. He answered. "Hello."

"Mac, you're a hard man to find," Prisha said, a note of relief in her voice. "I was starting to worry."

"You finally leaving that slob for me?"

"I've put that on the back burner. Just for the moment. Listen, something curious has come up. You remember the guy whose DNA was on that tube you brought me? Let's call him Pete—"

"*Prisha.*"

"C'mon, Mac, give me *some* credit. Doesn't matter. You know how I roll on confidentiality. Pete's safe. At least from me. Any consequences, that's your call. And Adam's. Anyway, as you may remember, the Federal Officials database identified former Assistant U.S. Attorney Adam Simons as Pete's first-degree relative. Obviously, as we know, his father."

"Believe me, I'll never forget it."

"Well, we found another relative of Pete's. The computer spit it out yesterday, from the Upper Echelon Federal database."

"You mean Beth, Pete's mother?"

"No. I limited my search to living people. It's a girl, a second-degree relative of Pete's."

"Same father, different mother?"

"Yes. Like Pete, she's a first-degree relative of Adam. That makes her Pete's half-sister. Mac, did Adam have another child...a daughter...by another woman?"

Mac sighed. "Turns out he did, Prisha...but she's dead."

"Oh no, Mac. Last I knew she was very much alive."

"What are you saying?"

"Mac. I think you know Senator Talbot."

"*Jesus Christ*. You're not telling me *Bill Talbot* came up as a first-degree relative of Adam Simons."

"Oh no, Mac. Not Senator Talbot. It's Jennifer. Jennifer Talbot."

Alan M. Wishnoff

ABOUT THE AUTHOR

Alan Michael Wishnoff is a trial lawyer living in Williamsville, New York. He graduated from McGill University and the State University of New York at Buffalo Law School. He began his legal career at the New York Court of Appeals and ultimately became a partner in a Buffalo law firm. For many years, he also played violin in a klezmer band, most recently known as "Bupkes."

Alan M. Wishnoff

Enjoy more novels and short stories from

https://www.twbpress.com

Science Fiction, Supernatural, Horror, Urban Fantasy, Thrillers, Romance, and more